DISTRESS SIGNALS

Catherine Ryan Howard was born in Cork, Ireland, in 1982. Before writing full time, Catherine worked as a campsite courier in France, a front-desk agent in Walt Disney World, Florida, and, most recently, a social media marketer for a major publisher. She is currently studying for a BA in English at Trinity College, Dublin. Find out more at www.CatherineRyanHoward.com or follow her on Twitter @CathRyanHoward.

DISTRESS SIGNALS

CATHERINE RYAN HOWARD

Printed in the United States of America
First printing: 2017
ISBN 978-1-5047-5752-2

1 3 5 7 9 10 8 6 4 2

CIP data for this book is available from the Library of Congress

Blackstone Publishing
31 Mistletoe Rd.
Ashland, OR 97520

www.BlackstonePublishing.com

This one's for you.

ADAM

I jump before I decide I'm going to.

Air whistles past my ears as I plummet toward the sea, dark but for the panes of moonlight breaking into shards on its surface. At first, I'm moving in slow motion and the surface seems miles away. Then it's rushing up to meet me faster than my mind can follow.

A blurry memory elbows its way to the forefront of my thoughts. Something about how hitting a body of water from this height is just like hitting concrete. I try to straighten my legs and grip the back of my thighs, but it's a moment too late. I hit the water at an angle, and every nerve ending on the left side of my body is suddenly ablaze with white-hot pain.

I close my eyes. When I open them again, I'm underwater.

It's nowhere near as dark as I expected it to be. Beyond my feet, yes, blackness, but here, just beneath the surface, it's brighter than it was above.

It's clear, too. I see no dirt, no fish. I twist and turn, but I can see no one else.

As I look up through the water, the hull of the *Celebrate* looms to my right, the lights of its open decks twinkling. I have a vague idea where, in the rows of identical balconies, my cabin is, and I wonder whether it's possible for two people to leave the same spot on such an enormous ship, fall eight stories, and land in completely different places.

It must be, because I seem to be alone.

I drift down, toward the darkness. Pressure builds in my chest. I need to get to the surface so I can take a breath. So I can call out and listen for the sound of legs and arms splashing, or for someone else calling out to me.

I move to stretch both arms out—

A hot poker has lodged itself deep inside my shoulder. The pain makes me gasp, pulling water into my throat.

Now all I want to do is take a breath. I *must* take a breath. I can't wait any longer.

But the surface is a good ten or twelve feet above me. I start to kick furiously. My lungs are screaming.

I'm not a strong swimmer; I'm going nowhere fast. My efforts just keep me at this depth, neither sinking nor ascending.

The surface gets no closer.

The urge to open my mouth and breathe in is only a flicker away from overwhelming. I start to panic, flailing with my right arm and both legs.

I lift my face to the light as if oxygen could reach me through the water the same way the moon's rays are doing.

And that's when I see a shadow on the surface.

A familiar shape: a life buoy. Someone must have thrown it down. I wonder what that someone saw.

The edges of my vision are growing dark. Everything is cold except for the spot where my left arm meets my torso. There, a fire burns. The pressure in my chest feels as if it were pushing my lungs to rupture and burst.

I tell myself, *I can do this.*

All I need to do is get to that floating ring.

Somehow, I kick harder and stronger and quicker now. Soon, the *Celebrate* starts to grow bigger. I keep kicking. Then the moon gets bigger, too, the water around me brighter still. I keep kicking. And just before I'm sure that my lungs will burst, when my diaphragm has already begun straining and spasming—

I break the surface. Gasping, sucking down air while my body tries to expel it, coughing, choking, retching, sputtering …

I can breathe.

I'm close enough to the life buoy to reach out and touch it. I grab it with my right hand and throw my left—hanging limp, the elbow at a disconcerting angle— over. The hot poker twists in my shoulder.

But now all my weight is on one side of the buoy, and it starts to flip.

I know it's only assistance, not salvation, and that even though I'm utterly exhausted, I'll have to keep my legs moving just to hold my head above water.

I'm not sure how long I can do this.

One thing at a time. Relax. Just relax.

I'm panting, hyperventilating, so my first task is to slow my breathing down. *Breathe in.* The right side of my face is stinging. *Breathe out.* My teeth are chattering. *Breathe in.*

I can't see anyone else in the water.

In the distance off to my left, the lights of Nice are emerging from around the *Celebrate*'s bow. First the amber streetlights following the curve of the promenade, and then, crowded into every available space beyond, hotels and office buildings and apartment blocks. Behind me, nothing but sea for hundreds of miles.

The ship is a colossus rising two hundred feet above my head. I think perhaps I can hear tinkling music drifting down from her decks. The only other sounds are my breathing and the splashes I make in the water.

I try to be still and listen for *someone else* making those same splashing noises, someone calling out …

I hear it then, faint in the distance: *whump, whump* …

I know the sound, but I can't remember what makes it. I'm trying to remember when I see something maybe fifteen or twenty feet beyond my left arm: a dark shape bobbing on the surface.

Whump, whump, whump … The noise is getting louder.

As I stare at the shape, the gentle rippling of water and the moon conspire to throw a spotlight on it, just for a second. I catch a glimpse of short brown hair.

Hair, I know, looks lighter when it isn't soaking wet.

The body it belongs to is facedown in the water and, as far as I can tell, moving only because of the gentle waves beneath it.

Whump-whump-whump-whump …

There's a blinding glare as a helicopter bursts into the sky above the *Celebrate*, the rotor beating so loud now that I can feel it thundering through my chest.

Its search beam begins sweeping back and forth across the water.

They've come for me.

My time is almost up. I wonder how they could possibly have gotten here so fast. Didn't I just hit the water a minute or two ago? Have I been here longer than I think? Or are they here for someone else?

Whump-whump-whump-whump-whump …

Above me now, the helicopter dips to hover close to the surface, kicking up radiating waves that push me off course and splash cold, salty water in my face. I kick harder. The body disappears from view and undulating waves take its place. I blink away a splash. The body reappears. A wave rolls over me. When I open my eyes a second time, the body is gone again.

Whump …

The sound is tunneling a hole in my brain. It's not above me anymore; it's *in* me. I feel as if it were coming from inside my head.

Then, the grip of a hand on my arm.

Everything is filled with dazzling white light now. Am I hallucinating? Is that what happens when you go into the water from several stories up, possibly dislocate your shoulder, nearly drown, and then exhaust yourself trying to stay afloat in open sea?

But no, there really is someone by my side: a man in a wet suit, with an oxygen tank on his back. All I can see of his face are his eyes through the foggy plastic of his mask. He lifts it up over his nose and says something to me, but the words are lost in the helicopter's roar.

I turn away from him and try to find the body again. I scan the surface, but I can't see it now.

A bright red basket is coming down on a rope. The wet-suited man grips me under the arms and pulls me toward it.

He speaks again, this time shouting into my ear from directly behind me.

This time, I hear him.

"Is there anybody else in the water? Did you see anybody else in the water?"

I say nothing.

I focus on the belly of the helicopter. It's navy blue and glossy. I think I see a small French flag painted on the underside of its tail.

"Was it just you?" he shouts. "Did you go in alone?"

We reach the basket and another wet-suit man. Together they lift me into it.

I'm now looking up at the night sky. It seems filled with stars. The man's face appears above mine, blocking my view of them. "Can you hear me?" he asks.

I nod.

"Were you alone in the water? Did you see anyone else?"

Above me, the helicopter's blades spin. *Whump-whump-whump-whump-whump-whump.* Out of the water, the pain in my shoulder stabs deeper. I start to shake.

All I wanted was to find Sarah. How has it come to *this*?

"No," I say finally. "It was only me in the water. There's no one else."

PART ONE

LOVE IS BLINDNESS

CORINNE

Even at 5:45 a.m., the *Celebrate*'s crew deck wasn't empty.

Something fleshy and pink and snoring was splayed on an inflatable chair bobbing at one end of the swimming pool. A young stewardess reclined on a sun lounger, smoking, her red and yellow uniform revealing that she worked the breakfast buffet and either slept in her clothes or stored them in a ball on the floor of her crew cabin. Huddled around one of the plastic tables, three security guards argued in English about a soccer match and some goal that should never have been allowed.

Shifts ran constantly and around the clock, the midnight buffet clear-up finishing only minutes before the breakfast prep had to start. It was always someone's spare moment before work, or smoke break, or post-shift crash. With the crew quarters impossibly cramped, below the waterline, and always smelling faintly (and sometimes not so faintly) of seawater and sewage, everyone dashed outside to the crew deck whenever they could.

Blinking in the sunshine, Corinne stepped out onto it now and paused for a moment while her eyes adjusted to the light. On the portside was an unoccupied table. Careful not to spill either of the two coffees she was carrying, she headed for it.

Passing the table of security guards, Corinne felt the gaze of one of them, crawling up her cabin attendant's uniform to her face. The flash of him she had caught in her peripheral vision left a vague impression of youth, broad shoulders, and closely cut blond hair. The man's eyes, she felt sure, stayed on her all the way to the table and lingered after she sat down.

She didn't entertain for a second the notion that this attention was down to admiration or attraction. He was at least three decades her junior, and Corinne's face wore several more years than she had lived. On top of that, her hair was gray, her body weak and painfully thin. That left mild interest (*What is a woman of her age doing working on a cruise ship?*), which was fine, but also suspicion (*What is she* really *doing here?*) and recognition (*Don't I know her from somewhere?*), which were not.

The table stood unevenly on its legs, and she had to weight it with her elbows to keep it from rocking. It was also missing its parasol, and one off-white plastic leg was pockmarked with cigarette burns—"crew grade," in company-speak. Everything the crew had was secondhand, from the flat, stained pillows on their bunks to the chipped crockery in their mess, all of it already used and abused by paying passengers until the Blue Wave Line deemed it no longer good enough for them.

Corinne sipped her coffee until she felt the inquisitive guard's attention wander. A quick glance confirmed that his focus was back on the football debate. Then she checked her watch. She had about five minutes before Lydia arrived, wired and tired after her overnight shift.

Lydia was her cabinmate, and over the past week—the first for both of them aboard the *Celebrate*—they had fallen into a pleasant routine. They met for coffee on the crew deck just after Lydia finished her shift and before Corinne started hers, and again in the mess just as Corinne was ending her workday and Lydia was gearing up for a new one.

Lydia was young—just twenty-one—and had never been away from her home in the north of England. Corinne thought perhaps the girl found comfort in the company of a woman her mother's age. Not that Corinne minded in the least. Lydia was a warm, cheerful girl, and it was nice to have someone to talk to about normal, everyday things. The world outside the shadow.

There was just enough time. Corinne pulled a small notebook from a pocket in her uniform skirt and laid it on the table, beside her coffee cup, angling her body so that no one else could read what was on its pages.

Behind her towered the bridge. All the crew's outdoor space was sunk into the bow, another cabin attendant had told her, because there wasn't much else a cruise ship could do with the open deck immediately below the bridge. For safety reasons, you couldn't put bright lights there, and paying passengers needed bright lights. So, with the curving white walls of the bow rising up around them, the crew had the only swimming pool on board that didn't offer a view of the sea.

For all Corinne knew, *he* could be one of the officers at the *Celebrate*'s helm right now, boring holes into her back. From what she'd seen on TV and in the movies, officers on the bridge had access to binoculars. She couldn't take any chances.

The sea breeze blew the notebook open, flipping through a few pages in rapid fire. Corinne slapped her hand down on it to keep it from blowing away. It was a small diary, the week-to-a-view kind, with her own small, neat handwriting filling the spaces for the past four days with short notations:

Cabine 1002: lit parfait? Rien.

Cabine 1017: Valises, mais pas des passagers.

Cabine 1021: Ne peut pas entrer—le mari dit la femme est malade.

Sunday: the bed in 1002 hadn't been slept in. She'd found nothing out of the ordinary on Monday. Tuesday: belongings in 1017, but no passengers for them to belong to. Then, on Wednesday, a request through the door of 1021 that she not disturb them, from a male passenger who said his silent wife was sick in bed.

All these little oddities had come to nothing. She would keep looking.

In the little pocket at the back of the notebook was a single sheet of folded paper. Corinne took it out and glanced over her shoulder. No sign of Lydia yet. No one else on deck appeared to be paying her any attention. She unfolded the page, laid it flat on the table in front of her, and smoothed out the creases with the heel of her hand.

Then, as she did every morning, she looked at the black and white photograph printed on the lower half. She studied the man's features, then closed her eyes to recall the face from memory. She repeated the exercise a few times, until she could remember every minute detail.

Looking at him, she said silently, *I will find you. Maybe today will be the day.*

Then she carefully refolded the page, tucked it back in the notebook, and put the notebook back in the pocket of her uniform.

Lydia would arrive any second. Corinne couldn't afford to get caught.

ADAM

The night before Sarah left was unusual only in that we didn't spend it at home.

We nearly always stayed in on a Saturday, taking up our established positions on the couch for a relaxed evening of pizza, bad-singing-competition TV, and good subtitled Scandinavian dramas.

I didn't much like going "*out* out," as the kids called it—the "kids" being what I called anyone under twenty-five, ever since I turned thirty years old six months ago.

Officially, my stance was that Ireland's binge-drinking culture should be not a claim to fame we were proud to promote, but an embarrassing problem we were desperate to solve. Our newly graduated youth, blinking in the harsh light of the real world, was presented with just two options: join the queue for the dole, or join the queue for Canadian work visas. It would drive anyone to drink.

That had to be why they did it, right? To numb their pain? Because it couldn't be for *fun*, could it? A typical Saturday night's going *out* out, as far as I could tell, started with you being sad you were sober and ended with you wishing you weren't so drunk. And, in between, all you did was queue up for things: for service at the bar, to get into the club, to use the toilets, to buy a box of greasy fried chicken, to hail a taxi home.

That was what I said, anyway.

The real reason I didn't like going *out* out was because Cork felt like an ever-shrinking city where a run-in with an old school friend or former college classmate was never more than a street corner away. There was a limit to how many "What are you up to these days?" a guy could take when he wasn't up to very much.

"I'm writing," I would say. "I'm a writer."

Me: hating myself for how sheepishly I said it.

Them: confused frown.

"Screenplays," I'd add. "Movies?"

"Oh, right." The inquirer would nod. "Nice. But I meant, like, for work. What do you *do*?"

Sometimes, I skipped the writing thing altogether and confessed straightaway to whatever shite temp job I'd taken that week, stapling things together in some generic office or answering phones in a call center. The pimply teens I'd left behind me when I dropped out of university were now young professionals collecting good salaries from investment banks, legal firms, and software giants. They had graduated during the boom and avoided the land mines of the bust, mostly. Their news was about promotions and bonuses and company cars, while I was still excited about the fact that scrawled across the top of my latest rejection letter had been my name. My *name*! Personalization: progress at last.

But it proved difficult to explain the concept of failing upward to a casual acquaintance who really only wanted to know whether you'd gone back on the dole.

"God, so bloody *what*?" Sarah used to say in the cab on the way home, ducking underneath my arm so she could lean her head against my chest, her degree of exasperation varying directly with how many drinks she'd had. "I don't know why you let them get to you. *You* still have your dreams."

"Ah, yes," I'd say. "My dreams. What's the current exchange rate on those, do you think? My phone bill is due."

"Well, you also have a gorgeous girlfriend. Who believes in you.

Who knows you're going to make this happen. Who has no doubt."

"None at all?"

"None whatsoever. Can we get takeaway? I'm starving."

"But you've no evidence. And I think the takeaway is closed."

"That's what belief means, Ad. I mean, really." A poke in the ribs. "Aren't you supposed to be a *writer* or something?"

I joked about it, yes, but the truth was, it got to me. I'd been trying to make this writing thing happen for *years*. Fantastical dreams were fine in your twenties, but I was thirty now. When even *I* had started wondering whether I should let my fanciful notions go, talking about them with people who had already moved to the Real World made it harder to convince myself that no, I shouldn't. Not yet.

I started making excuses, coming up with reasons to stay in on Saturday nights. I was tired. I was broke. *We* were broke because of me. Whatever my story, Sarah would nod, understanding, and our conversation would move on to deciding between a box-set rewatch or tackling our Netflix queue. Sometimes, she went out with the girls. And I was glad she did, because I wanted her to do what she wanted, and those nights typically won me a few weeks' reprieve. We still went out together every now and then, but eventually our go-to pub had a new name and our go-to club had closed down. I no longer recognized the songs that won especially loud cheers from the crowd when the DJ played them, and had no clue why we all were suddenly drinking out of jam jars with handles.

But that was before. Now things were changing. Finally.

"I bet it's like turning eighteen," Sarah said as we maneuvered around each other in the bathroom, getting ready. I was already dressed; she was wrapped in a bath towel. "From the moment you can produce legal ID, nobody bothers asking for it."

"So tonight no one's going to go 'But what do you actually *do*?' because for once I actually want them to?"

Oh, me? I'm a writer. Screenplays. Yeah, not doing too bad, actually.

Just made a sale. Major Hollywood studio, six figures. For a script I wrote in a month.

"Exactly." Sarah was putting on an earring, fiddling with the back of it. "They all know already anyway. You were on the cover of the *Examiner,* remember?"

I moved behind her, met her eyes in the mirror over the sink. "And," I said, "the back page of the *Douglas Community Fortnightly.*"

"And that advertiser thing you get free in shopping centers."

"That was the one with the very good picture."

"That wasn't of you."

"Still," I said. "It was a very good picture."

Sarah laughed.

"So who'll be at this thing?" I asked. "Anyone I know?"

We were going to a going-away party. If the pubs and clubs of Ireland had worried that austerity would damage their trade, they needn't have—there were enough preemigration shindigs these days to keep the industry afloat all by themselves. That night, it was the turn of Sarah's colleague Mike, who was heading to New Zealand for a year.

"Susan will be there. James—you met him before, didn't you? And Caroline. She's the girl we ran into the night of Rose's birthday. You know Mike, right? Don't think you've met the rest of them …"

While Sarah was saying this, I wrapped my arms around her waist and rested my chin on her shoulder, savoring the fruity smell of some lotion or potion.

There was no long fall of blond hair to move out of the way. Just that afternoon, Sarah had walked into a hairdresser's and asked to have it all chopped off. That morning, the ends had been tickling the small of her back. Now they couldn't tickle her neck. The cut had exposed more of her natural warm brown color, and I think it was this that made her eyes appear bigger and bluer than before. She also seemed more grown-up to me, somehow, and there was something wonderfully distracting about all that exposed skin …

I pressed my lips against the spot where her neck met her left shoulder.

Sarah said she had decided to get the haircut on a whim, after seeing a picture in the salon's window as she walked by. But a week from now, I would learn that she had made the appointment with the salon a week in advance.

"Just don't abandon me, okay?" I murmured.

I was expecting one of Sarah's trademark eye rolls and a sarcastic comeback. Maybe a reminder that I was now, technically speaking, a big shot Hollywood screenwriter and could surely hold my own in conversations about Things Adults Do, instead of standing on the periphery, smiling at the right moments and rearranging the ice cubes in my drink with a straw. Or perhaps Sarah would point out that tonight I didn't *need* to go to this thing. It was a work night, anyway, and she had planned on going by herself. But I moaned so pitifully about staying home alone the night before she was leaving for nearly a week, that she finally said fine, tag along.

But instead, she turned to face me, wrapped her arms around my neck, and said, "I would never abandon you."

"Well, good. Oscar night will be stressful enough without having to find a date for it."

I kissed her, expecting to feel her lips stretched into a smile against mine. They weren't. I moved my mouth to her jawline, down her neck. There was a faint taste of something powdery, some makeup thing she must have just dusted on her skin. I brought my hands to her waist and went to untuck the towel.

"*Ad*," Sarah said, wriggling free. "I booked a cab for eight. We don't have time."

I looked at my watch. "I suppose I should take that as a compliment."

"Funny." *Now* the eye roll. "Can you grab Mike's card? I think I left it on the coffee table. I'm nearly done here. I just have to get dressed."

I turned to leave.

"Oh, Ad?"

I stopped in the doorway.

Sarah was in front of the mirror, twisting to check her hair. Without looking at me, she said, "I meant to tell you, the others aren't exactly delighted about me being the one who gets to go to Barcelona. They've all been milking it with their honeymoons and maternity leave, but God forbid *I* get to have a week out of the office. I mean, it's not like I'm off. I'm there to *work*. Anyway, I've been trying not to go on about it, so …"

"Don't worry," I said. "I won't bring it up."

I smiled to myself as I crossed the hall into the living room. *Honeymoons and maternity leave.* Now that I'd sold the script, we could finally start making our own plans instead of being forced to watch as the fulfillment of everyone else's clogged up our Facebook feeds.

But first …

I collected Mike's card from the coffee table, then dropped into my preferred spot on the couch. It offered a clear line of sight to my desk, which was tucked into the far corner of the living room and so, crucially, was only a few feet from the kitchen and, thus, the coffeemaker.

A stack of well-thumbed A4 pages was piled on it, curled sticky notes giving it a neon fringe down its right side. I got a dull ache in the pit of my stomach just looking at it.

The rewrite. I *had* to start it tomorrow. And I would. I'd drive straight home after dropping Sarah at the airport and shut myself in, make the most of the few days and nights that I would have the apartment to myself.

Sarah emerged from our bedroom, wearing a dress I hadn't seen before.

The money from the script deal hadn't arrived yet, but ever since I learned it was on its way, I'd been melting my credit card. Sarah had supported me for long enough, paying utility bills and covering my rent shortfalls with money she could have been—*should* have been—spending on herself. That morning, I had sent her into town with a gift card for a high-end department store—the kind that comes wrapped in delicate tissue inside a smooth matte-finish gift bag.

"This is just a token," I had said. "Just a little something for now, for tonight. You know, when the money comes through …"

"Ad, what are you doing? You don't know how long that money is going to take to arrive. You should be hanging on to what you've got."

"I put it on the credit card."

"But you might need that credit yet. I really wish you'd think before you spend."

"Look, it's fine. We'll be fine. I just wanted to …" Sarah's mouth was set tight in disapproval. "Okay, I'm sorry. I am. It's just that I don't want to wait to start paying you back for … for everything."

She had seemed annoyed. Disappointed, too, which was worse. But then, later, she had come home with a larger version of the same bag, and now she was twirling around to show me the dress that had been inside it: red and crossed in the front, the skirt part long and flowing out from her hips.

"Well?" she said. "What do you think?"

She looked beautiful in it. More beautiful than usual. But with the new hair, not quite the Sarah I was used to.

"Nice," I said. I pointed to my jeans and my dark, plain T-shirt. "But now I feel underdressed."

"Change, if you want to."

Our buzzer went. The cab was here. "No, it's fine," I said. "Let's just go."

Aside from the clothes Sarah was wearing when I drove her to the airport the next morning, that red dress was the only item that I could tell the Gardaí was missing for sure.

Cork International Airport, all eight gates of it, is perched on a hill southwest of the city. Each year, it begins one in every three days shrouded in the sort of thick, dense fog that delays takeoffs and that, only a few years ago, contributed to a fatal crash landing on the runway. In other words, it was a terrible place to build an airport. Ask any Corkonian about this, and they'll mutter something about how the airport's planning application must have come clipped to a bulging brown envelope stuffed with cash.

On that Sunday morning, the skies were clear but with dark clouds on the horizon, threatening showers later in the day. Typical August weather for Ireland: warm enough to be muggy, with the ever-present threat of torrential rain.

It was a ten-minute drive from our apartment to the terminal's doors. Sarah was at the wheel.

"I could be coming with you," I said as the car passed through the airport's main gates. "I could put the flight on the credit card, stay in your room."

"It's only supposed to be me in there."

"Who'd know?"

"The hotel, and so would work once they got the bill. In Spain, all guests have to hand over their passport so the front desk can make a copy. Every name has to go on the register."

"How do you know that?"

"I think Susan told me."

"We could sneak me in."

"*You* need to work."

"I could work while you do."

"*Adam*," Sarah groaned. She looked over at me to see whether I was serious.

"Relax," I said, holding up my hands. "Just kidding."

We had already talked about my going to Barcelona, back when Sarah found out she had to go. But the only way not to get her into any trouble would have been to book another hotel room just for me, and there was no way we could afford to do that. A week later, I sold the script. But selling it meant I had to rewrite it, and the rewrite was due just after the Barcelona trip. So now I didn't have *time* to go.

"Sorry," Sarah said. "It's just ... well, you know. The flight."

She didn't like flying and knew that rain clouds over the airport meant a bumpy takeoff. I'd been purposely avoiding the subject.

"How long is it?" I asked.

"Couple of hours."

"That's not so bad. And you're going straight to the hotel when you land?"

Sarah nodded.

"Text me when you get there."

"Yeah." She glanced at me. "So what were you and Susan talking about last night?"

"What? When?"

"When I came back from the bar, you two looked like you were deep in conversation."

"She asked me for advice," I said. "Turns out she's not just all breasts and hair. She wants to be a writer. Who knew?"

"Not me," Sarah said, pulling right, to the departures lane. "In all the years I've worked for her, I never heard her breathe a word about it. I don't think I've ever even heard her mention a *book*. Then, what do you know—my boyfriend sells a script and suddenly she's all over him like a rash, asking for advice." A pause. "So that was it?"

"What?"

"All you and Susan talked about."

"Yeah, pretty much. Why?"

"Just wondering."

"You aren't …" I raised my eyebrows and waited for her to look over and see.

"What?"

"I mean, I know I'm quite the catch, now that I can make a living in my underwear and everything, but you don't need to worry."

Sarah parked the car in the taxis-only lane outside the terminal, killed the engine, and turned toward me.

"Ad, what *are* you on about?"

"I'm just saying jealousy is a terrible thing."

"What the …?" Sarah stopped, getting it. "Yeah. You and Susan Robinson. *Right*. Although I suppose women will be all over you now that you're rich and famous."

"I think you mean poor and anonymous."

"You won't be poor soon."

"*We* won't be. Anyway, this is me we're talking about. If, by any chance, any girl makes the poor choice of being all over me, the moment I open my mouth they'll be on their way again. Remember when we first met? What did I start talking about immediately?"

A hint of a smile tugging at her lips. "*Star Wars?*"

I glared at her. "*Star* Trek."

"So that's different?"

"I'm not going to react to that, because I know you know it is."

"That's my point. Girls *love* that crap now. Geeks are in."

"I think you have to have a beard for that, though."

"Don't all writers have beards? You could grow one."

"I know I could, but you're thinking of novelists," I said. "And poets. Poets have the best beards. Screenwriters do it clean-shaven. We like baseball caps, and the combination of beard and ball cap is just too much. But maybe I could start wearing glasses, or—"

A horn blew somewhere behind us.

"Shit," Sarah said, twisting in her seat to look behind her. "Am I parked in the wrong place? I am. *Shit.*" She reached for her handbag on the backseat. "What time is your talk tomorrow?"

"The one you're missing? Twelve."

It had been a last-minute request from my university to talk to their film studies class—the university I'd dropped out of, mind you. Apparently, all was forgiven.

"You wouldn't have let me come anyway," Sarah said.

"You'd make me nervous. I can only talk in front of strangers."

"Didn't you say Moorsey was going?"

"He's not sure he can get off work yet."

"So you can talk in front of him but not me?"

I shrugged as if to say, *I don't make the rules.* I didn't want to get into my real motivation for inviting Moorsey. It was a test.

"Then you're just going to write?"

"As much as I can."

"I'll try not to disturb you."

"Don't," I said, taking her hand. "I want to hear from you. I'll miss you."

"I mightn't have time to. They've got me booked into I don't know how many sessions at this conf—"

A cacophony of angry horn blowing began behind us.

"Come on," Sarah said, letting go of my hand and pushing open the driver's door. "Before there's a riot."

We both got out of the car and met at the trunk. I pulled Sarah's case out for her and set it on the ground.

"What time do you get in Thursday?" I asked.

"One-ish, I think."

"I'll be here."

I held her as we kissed quickly, lightly. Behind us, the horn blowing grew more enthusiastic.

Sarah pulled away first. She grabbed the handle of her case and turned toward the terminal.

"Have fun," I said.

Over her shoulder: "It's work!"

I called after her: "Yeah, but it's work in Barcelona!"

I got back into the car and readjusted the rearview mirror until it filled with the angry face and extended middle finger of a taxi driver. I waved apologetically at him and pulled off. Sarah was just a few steps from the terminal doors as I drove away.

That morning, she was wearing dark blue jeans, a white T-shirt with navy horizontal stripes, and a pair of those cheap, flat shoes that women (and their podiatrists) love. She was also wearing a scarf—navy with white butterflies—not because it was cold, but because she *felt* cold, what with her newly uncovered neck. A beige trench coat hung from the crook of her arm. She had a small leather bag slung over one shoulder and was pulling a cabin-approved bright purple trolley case behind her. She had packed light, she said. It was going to be only four days.

That afternoon, at 4:18 p.m. Irish time, she sent me a text message saying she had landed safely and was at the hotel. She had gotten a schedule of the conference, and it was going to be an even busier and more demanding affair than she was expecting. I wasn't to worry if she didn't manage to call or text much, she said. I was just to get writing and stay writing. She would see me on Thursday.

The last line of her text message read,

I won't even get to see Barcelona! :-(

If I've learned anything this past couple of weeks, it's that the most effective lies are the ones that are *almost* the truth.

Moorsey didn't come to the talk.

I spoke for an hour to a class of a hundred or so film studies students who had packed into a lecture theater in the basement of the Boole Library. Row after row of eager faces, Apple products, and slogan T-shirts. En masse, they looked as if they could eat me alive.

I smiled nervously at the wall behind them while some professor or other introduced me. I'd never done anything like this before, but as soon as I started talking, I saw that in their eyes, I was the only one with the information they needed. Then I started to relax. Individually, they may have phrased their questions in slightly different ways, but essentially they all wanted to know the same thing: How had I come up with an idea for a screenplay, written it down, secured an agent, and made a sale—all from my little desk in Cork?

"The short answer," I quipped, "is one decade and the Internet."

That got a good laugh. I made a mental note to trot out that little gem again.

Afterward, a man who said he was the course convener—whatever that meant—caught me just as I left the stage, and asked if I'd be interested in coming back for a practical screenwriting session. Behind his back, students were hurrying to leave the theater, some of them smiling or silently mouthing their thanks to me as they left.

I felt thoroughly pleased with myself.

"We want to take full advantage of this," the convener said.

"Having a Hollywood screenwriter right here in Cork!"

I fished a grubby-looking business card out of my wallet and told him to call me anytime, as I made another mental note: *get new business cards.*

"I dropped out of here, you know," I said, still riding a wave of confidence.

"Oh?"

"Three weeks, I lasted. One of them was Freshers' Week."

"How long ago?" The convener—Eric something—couldn't have been more than a couple of years older than I.

"Two thousand and one."

"What course?"

"English."

The next line was supposed to be, "Maybe you'll go back someday." That was the way this conversation always went.

But this guy said, "Well, third-level education isn't for everyone. You must be thrilled, though. After all your hard work."

I admitted that yes, I was thrilled—and a little overwhelmed. I said it was as if I had spent my whole life insisting on the existence of an invisible friend, and now, suddenly, everyone else could see him, too.

Eric Something looked confused.

"Well, thanks for today," he said, shaking my hand. "And best of luck with it all. We'll be in touch."

Mental note number 3: *retire the "invisible friend" analogy.*

I pulled out my phone as I crossed the Quad, heading through the campus in the direction of Western Road, where I'd left the car. Drops of moisture landed on my screen as I checked for missed calls or new text messages.

There was still nothing from Sarah.

I had sent her two messages last night and one earlier today. Why hadn't she replied?

I thought back to what I'd sent her: inane updates about the finale of a TV show we watched, and my observation that the coffee she had brought home on Saturday from one of those giant German discount supermarkets actually didn't taste *too* bad, and I tried to see them as Sarah would: evidence that I wasn't writing. She was well aware of my procrastination problem. Her not replying might just be her way of not encouraging it. And she was busy, as she had told me she would be. But had she gotten the messages in the first place?

I opened WhatsApp and typed a quick message:

Talk went well. So is it true the rain there falls mainly on the plain? It's about to start pissing down here. X

As soon as I pressed SEND, a single check mark appeared next to my message. After Sarah read it on her end, there would be two. That way, I'd know that she had seen it, at least.

There *was* a text message from Moorsey, saying he couldn't get off work but that he was having his lunch in Coffee Station if I was free to join. I checked the time: just gone one o'clock. I texted him back and said I was on my way.

Moorsey—his actual name was Neil Moore, but even his own mother called him Moorsey, and he wouldn't respond to anything but—had done everything right that I'd done wrong. I'd known him since secondary school, where he'd studied hard to get maximum points in his Leaving Cert *and* an award for the highest marks in physics in the whole of Ireland. We'd both gone straight into University College Cork, but he had lasted the full four years and graduated with first class honors before getting some big job with the Tyndall Institute. Something to do with nanotechnology, although, typical Moorsey, he'd tell you it was mostly entering numbers on spreadsheets all day long—"boring, really." He had bought a sensible house (two small bedrooms in a commuter town, price slashed because the builders had run out of money and so the development was unfinished) and a sensible car (a people carrier, secondhand) before I had even managed to leave my childhood bedroom. My parents loved him, and they loved using him as the standard I should have aspired to. Moorsey and I joked that he was like the son they never had.

But I had always been happy for him. He had always worked hard, and he deserved it. Moreover, he had always listened intently while I rambled on about screenwriting books and McKee seminars and the latest batch of rejection letters that, following Stephen King's instructions, I kept impaled on a nail hammered into my bedroom wall.

Since the script sale, though, something felt off between us. I wasn't surprised he hadn't made it to my talk, or that my consolation prize was a limited block of time when conversation would be hampered by the chewing of food.

I found him sitting inside the window of the café, a Coke and a card saying "23" on the table in front of him, the card angled toward the waitstaff.

Moorsey was an Irishman straight from Central Casting: fiery-red hair, skin so pale it bordered on translucent, a spill of freckles all over his face. Today he was wearing jeans and a T-shirt with the molecular structure of caffeine on the front. (Not that I would recognize the molecular structure of anything. He had worn it—and explained it to me—before.) Whenever I began to worry that I was still wearing the same kind of clothes I had when I dropped out of college, that I didn't own the tailored blazers, inexplicably tight jeans, or expensive yet scuffed-looking brown shoes I saw all the other men my age wearing, I thought of Moorsey and felt better.

And tried *not* to think about the fact that he had a PhD.

"I ordered for you," he said as I sat down. "A club."

"Perfect. Thanks."

"How did the thing go?"

"Great," I said. "I was really nervous before it started, but once it got going, I was fine. I was good. I was *funny*."

Moorsey blew air out of his nose in a lazy laugh, but said nothing.

"They wouldn't let you out of work?" I asked.

"No, sorry. We have this big deadline on Friday. A project's due."

"It's fine," I said. "Don't worry about it."

"Next time."

"Yeah."

There was a beat of silence then, broken by the clink of ice cubes as Moorsey took a sip of Coke.

Another conversational dead end.

I asked after Rose.

A few months ago, Moorsey had finally found his balls and made a move on Rose, Sarah's best friend. We all had known each other since college, and Sarah and I had known that Moorsey liked Rose for about that same amount of time. I thought it was great they were together.

"Rose is fine," Moorsey said. "Actually, I have some news. We've, ah, moved in together."

"Have you? Wow." In all the time I had known Moorsey, he never lived with anyone besides his parents and his younger brother. This was a big deal. Things must be getting serious. "Wow," I said again.

"So you're wowed, is what you're saying?"

"When did this happen?"

Moorsey looked embarrassed. "Couple of weeks ago."

Couple of weeks ago. That stung, but I didn't let on. Why hadn't he told me sooner? I hadn't seen him much since then, but we had talked. Texted. Why hadn't he mentioned that his first-ever serious girlfriend moved in with him?

Come to think of it, why hadn't *my* girlfriend told me the news, seeing as she must have known, too?

"Moorsey," I said, leaning forward. "Have I been a total dick lately?"

"What?"

"Have I been a dick? About the screenplay thing?"

"No. Not at all."

"You're sure?"

"Trust me when I say I'd let you know if you were being a dick."

"Okay."

I sat back again.

Moorsey frowned. "Why do you ask? Did someone say something?"

"No, it's just ... I don't know. I thought maybe you were annoyed with me."

Moorsey snorted.

"Jesus, Adam. You know, I think the stress of Hollywood is getting to you. It might be time to move out of LA. Get a place on the coast—Santa Monica, maybe. Then we can stalk Jennifer Lawrence together, like we've always dreamed."

I laughed. "Okay, okay. Sorry. Maybe the stress *is* getting to me. They sent me notes, you know? After the sale. Honestly, there were pages and pages and *pages*." I hadn't said this aloud to anyone yet, but now I pushed out the words that had been running around inside my head for more than a week. "I wonder why they bought the script at all, because it seems like they want everything in it to be different. To be honest, the thought of it ... I'm struggling even to get started."

My phone beeped with a text message.

"Mum," I told Moorsey as I read it. "She's made a batch of curry and wants to drop some of it over tonight so I don't starve to death while Sarah's away. Great."

"I love your mother's curry."

"Feel free to come and collect it, then. I've been avoiding it since she started adding peas back in '98."

"You remember the year?"

"It was a traumatic time."

"Why not just tell her to leave them out?"

"She thinks they're her signature ingredient."

"But I've seen peas in lots of curry."

"I know, I know. I don't want to burst her bubble."

A waitress appeared with our sandwiches. I ordered a coffee from her.

"Where *is* Sarah?" Moorsey asked. "Rose said something about her being away with work?"

Later, replaying this conversation in my head, I would recall how he had looked out the window as he asked me that.

"She's in Barcelona. At a conference."

"Nice. You didn't want to go, too?"

"I couldn't. I have the rewrite."

"How's she getting on?" Moorsey asked his sandwich.

"Actually, I don't really know."

I picked up my club and started pulling out the chunkier tomato pieces, eyeing my phone on the tabletop as I did. Still no new calls or texts. By now I hadn't had any contact with Sarah for nearly a whole day.

When I looked up again, Moorsey was looking at me questioningly.

"She knows I need to write," I said. "She's trying not to disturb me."

When my phone rang late Tuesday morning, the sound jerked me out of a deep sleep. I'd been up until four thirty, trapped in a cycle of checking Twitter, admonishing myself for checking Twitter, and then staring at my script on the screen until I gave in and checked Twitter. This had gone on for hours until, finally, I crawled into bed, defeated.

Groggy and disoriented now, I peered at my phone's screen.

The call was from a blocked number.

I thought, *Sarah*. And, *It's about time.*

"Hello?" It came out as an incoherent croak. I coughed and tried again. "Hello?"

"Adam, is that you?"

A woman's voice. Older. It took me a moment to place it. "Maureen. Hi. How are you?"

I sat up, rubbing the sleep out of my eyes and wondering why Sarah's mother could possibly be calling me.

Sarah had only one sibling: a brother named Shane, who lived in Canada and was nine years her senior. If you listened to the conspiratorial whispers of the relatives who cornered me at O'Connell family weddings and squealed, "You two'll be next!" Shane's arrival had been deliberately postponed, and then Sarah's had come as quite the surprise. My own parents had taken a different tack: they got married young, had me nine months later, and then bided their time until I turned eighteen—or twenty-two, as it turned out—when they got their lives back, duty done. As a result, our two sets of parents seemed to me to be of entirely different generations. Mine were vibrant, strong, and active while Sarah's were quiet, subdued, and frail. I wanted to reel mine in sometimes while I felt that hers needed some looking after.

"God is good," Maureen said. "Yourself?"

"Grand, thanks."

"How's the film going?"

Like all Corkonians, Maureen pronounced it *fill-um*. I'd taken to saying "movie" instead to avoid embarrassment.

"It's fine," I said. "Going well."

I'd long given up correcting her and Jack's misperception that what I was doing was moviemaking. Positive-sounding generalities were the way to go.

"Were you doing something yesterday, did I hear?"

"Yeah. A talk. In UCC."

"UCC? Really? Well, isn't that great. Good for you, Adam."

I smiled at this. Although I knew they liked me—they thought I was nice and kind and well brought up, Sarah said—Jack and Maureen had always frowned on my wanting something other than a nine-to-five job, because in their minds, those were the only jobs around. As far as they knew, the sole equation that worked was good Leaving Cert + college degree = a pensionable job. And they prayed (literally prayed—novenas, mostly) that I would realize this before wedding invitations were ordered and hat-shopping began. The script sale, then, was like a stress test for everything they believed about how to get ahead in life, and I knew they were struggling now with how to respond to it. Maureen had just paid me a kindness.

"Is herself awake?" she asked.

"Her ... Sorry?"

"Sarah. Is she awake? I said to myself, she's probably asleep, so I called your phone instead. Are you at home?"

"I ... I am, but ..."

She thinks Sarah's here?

She had forgotten that Sarah was in Barcelona, and, what, thought she could be sleeping this late on a weekday morning? Maureen was famously forgetful, but this seemed odd even for her. Had we graduated from looking for reading glasses that were on her head, and circling Tesco's car park twice to find the car, to forgetting that her own daughter was in another country?

"But, Maureen," I said. "Sarah's in Spain."

"What, love?"

"Sarah's in Barcelona," I said. "With work. There's a conference on, Monday to Wednesday. She flew out Sunday morning and she's back Thursday lunchtime." *Remember?* I waited for her to say that she did. When there was no sound on the line, I said, "She didn't tell you?" even though I didn't think for a second that it could be true.

Away from the receiver, Maureen said, "He says Sarah's in *Spain*."

A gruff male voice in the background: *Jack.* "What? But, sure, that doesn't make any sense."

"Are you looking to talk to her?" I said. "She has her phone."

Maureen, back to me: "We've been calling it. We can't get through."

A rustling sound as the phone changed hands. Now Jack's voice was loud in my ear. "We've been calling her since this time yesterday. There's no answer."

"Well, I'm sure she's just busy. There's the conference—"

"First it was ringing and ringing, but now it goes straight to the answering machine. Maureen sent some texts and left a message, but she didn't call us back, so we rang the office just now. The receptionist told us Sarah's out sick. Has been since Monday. We presumed she was at home, so we called you. Now you say she's in *Spain*?"

"She is." I repeated to Jack what I'd already said to Maureen: Barcelona, a conference, back on Thursday. "It's a big office, Jack. I'm sure whoever you spoke to had just gotten the wrong end of the stick. It's them that sent her there. I can call them for you, if you—"

"You've been speaking to her?"

I hesitated. "Yeah."

"Today?"

I pulled my phone from my ear to check for any new missed calls or messages. "No. Not today."

Sarah had sent me only one text message since she landed, and that had come in on Sunday afternoon. It was nearly Tuesday afternoon now. Forty-eight hours with no communication. Could she really be so busy that in two days she hadn't found sixty seconds to type me a quick text?

I opened WhatsApp and looked for the double check mark. There was still only one beside the message I'd sent.

She hadn't read it yet.

I ran through the logical explanations. Maybe her phone wasn't working abroad. Or maybe it was dead and she had lost her charger. She could have forgotten to bring a European plug adapter and was too busy to find a place where she could buy another one.

Someone would later tell me that denial, the first stage of grief, isn't big and simple, like refusing to accept that someone is dead when all the evidence overwhelmingly points to it. No. The *real* work of denial, the true intricacy of it, takes place beneath the thoughts your consciousness articulates in the nanoseconds before those thoughts form. It happens when you are presented with a set of circumstances that any person *not* in denial would immediately find worrisome. But because you are in the midst of it, the roots of every fear bend and break, reforming into plausible explanations that allow you to put off being concerned. Denial is forcing boring, pedestrian explanations out of your synapses, growing them thick and uncontrolled like vines on a time-lapse video—and doing it constantly and quickly, so nothing logical has a chance to squeeze through.

It just *didn't occur to me* that Sarah could be anywhere but where she had said she would be, or that the reason she wasn't answering her phone was because she (a) wouldn't or (b) couldn't. But, I realize now, this was *all* that was occurring to Jack.

"Where is she staying?" he asked. "We'll call her there."

I wondered what the urgency was. What couldn't wait?

"Is everything okay, Jack?" I asked. "Is something wrong? Has something happened?"

I wasn't getting it yet, but *this* was what was wrong.

This was what had happened.

After Jack hung up, I lay down and tried to go back to sleep, sure that he and Maureen were overreacting. But after less than a minute, I was staring at the ceiling and feeling responsible for their panic.

I couldn't remember the name of the hotel where Sarah was staying. Truth be told, I couldn't remember whether she had ever told me.

I imagined Jack and Maureen in their paisley-covered living room: Jack pacing back and forth in front of the fireplace, Maureen pulling the rosary beads she had bought in Lourdes through her fingers. It didn't matter that they didn't *need* to be worried, only that they were. Sarah would be devastated to find out what she had inadvertently caused with her radio silence—a silence quite likely intended to help me.

This could be all my fault.

I scrolled through the contacts on my phone until I found Rose's number. My call to her went unanswered. I sent her a text instead, asking whether she had heard from Sarah in the past couple of days, and if she hadn't, could she by any chance remember the name of the hotel in Barcelona where she was staying?

They would be able to tell me the name of the hotel at the office. Jack and Maureen had probably just spoken to the receptionist, who could hardly be expected to know the whereabouts of every employee. A hundred people worked at Sarah's firm. I could call them myself and make sure I got put through to her department, maybe even disguise it as a follow-up with my new best friend, Susan the "Sudden Scribe" Robinson, Sarah's manager. But then I pictured Sarah's face as I explained my reasons for calling her boss, and decided instead to wait and see if Rose knew the name of the hotel.

Besides, Jack and Maureen had already been on with the office. Them *and* me in the same day? Sarah would be mortified when she got back.

I padded into the living room and woke up my computer.

Sarah had bought me a laptop a couple of Christmases ago. She had one of her own, but only mine was connected to a printer. I'd seen the icon on my desktop already—a PDF file named as a string of random numbers. Sarah's boarding passes.

I opened them now:

EU/EEA Passenger: Sarah O'Connell Booking reference: EHJ9AM
10 August 2014
EI802: ORK-BCN | Zone B | Seat 18B
Departs: 10:55 | Gate closes: 10:25

EU/EEA Passenger: Sarah O'Connell Booking reference: EHJ9AM
14 August 2014
EI804: BCN-ORK | Zone C | Seat 23A
Departs: 11:40 | Gates closes: 11:10

I printed them off and set the page aside. Sarah would no doubt make contact any second, but seeing the boarding passes might make Jack and Maureen feel a bit better in the meantime.

I might go over there later and do some reassuring in person. Although Sarah would probably call long before then.

I tried her number now, but after a beat of dead air, voice mail kicked in: "Hi, you've reached Sarah—sort of, because I can't answer my phone right now. But please leave me a message and I'll call you back just as soon as I can." I hung up without saying anything.

So her phone *was* dead. Or switched off, at least.

I looked at my own mobile, turned it over in my hand, studied it. An item easily lost or damaged, kept alive by another item even more easily lost or damaged. If Sarah didn't have one, if every other person in the Western world didn't have one, too, would Jack and Maureen be worried about their grown daughter right now? Would it be at all odd that she had been away for a couple of days and hadn't contacted them? As my father liked to say, what did we all do before mobile phones, eh?

We waited for people to come home. How else could you contact someone if they didn't have their mobile phone? Sarah only ever emailed me links to articles she had found online and thought I would like, but I swiped a finger across my phone's screen and checked my inbox, just in case. All that had come in the past couple of days were circulars from online stores, notifications of new comments on my blog, and, three hours ago, an email from my agent.

The subject line said "*Rewrite?*"

I ignored it for now. One problem at a time.

I checked my Twitter and Facebook apps. Sarah had accounts on both, though she rarely used them. I saw that the most recent activity was from weeks before.

Even if her phone was dead, she was bound to be online, if only for conference-related work stuff. I sent her private messages on both networks, then an email, asking her to call me when she got the chance, telling her I missed her, reminding her that I loved her.

Back to the home screen.

Still nothing from Sarah, nothing from Rose.

I sent Moorsey a message, asking him to ask Rose to call me.

Then I realized there was a way I could find out where Sarah was staying. *Possibly* ...

The archive box was in my side of the wardrobe. Setting it on the bed, I riffled through utility bills, our lease, the finance agreement on my car. At the back was a bundle of bank statements and, stuck in the middle, the letter from Sarah's bank thanking her for registering for online banking, and giving her the eight-digit code she needed to access it.

Back at my computer, I navigated to her bank's home page. After clicking away a series of pop-up ads, I found a link to ACCESS YOUR PERSONAL ACCOUNT. I moved the cursor over it … and hesitated.

This was for Jack and Maureen, I told myself. I wanted to stick a pin in their panic, deflate the fear that was growing in that paisley-clad living room. Sarah would appreciate it. She would even forgive me for looking at her bank account.

Wouldn't she?

We didn't keep any secrets from each other anyway. We lived together, lived our lives together. How *could* we keep secrets?

I clicked on the link and logged on to Sarah's online banking.

The first thing that struck me was the balance on her current account. She had nearly fifteen thousand euro in there, and another five thousand in what looked like some kind of special savings scheme. I had less than a hundred to my name. What was she doing with so much money? How did she have so much while keeping both of us afloat?

I thought of our conversation about Barcelona. "*You can't afford it,*" she had said. *You,* not *we.* A few weeks ago, the flight might have been a hundred euro, at most a hundred and fifty. What was that out of fifteen grand? You wouldn't even miss it.

But as soon as this thought formed, I felt my cheeks warm with shame. This was her money. She had earned it. Sarah certainly wasn't under any obligation to spend any more of it on me.

I shook this discovery off and went looking for a list of recent transactions on Sarah's debit card. As soon as I found them, I knew that something was wrong. The narratives were all store and restaurant names I recognized. I knew them because they were all here, in Cork. They were all from before Sarah left for Spain. I could even see a charge from Brown Thomas, the store where she had bought the red dress on

Saturday. She must have used the gift card I gave her for part of the payment—apparently, women's dresses cost a lot more than I thought.

The exception was one charge from Sunday morning, something called HMS Host. The letters "POS" were displayed next to the transaction, meaning that it was a point of sale where Sarah had physically handed over her card at the cash register. I thought it might mean something, until I Googled it and discovered that HMS Host was just the operator of the café in the departures lounge of Cork Airport.

Sarah hadn't used her card abroad at all. How was that possible? Or was I just looking in the wrong place?

I scanned the screen until I found a link to PENDING TRANSACTIONS. There were just two:

10/08/2014	VDA-AEROPUERTO BCN	653.00 DR
10/08/2014	VDA-PLYAPRINCESSHTL	50.00 DR

I opened another browser window, typed "*plyaprincesshtl barcelona*" into Google, and hit ENTER.

Did you mean Playa Princess Hotel Barcelona?

I found the hotel's contact information on its website and called the front desk. It rang only once before a recorded message in Spanish kicked in. Not understanding a word, I hit the standard option for getting a human being: zero.

"Hotel Playa Princess, *buenos días*," a female voice said.

"Ah, *buenos días*," I said. "Er, *¿habla inglés*, um, *por favor?*"

"Yes, of course, sir. How may I help you?"

"I'm trying to reach a guest of yours. Sarah O'Connell. Can you put me through to her room?" I spelled the name.

"One moment please."

Tranquil hold music came down the line. Expecting to hear Sarah's voice next, I was gearing up to say something sarcastic about the whole point of having a mobile phone at all when, abruptly, the agent came back on the line.

"I am sorry, sir. We have no guest by that name."

"Are you sure?" I spelled the surname out again.

"Certain, sir. Perhaps she is in a different hotel?"

"Maybe it's under her employer's name …" I spelled out "Anna Buckley Recruitment."

"Let me see …" I could hear the soft clacking of computer keys. "No, sir. I have nothing under that, either."

"But she's definitely there," I said. "You charged her debit card. Fifty euro on Sunday. Why would there be a charge on her card if she's not staying there?"

"Perhaps she dined here." A pause. "Is there anything else I can assist you with today?"

"Look," I said, lowering my voice. "I don't want to get you in any trouble, but it's really important that I contact her. We have a bit of a family emergency here and she's not answering her phone."

There came a long pause, then a barely audible sigh. "One moment, please."

I waited through more computer key clacking—much more this time.

"Ah, okay," the agent said eventually. "I think I found her. Sarah O'Connell, arrived Sunday the tenth."

"That's her!" An unexpected surge of relief flooded through me. Perhaps I'd been a *little* worried that this was about more than a dead phone or a lost charger. "Great. Thank you. Can you put me through to her room?"

"Ms. O'Connell has already checked out."

"What?"

"She stayed with us for only one night."

I frowned. "Are you sure?"

"*Yes*," the agent said, a little indignantly.

"Did she check out early? Can you tell?"

"Sir, I'm sorry—"

"Do you have a conference on this week?"

"No. We do not have the facilities. We are only a small boutique hotel of thirty-five rooms."

I mumbled my thanks and ended the call just as my phone beeped with a message from Moorsey:

Rose at work til 6. Everything ok?

I wasn't sure. I had the name of Sarah's hotel, yes, but also confirmation that she had left it after just one night's stay.

Why? Where had she gone then? Where was she now? Why hadn't she called or texted me? Why hadn't she called or texted her parents? Was it possible that she hadn't told them she was going to Spain? Why wouldn't she?

What the hell was going on here?

Before now, whenever I heard people say, "I didn't know what to think," I thought they meant, "I couldn't decide on a likely explanation from all the possibilities that were running through my head at the time." But now I understand that it's far more literal than that. You experience a blankness, an absence of thought. The voice in your head goes silent because your mind is so overloaded with fragments of information that make absolutely no sense. Thus, it fights them all at once, pushing them away until only a silent, empty space is left. The voice in your head goes away because it doesn't know what to say. It doesn't even know where to begin. You don't know what to think, so you think nothing at all.

While we're on the subject, the same goes for "weak at the knees." Love songs and rom-coms have us thinking that it's all to do with love and butterflies and joy. But it's actually what happens when you get such a shock, your brain momentarily forgets to keep telling your legs to stand, and you collapse, sliding or dropping straight to the floor and landing in a tangle with your legs underneath you.

But that realization was still ahead of me.

A few seconds of contact with Sarah would clear all this up. I glared at my phone, willing it to come alive with a call from her. I refreshed my email, willing a new message from her to appear. I picked up the printout of the boarding passes and studied it, willing the black print to reveal something to me I hadn't seen before:

EU/EEA Passenger: Sarah O'Connell Booking reference: EHJ9AM
10 August 2014
EI802: ORK-BCN | Zone B | Seat 18B
Departs: 10:55 | Gate closes: 10:25

EU/EEA Passenger: Sarah O'Connell Booking reference: EHJ9AM
14 August 2014
EI804: BCN-ORK | Zone C | Seat 23A
Departs: 11:40 | Gates closes: 11:10

And then it did.

The first time I had looked at the boarding passes, I saw only what I had expected to see: that Sarah had been on the flight I dropped her off for on Sunday, and was due to be on the one that would land at lunchtime four days later.

But now I saw something else, too—something wrong.

No.

My phone began to vibrate, but it wasn't Sarah's name on the screen.

"Rose," I said flatly.

"Hey, Adam." Her voice was airy with artificial nonchalance. "Moorsey said you were trying to reach me. I'm at work, but I'm on a break. What's up?"

"You tell me."

At least five full seconds of silence followed. Then, quietly: "I'm not sure what you mean."

"She booked a middle seat, Rose."

"What?"

"On her flight to Barcelona. B is a middle seat. Why would she do that? No one *wants* a middle seat."

Unless, of course, you wanted to sit next to someone who had already booked the aisle or the window.

I didn't have any answers yet, but I had just figured out one of the questions.

"Where's Sarah, Rose?" My voice wavered, so I called on the added force of an expletive to steady it. "And who the fuck is she with?"

ROMAIN

Deavieux, Picardy, 1989

All Romain wanted was to be a good little boy.

According to Mama, Jean was the *best* little boy. This was clearly not true, because Mama didn't know all the little boys in the world, and anyway, Jean wasn't really even good. He was just pretending. He did as he was told, just because he knew it would get him sweets or extra TV time. He wasn't *actually* good, not inside. But Mama didn't seem to see this, and whenever Romain tried to tell her, she looked up at the ceiling and said, "If only you were *half* as good as your brother is ..."

But she never finished the sentence, and so he didn't know what would happen if he was.

Maybe that was why Jean felt so tired all the time. He and Romain shared bunk beds, and Jean was always asleep before Romain. And yet, every morning when Mama came to wake them up, Jean said he wanted to stay in bed longer and sleep more. Being good must be exhausting. The sweets Mama bought were the hard ones with no chocolate on them, and the TV didn't even have the children's channels with the cartoons, so why did Jean even bother pretending to be good?

Romain couldn't figure it out.

Papa worked in the city and was home only on weekends. Every Friday evening, Mama packed them all into the car and drove to Compiègne to collect Papa from the train station. This was Romain's favorite time of the week, because Papa was *his* favorite, and when he came walking out of the train station, it was the furthest moment from the moment when he would have to go back again.

Sometimes, though, Mama ruined it.

Papa would always drive back, and Mama would sit beside him and tell him about her week. She always talked about Romain as if he weren't sitting right behind her, listening. He did this; he wouldn't do that; I don't know what's wrong with that boy, but something is. Don't you see it? What are we going to do with him? What *can* we do? What can I do, at home all week by myself?

She was always going on about Felix, the Lauriers' cat, even though she hated cats. Romain had seen her chase Felix out of their garden more than once. He had been missing for ages when she found the cat's collar in the fort Romain and Jean had built down by the lake. Mama must think Papa had a terrible memory, because she told him the same story over and over again, and Papa always said the same thing. *So what? That cat was always around the place.* Mama said yes, except that the collar hadn't been torn or cut, but carefully unbuckled and removed. Papa said she had an overactive imagination and that that furry lump of fat probably died of heart disease. Then he would tell her to stop going on about it, because children understand more than you think.

Then Papa would wink at Romain in the backseat, and whenever Mama caught him doing it, she would tell him he needed to decide whose side he was on.

This Friday, though, she had something new to say.

"Ask him about the bird, why don't you?" she said to Papa. "Get him to tell you what happened to the bird. Then let's see who has an overactive imagination."

* * *

Yesterday was the first day without rain in a week. After being cooped up with Mama and Mikki and Jean in the house for so long, Romain was excited to get outside, to get away from them. He preferred the world when it was quiet.

The path to the lake went past the old shed at the end of the garden, where Papa kept things he never used. There was a big rusty lock on the door, and Romain and Jean knew they weren't allowed inside. At the back of the shed stood an old plastic rain barrel.

As Romain passed it, he heard a strange flapping noise coming from inside. Splashing … chirping?

Romain had to stand on tiptoe to see over the lip of the barrel. It was a third full of greenish water and smelled funny, and a little bird was near the bottom of it, drowning.

It looked like a robin, but Romain wasn't sure. He didn't know a lot about birds. He thought they *liked* water, but this one didn't seem to. Only its head and the ends of its wings were above the water, and it was chirping and flapping and hopping up and down, going crazy trying to get out.

Romain spent a few seconds thinking about what he could do. He could do nothing and carry on down to the lake, but then the bird would probably die. That wouldn't be very nice. He could try to find something to pull the bird out with, but he wasn't sure he was tall enough to do that. He could go get help, but if he told Mama about this, he'd probably get in trouble for it somehow. He always did. She'd find a way.

How else could he get the bird out of the barrel?

That's when Romain got the idea to pull the barrel over so all the water and the bird would come out.

It took a while, because he wasn't strong enough to pull it over all by himself. In the end, he had to hang from the side of the barrel with his arms outstretched, pulling on it with all his weight, before it tipped over. He tried to jump out of the way then, but the water came out fast. He felt it, cold and slimy, splashing against his legs. There was much more of it in there than he had thought, and it went everywhere in just a second, crashing out of the barrel and spreading all over the ground.

Everything went quiet. Even the chirping had stopped. At first, Romain thought the bird had flown away, and this made him happy. His plan had worked! But then he heard the flapping noise again—quieter now and slower, too, not *flap-flap-flap* like before—and when he followed it, he found the bird lying on its side in the muddy grass.

He could see its little chest going up and down, as if it was panting. He wondered if it was just tired after all the chirping and just wanted to sleep now.

"Romi, what the hell are you doing?" It was Mama's voice.

Romain's heart sank.

He turned toward her. She was looking around—at the barrel on the ground; the wet, muddy grass; the stains on his jeans where the water had splashed him.

"What's going on here, Romi?" She peered over his shoulder. "What's that, down there?" She took a step forward, careful where she put her feet, and looked down into the grass behind him. "What the ..."

By now the flapping noise had stopped, too.

Mama took a quick couple of steps back, away from the bird, putting one of her sandals right in the mud.

"Romi, I asked you a question. Answer me. What did you *do?*"

"It was drowning, Mama," he said, looking up at her. "The bird was drowning. But now it's not anymore."

* * *

Papa told him about the Sleepover School the very next day.

"It'll be fun," Papa said. They were on the rowboat out on the lake, eating chocolate bars with footballers on them that Papa had brought home from the city. "You'll do your schoolwork and play with your friends and eat dinner and sleep, all in the same place. It'll be like being on holiday."

"But there's no school on holiday," Romain said.

"Yes, well … Look, Romi, it's hard for your mother, okay? Being here all week without me, trying to look after the three of you by herself. We need to figure out a way to help her."

"Send *Jean* to Sleepover School, then. He'd love to go. He'd get to stay in bed even longer because school would be right there."

"He's too young to go now. It's a big boys' school."

"Please, Papa. I don't *want* to go. I want to stay here. And if I go there, I won't be here when you are."

Papa looked away, out over the lake.

"Well, I'll try to talk to your mother, Romi. Okay? I'll try. I'll see what I can do. But you'll have to do something for me in return. You'll have to start being good. *Really* good. All the time, no matter what. Like Jean. And if you can manage that for, say, a whole month, then we'll see about school."

"But Jean isn't good! He just *pretends* to be."

Papa frowned. "What do you mean?"

"He's just good to get things. Like yesterday, Mama said whoever ate all their dinner would get some ice cream, so Jean ate all his dinner to get the ice cream, and then Mama said he was good. But he wasn't! He just wanted the ice cream."

"Did *you* eat all your dinner?"

Romain trailed his fingers in the water, watching the ripples they made. "No."

"Why not?"

"Because I don't like ice cream."

Papa looked at him funny for a second and then laughed.

"Okay, Romi," he said. "Fair enough. But what do you think? Are you going to be a good little boy for me? For your mama? Will you promise?"

Romain *really* didn't want to go away to Sleepover School, so he promised Papa that he would try his best.

* * *

At first, it was easy. Come Monday morning, he got dressed without delay and brushed his teeth before going downstairs. He ate all his breakfast without complaining that the cornflakes were soggy, even though they were *really* soggy, and when he was done he brought his and Jean's empty bowls to the sink. He left for school before Mama had to tell him, and while he was there he stayed quiet and in his seat. He didn't listen to the teachers—he never did—but Mama wouldn't know that. The teachers didn't even know. After school, he walked straight home without stopping, and as soon as he got in, he changed out of his uniform and hung it up in the wardrobe.

But then, in the afternoon, things started to go wrong.

Papa had told him to be good like his brother, so Romain started watching Jean to see what he did, so he could copy him. They would *both* be pretending then, but things would be easier for Mama, and Romain wouldn't have to go away to any awful Sleepover School.

He watched from the doorway while Mama sat down to look at the TV. After a while, Jean left his toy trains abandoned on the floor and climbed up beside her on the sofa. He snuggled up against Mama, who smiled at him and put an arm around his shoulders and gave him a squeeze.

Watching them gave Romain an ache in his belly. Mama never hugged *him* like that. He hadn't really thought about it before, but he realized now that he wanted her to.

So he went to the sofa and climbed up on Mama's other side and smiled at her exactly as Jean had.

But Mama didn't hug him or squeeze him. She looked away from him and got all stiff instead. A few minutes later, she told Romain to go sit on the armchair across the room instead, on his own.

Romain didn't know what he had done wrong.

Soon after that, it was dinnertime. Chicken stew, Romain's least favorite. It looked like the muddy water from the lake, and it would taste like it, too. Mama never made anything nice. Dessert was chocolate mousse in pots, but only if their plates were clean. Romain didn't like chocolate mousse, and he would probably feel sick if he tried to clear his plate, but he remembered what Papa had said. He was supposed to be good. He was supposed to do what Jean did.

So when Jean clapped his hands and said, "It's my favorite, Mama!" Romain did exactly the same a moment later.

Mama turned to stare at him.

"What are you doing, Romi?" she asked. "What is this? What are you up to now?"

"Copying Jean," Romain said, because that was the truth.

"Copying … *Why?*"

"Because Papa said to."

"*Papa?*" Mama said. "Because *Papa* said to?" She sounded as though she was making fun of him.

Romain wasn't sure what he was supposed to say now, so he said nothing. He stayed quiet for the rest of the meal. Mama did, too. He cleaned his plate but didn't get any mousse, which was good because he didn't want it anyway.

Afterward, while Mama was doing the dishes in the kitchen, Mikki started crying. He was only a baby, so he was always in his cot in the living room. And now Jean and Romain couldn't hear the TV over him.

Jean went into the kitchen and asked Mama to turn up the TV, but she said no and told him to make his baby brother quiet instead. Jean went back to the cot and held Mikki's hand and made funny faces, but Mikki didn't stop crying. He just started doing it louder.

So Romain tried.

He had seen Mama make Mikki quiet lots of times. Whenever he was crying, she would take him out of his cot and hold him in her arms and walk back and forth across the floor, shaking him up and down and saying "*ssshhh*" a lot.

Mikki was heavier than Romain thought he would be, and his arms got tired right away, but he remembered his promise to Papa, so he did it anyway—and it worked!

After a few minutes, Mikki stopped crying. He looked as if he had fallen asleep. Careful not to wake him up again, Romain gently put him back in his cot and covered him with a blanket.

But when Mama came into the room a while later, she wasn't happy at all.

She looked at Mikki and starting shaking her head and saying "No" a lot. And then, when she picked him up, she started screaming and crying. And then she knelt on the floor with Mikki in her arms and shouted at Romain.

"What have you done this time, you evil little shit? Oh, God. And to think I was out there feeling guilty about you! Oh, God. No. Please, no. What have you done . . .?"

Papa was called and told to come home right now, and doctors came in an ambulance for Mikki, and Mrs. Laurier came from next door to bring Jean and Romain over to her house, and a week later Romain got sent to Sleepover School anyway, and Papa didn't talk to him at all in the car the whole way there.

Even though Romain had kept his promise. He *had* tried his best.

All Romain wanted was to be a good little boy. He just couldn't figure out how.

ADAM

I always knew when someone was outside our apartment, because the building had a tell. Whenever the fire door at the end of the hall was opened, our front door got pulled outward, the wood meeting wood in a loud *clunk*. Some kind of suction thing. When I heard it that Tuesday evening, I held my breath, waiting for a key to turn in the lock, or one of my neighbors' doorbells to sound. But neither sound came. There was only a pair of voices, whispering furiously in the hall.

I tiptoed to the front door and looked through the peephole.

Moorsey and Rose were on the other side.

I turned my head and pressed an ear to the door.

"You have to tell him," Moorsey was saying. "You know it's the right thing to do."

"I don't *have* to do anything."

"But you should."

"Sarah's my best friend."

"And I'm his."

"*You* tell him, then."

"Maybe I will."

"Maybe I'll move back out."

"Aw, Rose, please."

"I'm sorry. I just don't know what to do here. What are we supposed to do?"

The talking stopped. I put my eye back to the peephole and saw them hugging. When they broke apart, Moorsey kissed Rose on the cheek and then Rose reached for the doorbell.

I opened the door just as she pressed it.

"I thought I heard voices out here," I said.

I turned and walked into the kitchen without another word, sensing a silent exchange of meaningful glances behind my back. Footsteps on the hall's hardwood floor followed me. Someone closed the front door and snapped the lock into place.

I took a seat at the head of the kitchen table. Moorsey sat on my right, Rose next to him.

I looked to Rose. Everyone always said she and Sarah could be sisters, they looked so much alike. Blue eyes; brown hair with blond highlights; small, full mouths. But that evening, nothing about Rose was familiar, not when she was sitting in our kitchen with no Sarah in sight.

"I don't know where she is, Adam," she said. "Not if she's not at that hotel. Really, I don't."

"But you know more than I do about where she's been."

"I don't *know* anything. Not for sure."

"You know who she's with."

Rose looked to Moorsey for help.

"What's going on, Ad?" he asked me. "What's happened?"

I told him about not being able to get through to Sarah's phone, about Jack and Maureen not hearing from her, either, about the one-night stay at the hotel, and the prebooking of a middle seat on the plane.

"The hotel says they don't even do conferences," I said. "And when Maureen and Jack called Anna Buckley—"

Rose's head snapped toward me. "They called her *office*?"

"Oh, it gets much worse than that. They're completely freaking out. If they don't hear from her soon, they'll probably call Interpol to launch an international missing-persons operation."

The color drained from Rose's face until the pink powder on her cheeks stood out on her blue-white skin.

"But *why?*"

"Because they think something terrible has happened to their daughter." I heard my voice rise. "Has it, Rose? Has something terrible happened?"

"This wasn't how it was supposed to go."

"How *what* wasn't?"

"I can't tell you." Rose's eyes blurred with tears. "I'm *Sarah's* friend."

I turned to Moorsey and said, "And I thought you were mine."

"You have to tell him," Moorsey said to Rose. "This is Sarah's fault, not yours. She shouldn't have put you in this position. Just tell him what you know, and let her pick up the pieces when she gets back."

"But I *can't.*"

"Do you think she'd want her parents to be worried about her like this?" Moorsey said. "We have only two possible outcomes now. Which one would she prefer?" He put an arm around Rose's shoulders, pulled her toward him. Whispered in her ear. "Just tell him what you know, lovely. You can't do anything else."

I hadn't been around them much since they got together. I'd never seen them like this. He called her *lovely?* I felt a pang of regret that I'd never thought of calling Sarah that. What would I be calling her now, after this? What *was* this?

"Okay," Rose said. She sniffed, wiped at her eyes. Slipped out from under Moorsey's arm, sat up straight, and looked at me. "Sarah *is* in Barcelona, but not for work. That was just …" A pause. "That was just her cover story."

Her cover story. I knew then that everything was about to change.

"Adam," Rose said, "this may hurt."

She paused before she spoke again. And while that beat felt like eternity at the time, there is nothing I wouldn't do to go back to it now. Now ignorance seems like a nice place to hang out. Although

I didn't know it then, that pause marked the end of my Before and the beginning of this awful After. A moment of silence that the universe had the good manners to observe before it tore the fabric of my life to shreds.

"Sarah's seeing someone else," Rose said.

I honestly think my heart stopped, just for a couple of beats.

"I don't know much about him," she went on, in a rush now that she had blown the dam. "I do know that he's American, and he's married. Or *was*—I'm not sure which. She met him through work. He lives in Dublin, I think. I don't know his name. She just called him 'the American.'"

My heart cranked back up, making up for lost time now ... harder ... louder.

The noise of it in my own ears was deafening. Couldn't Moorsey and Rose hear that thumping?

"They started texting each other," Rose said. "Emailing, things like that. This was maybe two, three months ago? It was innocent, at first. They met for coffee a few times, then ... Well, I don't know all the details. Sarah felt bad enough as it was, without gossiping about it to me. But seriously, Adam, how long did you expect her to wait?"

I wanted to ask, *Wait for what?* but didn't feel confident that I could speak just yet.

"She didn't want to hurt you," Rose went on, "and she didn't want to leave you alone to fend for yourself. She cares about you so much, Adam. You don't even know how much. I told her if she wasn't feeling the same as she had before, she should leave. That if she felt like you two were more friends than anything else, then you should break up. But you know what she said? She said she couldn't do that to you. She was tearing up just at the thought. But then your script sold ..." Rose shifted in her seat, glanced at Moorsey before continuing, "You'd have your own money. You could afford to get your own place. Your career would be taking off. Sarah wouldn't ... wouldn't have to worry about you. But there was still some waiting to do, and I just think … Sarah couldn't wait anymore, okay? She'd waited long enough. He had to go to Barcelona for work, and he asked Sarah to go with him. She said she would. It was time to start thinking about *her* for a change. She'd tell you she was going to a conference, and call in sick to the office. She didn't say anything to Jack and Maureen, because they'd only be asking questions. She rarely sees them during the week anyway. She'd only be gone for a few days. They could speak on the phone and not even know she wasn't here. She didn't …" Rose bit her lip. "She didn't want to have to tell any more lies than she had to."

"Stop," I finally managed to say. "Stop talking."

Scenes from the past few weeks were flashing through my mind in a sped-up slide show, looking all wrong and feeling strange. Sarah and I had been together for ten years, lived together for the past eight. Almost the only time we didn't spend in each other's company was when she was at work, and yet I hadn't the slightest inkling that anything like this could be going on.

I thought I knew everything about her, everything about her life.

How had this happened without my noticing? When had it? Was I just that stupid, or was she just that good?

Sarah's face, framed by her new short hair, looking up at me. *I would never abandon you.*

"You're wrong about one thing, though," Rose said to Moorsey. "This isn't Sarah's fault." She looked to me. "Adam, you know I think you're a nice guy. A good guy. Everyone does. But what the hell have you been *doing* for the last ten years? Chasing your dreams, yeah, we know. But at Sarah's expense. And I don't just mean financially. What about *her* dreams? Did you ever think about those? Did you ask her about them? Did you even consider that she might have some, too? I never understood that about you. You've always seemed to think you're the only one with a dream and that everyone else is just happy to settle."

"Rose," Moorsey said. "Stop."

I got up from the table, went to the kitchen sink and stood looking out the window. We were three floors up on a hill overlooking a city that mostly liked to stick to one or two stories. Roofs and spires spread out before me in gentle rolling hills before scrambling up the sharp rise on the other side of the river valley. How many nights had Sarah and I sat wrapped together in a blanket on our tiny balcony, looking at that same view and talking about the future? About *our* dreams?

Many, many nights. But when had we *last* done it?

We had a deal. Sarah had supported me these past few years, and from now on, in exchange for that, I would take care of her forever. The first stage payment from the script sale would be in my bank account within a fortnight, and the very first thing I planned to buy was a ring.

And Sarah knew that … didn't she?

It was Rose who hadn't a clue. She saw Sarah maybe once a week. I lived with her. She slept in *my* arms. *We* were the ones sharing a life.

This had to be some kind of awful misunderstanding. All we needed to do was get Sarah on the phone. She'd clear everything up.

"When did you last speak to her?" I asked, still looking out the window.

"Sunday morning," Rose said. "I sent her a text message and she texted me back. She was at the airport."

I saw Sarah walking in the terminal doors. Waving goodbye to me. Kissing *him* hello. I gripped the edge of the countertop.

No.

"Have you tried calling her since?"

"I tried a few times after you texted me," Rose said, "but it went straight to voice mail. But then Moorsey said she told you she wasn't going to disturb you, because you were doing your rewriting thing. I think the phone is probably off. I think she turned it off. On purpose. You gave her the perfect excuse to do that."

"What am I going to tell Maureen and Jack?"

"We obviously can't tell them about any of *this,* so I was thinking, how about I call them and say I've heard from her, that her phone is broken or something and that she's sorry for worrying them and she'll talk to them when she gets back? You can intercept her at the airport on Thursday and explain why we did that. You're still planning to meet her there, aren't you? You'll have to. And you can't tell her I told you this. You'll have to make something up. I mean it, Adam. She's my best friend."

There was silence then.

When I turned around, Rose and Moorsey were looking at each other, hands clasped together on the tabletop.

You've always seemed to think you were the only one with a dream.

But Sarah was my dream. None of the rest of it mattered without her. This was all for her, for *us.* She knew that.

But had she stopped *wanting* it?

Another thought: Sarah, *my* Sarah, naked in a hotel bed, a faceless man on top of her, touching her skin …

I shut my eyes, but the image wouldn't go away.

I turned back around just in time to throw up into the sink.

Thursday at lunchtime, thick gray clouds pregnant with rain hung over the city, threatening to unload at any moment. I parked in the airport's multistory garage and followed the covered walkway into the terminal. Inside, the noise of heels and wheels meeting the hard floor blended with indecipherable PA announcements and distant Muzak.

The bank of screens suspended from the ceiling just inside the main doors flickered as I stopped to study them, changing the listing for Sarah's flight home from "Expected 13:15" to "Landed 13:05." She was here. I remember thinking that.

I made a beeline for the coffee kiosk. I needed a caffeine fix after a second night of broken, fitful sleep, tormented by what Rose had told me the day before yesterday, unsure what to do about it or even whether to believe it. I had decided just before dawn that all I could do was wait to see Sarah, wait to give her a chance to tell me herself what was going on. Maybe not all was lost yet, or maybe it had been for ages. I just didn't know.

I took my coffee to an empty chair in the first row of seats facing the arrivals doors—the last barrier between airside passengers and the landside public waiting for them. Sitting down, I pulled out my phone and dialed Sarah's number for the umpteenth time this morning.

Straight to voice mail. *Again.* I didn't leave a message. *Again.*

When was she going to turn it back on?

Before I could relock the screen, the phone vibrated with an incoming call. *Jack.* He was talking before I could even get the phone to my ear.

"Is she there? Is she with you? Maureen saw on the Internet that her flight has landed."

I had vetoed Rose's plan to lie to Maureen and Jack that Sarah had made contact with us, informing us of a lost or broken phone. It seemed both an unnecessary evil and too good a deed to do for someone who had lied to me—even though I was still holding out hope that there was an innocent reason for it all and Rose just had an overactive imagination. Instead, I had convinced Sarah's parents that the simplest explanation was the most likely one: Sarah had a problem with her phone, and we should just sit tight until Thursday lunchtime and wait for her to come off the plane.

Which was supposed to be now.

"It *just* landed," I said. "She hasn't come through yet."

"You'll get her to call us as soon as you meet her?"

"It'll be the first thing I say to her."

He thanked me and ended the call.

I meant what I said. The most unbelievable thing about all this was how Sarah was treating her parents. Hadn't she realized they would worry when they couldn't contact her? Why hadn't she contacted them? It was unbelievably selfish—although that would make two of us, if I believed what Rose had told me.

The coffee sloshed around in my empty stomach. I dumped the half-full cup in the nearest bin and went to stand at the railing in front of the arrivals doors.

A minute or two later, passengers started coming through.

Would they both be on this flight? Sarah had a window seat coming back, but maybe that was just because they couldn't book two seats together, or they had swapped over and *he* had booked the middle one. Would I recognize him? Would he recognize me? Sarah knew I would be waiting, so they wouldn't be coming through hand in hand. They would pretend to be strangers, but they would probably struggle with the act.

I studied faces and body language, looking for clues to which passenger was the other guy having sex with my girlfriend. The first to come through was a prime candidate: attractive man, maybe five years older than I, pulling a small trolley case, with a bulky laptop bag slung over his shoulder. As he passed me, I saw the airport code on his luggage tag: BCN. Sarah's flight. His eyes darted around as if he was looking for someone, and he moved fast.

This could be the guy.

But then he spotted someone holding a "GD Investments" sign and broke into a smile, waving at them.

What was I doing? Sarah wasn't cheating on me. She would never. She loved me.

I would never abandon you.

The rest of the passengers came spilling out in much the same order that they must have boarded the plane on the other end. First, first class, well dressed and relaxed. They had only carry-on because they knew how to travel, and there was no one to meet them but hired drivers. Next, harried young parents with buggies and bags that outnumbered the kids, who were on their last nerve after a week of round-the-clock family time. Then the masses. A mix of travelers, vacationers, and low-fare opportunists, sunburned but (mostly) smiling, carrying copies of the in-flight magazine, tablet computers, and clear, sealed plastic bags of duty-free purchases. Finally, the crew. Four men and three women, all wearing bright-green Aer Lingus uniforms and an air of superiority, the men flashing their straight white teeth and the women modeling various shades of harsh red lipstick.

None of the passengers took any special notice of me or appeared to be acting strange, and none of them was Sarah.

I waited another ten minutes, but no one else came through the doors except for flak-jacketed airport staff and a woman with no bags, who started moaning loudly about lost luggage and delays to the man who was there to meet her.

I waited another fifteen.

I imagined Sarah on the other side of the frosted glass, staring in disbelief at the phone she had just switched back on, blinking through tears at the influx of text messages, emails, and notifications of missed calls. Devastated at the pain she had inadvertently caused with her silence, wondering what the hell I must be thinking, trying to find the words to begin her apology.

Or maybe just confused to find that she hadn't gotten away with her lies.

Don't.

I shook my head as if to physically dislodge the thought.

She wouldn't. This is Sarah *we're talking about.* My *Sarah.*

I tried her phone again. Straight to voice mail. But then, she could be on the phone to Maureen and Jack …

I opened WhatsApp. Still only one check mark.

I started to feel self-conscious. I had been standing in the same spot for a half hour now and hadn't stopped checking my phone. If any CCTV cameras were trained on this spot, whoever was monitoring them had undoubtedly picked me out by now as a potential suspected something-or-other.

How much longer should I wait?

Cork Airport was small. Yes, the Celtic Tiger era architecture was impressive, but I'd been in the glorified sheds of really old airfields and seen more gates than here. Each year, when they announced the passenger numbers, I wondered how they managed to funnel everyone through just eight of them. Here there were no endless corridors, no warnings about allowing enough time to get to your gate, no need for a single moving sidewalk in the whole building. If you could waltz through passport control and you had only carry-on, it was a five-minute walk from the tarmac to the taxi rank.

So where was she?

I began looking around for someone who might be able to tell me whether Sarah had been on the plane in the first place. A middle-aged man in a high-visibility vest walked past. I stepped toward him.

"Excuse me," I said. I explained that I had been expecting someone who was supposed to be on the Barcelona flight but hadn't appeared. Was there someone I could talk to?

He pulled a walkie-talkie from his belt and barked jargon into it, then translated the squawk that came bursting back out: all the passengers from the Barcelona flight were through. They had cleared Immigration and Customs, and a cleaning crew was already aboard the plane.

"You're sure you've the right flight, son?" he asked. "Maybe she missed it." He shrugged and walked off.

My phone rang: a blocked number.

Here we go.

"Hello?"

"Hey, buddy, it's Dan. Goldberg. In New York. Can you talk?"

I winced. Dan was the agent who had brokered the script sale—the same agent who, right about now, was surely wondering where the hell the rewritten script was. He wanted to see it before I sent it to the studio, and the studio was expecting it in ten days.

"Not just now, Dan, to be honest."

"I wanted to check in. You know, since I haven't heard from you." A pause. "At all."

"I know, it's just—"

"It's your first time. It's imperative that you deliver *on* time."

"I will."

"You're going to show it to me first?"

"Yes."

"You won't send it directly to them?"

"No."

"When will I see it?"

"Soon. Dan, sorry, but I kind of have, uh, a family emergency going on at the moment."

"Really? Fuck. Is everything all right?"

"I'm sure everything will be fine, but I just can't talk right now. Sorry. I'll call you back as soon as I can."

"Is there any—"

I hung up on him. Then I looked down at my phone in surprise, as if I couldn't believe what I had done. I had waited ten years for someone like him to start calling me, and now I was hanging up on him. What was I thinking?

But then my phone rang with Jack's number yet again, and I remembered that on my list of new and pressing problems, Dan was currently sitting at number two. I'd call him just as soon as I spoke to Sarah—as soon as I knew what the hell was going on.

I waited another ten minutes. I tried Sarah's phone again on the way back to my car, slowing down the closer I got, hoping my phone would ring and I'd have reason to turn back around.

It didn't.

I drove back to the apartment with an empty passenger seat and new company: a question in my mind, repeating over and over like a snippet of lyric on a gouged-out CD.

Where is she? Where is she? Where is she?

Jack rang me three more times during the ten-minute drive from the airport to the apartment.

I didn't answer. I didn't know what to say to him now or what to do next, or even what to think.

I pulled into the first empty parking spot outside our building, killed the engine, and called Rose.

"She wasn't on the flight," I said as soon as she answered.

"What do you mean?"

"I mean *she wasn't on the flight.* She didn't come home. She hasn't come home."

There was a long silence on the line.

"Rose? You there?"

"Yeah, I … I just don't know, Adam. Maybe she missed it. Is there another flight from Barcelona today?"

"I don't know."

"I'll check. Where are you now?"

"I just got home. Listen. That … that stuff you said. About Sarah and the American guy."

"Yeah?"

"Is there any chance …"

"What?"

"How sure are you about it? Could she have been lying, or

something? Making it up? Or maybe they're just friends and you misunderstood? You said she didn't talk about it much with—"

"Adam …" A long sigh. "I'm sorry, I really am, and I'm sorry for the way that I told you, and some of the things I said, but she *is* seeing someone else. She met him through work and she went to Barcelona with him. That's all I know. But she *was* coming back today. Of course she was. She's getting ready to …" Another sigh. "To leave you. God, I'm sorry. This must be awful for you to hear. I feel terrible. I do. But she is. And anyway, where else would—"

I took the phone from my ear and pressed the virtual red button to end the call. I couldn't listen to it anymore.

Something clutched in my chest as I realized that the last time I would hold or kiss or touch Sarah had probably already happened. I would never get to do it again.

There went my entire future, destroyed by a dead phone, an online banking password, and a missed flight.

Sarah, what have you done? What have I done to you?

I ached for her. I wanted to hold her. Kiss her. Touch her. To have her next to me in the car, to reach over and squeeze her knee at a red light. I needed to speak to her. The list of little things I wanted to share with her, the anecdotes and observations and jokes I'd been saving up while she was away was already long, and I wouldn't be able to remember them all for much longer.

I missed her. I just *missed her.* Had been missing her for the past four days. I hadn't paid the feeling much attention, because I knew it was temporary, that it was going to come to an end. Today, supposedly. And now, all of a sudden, there was no end in sight.

If what Rose said was true, my Sarah might be gone forever. Now every evening and weekend and birthday and fortnight's holiday and special occasion was stretching out in front of me, empty and cold and dark. A drowning depth of loneliness. An endless abyss.

I had been with Sarah so long, I could barely remember what it felt like to live without her. I didn't know if I *could*. I didn't want to have to try.

But then, her and a faceless him, together in a hotel room.

My phone buzzed in my hand. Jack, calling again. I put the phone on silent, slipped it into my pocket, and got out of the car.

I typed the entry code into the keypad for our block and waited for the electronic *click* that signaled success. I pushed the door open, blinked in the dim light of the lobby, and, after a second, noticed something in our cubbyhole.

We didn't have locked letter boxes, only open shelves in the foyer. One for each apartment. We rarely received anything that wasn't a slim white bill or a thick brown packet covered in Amazon logos, so the small padded manila packet immediately got my attention.

When had I last checked the post?

I couldn't remember. Maybe Monday, when I'd gotten back from the talk at UCC, if even then.

I pulled the packet out, turned it over in my hands.

French stamps. Postmarked Nice, two days ago. Tuesday, August 12. A sticker with a tracking number and the word "*Priorité.*" Addressed to me in handwriting I didn't recognize.

The packet was about the size of a slim paperback book, but I could feel something smaller than that through the paper. Something thin and hard, sliding freely around inside.

There was a pull tab on the flap. I tore it open, pulled one side of the packet toward me so I could look inside …

And saw the wine-colored cover of an EU passport.

Slowly, using just my fingertips, I extracted it from the envelope. The passport had a harp on the front, above the word "*Pás.*" It was an Irish one.

I turned it over and opened it to the photo page.

The image shook in front of me—because my hands were shaking.

I let the empty packet flutter down to the floor so I could hold the passport with both hands.

By my right thumb, Sarah's face. By my left, a note in her handwriting.

A sticky note, white, square, with some kind of blue logo at the top. Two small wavy lines, centered.

I didn't recognize it at the time. I don't think I had ever seen that logo before.

Underneath it, three handwritten words—well, two words and an initial:

I'M SORRY—S.

I stared, disbelieving.

And then I learned what "weak at the knees" *really* meant.

PART TWO

LOST AT SEA

CORINNE

The cabin attendants' preshift meeting took place every morning at seven-thirty in the crew bar.

Fifty or more cabin attendants assembled, all in uniform (navy and white dress with white tights for the women, navy trousers and white T-shirt for the men, white soft-soled shoes for everyone). All were chatting in various languages, all saying different versions of essentially the same thing: that they were not looking forward to work today. It was Changeover, when the couple of thousand passengers on board would leave the ship to make way for the couple of thousand *new* passengers who would start streaming onto it this afternoon. This meant checkout cleans, which were considerably more work than stay-overs. And with boarding starting at two, they had to happen in double-quick time.

But Corinne rather liked the extra pressure. It meant there was less time to think.

The crew bar had closed only a few hours ago, and the air still smelled of stale cigarette smoke and spilled beer. As Corinne picked her way through the crowd, she felt the soles of her shoes stick to the linoleum.

"Changeover day, guys," Michael, one of the accommodation supervisors, called out from the front of the room. He always spoke in English, the working language of the ship.

A hush fell.

"Everyone's favorite, I know," he continued. "Now"—he glanced down at his clipboard—"we have a few issues today. The aft B elevator bank is only going as far as twelve. We are still having an issue with the air-conditioning on six—I hear it's blowing warm, so probably best to leave it in the off position. Laundry had a breakdown with one of the ironing machines, so we're a little short on the double sheet with the piping." A groan rippled through the room. "Guys, come on. We can manage. And finally, whoever has the junior suites on eleven, come see me—you've won a protein spill kit!"

A smattering of applause, but it was sarcastic. "Protein spill" was Blue Wave–speak for a bodily fluid no longer in a body. Nine times out of ten, this meant vomit. The other time, the cabin attendant might well threaten to quit on the spot.

Corinne collected her electronic master key and headed for the forward service elevators. One of them would take her to her charges: a cluster of exterior deluxe cabins, built back-to-back near the bow on deck ten.

Most attendants had cabins lined up one after another in a row, which meant walking to one end of them and then slowly working your way back. If, toward the end of your row, you encountered a DND—a "Do Not Disturb" sign—you had to walk the length of your section twice, going back to the DND later in the day. Corinne much preferred her tight loop of cabins. Better yet, they were right by a landing—the hidden area off the guest corridor where attendants' carts and supplies were stored and where the service elevators stopped.

Corinne was lucky in that regard. She might not have managed otherwise. These days, every little thing made a difference.

She collected her cart now: a chest-high plastic storage unit on wheels. Every day it seemed to get heavier and harder to push. She used her key to open the small storage closet where the vacuum cleaners were kept, and picked the one with the white stripe of correction fluid across the handle—the one that she knew worked for sure. Michael had promised a delivery of brand-new ones waiting for them at port today, but Corinne would believe it when she saw them. Supplies of everything were always limited.

After a deep breath, Corinne hoisted the vacuum cleaner onto the hook at the side of the cart. She paused a moment to recover from the exertion and then slowly pushed the cart as far as the first cabin on her list: Deluxe Superior #1001.

She rapped on the door—two firm knocks. Waited a moment or two, listening for signs of life on the other side. Nothing. Confident the cabin was empty, she pulled her master key from the elastic cord clipped to her waistband, and unlocked the door with a swipe.

Following regulations, Corinne turned to pull her cart across the door behind her. This was so other crew members and passengers would know she was inside.

Her eyes flicked to the strip of black plastic on the side of her cart, and the raised white letters that read, "DUPONT, CORINNE."

At most, it was the size of a nail file, but to Corinne it might as well have been a giant flashing neon sign. Thousands of people were aboard the *Celebrate*. What were the chances that not one of them would recognize the name? Everything was on the Internet these days, and then there were those documentaries, replayed and repeated on cable channels all over the world, all the time. It was only luck that she hadn't been identified so far. How much longer would that luck last?

Time was running out for her in more ways than one. She turned and went into the cabin, and her heart sank.

There was rubbish everywhere. Empty water bottles overflowing the bin, discarded shopping bags lying on the floor, the remnants of what may have been a jam doughnut, walked into and across the *Celebrate*'s carpeting. The sheets hung off the bed, one of the pillows was out on the balcony, and every single towel, amenity, and toilet roll in the bathroom had been used. The occupants hadn't even bothered to flush the toilet before they left.

Seeing this and knowing how much energy she would have to find to clean it, Corinne felt a wave of exhaustion sweep over her. The strength went out of her legs. Putting a hand on the wall for support, she gently lowered herself into a sitting position at the end of one of the beds.

She just needed a minute. *One* minute, and then she would get going.

Corinne hadn't had any breakfast, which, she now realized, had been a mistake. But eating no longer appealed to her, and so she regularly forgot to do it. She couldn't even recall what having an appetite felt like. When she looked at food now, she just saw an inanimate object, like a book or a piece of furniture.

But still, she had to eat. She had to stay strong for as long as it took.

She glanced around the room, searching for a forgotten chocolate bar or a fizzy drink. Guests often left unopened snacks or drinks behind.

Slowly and carefully, Corinne bent down to look under the bed.

There was something under there, but it wasn't a forgotten bag of chips.

With her foot, she nudged it out from under the bed.

It was a photograph, lying facedown. Small and almost square, with white borders around black. A Polaroid. Hadn't they stopped making those?

She straightened back up, turned the photo over.

She couldn't comprehend what she was seeing. She blinked, looked again.

It was a family portrait, its subjects arranged by descending height in front of a fireplace: a young husband and wife and two small boys. The mother had a baby in her arms.

It had been taken on a Christmas morning many years ago. She knew this because she remembered it being taken.

Corinne was sitting on the edge of a bed in Deluxe Superior #1001, one of more than a thousand cabins on the *Celebrate,* holding a photograph of her younger self.

How is this possible?

Her hands began to shake. She knew how it was possible. There was only one way.

He *was* here. This was confirmation. He was here, and now he knew that *she* was, too.

That evening, there was no sign of Lydia in the crew mess.

ADAM

The next morning—Friday—Jack, Maureen, and I met at Angelsea Street to file a missing-persons report.

"Angelsea Street" meant Cork's Garda headquarters, even though the city council offices, district court, and a host of businesses all shared the same address. It was a site I passed often but had never been inside. Garda HQ was an imposing gray block sat on a corner, its design all no-nonsense symmetry. I imagined that the architect's front elevation sketch looked a lot like the houses you drew in crayon or built in Lego as a kid: a large rectangle with one big door in the middle and neat, evenly spaced rows of square windows on either side. An Gardaí, its headquarters warned, didn't have time for frivolous aesthetics. They had crimes to solve, criminals to catch. We waited in the reception area, an indulgence of stone slab flooring and natural light made possible by an atrium well hidden behind the no-frills façade. It was eerily quiet, like a cathedral. Watching TV and movies, it turned out, was pathetically ineffectual preparation for what Irish police stations were actually like.

Jack left Maureen with me while he went to the reception desk. Behind it, a male garda, who looked as if he still had to show ID to order a pint of beer, stood flipping idly through a tabloid newspaper. He didn't look up as Jack approached, although he had to know he was there. But Jack, dressed for an early bird special and a night in the bingo hall—plaid shirt, shorts, socks and sandals—had shuffled up to the desk and was taking a second to smooth down the wisps of steel-gray hair over his spreading bald spot. If I didn't know better, I would have guessed he was there to get a passport form stamped. That's probably what the garda thought, too.

"Good morning," Jack said. "I'm here to …" He faltered. "My daughter is missing."

Missing.

The word echoed around the chamber.

"Oh, God," said Maureen, beside me. Her hand was on my right arm, squeezing it, leaning on it. Unlike her husband, she had let her appearance drop right off her list of priorities. Her hair—blond like Sarah's at the ends, gray at the roots—looked uncombed, and without her usual makeup, her eyes were small and sunken, the skin around them hanging slack, in folds. The old cardigan she had thrown over her shoulders smelled faintly of something medicinal.

I didn't want to think about what I looked like, not having slept much or shaved and still in yesterday's clothes.

"It's okay," I said, on autopilot. "It's okay."

I had spent the night thinking, among other things, about what a strange concept a *missing person* was—at least, the adult version of it. You could be fine, perfectly okay, even happy, but just because a selection of other people didn't know your current location, you were a cause for concern, potentially for the police.

Wasn't that odd? Wasn't that like saying it was against the law to leave us?

Maybe it wasn't. Maybe it made perfect sense. Maybe it was just that I hadn't slept for longer than thirty minutes at a time in the past thirty-six hours.

The cherub-faced garda came out from behind his desk and ushered the three of us into a conference room one floor up.

Sunlight was streaming in the windows, slowly cooking the space. A wall of stale, hot air hit us the moment we crossed the threshold.

Garda Cherub hurriedly pushed open the windows and dropped the blinds down halfway, leaving a waist-high sunbeam to illuminate the currents of gently swirling dust. We took three seats on the same side of the large table—the only ones in the shade. He offered us water from the dispenser in the corner, which came served in translucent plastic cups that caved and bent under our fingertips.

These are the kinds of details you remember when you don't want to remember the rest.

Someone would be with us shortly, Garda Cherub promised. Then he left us there for half an hour.

Sweat began to pool in the small of my back and in my armpits, gluing my T-shirt to my skin. The water from the dispenser was lukewarm. We didn't speak much while we waited, although Maureen did pray. I could hear the clink of the rosary beads moving through her fingers, hitting the edge of the table from time to time.

At one point, Jack got up and started to pace.

I kept my phone on the table in front of me, in case Sarah called or texted. The charger for it was in my pocket, in case the battery started to drain. Rose and Moorsey were back at our apartment, in case Sarah showed up there.

The door opened abruptly and a female garda entered the room carrying a sheaf of documents and smiling brightly at us, as if we were there to talk to her about booking a sun holiday.

"Garda Cusack," she said, reaching across to shake hands with each of us in turn. Her palm was damp. She took a seat on the opposite side of the table, facing us, blinking in the glare of the sun. "Hot out there today, isn't it? And there was me thinking that downpour last night would break the heat." She pulled a small leather notebook from a pocket and flipped it open to a clean page. A ballpoint pen was stuck inside it. She clicked it, saw that she had retracted the nib, and clicked it again. "So. I'm told you want to file a missing-persons report?"

Cusack was my age, I guessed. She looked like someone wearing a garda uniform on a dare. Her yellow-blond hair was pulled into a half-arsed attempt at a ponytail, leaving wayward strands of it hanging limp around her face. She tucked one behind her ear now. Cusack was heavyset, or at least appeared to be in her shapeless garda blues: navy wool trousers, cornflower short-sleeved shirt with epaulettes, and chunky black leather belt with various pouches hanging from it. Her cheeks were bright pink, and a thin sheen of sweat glistened at her temples.

"Our daughter is missing," Jack said. He had sat down at last. "We think she might be in some trouble. We called our local station yesterday and they told us, if we hadn't heard from her by this morning, we should come here first thing and make a report."

"We have pictures," Maureen said suddenly, "I brought some." She started rooting in her handbag. "You'll need those, won't you?"

I had the passport, the note, and the envelope they had come in stored carefully in a clear Ziploc bag. I took it from my jeans pocket and slid it across the tabletop toward Cusack.

"This came yesterday." It was surprising to me how steady and normal my voice sounded when, underneath it, anxiety was running amok through every vein. "It was delivered to our home. It's Sarah's. There's a note inside, in her handwriting. But the handwriting on the envelope isn't hers. And she's not in France; she's in Spain. She's supposed to be, anyway. Barcelona. She flew there last Sunday. Possibly with … with …" I glanced at Maureen and Jack. "A friend."

There was a beat of silence while Cusack just looked at us, moving from face to face in turn. Then, "Why don't we start at the beginning?" She held the clicky pen over her notebook. "What's Sarah's last name?"

"O'Connell," we said in unison.

Cusack directed her next question to Jack. "And she's how old?"

"Twenty-nine," he answered. "She'll be thirty in November. The eighteenth."

"Can I have your first names?"

"I'm Jack, and this is my wife, Maureen."

"And you're O'Connell, too? Both of you?"

Jack confirmed they were. He seemed confused, as if he didn't understand how there could be another option.

Cusack looked at me. "And you are?"

"Adam. Dunne. I'm her boyfriend. We live together."

"How long have you done that?"

"About eight years."

"Do you live locally?"

"On South Douglas Road. By the post office."

"The apartments in behind there?"

"Yes."

"Is Sarah on any medications? Does she have a history of mental illness? Would you consider her to be a vulnerable individual for any reason at all?"

I shook my head. "No."

Cusack looked to Jack and Maureen. They shook their heads, too. "Has anything like this ever happened before?"

All heads shook again.

"Does Sarah have any brothers or sisters?"

"One older brother," Maureen said. "He lives in Canada."

"Have you spoken to him?"

"Yes," Maureen said. "He said the last time he heard from her was a fortnight ago." She leaned forward. "Should we ... I mean, do you think we need to ... Should we ask him to come home?"

"I'm sure that won't be necessary," Cusack said. She flashed a quick smile. Probably aiming for reassuring, but to me it seemed dismissive.

"The passport," I said. "She can't travel without it. And it's postmarked Nice. In France. That's nowhere near where—"

Cusack held up her hand. "We'll get to that in a second. When did you last have contact with Sarah? Mr. and Mrs. O'Connell, why don't you go first?"

"She calls us every couple of days," Jack said. "Or texts. Maureen talked to her last Saturday morning, but there's been nothing since. We tried her on Monday. No answer. When we couldn't get through to her mobile, we rang her at work. That was, eh, Tuesday morning, Maur, wasn't it?" Maureen nodded. "Now, I don't know who we spoke to at the office, but it was a girl—a young girl—and she said Sarah was out sick. That day and the day before. So we called Adam, thinking he'd be at home with her, and that's when he told us that Sarah was in Spain. For work. A conference. She'd never said anything to us about going anywhere. And she would've. Of course she would've." Jack threw me a sideways glance. "Very unlike her, it was. *Very* unlike her."

"She flew to Barcelona on Sunday morning," I told Cusack, trying not to sound defensive. Jack seemed to be implying that there was a chance I was making this up. "I dropped her at the airport. Well, she drove there and I drove back." I had brought a copy of the boarding passes. I took it out now and laid it flat on the table next to the Ziploc bag—which Cusack still hadn't touched—and swiveled it around so she could read it. "I saw her go into the terminal. She sent me a text that afternoon, just after four o'clock, to say she'd landed and that she'd checked into her hotel. I know she withdrew cash from the ATM at Barcelona airport—"

"How do you know that?" Cusack asked.

"Her online banking. I checked it because I couldn't remember the name of the hotel she was staying at, but I thought she might have paid for it with her debit card, and so the name of it would be on there."

"Was it?"

"There was a charge for incidentals. I got it from that. They take it on check-in, apparently."

"Did she tell you that she hadn't told her parents she was traveling?"

"No. I assumed she had."

"You've tried calling her since yesterday lunchtime?"

All three heads on my side of the table nodded.

"Lots of times," Maureen said. "I'm still trying. I tried just before we came in here."

"Does it ring?"

"No," I said. "It goes straight to voice mail. It *did* ring at first."

"Does she have her charger with her, do we know?"

"I think so," I said. "I haven't found it at home."

"What about email, Facebook, things like that?"

"There's been nothing. No activity, no messages. I sent her some messages myself, asking her to get in touch. I sent her a text using WhatsApp, which she hasn't read yet." When Cusack frowned, I added, "There's a way to tell."

"When did you send that?"

"On Monday."

Cusack looked down at her notes. "Hmm."

"Also …" I cleared my throat. "She only stayed at the hotel for one night. The first night. Sunday."

"And how do you know *that*?"

I told Cusack about calling the hotel.

"But she was due to fly back yesterday," Cusack said, nodding at the boarding pass printout.

"Yeah, but she didn't. At least, I don't think she did. I didn't see her come through into Arrivals, and I waited until everyone was off the plane. I checked that they were. Then, when I got home, the passport was there. With the note."

"What does the note say?"

"It just says 'I'm sorry' and it's signed with an 'S.'" I motioned toward the Ziploc bag. "It's in there. Stuck on the photo page."

"Does that mean something to you? Does Sarah have something to be sorry for? You said Sarah went to Barcelona with"—Cusack looked at me pointedly—"a friend?"

"Yes …"

I shifted in my seat, hyperaware of Jack's and Maureen's presence. Rose and I had done our best the night before to explain to them that as far as we knew, Sarah had made a new friend, and that friend was a guy, and even though neither of us knew anything about him —not even his name—Sarah had gone to Barcelona with him.

But I wasn't sure they understood exactly what we were saying, and I couldn't face the excruciating experience that double-checking would have been.

Cusack looked from me to Jack, to Maureen, then back to me again.

"You know what?" She pushed back her chair. "It's roasting in here, isn't it? I think we could all do with a nice cold bottle of water. I'll go get some. Won't be a sec." She stood up. "Adam, would you come and give me a hand with them?"

Cusack walked out of the room, leaving Maureen and Jack staring after her, openmouthed.

Then they turned to look at me.

Before they could say anything, I got up and followed her out.

We crossed the corridor and went into another, identical conference room. The only difference was that this one, mercifully, was dark and cool.

"Okay," Cusack said, standing in front of me with her arms folded. "Go."

I blurted out everything Rose had told me, ignoring the waves of shame and embarrassment that flooded my cheeks with color.

"So she was seeing another man," Cusack said when I was done. "And they"—she nodded toward the room where Jack and Maureen were—"don't know that."

"Rose and I called over to them last night and tried to explain, but I'm not sure they got it. Or maybe they didn't *want* to get it. I think they think she just traveled to Barcelona with some guy from work, maybe *for* work. But then they did call the office … Look, I don't know." I threw up my hands. "No offense, but shouldn't we be *doing something*? Shouldn't we get out there and start looking for her? Call the French police? I mean, the passport—why would she send that? Why would she want to part with it? And if the handwriting on the envelope isn't hers—"

"The day she left," Cusack said. "How was she?"

"Um, fine. I don't really—"

"Was she acting strangely? Said anything weird? Did anything that made you wonder if something was wrong?"

"Not that I can think of. But we just got up and drove to the airport. The flight was around noon."

"What about the day before that? That would've been Saturday. Think back. What did you do? Did you spend the day together?"

"We went out that night. To a going-away party."

"What about the daytime?"

"I was at home. She went into town. She got a haircut."

"A trim or a restyle?"

"I ... a what?"

"Did she just get it tidied up a bit, or did she completely change her hairstyle?"

"She changed her hairstyle."

"*Big* change?"

"She went from long to very short. Why does that matter?"

"Did she take much luggage with her?"

"No, she only had a small bag. A cabin bag."

"Did you see what she packed in it?"

"No. I could maybe make a list, though, see if I can tell what's missing."

"What about a driving license?"

"It's in her wallet, usually. So she probably has it."

"What did she tell *you* she was going to Barcelona for?"

"Work."

"Can you be more specific?"

"A conference. She was there to attend a conference."

"What does she do?"

"She works in recruitment. Anna Buckley. They have an office on the South Mall."

"Has she ever traveled for work before?"

"No."

"Did she seem excited about it?"

"I don't know. Not especially."

"You didn't want to go?"

"I …" *You can't afford to. You need to work.* "No. I mean, I couldn't."

"You said she made a withdrawal from an ATM in Barcelona."

"Yeah. At the airport."

"Of how much?"

"It was an odd figure. Six hundred and fifty-something, I think."

"Did you check her credit card?"

"She doesn't have one. She just uses her Visa debit."

"How long have you been together?"

"Ten years."

"Why aren't you married?"

"Well …" *Because we never made plans to do anything beyond waiting a bit longer for my dream to arrive? Because, as Rose had so kindly pointed out to me, I never thought of anyone except myself?* "How is that relevant?"

"What about her friends?" Cusack asked, ignoring my question. "Have you spoken to them?"

"Rose is her best friend, and she hasn't heard from her."

"Work friends?"

"I haven't spoken to anyone in the office. I figured your crowd would do that."

"My 'crowd'?"

"The gardaí, I mean."

"Is she pregnant?"

"*What?* No."

"Was she?"

"No, never."

"Women go abroad, Adam. Sometimes, things go wrong; procedures take longer to recover from than they should."

"This isn't that."

"You're sure?"

"Positive."

"What was your relationship like?"

"It *is* great," I said defiantly.

"So you don't believe she was cheating on you with this other man?"

"I don't think there's any point in believing anything until I've had the opportunity to talk to Sarah first. But we can't make contact with Sarah, and we don't know where she is. That's why we're here. We're here so you can help us find her, which I'd really like to start—"

"What does Rose think?"

"About what?"

"About where Sarah is?"

"She thinks … She says that Sarah would never have not come home."

"Has Rose ever met this man, the American?"

"No."

"Does she have reason to believe he may have hurt Sarah in any way?"

"I don't think so," I said, trying not to follow the phrase "*reason to believe he may have hurt Sarah*" down the rabbit hole—the same rabbit hole I'd been circling since I found the passport and the note.

"Does Sarah keep a diary?" Cusack asked.

"Not that I know of, no."

"Do you have access to her emails?"

"I don't know the password."

"But you knew the password for her online banking?"

"That was written down. It came in a letter."

"Tell me: If I asked you to provide me with evidence that this American man exists, would you have anything that didn't come from Rose? Or if I asked Rose the same question, would she have anything that didn't come from Sarah? For instance, has Rose ever seen this American man? Is she friends with him on Facebook? Ever overheard Sarah on the phone to him?"

"Rose doesn't even know his name," I said. "She said Sarah felt bad talking about it."

"What about when—"

"Wait," I said. "There is something. The middle seat. On the boarding pass. Sarah booked a middle seat for her outbound flight. I think because she wanted to sit next to whoever had already booked the aisle or the window."

"Why do you think that?"

"Because who wants to sit in the middle?"

Cusack frowned, considering this.

"What do you do?" she asked me. "For a living?"

"I'm a writer."

"A writer? Really? What do you write?"

I lifted my hands, let them fall again. "Does it matter?"

"No, I suppose not." Cusack cocked her head, indicating the corner of the room behind me. "There's a fridge over there. Grab a few bottles of water and let's go back."

Back in the first conference room, Jack was pacing again. I doled out the bottles of water, but no one opened theirs. Cusack and I resumed our seats at the table. After a beat, Jack did, too.

Maureen had spread the photos she brought of Sarah out on the tabletop. Cusack looked at them briefly before collecting them into a stack, which she slid beneath her notebook.

None of those photos looks very much like Sarah does now.

The thought shot through me like an electrical current. Was that why Cusack had asked about Sarah's hair, about whether it was a big change or not? Was that why Sarah did it: to disguise herself somehow, to make herself harder to find?

I almost laughed out loud at the idea. Sarah—*Sarah*—thinking ahead to a situation where her parents would be sitting in a garda station reporting her missing, and cutting all her hair off in order to prepare. The same Sarah who cared enough to handwrite relevant quotes into every greeting card she sent. The same Sarah who always offered to make tea at the point in *The Shawshank Redemption* where Brooks doesn't do too well for himself on the outside, because she couldn't stand to watch bad things happen to kind old men. The same Sarah who, after starting a tradition for us of birthday breakfast in bed, rolled up copies of *Empire* magazine and folded back the page corners at one end to make a "flower" to put on my tray, to match the single sunflower in a vase I always put on hers.

No, it wasn't possible. The haircut must have just been a coincidence. But then, what did the passport and the note mean?

"Here's what we're going to do," Cusack said. "I understand that you're concerned that you haven't been able to get in contact with Sarah these past few days. I don't blame you. But technically, Sarah has only failed to be where she was supposed to be for less than twenty-four hours. I need you to understand that in my line of work we encounter situations like this all the time. Every week. And you know what? Nine times out of ten, we don't have to take any action, because, before we can, the person makes contact or returns home."

"What about the tenth time?" Maureen asked.

Not hearing—or else ignoring her—Cusack pressed on. "It can be difficult, I know, to understand why someone would choose not to make contact with their friends and family, but sometimes people just need a break. Or they think they do. Or it could be something else entirely, something innocent. A misunderstanding. A lost phone and a missed flight. You never know, Sarah could think she booked Friday instead of Thursday, and in a couple of hours she'll come walking through Arrivals up at the airport, wondering where her lift is. She could have lost that passport and, not knowing that a Good Samaritan has already returned it for her, be in a queue at an Irish embassy right now, waiting for an Emergency Travel Certificate so she can fly home."

I could feel it: my side of the table sinking into the bliss of those explanations, pulled into the idea of this all being over by the end of today—gone, with no harm left in its wake.

But if any of those things were true, why hadn't she called to let us know? How would a Good Samaritan know her home address? Where did a note in Sarah's own handwriting fit in? What about the middle seat? The one night in the hotel? Calling in sick to work but telling me she was traveling *because* of work?

"Regardless," Cusack continued, "Sarah is an adult. She's

twenty-nine years old. She's perfectly within her rights to go where she wants when she wants, without informing everyone or anyone of her intentions. There's a common misconception about missing-person investigations. A missing person isn't just someone who can't be located. It's someone who can't be located *and* for whom there is a genuine fear or concern regarding their well-being or the company they are known to be in. I see no cause for that here—at least, not at this point. I also have to tell you that some of the actions she's taken could be construed as preparation for leaving. If that's the case, if she *has* left intentionally, then even if we did find her, we'd have to get her permission before we could let you know that we had."

"*If?*" Jack repeated.

"You are going to look for her, aren't you?" Maureen said, lurching forward in her chair. "We can't do it ourselves. We don't ..." She looked around, panicked. "We wouldn't know *how.* We don't even know where to *start!*"

"Here's what we're going to do," Cusack said, and I noted that this was the second time in two minutes she had said those words and we *still* didn't know what we were going to do. "I recommend that you go home, continue trying to make contact with Sarah through any channels you can think of—phone, friends, Facebook, and so on—and let us know if you hear anything from her. You can use our telephone number here for the contact information if you wish. I'd recommend that you do; don't put your personal phone numbers on anything you plan to post online. In the meantime, I'll liaise with the Department of Foreign Affairs—see if Sarah has made contact with any of our European consulates. I can also check whether or not she was on that inbound flight yesterday. Perhaps she was and you missed her, Adam. If nothing changes, we'll reconvene here on Monday morning and see where we go from there."

I thought: *Reconvene here on Monday? Is there really a possible version of this universe where another* two and a half days *go by without us hearing anything from Sarah?*

Cusack started collecting her things but didn't touch the Ziploc bag or the printed boarding pass.

"Don't you want to take those?" I asked her.

"Why don't you bring them with you on Monday, if we meet then?"

"The CCTV!" Jack blurted out. "You could check the CCTV at the hotel."

"We'll definitely talk about that," Cusack said. "On Monday."

"I can't wait until then." Maureen's voice sounded so small, it pierced me. "I need to talk to her now." She looked at Jack. "I need to talk to my daughter *now*."

Jack looked at his wife, helpless. He watched as she started to cry. Then his lower lip began to tremble.

I looked to the opposite wall. I couldn't watch.

The normal world, the Before world, was slipping away, sliding toward a position that would soon be beyond my reach. The abyss wasn't just stretched out in front of me now. It was all around me, above and below me, and I was falling, tumbling down, down.

And what could I do about it? At that moment, I couldn't think of one single thing.

Out of desperation, I picked up my phone and called Sarah's number even though I knew what I would hear: a beat of dead air and then her voice mail kicking in.

For fuck's sake, Sarah. Turn on your damn phone. Or call us from another one. Just do *something. End this. Make it stop.*

I opened WhatsApp then and—

What the …?

I kept my expression neutral, my face a blank mask. Brought the screen closer to my face, blinked, looked again. Made sure it was really there, made sure that my despair hadn't built a hallucination.

A double check mark where I'd been expecting only one.

The message I'd sent to Sarah on Monday.

It had been read.

I mumbled goodbye to Jack and Maureen, telling them I had something to do and that I would call them afterward. They just looked at me blankly. I made my way back down to the lobby of District HQ, out into the morning sun and into the first place I found where I could sit and think: the bar across the street.

Inside, it was empty and cavernous, the lunchtime rush a while away yet. I asked the bartender for a whiskey. It felt like liquid heartburn going down, and then acid indigestion once it had, but soon my edges began to blur and my senses retreated a step. I felt a little better. I ordered another one. I felt better still.

The bartender was studying me, not realizing that I could see him in the mirror mounted behind the bar. After my second one, he asked if I was okay, said he'd seen me coming out of the station. I wondered whether they always kept such a watchful eye out for customers who had come from a chat with An Garda Síochána, and whether he did that because sometimes they had trouble with the ones who had. I said I was fine, and asked for another one. The bartender said he'd bring me something to eat instead.

I sent Moorsey a text to tell him the gardaí would be no help. He asked me where I was. Fifteen minutes later, he climbed onto the bar stool beside me. He must have left Tyndall the moment I texted back, or run all the way here without breaking a sweat.

"Weren't you at work?" I asked him.

"Yeah, but it's fine." He asked the bartender for a Sprite. "They pretty much let us come and go as we please over there."

"Do they?" I drained what was left of my second drink, fixed my eyes on the empty glass. "Even when you have a big project deadline, like you do today?"

Moorsey was silent while the bartender set a bottle of Sprite and a glass filled with ice cubes down on the bar in front of him.

"You knew, didn't you?" I said as soon as we were alone again. I turned to face him. "You *knew* Sarah was seeing that guy. That's why you were being weird. I thought you were jealous or something. Or annoyed with me because I was being a dick. Is *everyone* telling me lies, Moorsey? Can I trust anyone at all?"

"Ad, look …" Moorsey sighed, but he wouldn't look at me. "I'm sorry, okay? But I only found out by accident. I overheard Rose on the phone to Sarah. I didn't even tell her for ages, and when I did, she freaked out. She said if you found out, it'd be all her fault, not mine. Anyway, Ad, I didn't really believe anything was going on. I mean, *Sarah*? *You* and Sarah, the golden couple? I didn't think there was a chance. Even now, I'm thinking there has to be some simple explanation for this."

"She read the message," I said, turning back to my now-empty glass and the plate where only the crumbs of a ham sandwich remained. I pushed both away. "The WhatsApp message. Its status is 'read' now. She's seen it."

"What? When?"

"The time stamp is from when I sent it. You can't see what time it's read."

"Can you figure it out? When did you last check it?"

"I know I opened WhatsApp last night, when I was at Jack and Maureen's house. The message wasn't read yet; I'm sure of it. But when I looked just now—well, about half an hour ago—the double check mark had appeared. So it must have happened overnight. Considering that the phone must've been on for her to do it, and that all the calls we made went straight to voice mail—it never rang—that makes sense. She turned the phone on either very late at night or very early in the morning, so she could check her messages but not alert any of us that the phone was on."

"Shit, Ad. That means she—"

"Read all the texts I sent her. The ones Rose and her parents sent her, too. Maybe even listened to the voice messages, checked her emails. But didn't bother responding to any of them. *And* didn't bother contacting her mother and father, either, even though I sent a text saying we were going to the gardaí." I got the bartender's attention and pointed to the coffee machine. My head was starting to feel as if it were encased in a fog. "It means she left on purpose. With *him*. That she did this to us. *Is* doing it."

"What did the gardaí say?"

"'She's a grown woman; come back Monday.'"

"What'll they do then?"

"Not much, judging by the reaction today. They've told us to go home for the weekend and put her picture up on Facebook and Twitter—that kind of thing. We could've figured that out by ourselves."

"They know she read the message?"

I shook my head. "No."

"Did you tell Jack and Maureen?"

I shook my head again.

"Ad, you need to tell them."

"Why? What good would it do? 'Hey, you know this horrific waking nightmare we're all going through? Well, good news: Sarah orchestrated it all by herself. Your daughter did this to you. You're welcome.'"

"At least they'd have the comfort of knowing that she's alive."

"Alive?" I scoffed. "Of course she's *alive*."

"Yeah, but Jack and Maureen—I bet their imaginations are

running riot. They're probably lying awake all night picturing the worst. If you told them she'd read the message …"

"They'd *still* be lying awake all night, wondering why Sarah did this to them."

We lapsed into silence for a while.

"But what about the passport?" Moorsey asked. "Aren't the gardaí concerned about that?"

"The garda we spoke to said that maybe Sarah lost it and is at this very moment standing in line in an embassy somewhere, getting emergency papers so she can fly home."

"But who sent the passport to your place?"

"A Good Samaritan, apparently. Who is also a psychic, because that's the only way they could have known Sarah's home address."

"Isn't this a *good* thing, though?" Moorsey asked. "That they aren't springing into action? That they don't seem that worried about her? That makes me think they hear stories like this all the time, but the people come back."

"What if she *doesn't* come back, though? How are we ever going to find her if we don't have their help? Where will we go from there? How can I …" My words caught on the lump in my throat. "How can I just go on with my life without knowing where Sarah is or how she is or why she did this? I can't even sleep without knowing, let alone … How do you expect me to live in that apartment or go buy milk at the store or write—Jesus Christ, *write*—without knowing where she is? What do I do with her stuff? What if I move on and then she changes her mind and comes back? What if she's sick, like mentally ill or something, and this is not a decision she's made, but some kind of episode she's suffering from, and she needs our help? We can't help her if we don't know where she is. We don't know what's happening if we can't talk to her. What if we're still here a month from now, none the wiser? Or in a year? *Ten* years? I haven't even told my parents yet, Moorsey. I don't know how. How do I start *that* conversation? Where are the instructions for living like this?"

Moorsey put a hand on my arm. "At least you know she's okay, though," he said gently. "If she checked her phone, she must be okay."

"But *why* is she doing this? Why won't she just call me and talk to me? If she wanted to leave me and go off with this other guy, why didn't she just *break up with me*?"

My coffee arrived. I lifted the cup with both hands and took a sip, very slowly. It was a chance to pull myself together.

"What about the American?" Moorsey asked.

"What about him?"

"Have you thought about trying to contact him? He might be easier to get to. He might have his phone on, for a start."

"How would we get his number?" I asked. "We don't know anything about him. We don't even know his name."

The prospect of talking to him, to the faceless American, gave me heartburn worse than the whiskey did. I didn't want to know anything about him. I preferred him as an idea, a faceless threat, a possible misunderstanding.

But if I could reach Sarah through him …

"There has to be a way, Ad," Moorsey was saying. "Think. If you were looking for evidence that she had been in contact with someone, where would you go?"

"To her phone," I said, "which we don't have. Her email account, which we can't access. Her wallet, which she took with her."

"Did you look at home? Through her drawers and stuff? Rose has this big hatbox thing where she keeps mementos and souvenirs and crap. Receipts. Does Sarah have anything like that?"

"I don't think so, no."

"Is there anywhere else she'd keep …"

He stopped just as I spoke. We'd both thought of it at exactly the same time.

"Her desk," I said. "Her desk at work."

It took us five minutes to walk from Angelsea Street to the doors of Anna Buckley Recruitment. It occupied an entire Georgian building on the South Mall, across from the majestic limestone columns of the AIB Bank building that sat at number 66. I went to reception and asked for Susan Robinson while Moorsey waited on the street outside. They directed me upstairs.

Susan was waiting for me outside her office door.

"Adam!" She pulled me in for a hug. "I asked Lisa to double-check the name. I was like, 'Adam Dunne? *Hollywood screenwriter* Adam Dunne? Are you sure?' What are you doing here? We never see you around these parts. Come to pick up Sarah's homework, have you? Is she feeling better? Nothing worse than stomach flu, is there? I suppose you tend to lose a couple of pounds, at least. Maybe I should get her to lick me or something? I've a christening next week. Ha! Come on in, come on in. Have a seat."

I did what I was told. I was exhausted already.

But I *did* have confirmation that Sarah had indeed called in sick.

Susan was in her late forties and making every effort to hide the fact. Today she was wearing a short, shiny, shapeless dress with some sort of geometric design printed on the front, towering heels that poised her feet at the same angle as Barbie's, and thick black eyeliner that I could see pooling in the inner corners of her eyes from three feet away. Her legs and arms were the same odd rust color, and her white-blond hair didn't move when she did. I wondered idly how flammable she was.

"Saturday night was fun, wasn't it?" she said. "God, I didn't get home until after three! The babysitter was a right bitch about it. I gave her an extra twenty, though, and that soon put the train-tracked smile back on her face. Sixty euro she went home with. Can you believe that? She makes more than me, if you go by the hour. We should all be babysitters, eh? I was lucky to get a pack of chips and a fiver when I was her—"

"Susan," I said. "Sarah isn't sick."

A moment of suspended animation as she stopped chattering in midsentence. A flicker of confusion crossed her face. Then, "She's feeling better, you mean?"

"No, she was never sick."

"Then why ... I'm sorry, Adam." Susan laughed nervously. "I think I'm a bit lost here."

"Sarah just told you she was sick. She actually went to Barcelona. She flew out there Sunday morning and was supposed to come back yesterday lunchtime, but she didn't. She wasn't answering her phone, and now it's switched off. No one has heard from her—not her parents, not her best friend, not me."

"Well, I'm sure it's just—"

"We went to Angelsea Street this morning, her parents and I. We've reported her missing."

Susan looked stricken. "But she said she was sick."

"When did she tell you that, exactly? Do you remember?"

"She emailed me over the weekend. Sunday morning. I remember because I thought to myself ..." Susan blushed. "I said to myself, 'She seemed perfectly fine on Saturday night.' God, I thought she was just hungover. I mean, it's not like I could blame her. I was *dying* myself Sunday morning."

Had I seen Sarah typing a message on her phone at any point on

Sunday morning? I didn't think so, but then, she'd been at the airport early. She could have done it there.

I tried to picture her face as she composed the lie to Susan, read it over, and pressed SEND, but I got only a collection of blurry, indistinct features where Sarah's face should be.

I couldn't picture it. I couldn't believe my Sarah would do that. But she *had*.

"Have you heard from her since?" I asked.

"No. Is she okay? Is she feeling okay? I mean, like …" Susan pointed to her head. "*Mentally?*"

Ignoring that, I said, "Do you think anyone else here would've heard from her?"

"I don't know. I can ask. Whatever we can do to help, Adam. Whatever we can. Just say the word."

"Would you know anything about an American man that Sarah might have met through work? That she became friendly with?"

I focused on a spot of bulletin board just over Susan's left shoulder while I said it, but she didn't reply until I made eye contact again.

"An American man? Why? Do you think they're … Are they *together?*"

"Do you know anything about that?" A creeping flush was heading for my cheeks. The leading edge of it was the embarrassment of asking if other people were aware long before I was that my girlfriend was cheating on me; the rest was the shame of being embarrassed about anything when the reason I asked was because I didn't know where Sarah was. "Did you have any training days where someone came in from outside the company? Or visits from other branches? How could she have met someone at work who didn't work here?"

"I don't … Adam, what's going on?"

"Can I take a quick look at her desk?"

"Her *desk?*"

"There might be something in there that will help us contact her."

"Like what?"

"I won't know until I find it."

"I ..." Susan looked flustered. "I don't know."

"It's okay," I said. "Just thought I'd ask. Probably better to leave it for the gardaí anyway. I think you can expect them Monday, they said."

"They're coming *here*?"

"Well, they need to search her desk."

I could see the conflict on Susan's face: gardaí swarming around the office would be exciting, yes, but the workday would also be completely disrupted while Sarah's colleagues huddled together to gossip and theorize.

"I suppose it'd be okay," she said.

"Can I go look now?" I pushed back my chair. "Her parents are freaking out, as you can imagine. The sooner we make contact with her ..."

"Of course, yeah." Susan stood up. "Follow me."

We took the stairs down to the ground floor and walked toward the rear of the building and out into a modern extension: an office space filled with fluorescent lights, gray cubicles, and young workers in off-the-rack suits, sitting at desks. They all looked up as we walked in. Susan shot them a collective stern look. *Turn back around. Get back to work. Mind your own business.*

I followed her to the back of the room, to a desk by a large window.

"This is it," she said.

The desk wasn't in a cubicle, but backed up to another desk so that Sarah sat facing her coworker. There was no one sitting opposite now, but a half-full cup of coffee and this morning's *Examiner* spread open across the desk suggested that someone had been recently and would soon resume doing so. On her desktop sat a large computer screen, and a phone, and some stationery: a pen pot, stapler, and notepad. There were no personal items, no clues that this was Sarah's desk.

"She's very tidy," Susan said. "Very neat."

I pulled out the chair and sat down, eyeing the three drawers by my left leg. If I was going to find something, it would be in there.

It felt weird, sitting in this place where Sarah spent most of her time. A place I'd never seen before. Pictured, yes, and heard about in great detail, but never actually seen for myself. A huge part of Sarah's life took place in this room—a part that I knew only from the bits she decided to share with me. But did I really know it? Had she told me everything that mattered? Were other secrets hidden here?

Susan was looking down at me with her arms folded across her chest.

"I'll just be a second," I said.

"Oh. Right. I'll, ah, wait over by the door. Holler if you need anything."

I waited for Susan to walk away before I opened the top drawer— and immediately saw why Sarah managed to keep such a neat desk.

It was filled to the brim with junk.

I poked through it. A couple of blank note cards, a jar of paper clips, a Leap bus card, a pocket calculator, a pack of chewing gum, a crumpled tissue, a pair of cheap sunglasses, a Nespresso Club catalogue, a pair of headphones, a pendant I hadn't seen her wear in ages and that now had a tangled, knotty chain, an appointment card for a hair salon …

I pulled out the appointment card. Lane Casey Design, a salon I had a vague recollection of seeing somewhere in the Huguenot Quarter, maybe on French Church Street. A time and date were handwritten on the card: "11:30 a.m., Sat. 9th August."

So much for cutting all her hair off on a whim. I pocketed the card.

The next drawer had only a stack of manila folders, held together with a rubber band. I put them on the desktop and went through them quickly. They were all candidate files: application packages put together by those who came to Anna Buckley looking for a job—the job it would be Sarah's responsibility to find.

I flicked through a few files at the top of the stack. Each had a small ID photo printed in the top right-hand corner, underneath the candidate's name. Nearly every one was a man in his twenties who looked like a boy in his teens, complete with the odd spot, oversize shirt collar, and excessive hair-gel application; or a young woman with bad eye makeup and bed-head hair that she had probably spent an hour teasing into position. Finding jobs for newly graduated, overqualified but totally inexperienced aspiring adults was apparently Sarah's area of expertise.

I put them back in the drawer and went to pull open the bottom one.

Locked.

For the first time, I saw the little round lock in the upper right-hand corner of this, the deepest drawer.

Where was the key?

I looked around the room. Every desk was the same. Would the keys be, too? The facing desk was still unoccupied. Susan was still by the door, but leaning down now to chat conspiratorially with someone sitting near it—I could guess what about. I quickly got up, went around to the other desk, and pulled out the small silver key from the lock in the bottom drawer. It was the kind you get with a cheap padlock.

I sat back down at Sarah's desk and tried the key. It turned easily in the lock.

I pulled on the drawer.

The first thing I saw in there was my own face, smiling up at me. A framed photo that Sarah must, at some point, have kept on her desk. In it, I was sitting on our couch, smiling at the photographer. Her. It was from a couple of years ago, at least.

I turned it over and moved on to the rest.

A travel mug with a quip about Monday mornings printed on it. A box of highlighter pens. A pack of five A4 refill pads, still wrapped in plastic. A half-empty jar of hard candies with a sticker that read *The*

Olde Sweet Shoppe. A USB cup warmer shaped like a cookie, which I had given her last Christmas as a joke.

Why bother locking any of this stuff away?

I lifted up the pack of refill pads. There was a single envelope lying underneath. White and long, with a window. A bill. It had already been opened, and I pulled the contents out now.

Saw the familiar "O2" logo, Sarah's name, and our home address. It was her mobile phone bill.

Sent to our apartment, brought in to work, kept in a locked drawer. But why?

I spread the pages across the desk. There were four of them, each printed front and back. The cover page had a summary of charges and showed the amount owed. The billing period, a line of bold text said, covered the month of July. The other pages showed Sarah what she had to pay for: line after line of activity, arranged chronologically. Calls to other O2 numbers, calls to other mobiles, text messages, media messages, the odd international text, data usage …

And suddenly, I knew why.

"How are we going to do this?" I said to Moorsey. "We can't call them all."

We had walked to the Parnell Bridge end of the South Mall and settled on a bench by the river. The sun was shining and the tide was low. The putrid stench of the muddy green water in the Lee wafted up our nostrils.

"We don't have to." Moorsey had pulled a pen from his backpack and was already leafing through the pages. "We should be able to narrow it down." He handed the pages to me. "Go through them and cross off any numbers you recognize, your own included."

I did as I was told. Afterward, half the bill had lines through it. "Now what?"

Moorsey motioned for me to give him back the list.

"Now," he said, "I'm going to call out each of the remaining numbers to you and you're going to type them into your phone. If they're in your contacts already, the owner's name will come up as soon as you press CALL. That should get rid of a few more. Just try to hang up before they ring, or we'll be here all day with people seeing the missed call and ringing you back."

Using this method, we managed to eliminate several more numbers, including those for Sarah's parents, a couple of her friends, and common contacts such as our landlord and the management company who looked after our apartment block. But that still left many unknowns.

"What we need," Moorsey said, "is a time. These are all stamped with time of day, date, and duration. When would it have been unusual for Sarah to be making a call or sending a text message? Can you think of a time?"

I knew instantly: Saturday night. It was the one evening a week when we were almost guaranteed to be together, home alone. The going-away party had been our first time out together in weeks, so the four Saturday nights in July were probably safe bets. Possibly, Sarah had gone out with the girls on the first one, but that left three when I was all but positive we both were home, both watching TV, both making a conscious effort to stay off our phones. Phones during TV time annoyed us both.

I took the bill back from Moorsey and started scanning. Only one number had been called after eight o'clock on the night of Saturday the thirteenth, but it turned out to be a driver for a pizza delivery. We had missed his call, and Sarah had called him back. On the evening of Saturday the twentieth, she had called her mother twice. The second call was short, as if she had forgotten something the first time around. And later, she had sent a string of text messages to Rose.

But on the night of Saturday the twenty-seventh—a night I could actually remember, because we had spent it watching the end of the first season of *The Bridge*—Sarah had sent seventeen text messages to the same number between 8:15 p.m. and 11:23 p.m.

Seventeen texts.

That was one side of a long conversation.

"This is the guy," I said, tapping the paper. "It has to be. We were at home that night, watching TV. I would have noticed if she'd been using her phone that much. She must have sent them when I was in the bathroom. Or when she was. Look."

Moorsey took the bill back and studied it.

"There's calls to that number at other times," he said, "but not a lot. Mostly, it's text messages. Lots of them. Sent mostly during the daytime, while ..." He glanced at me. "While she's at work."

"So now what?"

"Now you call him."

My stomach clenched. Whether it was the toxic reek of this stretch of the River Lee, or the prospect of finding a real, live man who had been having sex with my girlfriend, I didn't know.

A combination of both, perhaps.

"And say *what*, exactly?"

"Just ask to speak to Sarah."

I unlocked the screen on my phone. I shook my head, not quite believing that I was doing this.

"He might hang up on you," Moorsey said, "so I'd get in there quick with something about how worried her parents are and that you've gone to the gardaí and stuff like that."

"Why don't I just text him?"

"Because we don't know if it's him yet."

I slowly keyed in the number, double- and triple-checking that I'd entered it right.

I looked at Moorsey. He nodded encouragingly.

"Okay," I said. "Here goes."

I pressed CALL. It rang once.

I got up and walked to the railing. Bad plan. There, the smell of the river was even worse.

It rang again. Then, "Hello?" A man's voice. "Hello? Is someone there?" An American accent. He had an American accent.

I said nothing. I couldn't say anything. My mouth had gone dry, my mind blank.

Well, almost blank. There was *something* in there: an image of Sarah and this man together, naked, in tangled sheets.

I turned to Moorsey, who was looking at me questioningly. He motioned with his hands.

Is he there?

I nodded.

Then talk to him!

I needed to find out who this man was. I was supposed to ask to speak to Sarah. Get it out as quickly as possible that her parents were very upset and that the gardaí were involved.

I took a deep breath, opened my mouth …

"Sarah?" the man said. "Sarah, is that you?" I jerked my head away from the phone, as if it burned. "Please, talk to me, Sarah." The voice was smaller now, tinny, coming from the phone I was holding away from my ear. "Just talk to me. *Please.*"

I threw the phone.

It smacked up against the bench with a loud *clack,* bounced onto the pavement, and skidded beneath Moorsey's legs.

"Adam," he said, getting up to retrieve it, "what the …"

Sarah, is that you? Please, talk to me, Sarah. Just talk to me. Please.

Wasn't Sarah *with* him? If she wasn't, where was she? And why did he sound worried?

"You cracked the screen," Moorsey said, handing me the phone. "What happened?"

"I don't … I don't know …"

The phone began to vibrate in my hand.

Jesus Christ. He's calling back.

I hit Accept.

"Who is this?" I said into the microphone. "Who are you?" Now it was my turn to listen to silence on the line. "Where is she, you fucking prick? Her parents are worried *sick.* We've been to the gardaí. If I don't find out what your name is, then they—"

A *click,* followed by a dial tone. He had hung up.

"'Fucking prick'?" Moorsey said. "Way to stay calm, Ad."

"She's not with him."

"What?"

"She's *not with him.*"

I repeated what the American guy had said.

"That's ..." Moorsey shook his head. "I don't get it."

"Neither do I."

"She's not with him, either. Does it make you feel better or worse?"

"I don't know," I said. "Better, I suppose, because ... well, because she's not. Worse because we're back to square one. But why ..." I stopped. "God, I am so *sick* of asking questions. I don't remember what it was like not to have a million of them running through my head constantly, all the time. It's *exhausting*. Worse, I don't know when it's going to stop—*if* it is. This could just go on and on. This could ... Fuck it, Moorsey, this could be my life now."

He slung an arm around my shoulders and patted my back.

"I miss her," I said, feeling tears sting my eyes. "I just *miss her*."

"I know."

"Can you wake yourself up when you're having a nightmare? Like, can you tell it's just a dream? I've always been able to. I realize, in the nightmare, that I'm just asleep and I can wake up and the crazy guy with the knife or the T. rex or whatever will stop chasing me."

"The T. rex?"

"I have a lot of *Jurassic Park*–based dreams."

"That's, uh, weird."

"What I do is, I force myself to make a loud noise, like shout out or moan or whatever, and that wakes me up. Nightmare over. Just like that." I clicked my fingers. "Do you think that would work for this?"

Moorsey looked at me sadly. "You should really talk to Rose."

"About what?"

"About *why*."

"She blames me for this. Don't you think I have enough to deal with right now without having to listen to her litany of why I'm the world's worst boyfriend?"

"I think she'd have more to tell you about Sarah than about you. It might help you understand."

"She said it was all my fault."

"She was upset, Ad. If you're not going to talk to Rose, what do you want to do now?"

"Well, I don't *want* to, but I have to tell Mum and Dad. We're going to have to do what the gardaí suggested: put an appeal for information on Facebook and stuff. I don't want to give my mother a heart attack when she goes online to do Telly Bingo and sees Sarah's face staring up at her under the headline 'MISSING PERSON.'"

But first, I tried calling *him* one more time. There was a long pause before a recorded female voice said, "The person at this number is currently unavailable. Please try again later."

I would never get through to that number again.

It's Saturday morning, and Sarah is beside me in the bed. Her back is against my stomach. Her hair is long again. She's wearing the red dress. I whisper in her ear, but she doesn't stir. When I put a hand on her shoulder, I realize her skin is ice cold—

I woke up with a start.

I was in our bed, alone. Even so, I had confined my limbs to my side of it while I slept.

The room was dark but for a sliver of sunlight pushing through a gap in the curtains. Had I managed to sleep through the night?

An angry vibration from the nightstand signaled that I was getting an incoming call. I didn't remember putting the phone on silent, but then, I didn't remember leaving myself a glass of water and a blister pack of Tylenol, or a small bottle of Bach's Rescue Remedy, or a packet of Kleenex. Mum had struck again. She and Dad had as good as moved in last night. She probably crushed up sleeping tablets and sprinkled them over that curry she forced me to eat.

I picked up the phone. A blocked number.

Could this be ...?

I hit ACCEPT.

"Adam? It's Dan. Don't hang up."

"Dan." I pulled myself up into a sitting position. "Isn't it the middle of the night there?"

"No, it's just after nine in the morning."

"But that means it's …" I pulled the phone from my ear to check the time. Three minutes after two in the afternoon. *What the hell?* "Uh, listen, sorry about the other day. I was just—"

"That's why I'm calling. I'm not going to ask you what's going on, Adam. I don't want to know, because if I don't, it means I can look at this situation objectively and give you the advice you need. That's what you're paying me for. I don't know what's happening over there, but I do know this: the script needs to get to the studio by close of business Friday. I need to see it first, and we have to allow for changes to be made before I pass it on. You know what that means? That means I need the script right *now*. Yesterday, ideally, so I could have brought it home to read over the weekend."

"I'm sorry, I just—"

"How far in are you?"

"Dan, the thing is that my girlfr—"

"I said I don't want to know. That's not me being a grade-A asshole, Adam. I hope you understand that. I just want what's best for you. I want this to work out. I want to be able to tell you what you *need* to hear, not just what you want to."

"I understand, Dan. I do. I just don't know if there's going to be—"

"There'll be no second chance here, Adam. You realize that, don't you?"

"Yes."

"This is it. One shot."

"I know."

"Like the Eminem song."

"I … If you say so."

"LA is a small town when it comes to business," Dan said. "People don't forget. They won't."

"I understand."

"A screenwriter gets his foot in the door with a spec, yeah, but he makes a *career* out of getting hired. Taking that one-word idea some idiot exec had in the shower this morning and turning it into a five-picture franchise. One of my clients, John Stacy—know him?—he's locked in a sweat lodge out in the Arizona desert right now, turning the phrase 'jungle subway' into a summer blockbuster. That's all the studio gave him, Adam. Two words. And they were 'jungle' and 'subway.' *You* only have to finish tweaking your own script. Who's going to hire someone who missed the deadline for *rewriting his own script* when there's the likes of John Stacy out there pulling Untitled Jungle Subway Project out of his ass for one hundred against three hundred, complete with an ending that leaves the door open for a sequel or six?"

"I understand that, Dan. I really do, but—"

"My advice is to do whatever you have to do to get this finished, and get it finished on time. Switch your brain off. Bottle your feelings. Take something, if you have to. Just *get it done.*"

"But you see—"

"Do you want all this to go away before it even gets started?"

"No, of course—"

"Payment is on delivery."

"I know, it's just that right now—"

"Kevin Williamson wrote *Scream* in a weekend."

"Actually, that's a myth. It was just the treatment."

"*You* don't even need to write anything new. You're *rewriting.* A hundred and twenty pages of mostly negative space. If you pulled out all the stops, you'd have this done in two or three days, and that's if you hadn't started it yet. But you *have* started it." A pause. "Haven't you?"

"Of course I have," I lied. "But the thing is, my gir—"

"Whatever's happening over there, Adam, it's not going to be happening forever. It'll come to an end. This, too, shall pass. And what will you be left with then? *Nothing,* if you don't get this done."

"But, Dan, it's serious. She's—"

"I'm hanging up now. I'll call again tomorrow, same time. Answer your phone when I do. You're going to thank me for this."

"But she's missing, Dan, okay? My girlfriend is *missing*! How am I supposed to think about a bloody screenplay when I don't know where my girlfriend is? And haven't known for nearly a *week*?"

Silence.

"Dan?"

I pulled the phone from my ear. He'd hung up. *Shit.*

I dialed Sarah's number.

"Sarah, for fuck's sake," I spat as soon as the voice mail kicked in. "What the *fuck* are you doing? Call me when you get this message. Just *call me*, okay? I *know* you're checking your phone. I saw that you read the WhatsApp message. This has to stop. Your parents are in bits; the gardaí are involved; I've just had Dan Goldberg on the phone. You *know* how much this means to me, how long I've waited for—" The room blurred, and I realized I had tears in my eyes. "Sarah, please. I don't know what's happening here. I don't know what to do. I don't know what I'm *supposed* to do. Just call me. You don't have to talk to anyone but me. I won't even tell anyone we spoke if you don't want me to. But please. Call me. *Please.*" I took a breath. "Sarah, you're scaring me."

There was a gentle knock on the bedroom door. It swung open to reveal Rose, carrying a steaming mug of something and a plate of toast.

I quickly ended the call and put the phone down on the bed.

"Your mother sent me," she said. "Can I come in?"

"Sure."

"Did I hear you on the phone?"

"My agent," I said. "Don't ask."

Rose handed me what I now saw was coffee. She placed the toast on the nightstand, pushing my mother's panic paraphernalia to one side so she could.

"It's good you slept so long," she said. "You needed a rest."

"Any news?"

She shook her head. "No, nothing."

Something crashed in the kitchen. "Who's out there?" I asked.

"Your parents. And Moorsey. Jack and Maureen are on their way over—your mother called them, apparently. She wants to force-feed them dinner, make sure they're okay."

The substance in my cup was flecked with black flakes. Mum didn't drink coffee. If I had to guess, I'd say she prepared fresh grounds the way you were supposed to make instant.

Rose moved to go.

"Wait," I said. "Can we talk?"

After a beat, she sat down on the very edge of the bed. "Moorsey told me that Sarah read the WhatsApp message," she said.

"She did."

"And that she's not with the American guy."

"Doesn't look like it, no."

"She does love you, Adam."

I laughed softly. "Yeah. Seems like it, doesn't it?"

"She *does*. But not like … not in the same way she used to. She cares about you."

"Is she going to leave?"

Rose bit her lip. "Yes."

"When?"

"When the money comes in. Your money. When you can afford to live here by yourself."

I looked around the bedroom. It had been a blank canvas when we moved in, and would still be if not for Sarah. She had bought the colorful bed linens, the coordinating bedside lamps, the floral art print that now hung on the opposite wall. The dressing table was home only to a scented candle and a ceramic bowl filled with various pieces of Sarah's costume jewelry. Her clothes took up most of the space in the wardrobe. Those were her paperbacks gathering dust on the windowsill.

And yet, she wanted to leave this home, to leave me here alone.

"Why?" I asked.

"She just isn't … She isn't *sure* anymore. That you two are the way it's supposed to be. You've been together for ten years, Adam. *Ten years.* And she's only twenty-nine. She was nineteen when she met you."

"I can do math, too, Rose."

"Are you the same person you were when you were nineteen?"

"Who else would I be?"

"You know what I mean." Rose shifted her weight on the edge of the bed. "Sarah and you—you've grown up since you first met. That's what you do in your twenties. If you do it with someone you met before any of that changing even began, well, what are the chances you'll both come out the other side having grown into two people who still want to be together?"

"*I* did."

"That makes one of you, then."

"Sarah and I had a deal. Did she tell you that?"

"You mean the arrangement whereby you had the luxury of avoiding the responsibilities of adulthood while the rest of us were forced to figure out how to carry them on our backs? That one? Yeah. She did tell me that. God, how nice it must be to be a man. No deadlines." She waved her arms. "Here, have all the time you want."

"I'll give Sarah all the time she wants, too."

"That's nice of you, but Mother Nature isn't as generous." Rose waved her finger back and forth. "Tick-tock, biological clock. If you're a woman and you ever plan on having kids, your time to run off and have adventures and chase your dreams comes with a best-before date. Sarah's worried about hers. That's normal. You don't seem worried at all. I'd bet you haven't even thought about it. That's not."

"But why didn't she just *talk* to me about it? We could've figured this out."

"I think her mind is made up."

"Then why not just tell me?"

"She doesn't want to hurt you, Adam. Or embarrass you."

"And *this* isn't hurtful or embarrassing?"

"If Sarah came in that door this minute and said she wanted to break up and you had to leave, where would you go?"

"I'd figure something out."

"She was waiting until you wouldn't have to figure something out, until the money was in your account. Until you'd taken care of yourself. *Could* take care of yourself, after she left you to your own devices."

"Then where is she? Hiding out until that happens?"

"I don't know where she is," Rose said. "She was supposed to come back."

"Why send the passport?"

"I don't know."

"What does the note mean?"

"I don't—"

"Why hasn't she called?"

She threw up her hands. "Adam, I *don't know*."

"Do you think she's in trouble?" I asked quietly.

"The gardaí don't seem to think so," Rose said after a beat.

"That's not what I asked."

"I think …" She drew a slow breath and let it out. "I think we're all going to be smacking ourselves in the forehead when we find out what's actually going on here. It's like the time a few years ago when my sister—she was just nineteen or twenty then—didn't come home from a Saturday night out. My mother could never fall asleep until she did, so she lay awake, three, four, five in the morning. She started calling her. Texting her phone. Got no reply. No response. When it reached a reasonable hour, we called the friend she'd gone out with, and she told us she hadn't seen Ruth since they got separated in the club, around midnight. Ruth had work at eleven, and her uniform was at home, so when she hadn't come home by ten o'clock, we were all worried sick. We rang the place where she worked, as soon as they opened, thinking she might have gone straight there. But they hadn't heard from her, either. She'd never missed a day of work in two years. My mother was *literally* just about to call the gardaí when Ruth walked in the door, looking for cash to pay the taxi driver. Her bag had been stolen in the club—so no phone—and she'd slept at a friend's. They were drunk, so they *over*slept. She'd only woken up fifteen minutes ago and had no idea we were all at home, panicking, imagining a future of missing posters and underwater search teams. It was so real, Adam. My mother was about to dial nine-nine-nine. We were all convinced something awful had happened, and we started thinking it just because someone wasn't answering their phone. But absolutely *nothing* had happened."

"Sarah's been gone a lot longer than a few hours."

"I didn't say it was exactly the same."

"What if she never comes home? What would you have done if your sister didn't show up?"

"Let's not indulge in the hypothetical," Rose said. "Worry is the most pointless human emotion. Didn't anyone ever tell you that? Want to guess who told *me* that? I'll give you a clue: she wrote it in a "thinking of you" card she gave me back when I was convinced I'd failed my final-year exams."

"Yeah, well ..." I sighed. "Easy for her to say."

There was another knock on the door. Rose and I both looked toward the sound.

This time it was Moorsey, waving his iPad. I could see from the blue banner at the top of the screen that the device was logged on to Facebook.

"Adam," he said. "You need to see this."

ROMAIN

Marly-le-Roi, Paris, 1993

The snow in Paris was different from the snow that had fallen over their old house. Out in the countryside, snow lay undisturbed on the ground for days, thick and pure. Here in the city, workers started plowing paths through it just as soon as it fell, and with so many people around, it didn't take long for what was left to turn into a dirty, slushy mess.

The day before Christmas Eve, Romain picked his way through the slush, en route to school. Temperatures had dropped to freezing overnight, so there was a good chance that some of what looked like harmless melted snow was actually rock-hard ice. He had reminded Mama again and again that he needed new winter boots, that he had outgrown the pair he wore last year, but unless it was something about Mikki—which pills he was supposed to take at which time, how to clean the feeding tube, when the battery on the back of his chair needed changing—nothing seemed to take root in her head these days. She would just forget.

Just this morning, he had told Papa, who promised to pick up a pair for him later, on the way home from work.

"These will do in the meantime," he had said, pulling a pair of his own thick, knobbly woolen socks over Romain's sneakers. "Just go slow, okay? And be careful."

Romain *did* go slow—so slow he didn't get to school until after the bell. And he *was* careful, but the wetter the socks got, the more slippery the ground beneath them felt. Right outside the school gates, his left foot slid off the path, and his balance went with it.

He yelled out. He fell over. He hit the footpath hard, coming down on his right side. Tears sprang to his eyes. His hip throbbed. His elbow stung, and the skin on both palms was scraped.

Romain could feel the cold wetness of the snow seeping into his trousers. With a sinking feeling, he realized that when he stood up he was going to look as if he had wet his pants.

He pulled himself into a sitting position and waited for the pain to subside a bit. At least he was late. Everyone else was inside already. The only thing that could make this worse was …

"Hey, look! It's Romain the Retard!"

Bastian Pic was coming down the path with two of his friends following behind. Bastian was in *quatrième,* two years ahead, and lived in the house across the street from Romain's. He was mean to all the boys in the younger classes—he was always getting into trouble with the teachers for it—but, for some reason, he was especially mean to Romain.

"What the fuck happened to you?" He was standing over Romain now, kicking him with one of his heavy boots. "I think you've been spending a bit too much time with that little brother of yours. Should I go and get his *wheelchair* for you? Or"—a burst of laughter—"is it his *nappies* that you need?"

The other two boys started laughing, too.

Romain tried to haul himself up, but Bastian pushed him down again.

"You better stay there," he said. "Wait for the retard ambulance to come and collect you."

"Boys?" One of the teachers was standing at the gates. "What's going on over there?"

"Nothing, Madame," Bastian called out. But when he turned to say this to her, he revealed Romain sitting on the ground. The teacher came rushing over.

"What happened? Are you all right?" She helped Romain up, then turned to Bastian. "Are you *trying* to get another suspension?"

Bastian held up his hands in a show of innocence. "I was just helping him up, Madame Berri."

"Oh, you *were*, were you?"

"I was." Bastian looked to his two goons for backup. "Wasn't I?" The two other boys nodded obediently.

Madame Berri turned to Romain and demanded that he tell her what happened. Behind her, Bastian was glaring at him.

"I want to go home," Romain said. "Can I just please go home?"

"Tell me what happened first. And I want the *truth*."

Romain was cold and wet, and his side was really hurting. He just wanted to be back in his bedroom, to crawl under the blankets and wait in the darkness for Papa to finish work.

"I fell on the ice," he said flatly. "He was helping me up."

"Romain, look at me." Reluctantly, Romain lifted his eyes. "Now, tell me again. What happened here?"

"I fell on the ice," he repeated. "Bastian was just helping me."

"*See?*" Bastian snarled. "I *told* you."

Madame Berri ordered Bastian and the other two boys inside, then helped Romain into the school and to the principal's office. He could walk okay, but the pain in his side was getting worse.

They told him they had called his mother and that she was going to come pick him up. He was to wait for her in a chair outside the principal's office. They gave him a cup of hot chocolate to drink and a scratchy blanket to put around his shoulders and told him his mother wouldn't be long.

They lived only a few streets away. She shouldn't have been long. But Mama took more than an hour to get there, and when she did, she didn't ask him how he was or what had happened. She just hurriedly thanked the principal's secretary, grabbed Romain's hand, and said they had to hurry back because it was nearly time for Mikki's bath.

* * *

Christmas was okay. Romain got a PlayStation and some new books and clothes. Jean got a set of WWF action figures he had yet to leave out of his sight. He was even sleeping with them. Mikki had what Mama called a Good Day, which meant that nothing went wrong with his chair or his medicine or his food and that he remained calm for the most part and didn't get stressed or agitated. It was his first Christmas at home; he had been staying at a special hospital for kids like him until a few months ago. That was why they had moved from the countryside: to be closer to him. Now they were all back together, and Romain suspected that this was why even Mama seemed to be in a good mood. She drank wine in the evening with Papa and hadn't gotten upset or shouted at anyone.

A deep purple bruise had spread all over Romain's right side, but it didn't really hurt anymore—not as much as it had, anyway.

He hadn't shown it to anyone.

"Hey, Romi," Papa said to him the day after Christmas. "I hear the park is open again this morning, and all the kids are in there making as many snowmen as they can. They're trying to build an army of them. Want to head down there?"

Romain shook his head. If "all the kids" really were there, that meant Bastian Pic probably was, too.

"Why not?" Papa asked.

"It's cold."

"Building snowmen is hard work. You'll soon warm up."

"I don't want to build snowmen."

"Then you can just watch."

Romain shook his head again.

"Ah, come on," Papa said. "It'll be fun. You can take Jean with you."

At the mention of his name, Jean looked up from his action figures. The toys were all laid out on the living room floor around a plastic wrestling ring, except for one, which was lying flat on its back inside it. Pink and black gear. Bret "the Hitman" Hart.

"I don't *want* to go," Jean whined.

"Listen, boys, you two have been stuck inside since school ended. You need to get outside. Romi, what did I buy those boots for? It wasn't to keep your feet dry on the living room carpet. And, Jean, you can take the wrestlers with you. They can fight on the ice, can't they?"

"No," Jean said sullenly.

But Papa was adamant that they go outside for a while. He dressed them both in heavy layers, slipped Romi a few francs so they could buy sweets in the shop, and told them to stay out for at least a half hour.

It was all a bit strange, but Romain did what he was told. He always did, nowadays.

The two boys dutifully trudged their way to the park. It was only a five-minute walk from their house. Romain got Jean to walk on the inside of the footpath, away from the road, and held his hand the whole way.

The park *was* full of kids, and they *were* all building snowmen. Romain counted nearly twenty of them in the open area just inside the gates. Some had accessories: scarfs, hats, carrots, twigs, coals. The park had been closed yesterday, and so the snow had had a chance to build up, white and thick. It reminded him of how the garden around the old house used to look during winter.

Jean had no interest in the snow or snowmen. He just wanted to play with his action figures. Romain suggested that they cut through the park to the shop, buy some sweets, and then start back home again. If they walked slowly, it would take the half hour that Papa had insisted they stay out for.

"What about the ice?" Jean asked.

"What ice?"

"Papa said I could play wrestling on the ice."

"Well …" Romain looked around. The pond was straight ahead. They could skirt around it to get to the exit by the shop. It would take a little longer, but that would only please Papa. "Okay, come on. Just for a minute, though. I want to get back."

The pond wasn't frozen, only frozen over. The layer of ice on its surface was thin and translucent and full of cracks and gaps. There was no one around.

Over the shallow part by the edge, the ice was fairly thick, so Romain told Jean he could put his figures there.

"You stay on the path, though. Don't go on the pond. Only the wrestlers can do that, okay?"

Jean nodded. "Okay."

He crouched down and started organizing the figures on the ice.

"I don't *believe* it," a voice said. "You again."

It was Bastian Pic, coming toward them along the side of the pond. Alone, but then, his stupid henchmen were never too far away.

"Jean," Romain said. "Sorry, but we have to go."

"But the referee hasn't even rung the bell."

"You can have that match at home. Come on."

Bastian was on them now. He looked down at Jean. "How many of you retards are there?"

Jean's face fell.

"Leave him alone," Romain said.

"Oh, leave him alone?" Bastian put on a high-pitched, girly voice. "You want me to *leave him alone*?" He stepped toward Romain until his face was inches away. He was close enough that when he spoke, Romain felt droplets of saliva hit his face. "You don't fucking tell me what to do, okay? Don't even *think* about it."

In a small voice, Jean said, "Romi?"

"We're going now, Jean. Pick up your toys."

"You're not going anywhere," Bastian said. "You know I got detention over you, you little shit? I didn't even *do* anything. *You're* the idiot who fell. When I saw you leave your house a while ago, I thought now was a good time to collect what you owe."

Romain said nothing. He thought of the money Papa had given them for sweets. Was that what Bastian meant?

"Romi?" Jean said again.

"If I'm going to get in trouble for kicking your pathetic ass," Bastian said, "I should at least get to kick it."

No, he didn't mean money. He was going to beat Romain up.

"Romi?" Jean said. "Romi, what's—"

Bastian swung around and roared, "Will you just *shut the fuck up!*"

Jean's eyes grew wide with fright; then his face crumpled. He looked at Romain helplessly as a dark stain began to spread between his legs.

Bastian started laughing. "No way. Seriously? *You're* not toilet-trained, either?"

The elastic snapped. That was how Romain would describe it later. That was the only way he could. It was as if everything he had been keeping inside since Mikki's accident, all the times he had held back his anger at the shit he took from Bastian and the other boys, all the words he'd had to swallow so he could try his best to be good—all of it had been bundled up, hidden away, kept back, held tight inside this stretch of elastic.

And where had it gotten him?

All but ignored by Mama. Bullied at school—Bastian hadn't been the first. And now here was poor Jean, shouted at, frightened and humiliated, all by this dumb, mean shit smear of a—

Romain pulled his right arm back and punched Bastian as hard as he could in the face.

After that, everything seemed to happen in slow motion.

His fist connected with the underside of Bastian's jaw and kept going, into the soft flesh on the side of his neck.

Bastian's eyes widened in surprise and he fell backward, over the edge of the pond.

Jean grabbed his action figures just before the thin layer of ice they were on smashed with the force of the impact.

The rage roared like a fire through Romain's veins.

He didn't feel like himself. It felt as if he were standing a few feet away, watching himself from afar.

He lifted his boots over the edge of the pond and stepped into the shallow water on the other side. He felt like a giant, towering over Bastian. He felt strong, *impossibly* strong, as though he could snap the boy's neck if he really wanted to.

Bastian was sitting in water up to his armpits. He was splashing around, trying to get up, but already the icy water was affecting his breathing. He had started to pant loudly.

He looked up at Romain, confused and scared. "What the hell are y—?"

Romain bent over and pushed Bastian back down under the surface, both hands on the boy's neck. A knee digging into his chest.

Behind him, on the path, Jean started to wail.

Romain could feel Bastian thrashing under the water, trying to come up. His hands were above the surface, smashing at it desperately, sending icy droplets flying everywhere and making splashing sounds, clawing at the skin on the back of Romain's hands.

Still Romain held him under. He did it until the thrashing stopped.

Then, tentatively, he lifted his knee. No movement. He released his hands from the boy's neck. Still none.

He pulled his hands out of the water and looked down at them, turning them over, studying the palms. They were turning blue with the cold, and the skin on the pads of his fingers was all crinkly. He looked beyond them, into the water.

Bastian's gray face was floating beneath the surface, eyes open wide.

And Romain was suddenly back inside his own skin. He wasn't

watching from afar anymore. This was happening. This was real.

He looked at Jean, then back at Bastian, then back at Jean again. What had he done *now?*

Romain got out of the water, grabbed his brother's hand, and ran the two of them out of the park and all the way home.

At first, it seemed as though the house was empty. Mama had taken Mikki to the hospital for an appointment; Romain knew that. But where was Papa? He called out for him but got no answer. The TV was on in the living room. Papa wouldn't have gone out without turning it off, would he? So where …

Romain saw him then, out the window.

Papa was in the back garden, stringing netting between the poles of a trampoline.

A *new* trampoline. That's why he had sent them out of the house. As he watched Papa prepare a surprise for them, Romain realized that he had ruined everything. *Again.* He had let the darkness out, just for a minute, and destroyed everything. *Again.*

Jean lifted his hand to knock on the glass, but Romain stopped him.

"Don't," he said. He put a finger to his lips. "Be quiet, okay? We're going to sneak upstairs. We can't make any noise, though. It's a game."

They went to their room and changed into clean, dry clothes of similar colors to the wet ones, hoping Papa wouldn't notice the difference. He *would* notice if their winter boots were missing, though, so they stuck their feet into the plastic bags Mama put in the bin in the bathroom, before sliding them inside their soaking-wet boots again.

Jean carefully transferred his wrestlers from the pockets of his wet coat to the dry one he had on now.

"Romi," he said. "Where's Bret Hart?"

"What?"

"Bret Hart isn't here."

"Are you sure?"

"He's not *here.*" Jean's voice started to rise. "He's not *here!*'

"Jean, please. Be quiet. Don't forget the game. I promise I'll get you another one, okay?"

"But I want the one I had. Where *is* he?"

"Maybe you dropped him on the road outside. We'll go look, okay?"

Romain put all the wet clothes in his gym bag and stuffed it down in the back of the wardrobe.

Then he went to the window. Papa was still outside. The trampoline was nearly assembled.

They hurried down the stairs and back out the front door, walked around the block a couple of times, and came back, this time ringing the doorbell.

"Boys!" Papa said when he pulled back the door. "How was the park? Did you have fun? Did you build a snowman?" Before they could answer, he beckoned them down the hall. "I have a little surprise for you—well, a big one. It's out in the garden. Père Noël was supposed to bring it, but it got delayed at customs, so …"

Behind Papa's back, Romain and Jean exchanged a glance.

Romain put a finger to his lips.

After a moment's hesitation, Jean nodded his head, just once, in silent agreement.

* * *

By the next morning, Bastian's disappearance was all over the news. Policemen were all over the neighborhood. Parents were getting together, conducting searches. Papa said he wanted to go, but Mama stopped him, saying he was needed more at home. Mikki was having a Bad Day. The battery pack on his chair kept beeping, and Mama couldn't figure out why. She was worried that it might go off at any moment. If it did, they would have to run to the hospital. Papa wasn't going anywhere.

Romain sat in the living room with him, watching the TV. The local news channel showed jerky helicopter footage of people walking through the snowy streets, across the school grounds, checking in ditches and drains, rifling through bins. Bastian's parents stood on their doorstep, holding each other and crying, pleading for information about their son's whereabouts.

A heavy lump settled in the pit of Romain's stomach. Dread was seeping out of every pore on his skin. It would be only a matter of time before they found the body. He wondered whether he should just run away, but he couldn't think of a single place to go.

Why had he done that awful thing? *Another* one?

To protect Jean.

Where *was* Jean? He had been avoiding Romain all day, but that was understandable. Although he wasn't sure whether Jean had really understood what he had seen. Maybe he was scared of his big brother now. Or maybe he was just playing with those damn wrestlers.

Which reminded him: he had to get another Bret Hart. He had some pocket money saved up; it would be enough. He just didn't know where to get one. He would have to figure it out.

The announcement came just after lunch: Bastian Pic's body had been found in the pond in the park. Police were looking to speak with anyone who had been in or around the park between lunchtime and six o'clock the day before. There had been a large crowd building snowmen. Were you or any of your children one of them? They were particularly interested in speaking to anyone who had lost an American wrestling action figure in or around the area by the pond. Apparently, Bastian had been found with one on his person, even though he didn't own such a thing himself.

The TV screen went blank. Papa had turned it off with the remote.

"An American wrestling action figure," he repeated. "In the park ..." Romain held his breath as his father's head turned slowly toward him. "Romi?"

It was just one word, but it was soaked in sadness. Romain didn't dare turn to face his father. He couldn't.

After Mikki, Papa was the only one who had stood up for him, who had defended him to Mama. *She* wanted to send him away. *She* wanted him punished. *She* never wanted to see him again. *I knew something was wrong with him. Didn't I always say it? Didn't I? And you told me to calm down.* But Papa had made her see that Romain was just a child, a child just trying to help, copying what he'd seen grown-ups do, not understanding his mistake.

Papa had understood what really happened with Mikki. But would he this time?

Romain could say it was an accident. That Bastian had been saying things to Jean when he slipped and fell. What would be Romain's excuse for not helping him, though, for not running to get help? He could say he was scared. He *had* been scared. That was the truth.

"Romi?" Papa said again. "Romi, did you—"

The door to the kitchen swung open.

Mama stood on the threshold, tears running down her face. She looked angry and scared and sad, all at the same time.

She was holding the gym bag of wet clothes in her hand. Jean was holding her other hand.

He was standing just behind her, against her leg, hiding almost in the folds of her skirt. Sucking his thumb, just as he used to when he was younger.

He wouldn't look at Romain.

"The police are on their way," she said to Romain.

"What!" Papa stood up. "What are you talking about?"

"*He* knows," Mama spat, nodding at Romain. "You can ask him. And don't you dare speak to me. I listened to you the last time, and look what's happened now. He is *not a boy*, Charlie. I've tried time and time again to tell you that. He nearly killed Mikki and now he's *actually* killed that boy—and he did it *in front of Jean!*"

Papa looked bewildered.

Romain started to cry.

Jean tugged on Mama's hand and said, "*Now* can we go get a new Bret Hart?"

ADAM

"'I know it's unlikely,'" I read aloud. "'And my husband said I shouldn't be bothering you. But she had a Cork accent and said her name was Sarah. She was on her own for dinner, sat next to us—the Pavilion Restaurant only has tables for twelve, and they fill them up as guests arrive. I saw on your post that your Sarah was on a flight from Cork to Barcelona last Sunday, and so were we. I didn't see her on it, though. Then we boarded the *Celebrate* from Barcelona early Monday morning. Now, I might be wrong, God forgive me, but I'm convinced it was the same girl. Her hair was different though—short, like a boy's. I'm sorry I don't have any other information for you, because we only chatted about the ship—Paul and I had been on the maiden voyage, too, so we were giving her tips about what to do and where to go, that sort of thing—and then I didn't see her again. But it's a huge ship— two thousand passengers it can take! We stopped in Nice in France, and La Spezia in Italy, and then went back to Barcelona again. Disembarked Thursday morning. Three nights, four days. You can contact me if you think I could be of any help, but as I said, that's really all I know and maybe I'm wrong. I'll say a novena for you all anyway. Regards, Mary Maher.'"

I looked up from my phone. Cusack was sitting on the other side of the conference table, with an expression that seemed to say, *And ...?*

Then she actually said it.

"The logo," Maureen reminded me.

"Oh, yeah." I slid an A4 page across the table. Half of it was taken up with a photo of a middle-aged couple posing in front of a mural of a large cruise ship. The image was streaked with white lines—my printer was running low on ink. "This is Mary and her husband, on the ship." I tapped the bottom right-hand corner of the picture, where a logo had been superimposed. "See that?" I opened Sarah's passport to the photo page, where the note was still stuck. I laid it flat on the table, aligned it with the photograph. "The squiggly lines —they're waves. That's the Blue Wave logo. That's the company that owns the *Celebrate*. Sarah must've gotten that paper when she was on the ship."

To my left, Jack blew air out of his nose. When I turned to look at him, I saw his lips set in a tight line and his arms folded across his chest.

He looked annoyed, but with who? With Sarah? With *me*?

"So this message," Cusack said. "It came from the Facebook page?"

"Yeah."

On Friday night, Moorsey had set up a "Help Us Contact Sarah O'Connell" Facebook page. By Saturday afternoon, a Tipperary woman named Mary Maher had sent a private message to it, saying she had just returned from a Mediterranean cruise where she met a woman she thought was Sarah.

Mary's Sarah had a Cork accent and very short hair, and the ship—the *Celebrate*—had made a stop in Nice, from where the passport had been posted.

But still, a *cruise ship*? Why would Sarah have gone on one of those?

The Facebook page's inbox was quickly filling up with similarly ridiculous claims. The message that came in just before Mary's claimed that Sarah had been buying a trolley-load of ice in Tesco Mahon Point Thursday morning, and the one after was from a psychic who told us, hey, bad news, Sarah is dead, but *good* news, if you cough up two hundred euro in cash, you can communicate with her across the ether.

But then, when Moorsey went and looked at Mary's Facebook

profile, he saw that she had just updated her cover photo with an image taken aboard the ship. He recognized the logo instantly. We had messaged Mary back, then later spoke to her for a few minutes over the phone. Next, we called Garda Cusack to tell her we had new information, and she agreed to move our planned Monday meeting up. Now it was Sunday morning, we were back in the same stuffy conference room in the District HQ on Angelsea Street, and Cusack was not reacting to this the way I had thought she would.

In fact, she was barely reacting at all to the news that we had traced Sarah to a cruise ship in the Mediterranean.

Cusack picked up the printout of the photo now, brought it close to her face, studied it. Put it down again. Picked up the passport, flicked through its pages. Stopped on one page. Raised an eyebrow. Rotated the passport to get a better look at whatever was there.

"I found the, ah, friend, too," I said. "I got his number from Sarah's phone bill. She isn't with him. I have his number, if you want it. But I haven't been able to get through to it since Thursday."

Cusack said nothing.

"And she read the message," I said, pushing on. "The WhatsApp message I sent her? Its status is 'read' now. I think she read it Wednesday night, or early the next morning. And we know for sure she called in sick to work, so—"

"That's good," Cusack said. "That's all good news. But I'm a bit confused. What is it you think we can do for you at this point?"

"Well, we need you to confirm that she was on the ship," I said, swallowing the word "*obviously.*" "We called Blue Wave, but they won't give out any passenger information. They must know where she got off. *When* she got off. Who she was with. Whether she reported to them that her passport had been lost or stolen while she was there. Or maybe she had an accident or got sick during the cruise and had to be transferred to a hospital." I felt Maureen beside me, reacting to this scenario. "You could find out who owns the phone number, the one for Sarah's ... friend. Find out who it's registered to. We can't do that ourselves."

"I'm not sure we can do that, either," Cusack said. "You said Sarah isn't with him?"

"She's not with him *now*, no."

"What about the police in Nice?" Maureen asked. "And the consulates? You said you were going to check with them. Have you heard anything? Has Sarah been to any of them? When are you actually going to"—Maureen's voice rose—"start *doing something* about finding my *daughter*?"

Jack put a hand on his wife's arm. I couldn't tell whether he was comforting her or shushing her.

"I know this is difficult for you," Cusack said gently. "And confusing. But as I explained when we first met on Friday, we don't go looking for every capable adult who goes somewhere without telling anyone else. We don't send out search parties for people who turn off their phone. And we don't open missing-person cases unless there's a real concern that the person who can't be contacted has come to harm, could come to harm, or has plans to harm themselves. I don't see any evidence for any of that here. And that's a *good thing*." She exhaled. "Now let me tell you what I *do* see ..."

An Gardaí, it turned out, had their own names for things. We sat and listened while Cusack translated the events of the past week into garda-speak.

Sarah telling work she was sick, telling me she was going to a conference, and not telling her parents anything at all became "*purposely misleading loved ones about her whereabouts*." Withdrawing 650 euro (the odd three euro, Cusack explained, was the foreign ATM transaction fee) constituted "*having means*," and withdrawing cash instead of using her card was "*concealing her movements*." And the new haircut meant it would be difficult, if not impossible, to locate a photograph that accurately reflected what Sarah looked like now, which, in garda-speak, was *"actively taking steps to disguise her appearance."*

"No," I said. "Sarah wouldn't do this to us. She just wouldn't do it. I know her. She wouldn't leave us … leave us *feeling* like this."

"You told me yourself, Adam. She saw the WhatsApp message. It was marked as read. Presumably, she saw all the messages you'd been sending her, potentially read the emails, and listened to the voice mails as well. She got them all, and she chose not to respond to any of them."

"There has to be a reason for that," I said. "Maybe she *can't* respond."

"But she can go on a cruise?"

I didn't answer that.

"We've contacted the Department of Foreign Affairs," Cusack said, "and we will send a bulletin to Interpol tomorrow morning. But that's all we can do in this situation. That's all we *should* do, based on our review of it. And that's a positive thing."

"You keep saying that," Maureen said, "but I still don't know where my daughter is."

"What are we supposed to do?" I asked. "Are you seriously leaving us with *Facebook*?"

"Actually …" Cusack cleared her throat. "You might want to consider what may happen if you continue to appeal to the public—especially online—for help in contacting Sarah. People will find out about her last known location, and you know how quickly the tide can turn. You hear 'cruise ship,' you … well, you think 'holiday.'"

"Holiday?" Maureen gasped. "*Holiday?*"

Jack shifted in his seat.

"What about the passport?" I asked. "If she's on holiday, how is she going to get home without it? And who sent it? The writing on the envelope wasn't hers."

Cusack picked up the passport again, opened it to a middle page, and turned it around so I could see what was stuck to it: an airline luggage sticker, the kind used to trace a suitcase that's gone missing.

"This luggage tag has 'Cork' on it," she said. "If someone found this after Sarah lost it, they could easily use social media to track down the Sarah O'Connell who looks like the photo in it and who lives in Douglas, Cork."

"Oh, right, of course," I said. "And figure out her address *how,* exactly?"

"She's in the phone book."

The phone book? "*How?*" I didn't even know they still made those.

"It's just a check box whenever you get a landline installed," Cusack explained. "Did Sarah set up your phone or broadband account, by any chance?"

I nodded. Sarah set up everything because, more often than not, she was the one paying for it

"Well, there you go."

"There must be hundreds of other Sarah O'Connells living in—"

"Her Facebook page is set to 'public,' and she's checked in at your apartment complex in the past. It wouldn't take a detective to figure it out."

"Just as well," Maureen muttered.

I ran a hand through my hair in frustration. I thought about the last time we'd been in this room, all of us sitting in exactly the same positions, only with photos of Sarah fanned out on the tabletop between us.

"What about the note?" I asked. "How does that fit in if the passport is returned lost property?"

"Block capitals. Nondistinct. Signed with an initial. It could be—"

"It's her writing. I know it is."

"I know you believe—"

"It's *hers!*" I said, hitting the table with my hand. "I'm sure."

"Fine," Cusack said. "Let's pretend for a second that the note *is* from Sarah. And that the passport is, too, even though I can't think why she'd post her own passport home ahead of her. Whenever we do launch a missing-person investigation, we have one of two goals. If we believe something has happened to the missing individual, we want to find out what that was. If someone else was responsible for it, we want to apprehend them. If we think the individual has left of their own accord, then our end goal is to make contact. Contact is always what we're after, either directly between us and them, or between the missing person and their family."

Her eyes flicked to the passport.

"No," I said. "No."

"If this is from Sarah," Cusack said, "then that's what it is: contact. I don't believe it is, though. I believe this is, to use your words, returned lost property."

"But we still don't know where Sarah is. Or *how* she is. If she's okay."

"You have no right to know. I realize that's tough to hear and probably impossible to accept—for now, anyway—but Sarah is a grown woman. This may not be the nicest thing to do, yes, but she's perfectly within her rights to do it."

"Don't you get it?" Now *my* voice was rising. "You're talking about someone I don't know. A stranger. An alien. I don't recognize Sarah in any of the things you say. She wouldn't do this. She *couldn't* do this."

"But she has."

I turned in surprise toward the voice that said this.

Jack was looking at Cusack, pushing his chair back from the table.

"We understand," he said to her. "Thank you for your time."

He stood up to go and motioned for Maureen to do the same. She looked helplessly from him to me, to Cusack, then back to Jack again.

"But Sarah," she said to him.

"Come on, Maur. Let's go."

I stood up, too. "Jack, what are you doing? We have to find her."

"How do you think we feel," he spat at me, "having to tell everyone that our twenty-nine-year-old daughter *ran away*? Putting her mother through all this. Not to mention what she was up to before she flew off to Spain for herself. Spain *and* France. Wake up, would you, son? The girl is *on holiday.* Jesus Christ. It's like the bloody Peru Two all over again. I don't *want* to know where she is or what she's doing. I don't care. This … this *embarrassment* stops now."

The so-called Peru Two were a pair of young women who had been reported missing from the island of Ibiza a year or so before. The family of one of the women had launched an appeal for information, which spread from Facebook to mainstream media outlets. Her face was everywhere alongside pleas from her loved ones, who said she would never go a week without calling home. An Gardaí, meanwhile, were conspicuously absent. Then, a week after the story broke, the Department of Foreign Affairs found their "missing person" imprisoned in a Peruvian jail, charged with smuggling something in the region of 1.5 million euros' worth of Class A drugs into the country, hidden in packets of food. The appeal—and the girls' family—instantly became the butt of Internet jokes.

"She doesn't deserve us looking for her," Jack said. "She doesn't deserve us *at all.* Now, *come on,* Maur."

Maureen stood up, her eyes on the floor.

"Thanks again," Jack said to Cusack. "Sorry for wasting your time." He took Maureen's arm, and together they started out of the room.

Cusack looked to me. "I know this is difficult …"

I didn't wait to hear the rest. I walked out, too.

Around seven-thirty Tuesday morning, I heard the telltale *clunk* of the front door being pulled outward by someone entering the corridor from the stairwell. I was already standing in my hallway, waiting, ready to go. The car keys jingled in my hand.

"I would shout, 'Road trip!'" Rose said when I opened the door, "but it seems inappropriate." She was holding two takeaway coffees and handed me one. "You ready to go?"

I had come straight home from Angelsea Street on Sunday and, after telling my parents of the conversation with Cusack, convinced them that I needed some time to myself. My father literally had to push my mother out the door, but they eventually left.

I went straight to work, trying to get someone in Blue Wave to talk to me about Sarah. I needed to know when and where she had gotten off the ship. Well, first I needed them to confirm that she had been on it in the first place, and *then* I needed to know when and where she got off. I had never been on a cruise. Did you have to wait until the end, or could you get off before that? What about the days when they stopped places? Could Sarah have gotten off and stayed off then? Would there be a way to tell? What about the American? Had he been on the cruise, too? Was he home already? Had they shared a cabin?

When was any of this going to start making *sense*?

I had spent the rest of that afternoon and most of Monday calling every telephone number I could find on Blue Wave's website, sending tweets to their corporate Twitter account, and even live-chatting online with something called a "customer experience ambassador." A futile experience—I felt I was either interacting with someone who couldn't stray an inch from a limited script of prepared responses, or merely generating automated answers based on keywords in the questions I had asked. Time and time again, I had been told that passenger information was confidential. Under no circumstances could they give out a single detail.

I was getting nowhere until, just before eight last night, an exasperated call center employee who must have been nearing the end of her shift told me to put my request for information in writing. She even gave me an address to send it to.

Blue Wave, it turned out, had its European headquarters in a business park two and a half hours' drive up the motorway, on the outskirts of Dublin. Wouldn't it be harder to dismiss me in person?

I had been debating whether to go when Rose and Moorsey knocked on the door, having come straight from work and bearing Chinese takeaway. Moorsey had already filled Rose in on what happened at the meeting with Cusack.

I had asked her what she thought.

"About Jack having a tin can for a heart?"

"About Sarah being on a cruise."

"Well . . ." Rose pushed a clean plate toward me and started pulling cartons out of a grease-stained brown paper bag. "In all the time I've known her, Sarah never even mentioned such a thing. I mean, *Sarah* on a *cruise*? Stuck in an enclosed space full of retirees watching cabaret shows put on by *X Factor* rejects, and stuffing herself at all-night high-calorie buffets? Does that sound like something she'd be into?" Rose shook her head. "Not the Sarah I know."

"That's just it, though, isn't it?" I said. "Who *is* the Sarah we know?"

"I think," Moorsey said through a mouthful of chicken curry, "it's safe to say she *was* on the ship. The flight to Barcelona, the one-night stay in the hotel, the logo on the note, and Mary Maher's story. It all fits. It would be too big a coincidence otherwise."

"Yeah," Rose said. "But what was she *doing* on that cruise?"

"She was with him," I said. "The American. I think we can assume that much. But then, for some reason, they went their separate ways. *After* the cruise. If we knew where Sarah got off the ship, we'd know where they separated. We'd know when. But Blue Wave won't tell me anything. They keep transferring me around and saying passenger information is confidential."

"So what are you going to do?" Moorsey asked.

"Well, their European headquarters are in City West."

"Where's that?"

"Business park just outside Dublin."

Rose raised her eyebrows. "You're thinking of going there?"

"Thinking about it, yeah."

"I'll come with you," she said. "We can go tomorrow. I'll take a day off work."

It was just as well that she did; otherwise, I would never have found their offices. City West was a sprawling, well-manicured maze of nondescript glass blocks, busy signage, and serial roundabouts.

We got there just before ten on Tuesday morning and drove around in circles until Rose happened to spot a tiny brass nameplate affixed to the front of an office building.

"There!" she said. "Didn't that say something about Blue Wave?" Stopping, I reversed a few feet.

"'Blue Wave Tours,'" I read aloud, peering at the lettering. "'Your friends at sea.'"

Afraid we might never find it again, we abandoned the car in the nearest empty space: Blue Wave's employee parking lot.

Just before we headed inside, I checked my phone for new messages.

"That would be amazing timing," Rose said, watching me.

"Wouldn't it? If she called right now and said, 'Hey, what's up? Oh, sorry. I meant *Tuesday*. I'm at the airport right now. Come pick me up.'"

I said, "Yeah," only because it was easier than admitting just how far past misunderstandings we now were.

The lobby was a mess. Bare concrete floor was exposed, presumably awaiting the plastic-wrapped roll of carpet leaning against the wall in one corner. Framed pictures of the company's fleet of cruise ships were stacked on the floor. They all looked the same to me: enormous, top-heavy, unlikely to float. All the lobby's furniture—a reception desk, a blue coffee table, six chairs with scratchy blue upholstery—were pushed to one side and covered in a fine layer of gray dust. The only sound was a radio talk show, playing at low volume from an unseen speaker.

The receptionist looked surprised to have someone to receive. She smiled and apologized for the mess. They were in the process of rebranding, she explained.

"This is a corporate office," she said. "If you're interested in traveling with us, I'm afraid you're in the wrong place. I can give you a number to call, though." She reached for a neat stack of business cards atop the reception desk.

"My girlfriend is missing," I said. "The last place we know she was for sure was on one of your ships, last week. Is there someone we can talk to about that?"

The receptionist's mouth fell open.

"Let me just, um, make a call," she said, recovering quickly. "Please, take a seat."

We sat. The receptionist—"Katy," according to her name tag—left us waiting for more than fifteen minutes. When she returned, she took our names and a few details about Sarah and the cruise we thought she had been on. Then she disappeared for another half hour.

When she came back a second time, she asked if we happened to have Sarah's passport number. I was still carrying the Ziploc bag with the passport and note around with me, so I pulled it out of my jacket pocket. Katy seemed thrown by this at first but then carefully copied down the number. After that, she plied us with cups of coffee and left us waiting once again, this time for over an hour.

Eventually, a woman named Louise arrived to escort us elsewhere. No last name, no job title. She wasn't wearing a name tag. She was pretty, with big eyes and brown hair twisted back into a tight, perfect bun, but she looked skinny in that hard, sharp-angled way. A little older than we were—maybe mid- to late thirties. Her heels clacked loudly on the bare concrete as she walked toward us.

She greeted us both with sympathetic smiles, but they seemed to stay on her lips and keep well away from her eyes.

"Sorry about the mess," she said, extending a hand to me. "We're just—"

"Rebranding," I finished. "Yeah, we know."

She led us deeper into the building, down a long, gray corridor. It was just as quiet. I heard no sound but our footsteps and occasional traffic noise from outside. Louise directed us into a meeting room where more coffee, along with sparkling water and a plate of muffins, had already been laid out.

This felt like the Case of the Escalating Snacks.

Louise motioned to two seats on the far side of the large polished table in the room's center and then slid into a chair across from us. A thin manila folder, closed, was waiting on the tabletop in front of her.

"I'm so sorry to have kept you waiting," she said.

"We don't mind," Rose said. "We just hope you can help us."

Louise flashed another cosmetic smile. "I hope so, too."

I caught a blur of color in my peripheral vision. A fourth person had entered the room: an older man in a suit. Without a word, he walked past us to the far end of the table, took a seat there, and hoisted a briefcase onto his lap so he could take various things out of it: a yellow legal pad, a tablet computer, a tape recorder.

"That's just Simon," Louise said, waving a hand dismissively. "You'll have some coffee?" Before we could respond, she started pouring.

Simon got no further explanation, and as far as I could tell, he wasn't even going to acknowledge that Rose and I existed.

It was odd, yes, but then, so was this whole situation. I was getting used to odd. Odd was the new normal. A mute suit recording our conversation with Blue Wave? Not the weirdest thing that had happened to me. Not even the weirdest thing that had happened to me that *week*.

"Now," Louise said when we all had been furnished with yet more caffeine, and Silent Simon had pressed a button on his little digital voice recorder. "Sarah. According to the *Celebrate's* manifest, we had a Sarah O'Connell on our three-night, four-day Mediterranean Dreams cruise departing Barcelona on August eleventh last. The passport number that was scanned into our system at embarkation appears to match the passport number you've provided. On this itinerary, the newest member of the Blue Wave fleet, the *Celebrate*, carries up to two thousand passengers from Barcelona, Spain, to La Spezia, Italy, and back again, stopping off for a day on the French Riviera en route. Sarah stayed in a junior suite with a balcony, close to the *Celebrate's* boardwalk promenade. It's an indoor space beneath a stunning atrium ceiling that lets you bask in sunshine during the day, watch the sunset turn the sky pink in the evening, and admire the glittering stars at night."

Rose and I exchanged a glance. *Was she trying to sell us tickets?*

Louise lifted the top item from her folder: an 8″ × 10″ color photograph. When she held it up in front of us, my breath caught.

It was Sarah.

Posing in front of a painted mural, a cartoonish "under the sea" tableau. She was smiling—laughing, actually—and wearing a blue dress I didn't recognize. It was the first I had seen of her since I watched her walk through the terminal doors at Cork Airport ten days ago.

The first proof that her life had gone happily on without me—

that it was going on even while I checked my phone so frequently it was becoming a nervous tic. I didn't know what to make of it. I was confused about why she had gone on the ship. Sure, it hurt to think of her enjoying herself while I worried at home, but mostly, I was just happy to see her face.

"I spoke to the *Celebrate*'s cruise director on your behalf," Louise said, "and he was kind enough to email me this." She tapped the photograph. "It was taken on the first evening of the cruise, Monday the eleventh, outside the Pavilion Restaurant. By one of our professional photographers. We thought you might like to have a copy." She slid the photograph across the tabletop to us.

Rose reached across me to pick it up. She studied it. "She's on her own," she said after a beat.

"Yes," Louise agreed. "Are you familiar with cruise cards?"

We were not.

"Passengers don't use cash or credit cards aboard Blue Wave ships," Louise explained. "Instead, they preload cash or tie their credit card to a system we call Swipeout. It's essentially a charge card they use on board for all purchases, and it's also an electronic key that opens their cabin doors. This also helps us maintain safety and security—passengers have their identification information stored electronically in their Swipeout, and it's checked against our system whenever they embark or disembark. This way, unauthorized persons cannot board the ship, and we have a continually updated manifest."

There was just a single sheet of white paper in the manila folder now. Louise glanced down at it as she continued. "I have obtained for you a copy of Sarah's Swipeout activity from the purser, as logged in our system beginning August eleventh last. It shows that Sarah entered her cabin for the last time at 10:42 p.m. on the Monday evening— departure day—and then disembarked at 7:36 a.m. the following morning, while the *Celebrate* was tendered at Villefranche-sur-Mer."

"Where is …" I'd forgotten it already. "That place?"

"The Côte d'Azur," Louise said. "Villefranche is just a few minutes down the road from Nice."

Nice. Where the passport had been posted.

"What does 'tendered' mean?" Rose asked.

"If there isn't a suitable port to dock at, we drop anchor offshore and ferry passengers to and from the coast in smaller vessels—tenders—instead. Nice is a popular stop, but its port isn't suitable for our ships, so we stop in Villefranche, which has the space in its bay, and the onshore facilities needed to receive our tenders. We bus our passengers into Nice, or they can explore the coast by train or private tour instead. Sarah, however, left the *Celebrate* at Villefranche, and according to this"—she passed the printout to me—"she did not return to the ship."

I looked at Rose, then back at Louise. "Meaning …?"

"Meaning she didn't return to the ship."

"Was she supposed to?"

"I'm afraid I don't have that information. We've been unable to access Sarah's booking detail."

"Which means what?" Rose asked. "In English."

Louise flashed a brief, oddly pleasant smile. "It means that for some reason, I can't bring up Sarah's reservation on our system. There's no booking under her name." She waved a hand. "It's probably just a glitch."

"But you were able to check the manifest," Rose said. "And find Sarah's Swipeout account?"

"Those are stored on different systems."

"But we need the booking information."

"I would stress that Blue Wave is not obliged to provide any information about our passengers. We have furnished you with the data from the manifest and the Swipeout account as a gesture of goodwill. We are going above and beyond already in providing you with that."

"Why *are* you providing us with it?" Rose said. "If passenger information is so confidential?"

"What Rose means," I said, shooting her a look, "is, 'Thank you.' We really appreciate this. What, ah, what about luggage? Did Sarah leave luggage behind? She only took one of those little cabin-approved trolley cases with her."

Now Louise and Silent Simon exchanged a glance.

"I have no information about that," Louise said. "But she could have brought that on the tender with her. It sounds small enough."

The questions were stacking up in my head. I regretted not bringing something to take notes with. There were so many details we needed to know.

When was the cruise booked? *How* was it booked: online or with a travel agent? I suspected travel agent, because I had seen no payment to Blue Wave on Sarah's debit card. Did she put cash on her Swipeout card? If so, how much? Was that what the 650 euro were for? Was there any credit still on the card when she left the ship? Had she booked Blue Wave transport to Nice? Was there room for mistakes in the disembarkation identity checks? Was it definitely Sarah who got off at Villefranche?

Was the reason they couldn't find her reservation because there wasn't one under her name, only his?

Sarah, were you alone in that junior suite?

"I have so many questions," I said, "I don't know where to begin."

"I understand." Louise pressed her lips into another odd smile. "I do hope the information we've shared today has been of some assistance to you."

At the end of the table, Silent Simon shifted in his chair.

"It was," I said. "Thanks. But we really need to know about Sarah's reservation. Like, was she traveling with someone else, or—"

"As I said, I was unable to access Sarah's booking detail."

"But could you?" Rose asked. "Like, if we waited a while? We don't mind waiting."

Rose looked to me.

"No," I said. "We don't mind. We can wait."

"I don't think that's possible," Louise said. "I don't see us being able to recover that data anytime soon. Now, we have been very accommodating, but as I'm sure you understand, we have a commitment to our passengers, and an obligation under the law to protect the data of the private individuals who choose to travel with us. Your situation is no doubt distressing, and we want to help, but I'm afraid we have already helped all that we can."

"But I don't want any private information," I said. "I just want to know when my girlfriend booked this cruise."

There was a moment's silence. Silent Simon cleared his throat.

"It's a shame, then," Louise said to the tabletop, "that Sarah didn't tell you that."

I felt as if I'd been slapped across the face so quickly and so suddenly that I wasn't even sure whether it had happened. The only evidence that anything had happened at all was the stinging pain.

Rose, too, seemed stunned into silence.

"I am truly very sorry that you are unable to contact Sarah," Louise said, lifting her eyes. "On behalf of Blue Wave and on a personal level. But we have no obligation here. We do wish you both well, and, of course, we all hope that Sarah will make contact with you sooner rather than later."

Louise picked up the manila folder and pushed back her chair.

"But we're talking about a *missing person*," I said. "Your ship is the last place we know Sarah was for sure. We need to know everything so we can find out where she went after that. It might lead us to where she is now."

"According to the gardaí," Louise said, "there is no missing-person case. They told us they are attempting to make contact with her but that the working assumption is that she left of her own accord."

"Even if she did," Rose said, "we still need to find her. You're the only ones who can help."

Louise stood up.

A moment later, Silent Simon did, too.

"Who is this guy?" I said, pointing to our silent friend. "Is he your boss? What's he doing here? Does he talk?"

"I'm sorry," Louise said. "This meeting is concluded." She turned to leave.

"No," I said. "You can't do this. Don't you realize there is nowhere we can go from here? We have *no idea* where she went next. If you would just tell—"

Louise stopped halfway to the door and turned. "Mr. Dunne,"

she said, "we're finished here. Katy will come in a moment to escort you out."

She walked out of the room, followed by her silent friend.

I turned to Rose. "Did that just happen?"

She shook her head in disbelief. "What an absolute *bitch*."

"What about that booking thing?"

"Bullshit," Rose said. "It's complete bullshit. Even if someone else made the reservation, her name would still be on it, right? It's like a flight. You can't just have a lead passenger. You have to give all the names. They must be hiding—"

"Um, excuse me," a new voice said.

We turned to find Katy, the skittish receptionist, standing in the door, here to see us out.

The walk back to the parking lot was a silent one. Once we were both in my car, I stuck the key in the ignition but didn't turn it on.

"Rose," I said, "I just want to say thanks for coming with me. I really appreciate ..." She was looking out the passenger window, clearly not listening to me. "Rose? Rose, I'm trying to say a nice thing here. Hello? Hey, what are y—"

"*Ssshhh,*" she said. "Shut up for a second."

"Rose, what the hell?"

"Look."

She pointed at something, and I leaned over to see.

Five or six parking spaces down and one row across sat what at first glance looked like a bus stop but, on closer inspection, proved to be a smoking shelter for employees. Louise was inside, lighting up a cigarette and talking animatedly with an older woman. She carried herself very differently now—the way she was waving her arms about, the frequent drags on her cigarette, the quick shake of her head every few seconds.

She had been so composed inside. Now she looked anything but.

"Turn the key so I can roll down the window," Rose said. "Then duck down."

"Why?"

"So we can *listen,* obviously."

I did what I was told. Rose cracked the window open a few inches and then reclined the passenger seat. At this angle, even if Louise turned to face us directly, she shouldn't be able to see us.

Her voice, high-pitched and anxious, drifted into the car. She sounded like a different person.

"... before, didn't I? I told her I don't know how many times. It's *not my job.* I'm in PR. They called my degree studies in *media relations,* and this is the third one I've done! The *third.* I had to do that *Fiesta* boy ... Yeah, that was me, too ... I *know.* Can you even ..." A truck rumbled past, drowning her out momentarily. "... had enough. I really have ... No, I mean it this time. I can't do it anymore. *Lying* for a living? Like, what the fuck? Sorry, Marian. Excuse my French." There was a pause, presumably while the older woman spoke in a much quieter tone. "Yeah, I suppose ... talk to her ... *hate* this place."

There was a clatter of heels on tarmac as she and her friend walked away, back inside the building.

We waited until we were sure she was gone, then sat back up. Rose turned to me. "So she *did* lie to us."

"But why?"

"I don't know, but I think a more important question is why she didn't *only* lie."

"What do you mean?"

"If they don't want to give us the truth, why not just say they didn't find anything for Sarah? Why confirm she was on the ship and tell us about the times she went into and out of her room? They could've just said, 'No, sorry. No Sarah O'Connell here.' It doesn't make any sense."

"What about this does?" I lay back against the headrest and closed my eyes. I felt exhausted.

"What do we do now?"

"You know, I don't really remember what life was like before it was just about answering that same question, over and over."

"Sure you do." Rose buckled her seat belt. "And you didn't."

I turned to look at her. "Didn't what?"

"Answer the question."

"We go home, I suppose." I started the engine. "We just go home."

I dropped Rose back at Moorsey's. He was at work. My parents were still adhering to my alone-time wishes, although I figured I had only an hour or two before Mum finally succumbed to her maternal instincts and arrived back on my doorstep with a stack of neatly labeled Tupperware and a Tesco bag straining to hold boxes of breakfast cereal and packs of toilet paper.

I wondered if maybe I should call Maureen, but I feared Jack would answer the phone.

I wandered around the apartment, touching Sarah's things, picking up the odd item to examine it, as if searching for clues.

Where is she?

I felt it then, buzzing faintly, starting to gather strength beneath my outward calm, seizing the opportunity that silent inaction gave it: panic. *Dinner.* I would make some dinner. Yes, that's what I would do.

I wasn't hungry, but it would involve a series of steps—foraging, deciding, preparing, consuming, cleaning—that would distract me for at least a half hour if I did it right.

I was staring into the fridge when I remembered something we had overheard Louise say in the parking lot.

I had to do that Fiesta *boy.*

The *Fiesta.* Could it be another Blue Wave ship? It sounded as though it could be. Who was the boy she had been talking about?

Another passenger? Did she mean she'd had to talk to his family, too? About what?

I shut the fridge and went to my desk.

After a quick circuit of email, Twitter, Facebook—making sure Sarah hadn't been in touch since I checked five minutes ago—I typed the words "blue" and "wave" and "fiesta" into Google's search box and hit ENTER.

The screen filled with results.

They were nearly all links to official Blue Wave sites. Special offers: explore the other members of the Blue Wave family; book your summer 2015 cruise now! I clicked on a piece from the *Irish Independent's* website, written by their resident travel writer who had been invited to tour the *Fiesta* before it launched, and then watched a three-minute video tour of it on YouTube, filmed by what appeared to be a maniacally enthusiastic, overcaffeinated twentysomething American blonde named Megan who "you may know as the cruiser behind the Megan's Muster Station channel on YouTube!"

What I saw in the video was as confusing as it was impressive. I knew that cruise ships were big, but I had had no idea just how much they managed to fit on board. According to the video clip, the *Fiesta* had an indoor park with actual trees and a working carousel, a boardwalk promenade lined with old-fashioned arcades and strung with twinkling fairy lights, an enormous theater, three cinemas, an ice rink, and a shopping mall, as well as hundreds of rooms, dozens of restaurants, and five or six open decks jam-packed with rows of blue sun loungers and swimming pools—and, as Megan either promised or threatened depending on your point of view, "much, *much* more!"

How the hell did these things *float*?

I scrolled down and clicked through three pages of results, but saw nothing that could be related to the "*Fiesta* boy" Louise had mentioned.

Next I tried "blue" and "wave" and "celebrate" and got page after page of more of the same. The only real difference was that the ads for the *Celebrate* always referred to it as the "newest and biggest ship" in Blue Wave's fleet.

I went back to the first results page and clicked on a sponsored link that invited me to explore the *Celebrate*. I remembered that Louise had called the route Sarah took "Mediterranean Dreams."

That itinerary was listed at the top. I clicked on "Show Me More!"

A new page opened, dedicated to that particular cruise: Barcelona to La Spezia, with a stop at "Nice" (translation: a mile off the coast of Villefranche) in between. There were stats and dates and a map and ...

Passenger reviews.

It was a long shot, but I started scanning them, scrolling down as I went, looking for any mention of a new friend the reviewer had made on board who could be Sarah, for her face in the background of a user-uploaded photo.

Unsurprisingly, I found none, but around review fifteen or sixteen, I came across this: "Got a great deal on this cruise last minute so decided to go despite what Chris D. said on Cruise Confessions. SO glad I did!"

I typed "Cruise Confessions" into the Google search box.

It was a website that invited potential cruise ship passengers to get the lowdown on what it was really like to go on a cruise. Its home page listed links to sections such as "Which Cruise Company Is Best?" and "How to Prepare for Your First Cruise," and "Get Tips from the Insiders: Staff and Crew Reveal All!"

And then, right at the end: "Deaths, Disappearances, and Other Cruise Crimes."

I clicked on the link and got a 404 error message. The page no longer existed.

I went back to Google and typed "cruise ship deaths disappearances crimes" into the search box.

Then I spent at least a full minute blinking at the results:

Cruise Ship Deaths: Index by Year ... Cruise Crimes: Search by Cruise Line or Vessel ... Foul Play Suspected in Death of Woman, 43, aboard Atlantic Dreams Liner ... Disappearance of Teenager Throws Spotlight on Epidemic of Fatalities at Sea ... Search for Frenchwoman Missing from Oceanic Escape Called Off ... Murky Maritime Justice System Failed Us, Says Scott Family ... Cruise Company Helped Father's Killer Get Away with Murder Says Grieving Daughter ... Cruise Ship "Curse": Third Woman Plunges to Her Death ... FBI to Review Honeymoon Cruise Death ... Cruise FAQs: Staying Safe on Board ... Latest Fatality Prompts Concerns: Are Cruise Ships Deadly?

I felt sick but also, for some reason I couldn't quite articulate yet, as though I was onto something.

I scrolled back up to the top of the results and clicked on the first one: a list of suspicious deaths that had occurred or were suspected to have occurred on cruise ships.

Christ, someone was *collecting* these things.

The page had a short paragraph about each incident, next to a photo of either the victim or the ship involved. Just two or three sentences about each one, with a link to a relevant news story if one was available.

Not all of them, I soon realized, had links to news stories. In fact, most didn't. Did that have something to do with why I couldn't remember hearing anything about any of them? When the *Costa Concordia* sank, it had been the top story for a week, and in the news for months afterward. Sarah and I had watched a bloody hour-long documentary about it, for God's sake.

Why hadn't any of *this* been in the news?

May 12, 2011: Female passenger discovered dead in her cabin after suspected fall/head trauma. Victim's sister receives anonymous tip that suggests death occurred elsewhere, possibly in staff quarters. Coroner returns verdict of accident.

October 27, 2012: Female passenger becomes ill after drinking in casino bar. Crew member assists her with return to her cabin; subsequently subjects her to prolonged and violent sexual assault. FBI board at Port Canaveral but crew member is not located. He continues to be sought by authorities.

February 5, 2009: Male passenger is reported missing, suspected overboard. A large streak of blood is photographed by another passenger on victim's balcony railing; cleaning crews remove it before ship returns to port. Victim's friend charged with murder but found not guilty due to lack of physical evidence; judge criticizes cruise ship operator for lack of cooperation.

June 11, 2013: Male passenger is reported missing by family and search finds his body in lifeboat on Lido Deck with stab wounds. Cruise company claims security camera pointed at lifeboat was out of order at the time. Case remains open.

May 14, 2014: Adolescent male passenger, 16, falls overboard from pool deck after becoming inebriated. Cruise company admits "unreasonable" amount of alcohol was served to deceased's older brother, age 18, but deny liability. Civil action ongoing.

Could a sixteen-year-old be Louise's "*Fiesta* boy"? I followed the news report link and found mention of the *Fiesta* in the very first line.

It seemed that the older brother had been buying two drinks at a time for the evening, despite the barman's never seeing who the extras were for. Now the parents were suing Blue Wave for negligence. Both brothers had gone to one of the swimming pools afterward, and while they were there the younger one went to the railing, perhaps to throw up or look over. He had fallen overboard, his body never recovered.

An awful, tragic story, yes, but nothing to do with Sarah. The only connection seemed to be Louise, who presumably had had to talk to the boy's parents.

I went back a page and continued reading:

August 4, 2013: Female passenger is reported missing, initially presumed overboard. Cruise card activity subsequently shows that guest disembarked the ship at Nice but her whereabouts remain unknown. Owners refuse to release security footage to corroborate disembarkation. Last update January 2014: a civil action is ongoing.

Accompanying it was a picture of the only cruise ship I knew well enough to recognize: the *Celebrate*.

Underneath the photo was a link to a recent news story.

I clicked on It.

The Internet couldn't tell me where Sarah was, but it took only five minutes to find me the man whose wife had disappeared after disembarking from the *Celebrate* almost exactly a year to the day before Sarah apparently did exactly the same thing in exactly the same place.

It took only another minute after that to find me an email address for him.

My hands shook as I typed a message to Peter Brazier. According to LinkedIn, he lived in London. According to his profile on a financial services firm's website, he was a portfolio manager. According to news reports, his missing wife was named Estelle.

What to say? I introduced myself, briefly described the circumstances of Sarah's disappearance, and outlined what, I was beginning to realize, were horrifying similarities: August, the *Celebrate,* and Blue Wave saying she got off the ship in one piece. I mentioned my unproductive meeting with Louise, and the gardaí being no help at all. Finally, I signed off with my phone number and asked him to call me as soon as he could.

Then I pushed my chair back from the desk so I could put my head between my knees.

I had grown up in a loving, safe household in a nice, safe community. For most of my childhood, Mum left the doors open and Dad left the car unlocked. We lived in a country where, until the middle of the last century, murder was an annual occurrence, not a daily or weekly one, and when the murder rate began to catch up with the rest of the world in the 1970s, a terrorist group was the reason why. Crime, to me, was entertainment I saw on television. Evil was a Hollywood creation. Violence was what happened in foreign places fifteen minutes into the *Six One News*—so called because, here in Ireland, the evening news started a minute late so the bells of the Angelus could be played on national TV. Bad stuff happened to *other* people, in *other* places, all of them far, far away from here.

I didn't know where Sarah was, but I had assumed that whatever she was doing, she was physically okay. She had told everyone lies. She had cut her hair. She had checked her WhatsApp messages long after she stopped answering her phone. She had done *this*, whatever this was.

But what if, *while* she was doing this, something else had happened to her?

What if she hadn't walked off the *Celebrate*? What if she had slipped or fallen or been pushed off? What if the *Celebrate* wasn't a clue to where she was now, but the *reason* for her disappearance?

What if the same thing that happened to this Estelle Brazier woman a year ago had happened to Sarah, too?

The room suddenly felt airless. I stumbled out onto the balcony, gripped the railing, and gulped down the deepest breaths I could.

Where is she?

Then an onslaught of leaks from behind the wall that denial built: *What happened to her? Is she alive? Did it hurt?*

I'd been dumbfounded at Cusack's calm interpretation of events— no, *mis*interpretation. But what if I had been doing the same thing?

Despite all the lies, despite all the confusion, there was one fact that we all could agree on: none of us had seen or heard from Sarah in more than a week.

I thought of the angry voice mail I had left her, and my cheeks flushed with shame. I should have raised the alarm sooner. I should have known something was seriously wrong. I should have fought harder to get the gardaí to do something.

But the passport. The passport and the note inside it. Those block capitals were definitely hers. Unlike Cusack, I had no doubt. I wasn't a handwriting expert, but I had been looking at them—on notes on the fridge, in greeting cards, on shopping lists—for the best part of a decade. Sarah *had* written that note.

And then what? Decided she wanted the adventure of being abroad without travel documents?

And the American—how did he fit in? What if … What if *he* had done something to her?

We didn't know who he was or what he looked like. Was that just because Sarah had been keeping him a secret, or was that him covering his tracks?

My phone rang. The screen read, "Dan Goldberg."

"Oh, fuck off, Dan," I said, hitting Reject.

A few seconds later, it rang again. I didn't recognize the number, but the country code was 0044. A UK number.

I hit Accept.

"Hello?" I said uncertainly.

"Is … is this Adam?" A British accent.

"Yes," I said. "Is this Peter?"

It was. He sounded older than I and, for want of a better word, *posh.* I pictured him working in the city and driving a small but flashy sports car. He sounded anxious, his words coming fast at times and then slow, breaths taken irregularly and in midsentence.

I imagined it was what I would sound like if, in a year, I was still wondering where Sarah was. Then I tried very hard *not* to imagine that.

Before my email to him, Peter had heard nothing about Sarah. His first question was whether the authorities were involved.

"Not really," I said. "They seem confident that she left of her own accord, and, well, she did. Most likely. But since I read about your wife, I'm not so sure about the … the coming-back bit."

"Have *they* spoken to Blue Wave?"

"No. I went by myself."

"And they confirmed she was on the ship?"

"They have a Sarah O'Connell whose passport number matches. And they showed me a photo. And before all that, there was the Blue Wave logo on the note."

The silence on the line was so long and so absolute that I pulled the phone from my ear to check that we were still connected.

"Peter? Are you there?"

When his voice finally came down the line, it sounded small and faraway. He said just one word: "Note?"

"There's a note. It was sent here, to our home. Stuck inside Sarah's—"

"Passport," Peter finished.

"Eh, yeah. How did you …?"

"Did it have a postmark?"

"Yeah."

"Nice?"

"Yes …"

More silence.

"Peter? Peter, how did you know that?"

"The note," he said, the words sounding as if they'd had to force their way around a choking constriction of his throat. "Are you *sure* it's in Sarah's writing?"

"Positive. Although it wasn't her handwriting on the envelope."

When Peter spoke again, the words came tumbling out. "Estelle disappeared at the start of August last year. By Christmas, everyone was telling me I needed to move on with my life. We'd done everything: gone to Scotland Yard, done the media rounds, made posters, gone to France. I'd even instructed my solicitor to start proceedings against Blue Wave, to force them to release the CCTV footage of the tender platform that morning. My money was running out, and I knew I'd need it to get the thing to trial—which is where it was going, because Blue Wave were refusing to even talk to us—so I went back to work, tried to get back into the swing of things. It was impossible. I would come to and realize I'd been sitting at my desk for an hour or more, staring into space. How could I concentrate on something as trivial as a share price when Estelle was out there somewhere, alone? Turns out I couldn't. I stayed another week before they put me on leave." Peter made a scoffing noise. "But before I left, my secretary comes along with this archive box. Personal mail, she says. Turns out that ever since Estelle's story hit the papers, people had been sending cards and letters and prayers and things to the firm because, of course, they didn't have my home address. One day soon after, I was at home and … well, I was feeling pretty low. *Real* low. I started … thinking about things. Things you shouldn't think about." A pause. A cough. "But then I saw the archive box, and I don't know why, I don't know what made me pick it up, but I started going through it. And right at the top—it must have been only the third or fourth thing I picked up—was a brown envelope, addressed to me at the office, postmarked Nice."

My view of the cityscape started to slide upward. I gripped the balcony railing with my free hand to steady myself.

"It was Estelle's passport," Peter said. "My wife's passport, in perfect condition. I flicked through it and saw the note stuck inside. It was written on Blue Wave–branded paper. A sticky note. The same kind of pads they leave in hotel rooms."

"What did it say?" I pressed. "What did it *say?*"

But I already knew.

"'I'm sorry,'" Peter said. "Signed 'E.'"

The soles of my running shoes smacked unapologetically across the stone floor of the atrium at Angelsea Street. The same cherub-faced garda was standing behind the reception desk, but this time he was ignoring his tabloid newspaper. He was looking instead at the sweaty, panting red-faced figure running toward him. His mouth began to open in question.

"Cusack," I said when I reached the desk. My lungs were burning; coherent speech was a herculean effort. "Garda Cusack."

"Do you need"—Garda Cherub looked me up and down—"assistance?"

"Cusack," I said again, leaning against the counter while I tried to get my breath back. Garda Cherub leaned back from the other side. "I need to speak to her."

"You can speak to me."

"I want to talk to *her*."

"What's it in relation to?"

"She'll know."

"I'm afraid *I* have to know before I can—"

"For fuck's sake," I roared, slamming a fist down on the countertop. "Will you just fucking *call her*?"

The face grew less cherubic. His hand went to his belt, where a little canister of something was hanging, along with what looked like a baton.

"Sir, you need to lower your voice. *Immediately*."

"Sorry, I just … I just really need to speak to Garda Cusack, okay? She's the one we've been talking to. Is she here?"

"Talking about what?"

"My girlfriend. She's missing. And I just got new information from this man and his wife went missing and he got a note too and now I think maybe something awful has happened to her and I need … I need …"

I ran out of breath.

Garda Cherub slowly raised one eyebrow.

"Sarah," I panted. "Sarah O'Connell. That's her name." I pointed at the computer sitting on Garda Cherub's side of the desk. "Look it up."

He did while watching me out of the corner of his eye. He then directed me to a nearby row of chairs and told me to wait there. I collapsed into the first one and let my head drop between my knees.

Cusack appeared five minutes later, wearing jeans and a T-shirt.

She sat down in the chair next to mine.

"What's going on?" she said. "I was just on my way home."

"I think something bad has happened to Sarah."

"Adam …" A sigh. "We've been—"

"No," I said. "This is different. This is serious. Listen …"

I told her everything: about the visit to Blue Wave, Louise lying, what I'd found on Google about cruise ship crimes, and what Peter Brazier had said about Estelle. About how a woman with no connection to Sarah had also been on the *Celebrate* just before she disappeared. About how the man that woman loved had received her passport in the mail, too, also postmarked in Nice. About how the note inside had said exactly the same thing, only with a different initial. About how, a year later, that woman still hadn't come home.

"And you think what now, exactly?" Cusack asked when I was done. "That someone is out there kidnapping cruise ship passengers after they post notes home?"

"Oh, Jesus *Christ*." In my peripheral vision, I could see Garda

Cherub's head snap up from his sports pages. "What the hell do you need, to believe that something is going on here, Cusack? What will it take? Seriously, tell me. Bloodstained clothes? Video footage? A *dead body?*"

"There's no nee—"

"I feel like I could come in here and tell you I came home to an apartment full of someone else's blood and you'd be like, 'Well, maybe a butcher came 'round and mistook your living room for an abattoir.'" I rolled my eyes. "I thought the police didn't believe in coincidences. But you seem to see them everywhere. You see nothing *but* coincidences. So tell me: what does someone have to say around here to convince you people that a crime has been committed? I'm actually asking. Save me a fucking trip next time."

"Do you like flying?" Cusack asked.

"Do I ... *What?*"

"I *hate* flying."

"Well, that's just ..." I threw up my hands. "That's fucking wonderful, that is. Tell me some more utterly irrelevant things I don't give a shit about."

"You didn't swear at all when Jack and Maureen were with you. Did you know that?"

"Yeah, well, back then I thought you were going to help us."

"I hate flying," Cusack said again. "I'm terrified of it. Avoid it as much as I can. But sometimes you have to get on a plane, and in this job you might have to get in a helicopter from time to time, which is even worse. So I went on one of these fear-of-flying courses. One of the first things the instructor told us to do was to look at the faces of the flight attendants if we felt scared. Like, if there was turbulence or a strange noise. Because turbulence isn't a big deal, and the crew know that what sounds like the arse of the plane falling off is actually just the landing gear coming down. They know it's normal. That's why they can remain calm. So if you look at them, their faces will help reassure you, and you'll stay calm, too."

"Cusack, I'm sorry, but what the—"

"I'm *your* flight attendant, Adam. I'm the one remaining calm because I'm experienced enough to know that the chances of something being seriously wrong here are between slim and none. Do you know how many people were reported missing in Ireland last year?"

"Why would I know that?"

"No reason at all. But it's my job to know. It was 7,743. Want to guess how many were still missing at year's end?"

"I'm sure you're going to tell me any—"

"Fifteen people, Adam. *Fifteen.* One five. That's less than zero point two percent. You think I don't care, because when you come in here and tell me that a grown woman—who lies—went on a holiday and didn't come home, I don't immediately send out an international search party. But it's not because I don't care. It's not because the gardaí aren't interested in helping you. It's because I· *do* and we *are.* I'm here telling you there's no need to panic, because all the other times my colleagues and I have heard similar stories, the outcome wasn't what you fear it will be here."

"But this Peter guy," I said. "What about what he says? About the ship?"

"Leaving aside my concern that you are taking as fact something you read about online and then"—here Cusack made air quotes—"*verified* by talking to a stranger over the phone, I actually *can't* help you there. We don't have jurisdiction."

"So I need to call the French police?"

"You don't need to call *any* police."

"But if I wanted—"

"If you wanted to get politely listened to for a couple of minutes and then completely ignored thereafter, you could call them, yes. But there'd be no point calling the French. The last sighting of her was on the ship, right? While it was sailing? That's international waters. Maritime law applies."

"Which means what?"

"When at sea, all seafaring vessels fall under the jurisdiction of the country in which they are registered. If you get mugged in Times Square, you're not going to call the gardaí, are you? I should hope not. You'd call the NYPD. Same wherever you are in the world. If something happens, you get the local police. But what if you're not in any country at all? What if you're at sea? That's where maritime law comes in."

"Who do I call, then?"

"You're still not calling anyone, because it's up to the captain of the ship to invite an outside authority aboard. But if he or she did, then it would be the authority of the country where the ship itself is registered. The *Celebrate* is registered in Barbados."

There was a beat of silence while my brain—still processing the idea that there were essentially no police at sea—caught up with what Cusack was saying.

"How do you know that?" I said. "Did you call Blue Wave?"

"I know because of Shane Keating."

"Who?"

"I would have thought the name would come up in your Internet search. He was the boy who went overboard from a ship called the *Fiesta* a while back. Another Blue Wave ship. He was just—"

"Sixteen," I said. "Yeah. He did come up—just not his name."

"Initially, they didn't know he'd gone overboard. He just disappeared from the ship. A family member contacted gardaí in Dublin, and we contacted Blue Wave. They politely told us we had no jurisdiction. He'd disappeared while the ship was in the North Atlantic. Blue Wave have their European headquarters in City West, and their global headquarters in Florida, but the *Fiesta* was registered in Barbados, like all Blue Wave ships. Those big cruise ships are all registered in places like that—the Bahamas, Panama, Libya even—for tax reasons. 'Flags of convenience,' they call them. Two—what do you call them?

Barbadian, isn't it? Two Barbadian police officers were just about to get on a plane to go meet the ship when they discovered that he'd actually gone overboard. So they called in the Icelandic Coast Guard to start search and rescue instead." Cusack sighed. "So like I said, I *can't* help you."

"This is bullshit."

"This is *procedure*. Best practice, based on cumulative knowledge and experience. I've been a garda for ten years. You've been at this a week."

"So yet again, there's nothing you can do for us." I stood up to go. "You know, I always thought … Well, I never really thought about it, I suppose, but in the back of my mind, I had this idea that the gardaí would be there to help me if anything ever went badly wrong. Silly me."

"It's not that simple."

"We don't know where Sarah is. We need your resources to find her. Sounds pretty simple to me."

"Adam, wait." Cusack stood, too. "I know you're angry at us—at me—and that's fine. I get it. I really do. But I don't know how many other ways I can say it: this is how it works. We've contacted the Department of Foreign Affairs. They'll contact us the second they hear from her. We've sent out an Interpol bulletin, so if Sarah's name comes up in any police investigation anywhere in the world—whether it be a missing person or a car accident or a parking fine—we'll know about it, too. So no, there aren't any police officers walking the streets searching for her, but every police department in the world has an alarm on her name. We can't help you with the ship, but …" Cusack stopped.

"What? What is it?"

"I did do one thing you asked," she said. She reached into her jeans pocket and pulled out a slightly rumpled, folded piece of lined paper. "I looked up that phone number."

"*What* phone number?"

"The one that you said belonged to the guy Sarah was seeing." ·

I glared at the piece of paper. "Is that it?"

"You could've found it yourself if you dug around online long enough. He used to have it on an old profile on a jobs website. That's why I'm giving it to you." Cusack looked at me pointedly. "Because you could've found it yourself. Understand?"

"Yeah."

She handed over the paper. I began to unfold it, but Cusack put a hand on mine to stop me.

"Listen to me for a second, Adam. His name is Ethan Eckhart. He is American, and he does live in Dublin. This is an email address for him that I found. The telephone number seems to have been disconnected." A pause. "And there's something else."

"What?"

"It'll explain something for you."

"Go on. What?"

"Why Sarah was on that ship."

"She was on it with *him*."

"I mean why she went there with him and not, say, on a sun holiday or off to Paris on a mini break. It's a piece of the puzzle we were missing, that we have now. That's the way *you* need to look at it, too."

"Just *tell me*." My fingers tightened around the folded piece of paper. "Just say it."

"Ethan Eckhart," Cusack said. "He's on the *Celebrate* right now. He works there."

PART THREE

THE BAY OF ANGELS

CORINNE

It was midafternoon, and the crew mess was filling up with cabin attendants, relaxed and jovial now that they were done for the day.

Corinne was too exhausted to wait in line for the hot counter, so she took a prepacked salad from the fridge instead—a leftover from one of the cafés on board, no longer fresh enough to serve to paying passengers, but still perfectly okay to eat. She poured herself a coffee from the self-serve machine and then, on second thought, poured herself a second one.

It had been a long night with almost no sleep, and then, because of that, an even longer day. She was struggling to stay awake.

She found a table at the very back of the mess—an ideal vantage point for watching other crew members join the queue for lunch. With her eyes on the faces coming through the doors, she opened her salad, forked up a piece of torn chicken breast, and put it in her mouth. It had no discernible flavor. To Corinne, it tasted like chewing gum that had been chewed for too long.

Where was Lydia? That was all she could think about. *Why didn't she meet me here this time yesterday?*

That Lydia hadn't shown up wasn't in itself that big a deal. She could easily have overslept or been called on shift earlier than usual. They had no phones to contact each other with, and anyway, it wasn't as if their meetings were anything other than a comfortable routine they had fallen into over the past week.

Lydia could have had dinner with some of her colleagues instead, spent the time with friends her own age. She was a dancer in one of the stage shows—the Entertainment Department had nothing *but* young people in it. Who would want to hang around with an ailing sixty-odd-year-old French woman when there was such fun to be had? Corinne had worried that Lydia was having difficulty adjusting to life on the ship. She was just happy to see the girl settling in so well.

There was no way of checking whether Lydia had gone to work—crew weren't allowed into passenger areas while off duty—and Corinne found it impossible to tell whether the jumble of cosmetics on the girl's bed had been disturbed since yesterday. She had checked the cabin again just now, but perhaps Lydia hadn't been there because she was showering.

Which left only her absence on the crew deck this morning to explain away. Why hadn't she shown up for *that*?

Corinne hadn't seen her cabinmate for more than twenty-four hours now—not since just before she found the photograph in #1001.

Could that really be a coincidence? Or was this another message from *him*?

She should tell someone about this. But who? And what would she even say? Surely, if Lydia hadn't shown up for her shift last night, *someone* would have noticed already and ...

"Oh, my God." Lydia's voice, then the girl herself, dropping into the seat opposite. "The queue for the shower room was *insane,* Cor." She was panting, out of breath. Her makeup had been freshly applied, and her hair was still wet at the ends. "How's things?"

"Where ..." Corinne was at once flooded with relief and angry at the girl for making her worry. Then she was angry at herself for being so fretful. She swallowed all those feelings and said as cheerfully as she could, "I am very well, thank you. And you?"

"Good. *Great,* actually."

"Good. Are you going to have some dinner? I think I saw some pizza up there."

"Mm, I will in a sec." Lydia glanced over her shoulder. "When the line thins out a bit."

"Here." Corinne pushed the extra cup of coffee across the table.

"Are you sure?"

"Of course. It is for you."

"Thanks, Cor. You're a lifesaver."

"Did you, um, start early yesterday?"

Lydia took a sip of her coffee. "Early?"

"You weren't here."

"Oh, yeah. Well …" Lydia blushed. "I, uh, had a date."

"A *date*?"

Corinne couldn't hide her surprise. Lydia seemed so young, so naive. A child out alone in the wide adult world for the first time. She couldn't imagine her out on a date. But then, Lydia was the same age now that Corinne had been when she got married. She couldn't imagine *that*, either.

"Yeah. We work the same shift, so that was the only time we could meet."

"I see. Did you have a good time together?"

"A *very* good time." She burst out laughing. "Sorry, Cor. I don't know why I'm so embarrassed to tell you this, but I am."

"It is probably because I'm older than your mother. But I'm glad you had a nice time. Are you seeing him again this evening?"

"I think so. I …" Lydia's face changed. "Oh, Cor. You weren't waiting for me, were you? Out on deck this morning? Sorry, I thought … I thought that, you know, you'd be going out there anyway and it wouldn't matter if—"

"I was," Corinne said. She smiled. "No problem." She picked up her coffee. "So tell me about him. Your new friend."

"He's a security guard." Lydia's eyes sparkled. She was clearly delighted to have an opportunity to talk about him. "His name's Luke, and he's really nice. Really good-looking, too. Fit."

"Fit?" Corinne was puzzled. "You mean healthy?"

Lydia laughed. "It does mean that, but it can also mean, like, sexy."

Now Corinne felt herself blush.

"By the time you go home, you'll know all the slang," Lydia said. "I'll teach you. You'll be *so* down with the kids. But you'll have to teach me French in exchange. If things work out with Luke, between the two of you I might be fluent by the time *I* have to go home."

Corinne frowned. Between the English and the accent, it took her a second to put together what Lydia had said.

"Luke is French, too?"

Lydia nodded. "Yup. Funny, huh?"

"Yes …" The ship had very few French crew members. Indeed, Corinne had yet to meet one, and that included the crew she had encountered during the introductory training, which had been more like a convention, with hundreds of people attending. "Did you tell him your cabinmate was French?"

"Yeah. He wanted to know where you were from. It's Lyon, right?"

"Yes," Corinne said absently. "Lyon." It was the first town she had thought of when Lydia asked.

"Good. I wasn't sure I got it right."

"Which part of France is he from? Did he tell you?"

"Um …" Lydia made a face. "North of Paris, I think?"

"Do you know where exactly?" Corinne barely dared to ask. "Did he mention a town?"

"It was like *dev-oh* or something …"

Corinne tried not to react, but she was only partly successful.

Lydia mistook the dawning of horror on her face for recognition. "You know it, Cor?"

Corinne nodded silently. She couldn't speak.

ADAM

"We're he-re!"

A singsong voice, intruding on my sleep. Tugging me awake. "Sir? We are here."

Closer to me now, near my ear. Accented English. "Sir? It's time to go."

A hand on my left arm, gently shaking me. I opened my eyes.

"Sorry for waking you, sir." The Blue Wave rep had a wide, unnaturally white smile. She was young, eighteen or so, with tightly curled dark-brown hair. Potentially Spanish. "But we have arrived at the terminal. Welcome to Barcelona."

She pronounced it "Bar*the*lona." Definitely Spanish, then.

I began the process of freeing my limbs from the tiny space between the end of my seat and the back of the one in front. The Blue Wave shuttle from the airport was actually a fleet of spectacularly cramped minibuses, made worse by my choice of a window seat. I had taken it so I could turn my body away from the other passengers, plug in my headphones so I wouldn't have to listen to their excited chatter, and pretend to be asleep.

Then actually be asleep, since I hadn't slept much in the past forty-eight hours.

Everyone else was already off the bus and moving toward the terminal building, the children running ahead while the parents yelled after them.

Around me, the port was a hive of activity: buses coming and going, luggage stacked on the same little trucks you see at the airport, people swarming everywhere. Blue Wave reps, identified by their deep-blue T-shirts and aggressive friendliness, smiling and waving clipboards around. All views of the sea blocked by the enormous terminal building, a glass-and-exposed-pipe design that had probably been considered futuristic in the eighties but now seemed clumsy and obsolete. A giant sign outside its doors threatened that my Blue Wave adventure starts right now!

I headed that way, squinting in the midday sun. I had sunglasses in my backpack but didn't put them on lest he not recognize me. My entire knowledge of what Peter Brazier looked like came from the photos I had seen posted online alongside stories about Estelle. In each one, he was posed happily next to her, smiling at her or holding her or kissing her or doing a combination of those things. He was about a foot taller than his wife, broad-shouldered and invariably tanned, with the strong jaw and dimpled chin of an American named Brad who can make sound financial investments and chop wood with the same hair-flipping ease.

Together, he and Estelle looked like a Ralph Lauren ad campaign: all teeth and style and effortless beauty. They had a shine to them, as if they had been polished to a high gloss.

This was the image I had brought with me to Barcelona, but now, seeing him waiting for me outside the terminal doors, I realized that the Peter in all those pictures was the one from *his* Before.

Estelle had disappeared a year ago. Since then, the man had gotten thin—*too* thin. He was just skin and bones now, no muscle mass. The line of his jaw jutted out above a narrow, birdlike neck, and his cheekbones seemed to have been pushed up and out. He had let his hair grow and become unruly, curling around his ears and neck—still light brown mostly, but running gray in parts. Peter was unshaven, sporting a beard of patchy stubble that gave the impression that he had just rolled out of bed, and that the "bed" might have been a sheet of cardboard under a bridge. His linen pants and black T-shirt were wrinkled and misshapen, and the T-shirt had white crescents of old deodorant under the arms. His eyes were dull, the skin beneath them sagging in tones of gray and purple.

The guy was a wreck.

But then, maybe I would be, too, if I had been feeling for the past year the way I felt for the past ten days.

Ten days.

This time last week, almost to the hour, I had been at the airport waiting for Sarah. On the one hand, it seemed unfathomable that I had been living in a world that Sarah was missing from for so long. On the other hand, I couldn't believe that this nightmare was barely a week old.

"Adam!" he called out. He waved.

"Peter. Hi."

We shook hands. He grasped mine tightly, pumped it twice. We looked at each other until I laughed nervously.

"I don't really know what to say."

"Best not to say much for the moment," Peter said. "Not until after we're aboard."

"Right."

The terminal's automatic glass doors slid open for us, and a blast of cool air rushed out.

Peter went in first.

Inside, it was much like an airport: a huge hangarlike space thronged with people. A jagged white design cut in diagonal rows across a navy carpet, under the feet of hundreds of cruise goers shuffling along inside a maze of blue ropes, waiting their turn at the many check-in desks. Anticipation and the noise of excited chatter filled the air.

Peter stopped and nodded at something up ahead. "There it is."

I thought he was talking about the queue to board, until I lifted my head.

The far wall of the terminal, the one facing the water, was made entirely of panes of glass. *White-colored glass,* I thought for a second, until my focus shifted and I realized what I was looking at. The panes were clear; all that white was *behind* them.

Something gargantuan, something taller and wider than the terminal building itself. A gleaming monster that blocked out both sea and sky, that couldn't even be encompassed by hundreds of window panes.

The *Celebrate.*

It—*she,* I suppose I should say—was docked alongside the terminal building, which made sense now that I thought about it. We would simply check in here and walk aboard, just like that.

This was really going to happen. I was about to get on the *Celebrate.*

Or try to, anyway. Peter had concerns that one or both of our names could be flagged. I had booked two cabins, one under Peter's name and one under my own, without encountering any problems, but it might be a different story trying to physically board the ship. Peter explained that this was partly why he had never tried to go aboard before. The other reason was that he had cleaned out his bank account petitioning Blue Wave in court for access to its CCTV and then, after that failed, filing a civil suit.

Either way, our tickets were nonrefundable. My credit card was effectively melted down now.

We flashed our tickets to a security guard manning the start of a line for customs and immigration, then showed our passports to Spanish border guards.

We barely spoke while we waited. There was only one thing we wanted to talk to each other about, and we couldn't risk being overheard.

Afterward, we shuffled to a check-in counter, where our passports were scanned and our photos taken by a tiny camera mounted on the desk. I could feel Peter tensing beside me as the agent activated our Swipeout cards, but she said nothing to us except for an automatic-sounding "You're all set. You'll be in boarding area C." Then she handed me a blue plastic wallet and told us to enjoy our cruise.

The wallet had a Blue Wave logo on it, but it was different from the one on Sarah's note. They were rebranding, I remembered the receptionist saying back at the Blue Wave office. The tickets had the waves, so this logo on the wallet—an outline of a ship—must be the one they were replacing.

Up ahead, passengers were posing in front of a backdrop of the *Celebrate* at sea while a professional photographer hopped around them, shouting instructions and snapping his lens. When he was done, an overly enthusiastic Blue Wave T-shirt-wearing assistant scanned the relevant Swipeout card into a handheld machine while squealing the same line every thirty seconds, like one of those dolls with a pull string on the back: "Don't forget to stop at the Photo Shop on the Oceanic Deck, where prints start at *just* $9.99!"

"We should do it," Peter said. "Everyone does, and we don't want to stand out."

So the two of us stood in front of a picture of the ship where the women we loved had last been seen alive, and gave a big smile for the camera.

After that, there was one more security check, where our Swipeout cards were compared to our photo IDs, and our bags were scanned. Then escalators carried us up onto the terminal's mezzanine level.

Now we were alongside the first row of the *Celebrate*'s portholes. The crowd, getting more excited, moved faster here. We flowed outside, back into the warm Spanish sun and fresh sea breeze, and …

There she was, her whole side in full view now, towering above us as high as a skyscraper and as wide as a city block.

I saw balconies and orange lifeboats and blue and white bunting. At her highest point, a massive yellow funnel rose up into the cloudless sky and disappeared in the glare of the sun. On her hull, "Celebrate" was stenciled in blue lettering, broken up to look like crashing waves.

We made slow progress to the gangplank and then across it, through an opening in the side of the ship, close to the waterline. The queue was unrulier here. Kids jostled each other for position, a baby was squealing somewhere, and the woman behind me kept clipping my ankles with the front wheels of her baby's complicated-looking pram.

It was almost a relief to step into the hole in the side of the ship. Almost.

We emerged into a spacious area that looked like the lobby of a luxury hotel: patterned carpet, low lighting, overstuffed armchairs strewn about in a way that appeared casual but was undoubtedly planned to the last inch. Ornate polished wooden stairs curled up and out of the space, past a huge watercolor of the *Celebrate* over the landing.

Paired with the plush furnishings, the smell of seawater drifting in from the open hatch was disconcerting.

A line of Blue Wave crew members, dressed in the standard blue polo shirt and beige chino combination, stood by to greet us. I looked at each face in turn. Folded in my pocket was a printout of the profile page for Ethan Eckhart that Cusack had found on a website for cruise ship workers. I had stared for hours at the tiny head shot.

Ethan didn't look at all like what I had expected. In my imagination, Sarah had fallen for an underwear model—someone with the kind of honed and chiseled body that graced the covers of glossy style magazines and required endless hours in the gym and in front of the mirror and, before any of that could even begin, a winning ticket in the genetic lottery. That was why she had fallen for him: because he looked that way, because he was something so *other,* so different. She hadn't been able to resist him, because he was irresistible.

That's what I had been telling myself, anyway.

In reality, Ethan was perfectly ordinary. Dark hair cut close to the scalp, not unattractive but not especially attractive, either, his thin lips parted in a half smile. It was a professional's head shot. He was wearing a suit jacket, white shirt, and plain tie. He had nothing in the way of identifying marks, no stand-out feature. No eyewear, facial hair, piercings, or visible tattoos. Whenever I closed my eyes and tried to conjure up a description that would be of use to a police sketch artist or the operator of an Identikit machine, I could think of nothing more specific than *blue eyes, brown hair, white skin.*

Still, I felt confident I would recognize him if I met him in the flesh, but none of these guys looked anything like him.

When it was our turn, Peter and I found ourselves facing a guy of maybe twenty, twenty-one years. He had a big smile and a small tablet computer with a key-card device attached to its side. His name tag told us that this was Danny and his favorite Blue Wave destination was Istanbul.

"Welcome aboard the *Celebrate!*" He sounded English. "Are you excited to experience our Mediterranean Dream?"

In a moment that would have been amusing under other circumstances, Peter and I found ourselves able to respond only with blank looks.

"Well … that's great," Danny said. "I just need to see your Swipeout cards, sirs, please."

Peter handed over his card while I rummaged in the plastic wallet for mine. I had stupidly put it back in there after the last security check, thinking there would be no more.

Danny slid each through his little machine and waited until it beeped. He looked up at us, then down at the machine again. Satisfied, he handed back our cards. Peter reached out and took both of them while I struggled to get the plastic wallet to snap shut again.

"Mr. Dunne and Mr. Brazier, you are so welcome aboard," Danny said. "You will be staying in two of our deluxe junior suites up on Atlantic Deck: 801 and 803." He pointed with two fingers to a bank of elevators on his left. "Take the C elevators up to eight, turn right, and follow the signs. We're serving a buffet lunch in the main dining room on the Oceanic Deck—that's thirteen—and we start our Sailaway Party at six o'clock sharp on Pacific. That's the very top. If you're waiting for luggage, we hope to have it on board very shortly, but if you need anything in the meantime, the Central Park shopping mall on the Promenade Deck is open. There's also a comfort pack in your cabin, along with more information about the ship and this afternoon's muster drill. Do you have any questions?"

We both shook our head.

Danny nodded at the Swipeout cards in Peter's hand. "Just so you know, those are both charging back to the same account, but they don't open both cabin doors, so if you mix them up you might find yourself locked out. Replacements can only be issued with photo ID. Do let the crew know if you have any questions. And again, welcome aboard the *Celebrate!*"

"What the hell is a Sailaway Party?" I asked Peter as soon as we stepped inside the elevator.

"It's when the ship sets sail. Everyone goes up on deck to watch dry land disappear."

He pressed the button for ATLANTIC.

As the doors slid closed, he turned to face me. "Adam, are you okay?"

"Yeah. Fine."

Peter was staring at me. Studying me.

"I know it's weird," he said. "It's hard not to think, *Did she see this? Was she in this elevator? Where's* her *boarding photo now?*"

I had actually found it easy not to think those things, until he brought it up.

"On the phone," I said, "you told me there were things you wanted to wait and tell me in person?"

"Yes. We'll be able to talk soon. I just think it's safer to wait until we know there's no one around to overhear. Crew, especially."

"We can talk in one of the cabins."

"The walls are thin, and the balconies share partitions. I think an open deck might be the best option."

"They're rebranding," I said, holding up the plastic wallet. "Some stuff has the old logo, some new."

The elevator stopped.

"Atlantic Deck," an androgynous voice announced.

The doors slid open on a narrow, brightly lit corridor. Its walls were white, and one long, wavy blue line had been painted along it at waist height, as far as the eye could see. It had the faint smell of seawater, layered with something floral and sickly sweet, like air freshener.

We stepped out, turned right, and walked as far as the door marked "801." The door of 803 was right beside it.

"You're 803," Peter said, handing me one of the cards. "Shall I knock on your door in, say"—he looked at his watch—"twenty minutes? We'll find a place to talk then."

I said that was fine.

"And you might want to use your phone while you can. I don't think it'll work once we're sailing."

"Okay."

"We're going to find him, Adam."

Peter was staring at me again with that intense gaze. Uncomfortable in it, I shifted my weight.

"Yeah," was all I said. *But what are we going to do then?*

"Twenty minutes," Peter said, and disappeared into 801.

I unlocked 803 with my Swipeout. A Do Not Disturb sign was hanging from the inside handle. I opened the door again to hang it outside.

My cabin was narrow but long, and larger than I expected. Everything was blue, yellow, or white—or covered in a pattern that incorporated all three—and spotless. With my back to the door, the bathroom was on my immediate right. On my left was a narrow wardrobe. Walking farther into the room, I found a two-seater couch upholstered in Blue Wave blue, pushed up against one wall and facing a built-in desk with a mirror and flat-screen TV. A little round tray on the desktop held a small bottle of champagne and two glasses, with a spray of blue and yellow ribbon curls tied around the bottle's neck. Every flat surface had a little railing or a raised edge, presumably to keep things from crashing to the floor in stormy seas. The double bed had just enough space between its foot and the opposing wall to allow access to a pair of sliding glass doors, which gave onto the balcony. Was this the kind of cabin Sarah and Ethan had shared? Had they enjoyed a glass of champagne and watched the sunset on a balcony just like the one out there? Had they lain together on a bed like this? Had sex in it?

What had happened then?

I grabbed the remote control from the bedside table and turned on the TV. It was set to some sort of Blue Wave info channel. Scenes from the *Celebrate* were playing in slow fades set to gentle elevator music. Text at the bottom of the screen read, "Welcome aboard, PETER!"

I looked down at the Swipeout card I had tossed on the bed, and frowned. It said "DUNNE," but then, they both did. Peter must have just mixed them up and taken the cabin assigned to my name instead of his own, and handed me the key that opened the one assigned to him.

But it didn't matter; they were both the same.

I thought nothing more about it at the time.

"Tell me, Adam: How much do you know about maritime law?"

Peter and I had found a quiet spot on the Pacific Deck—a small bar with its shutters down that faced into a semicircle of tables and tub chairs, arranged in the chilly shadow of the ship's funnel.

Pop music played unobtrusively from unseen speakers. Happy passengers milled about, clutching glasses topped with impressively cut fruit, while, over the port rail, the cityscape of Barcelona shimmered in the afternoon heat. On the other side of the funnel, in the sun, we had walked past an expansive swimming pool, which was already filling up with children splashing and laughing and throwing inflatable things.

I couldn't help but scan the faces of the crew members I found in the crowd.

"I only know what Cusack told me," I answered. "The thing about the authority in charge being the authority of the country where the ship is registered, not wherever the ship happens to be."

"In charge," Peter scoffed. "If only."

"She talked about Shane Keating. Have you heard of him?"

"Yes, of course. Tragic, that. You have to feel for the brother."

"She said a couple of policemen from Barbados were about to head for the *Fiesta*, when the crew realized he'd gone overboard, and called in the coast guard instead."

"Yes." Peter took a sip of his drink and made a face. Two fruity watered-down cocktails had been thrust in our faces the moment we stepped out on deck. The easiest option had been to accept them. "The thing is, Adam …" He stopped, hesitated. "Let me ask you something. What do *you* think has happened to Sarah?"

"I've been trying not to think about it."

"Which I can understand."

"There's no scenario that makes sense."

"It seems that way, yes."

"It's as if I'm walking down a very narrow corridor, and the wall on my right is the best-case scenario: that this is all a misunderstanding of some kind, that Sarah did lose her passport, that there's a logical explanation for the note. That's she been in the hospital or had an episode or something, which explains her absence, but she's going to be absolutely fine. That this guy Ethan was just a friend who let her use his employee discount. Then the wall on the left is … well, it's the *other* end of the scenario spectrum. The worst possible outcome. And while the best-case scenario seems implausible at this point, I don't want to believe the worst one until I have to. Until I've no choice *but* to. So until then, I'm just walking down this corridor, trying to stay in the middle, trying not to touch either side, even though they're so close there's only inches to spare." I paused. "Sorry, that probably sounds a bit crazy."

"Not at all," Peter said. "It makes complete sense. And I know exactly what you mean. I spent enough time in that corridor myself. But those walls … I'm sorry, but I'm about to push you straight into one of them."

I didn't have to ask which one.

"Your policewoman was right about the Keating case," Peter continued. "The *Fiesta*, like the *Celebrate*, is registered in Barbados for tax purposes, so if a crime that took place in international waters needed investigating, two Barbadian police officers would board a plane and head for the ship—a ship filled with thousands of potential suspects and owned by an incredibly powerful corporation. *Two* of them. On their own. Away from their offices, support staff, et cetera. And that's if the ship's captain *invites* them aboard in the first place. Where was that one, Shane Keating—the North Atlantic?"

"I think so. It was the Icelandic Coast Guard that got called in, so yeah, it must be."

"That's, what? Four thousand miles from Barbados, give or take? How long would our two Barbadian PD friends need to get there? Let's say twenty-four hours. And while they're in a plane over the Atlantic, what's happening back on the ship? The crew could be unwittingly scrubbing potential crime scenes clean. Potential witnesses walk off to take a pleasant day tour or, worse, fly off home."

"But isn't there somebody on the ship who can start the investigation?" I said. "Isn't there security on board? There has to be *some* kind of authority on the ship."

"There are security guards," Peter said. "The same kind you see parading around shopping centers with their thumbs in their belts, and the power they think they have already gone to their heads. Blue Wave calls them 'security *officers,*' but that doesn't make them effective. Or change the fact that they're policing a property they are also supposed to be protecting for their employer—which is a huge conflict of interest. That's why, most of the time, crimes aboard cruise ships aren't investigated at all."

"How can that be?"

"Let's say you were physically assaulted in your cabin and then robbed. What do you do?"

"Go to a security officer."

"Go to a security officer, who may talk to you for a while, take a statement, and so on, and then take the matter up to the bridge. There, the captain will decide whether or not to do anything about it—but who says he has to do anything at all?"

I raised my eyebrows. "Um, the *law?*"

"So he's going to fly two police officers halfway around the world to find the guy who stole your wallet?"

"*And* assaulted me."

"That would only draw attention to the incident."

"You say that like it's a bad thing."

"To the captain, it would be, because he likes having a job. Cruises are supposed to be all fun and frolics at sea. There's nothing about thefts or assaults in the brochures I've seen. Or date-rape drug incidents, for that matter. No mention of sexual assaults. No disappearances. Those things just wouldn't be seemly in a floating paradise. Who'd want to go on a cruise if they thought they were walking into danger? An *enclosed space* full of it? If something happens, they try to keep it quiet. Most importantly of all, keep it out of the press."

"*How*, though?"

"More often than not, these incidents involve a wayward crew member, and crew can be fired. Problem solved. If the victim can be appeased with a free cruise or compensation for medical bills or whatever, better yet. They'll cough up any amount so long as it's kept out of court and you sign a nondisclosure agreement. It's in the cruise company's best interests to sweep all this under the rug and then stand over the bulge, smiling and pretending nothing's wrong." Peter looked around, presumably to make sure we were still alone before he continued. "Unless, of course, there's a murder."

I flinched.

"They wouldn't call it a murder, though," Peter said. "Not unless they had to. If there's no body, they don't. For a murder, you need a cause of death."

"Where would the body ..."

I stopped and turned my head toward the starboard rail. There it was: endless sea.

"The perfect dumping ground," Peter said. "If you pushed someone off a balcony in the middle of the night, who would even know? No one, until morning, when that person's absence is noticed. *If* it is. It might take longer if the person was traveling alone. They might not be missed at all until the end of the cruise. Meanwhile, the cabin attendants are cleaning away all the forensic evidence, and the ship's sailing farther and farther away from the body's location. The other passengers are oblivious. It's as if it never happened at all."

"Except that a person is missing," I said.

Peter clicked his fingers. "Exactly. That's just it. There's no evidence of a murder, but a person is missing. And what's a missing person minus a body? Not a murder. Oh, no. Never a murder. That's called a *disappearance*."

The word hung in the air.

I steeled myself. "You're saying …?"

No. I couldn't say it.

"Estelle didn't disappear, Adam. I know it. There's no possible way she would have walked off this ship and decided never to come back to her life, never to come back to me. She would never have left me living like this, in this hell of not knowing. And wouldn't you say exactly the same thing about Sarah?"

"But Sarah *did* walk off it."

Peter said nothing for a full three seconds. Then, gently: "How do you know that?"

"Because Blue Wave told me," I said. "They *showed* me."

"What did they show you?"

"The key-card activity. The Swipeout card thing."

"A piece of paper, you mean."

"Yeah."

"With things printed on it."

"What *else* could they have produced?"

"How about some CCTV? How about moving images, time- and date-stamped, of Sarah getting off the ship when they say she did? Every inch of this ship has cameras pointed on it. That tender platform was probably covered from every angle. Why not show you *that*?"

"Maybe it was because I didn't think to ask them for it."

"Well, I bloody well did, Adam. I asked them for it. More than once. I took them to *court* to ask them for it, and they still said no. Why? Could it be because they *don't have any*? Could it be because there's no footage of Estelle getting off the ship? Could it be that she *never did*?"

"If she didn't walk off the ship," I said, "then where did she go?"

"I think she's with Sarah. I think the same person took them both."

In the narrow corridor in my mind, the wall on the left was rushing toward my face.

I closed my eyes.

"It seems like no scenario makes sense," Peter said. "But *one* does. Unfortunately, it's the one we don't want to think about."

When I opened my eyes again, a British passport was on the tabletop between us.

"The envelope got thrown away," Peter said, "but it was postmarked 'Nice' too. Sent two days after I last saw Estelle. The same day she supposedly got off the ship."

I picked it up and flicked through it. It was the same in all the ways that mattered: the sticky note, the new Blue Wave logo, the two words.

But this note was signed "E."

"Like you," Peter said, "I didn't know what to make of it when it arrived. But I knew something had happened to her. Something awful. I knew it from the moment her friend Becky called to tell me they couldn't find her on the ship. So this"—he lifted his chin to indicate the passport—"was a torment. A piece of the puzzle I couldn't get to fit. The note—it's in Estelle's writing. Definitely. And you said you were sure the writing on yours was Sarah's, right?"

I nodded but didn't speak. I wasn't sure I could.

"So we have two women," Peter went on, "who don't know each other, who have no connection to each other, last seen in the same place, one year apart. Here, on this ship. They both write exactly the same words on exactly the same type of paper and stick them in their passports. And then, *somehow,* those passports find their way to you and me, the men who love them. Postmarked 'Nice,' where Blue Wave says they walked off the ship. How can that possibly be a coincidence? And then you find me and find out that Sarah came aboard with a man who works here. A man who would know this ship and the rules that govern it like the back of his hand."

Ethan.

"He's the connection," Peter said. "He's the one who did this."

Into the wall, face-first.

"Tell me what happened," I said weakly. My tongue felt thick and bristly, my throat tight and dry. "Tell me what happened to Estelle."

Estelle Brazier was thirty-two on August 3, 2013—the day she disappeared from the *Celebrate*. She had boarded the ship in Barcelona the day before, in a group of ten women. Among them was Becky Richardson Estelle's closest friend. They had known each other since they were toddlers.

"It was a last minute thing," Peter explained. "The trip was actually a bachelorette party for one of Becky's colleagues. Only three days before, one of the women broke her leg in a cycling accident and had to drop out. She was supposed to be Becky's cabinmate, so Becky was asked if she knew anyone else who might be able to come along instead on short notice. It was already paid for, no refunds. Estelle wangled a few days off work, and off she went. I often think, *What if that other woman hadn't fallen off her bike?* None of this would have happened. Doesn't the world turn on such small, small things?"

"Had Estelle ever been on a cruise before?" I asked.

"No, never. It wasn't really our kind of thing. To be honest, I didn't want her to go."

"Why?"

"I just didn't think she would enjoy it. Becky was the only one in the group she knew well. She'd never even met most of the others before. And stuck with them all on a ship, drinking and being silly and running around with veils on?" He shook his head. "That wasn't Estelle."

"But she must've wanted to go."

Peter's face hardened. "*Becky* wanted her to go. That's why she went."

I figured he wasn't a big Becky fan these days. Understandable, after what happened.

"They flew out from Gatwick together," he said. "Boarded the *Celebrate* here early on a Thursday afternoon. I think the ship had been in service barely a month at that stage. Still a few teething problems: lifts breaking down, a wave pool not open yet, glitches in the dining reservation system—things like that. They spent a few hours sunbathing by the Grotto Pool and had a late lunch in the Cabana Café alongside it. Then they all went back to their cabins to get ready for the evening, before meeting up again around eight in the Showcase Theater on the Oceanic Deck, to watch a variety show. After *that*, they went to Fizz. It's a cocktail bar."

The way Peter talked about the *Celebrate* reminded me of *Titanic* documentaries I'd watched where talking heads—historians, enthusiasts, director James Cameron—spoke of the A Corridor and the Grand Staircase and Orlop Deck as if these were places they had been visiting all their lives. Places they knew so well, they could navigate them in the dark. This despite the fact that the ship had sunk long before any of them were born.

Accounts—and, not coincidentally, inebriation levels—varied regarding what happened next, but it was generally agreed that sometime between 10:45 p.m. and 11:10 p.m. on that first night at sea, Estelle told the others she had developed a bad headache. One of the women would recall her looking "gray and sweaty," while another said she was slurring her words.

"She wasn't drinking alcohol," Peter said, "so we're talking about the effects of something else. My guess is, either Estelle had something slipped into her drink, or she was getting a migraine. She did suffer from those, from time to time. Either way, she told Becky she was going to go buy some aspirin, lie down for an hour, and then come back to the bar if she was feeling well enough. But she didn't come back."

"She wasn't in the cabin when Becky went back to it?"

"Becky spent the night in one of the group's other cabins so as not to disturb Estelle. When she finally did go back to theirs, it was nearly nine the next morning, and Estelle wasn't there."

"Had she slept there?"

"The bed was made. Becky assumed Housekeeping had come and gone. They were already tendered at Villefranche by then, and the plan for the day was to take a private bus tour around the coast. The driver was meeting them at the ferry terminal at half past ten. They all assumed that Estelle, being the only one among them who had an early night, had gotten up early and gone ashore. They thought she had figured on meeting them there."

"What about her phone?"

"Becky called it, but it went straight to voice mail. She thought maybe the phone hadn't managed to connect to a service in France."

"But when they got ashore and realized Estelle wasn't in Ville-franche ..."

"Becky went back to the ship. To the cabin. Had another look at the bed. She realized then it hadn't been remade—because it was never disturbed in the first place. And then she found the phone."

"Estelle's phone was in the cabin?"

"Yes," Peter said grimly.

It was a sign of the times that this detail seemed more significant than all the rest.

I said, "What about the rest of Estelle's stuff?"

"All her clothes and cosmetics were still there, many of them still in her suitcase. So was the aspirin that she'd presumably bought after leaving Fizz. Unopened. No sign of her Swipeout card." A pause. "Or the passport, of course."

Becky alerted a security officer, Peter explained, who brought her to the bridge to speak to his superior. A shipwide announcement was made over the PA system, asking Estelle to make herself known to a crew member. By now, time was ticking on. It was almost one o'clock, and no one had seen Estelle since around eleven the night before.

"It was at this point that Becky really started to worry," Peter said, "mostly because the crew seemed to be taking it quite seriously. There was talk of conducting a cabin-to-cabin search—with most of the passengers already on the coast, now was the time to do it. But then, all of a sudden, the cruise director shows up, brings Becky into a little room, and says it's all right; panic's over; Estelle got off the ship this morning. He gave her this."

Peter reached into his pocket and pulled out a letter-size sheet of paper, folded in quarters.

"Estelle's Swipeout activity," he said, handing it to me.

"Yeah," I said, "I got one, too."

I quickly scanned the page: a dense, tidy list of dates, times, and what I presumed were point-of-sale locations on the *Celebrate*. Three lines at the end had been highlighted in neon yellow, and alongside them, in the margins, were notations in handwriting:

03.08.13 11:23 4814 (CB) CRES Crescent CB=chargeback (tablets)

03.08.13 11:59 2391 (AP) 7012 Access point—40 mins???

04.08.13 07:28 9281 (ID) TENPLT4 Tender/ID check (CCTV?)

"According to this," Peter said, "Estelle entered her cabin a minute before midnight on Thursday, then got off the ship and onto a tender at twenty-eight minutes past seven the next morning."

"So they ... *faked* this?" I said, waving the piece of paper.

"Not necessarily. I think Estelle's Swipeout card got off the ship. Think about it: how hard would it be for a crew member to sidle up to one of his colleagues at the tender platform and distract him for a few seconds—long enough to slide a card through one of those handheld machines?"

In my mind's eye, I saw Ethan doing just that. Unlike Cusack's explanations, this theory actually made sense. Unfortunately.

"That would explain Blue Wave's willingness to let you have the Swipeout activity," I said, "but not the CCTV."

"Yes." He nodded encouragingly. "Exactly, Adam. Yes. Indeed."

He seemed *relieved?* Yes, relieved that I was agreeing with him. But then, this was probably the first time he had told anyone this and got a response other than pity or maybe a tactful query about his mental health.

"What's their excuse, though?" I asked. "I mean, what does Blue Wave say when you ask to have a look at the CCTV?"

"Officially, the footage contains '*sensitive operational procedures.*'" Peter rolled his eyes at the phrase. "And they tell me that if I'm looking for evidence that Estelle got off the ship, I already have it. But what I actually have is evidence that something happened to her while she was aboard."

I looked at the printout again, then back to Peter. "What am I missing here?"

"Look at the times." He pointed to the page. "Estelle buys the aspirin at twenty-three minutes past eleven—just after she leaves the other women in Fizz. But she doesn't enter her cabin until a minute before midnight—almost forty minutes later. I've studied the maps. The Crescent General Store is on deck twelve, aft of the D elevators. All Estelle had to do was walk twenty, thirty feet along a corridor, get into the lift, go down a few floors, and then walk another fifteen, maybe twenty feet to her door."

When I raised my eyebrows at this, Peter said, "I've had nothing to do but think about this. I've studied the floor layouts for hours. By now, I could probably navigate my way around this ship blindfolded."

"What are we talking in minutes?" I asked.

"Even if Estelle took her time, it would take five, ten minutes. Fifteen, let's say, if the lifts were especially busy. So why the forty-minute gap?"

"Maybe she stopped to look in a store or something."

"But she had a bad enough headache that she left the group and went to buy something to get rid of it. Does that sound like someone inclined to do a bit of shopping?"

"Well, I don't know, then."

"Neither do I, but I have a theory. If someone had her Swipeout card and used it to make it look as though she'd gotten off the ship and onto a tender, couldn't that same person have let himself into her cabin with it the night before?"

"Run me through it, then," I said. "What happened?"

"I think someone spiked Estelle's drink. That's why she was feeling unwell. Whoever spiked it then followed her out of the bar and into the Crescent General Store. Watched her. Perhaps got talking with her. Remember, she's on holiday on a cruise ship. She feels safe. Everything's all lit up and festive, everyone having a good time floating on the lovely, tranquil Mediterranean. It never occurs to her this is still just like meeting a strange man in a dark alley at the end of the night out. Then he either walks her back to her cabin and follows her in—which would also explain the delayed key-card entry *and* the unopened aspirin box—or he takes her somewhere else. She has a headache; maybe he suggests that some fresh air out on deck would do her good. And then … well, then he does it."

There was a beat of silence as we both tried not to picture "it."

Peter pushed on. "If it did happen elsewhere, then afterwards he uses her key to open her cabin door, thereby creating a record of it in the Swipeout activity. Does the same thing the next morning on the tender platform."

"But where do the passport and the note come in?"

"Well, it throws a wrench in the works, doesn't it? A communication that appears to be from Estelle, sent from the place she supposedly got off the ship. It diverts attention from the *Celebrate*. You think, whatever happened must have happened after she went ashore."

"But do you think … the notes … I mean, are you saying he forced—"

"I think it would be relatively easy for a crew member to get hold of a weapon. That's what I think. Just for a start, you have how many restaurant kitchens full of knives?"

My stomach twisted at the thought.

"Now," Peter said, "he's covered all the bases. There's no evidence, no body, and no police. Blue Wave says she got off the ship, so their hands are clean. It's the perfect crime. He waits a while, just to make sure. A year later, he does it again. Only this time, he selects his victim ashore and then maneuvers her *onto* the ship. And this time, her boyfriend finds his way to the husband of the first woman. And when we talk, we learn that we *both* got a passport with a note stuck inside. This time, someone figures out that the only connection the two women have is *him*."

It seemed a perfect fit for the hole in the jigsaw puzzle, but I wasn't ready to slot it in just yet.

Peter looked at his watch. "We sail at six," he said. "We'll start the search for him then."

I told Peter that now *I* had to go buy some aspirin. All the not sleeping and the traveling and the heat had conspired to start a thundering in my temples.

I listened while he told me where the nearest store was. I assured him there was no need to take me there himself. And then I fled.

Sarah dead. Murdered. The worst-case scenario. But also, the only one we had that made any sense.

Her eyes bulging in terror. Hands on her mouth and neck. Her clothes ripped. Her skin bruised.

There could be no avoiding it anymore. Holding back the worst thoughts was so exhausting, it was a relief of sorts to give up and let them in.

I hurried back down the deck, blinded by the sun, gasping in the heat. Trying to find a way inside as images of Sarah's death went off like camera flashes in my mind.

A body falling through the night air ...

I pushed past a young mother with her troop of three children and their assortment of inflatable swimming-pool toys. Streaks of sunscreen glistened on their cheeks. A faint scent of coconut.

Dropping like a stone into dark water, lost forever ...

I clipped the shoulder of a guy close to my own age, wearing board shorts and trying to keep three beers from sloshing. He swung around toward me and shouted, "Hey!"

Sarah, lost forever …

A Blue Wave crew member with flowers in her hair thrust a flyer in my face.

… cold, damaged, and alone.

"Why not join us tonight in the Horizon Room for a special screening of … sir? Are you okay, sir?"

Up ahead, I saw a set of double doors, propped open. I ignored her and made straight for them.

I followed the flow of people into a dim corridor. Tasting salt on my lips, I lifted my hand to them and realized that my face was wet.

When had I started crying?

I put my head down and walked faster. I just needed to get to a place where I could sit down for a second and think.

The corridor ended suddenly in a burst of light. I was on a paved garden path now, winding through lush green palms grown tall enough to bend and hang overhead. I could hear piped-in birdsong and the gentle trickle of an unseen water feature. And through gaps in the foliage, I saw the glint of a golden, twirling carousel. Above me, I saw what looked like two opposing cliff faces—cabins, their balconies stacked side by side and row upon row, all the way up to the atrium's ceiling.

I should never have come here. If Ethan had killed Sarah, what was I supposed to do when I found him?

I dug out my phone and powered it up. It had been off since I was back at the airport—*Cork* Airport. I couldn't take the chance that someone might talk me out of coming to Barcelona, because I knew they wouldn't have to try very hard.

Now I needed someone to talk me down.

The moment the phone connected to a service, it sprang to life, beeping and pinging as text messages, emails, and voice-mail alerts came streaming in. Ignoring them all, I went to CONTACTS and scrolled until I found Rose.

I spotted an empty garden bench set back from the path. While the call was connecting, I walked over and dropped into it.

"Jesus *Christ!*" Rose yelled when she picked up. "Where the hell are you? Your parents have been losing their shit. They think you're in a river somewhere, that you jumped off some bridge out of grief. What the hell, Adam? Didn't we *just* spend a week of our lives wondering where—"

"Rose," I cut in. "I need you to shut the fuck up for a second. Where are you right now? Are you at home?"

"I'm in town, Mr. Manners. On lunch. Where are *you?*"

"I'm on the ship. The *Celebrate.* At the port in Barcelona. It's getting ready to set sail."

Silence. Then, "What are you doing, Adam? Why are you there? You're not ... You're not planning on doing anything stupid, are you?"

"Rose, listen. I met a man. Found him, then met him. Peter. I read all this stuff online and then I saw that he'd been sent a passport too and now we're here and ... and Ethan! That's his name. Cusack found out who the number belonged to, and get this: *he works here.* He's on the ship. Right now. The man who ..." My voice began to waver. "... killed her, Rose. Who *killed her.* Oh, God. What if he did? What if she's dead? What am I going to do?"

The silence was longer this time.

"Adam, you listen to *me,*" Rose said. "Where are you right now? Are you sitting down? Are you alone?"

"I'm on a bench ... Yeah, alone."

"Okay. Start at the beginning. Go slow. Who is the man you're talking about? This Peter guy."

I walked Rose through the events of the past few days: remembering the comment about the *Fiesta,* Googling cruise ship crimes, finding out about Estelle, contacting Peter, him telling me he had received a passport and a note, too. An identical note but for the initial. I told her about Cusack giving me Ethan Eckhart's name and that he was working here, on the ship. Peter's theory about Ethan. Our plan to search the ship until we found him.

"And then what?" Rose asked. "What will you do then?"

"I came here because I thought he could fill in more blanks," I said. "Move the timeline along. Tell me where Sarah was going when she left him, and then go there. But now ... now I don't really know."

"You need to come home," Rose said. "*Now.*"

Through the leaves, I saw the carousel come to a stop. A moment later came the high-pitched voice of a young girl pleading with someone to let her ride it again. This was soon followed by an ear-piercing shriek that suggested her request had been refused.

"Adam?" Rose prompted.

"I'm here," I said. "Don't you think it's the only explanation that makes any sense?"

"It's not an explanation at all. It's only *speculation*. The baseless kind. This is real life, Adam. Not one of your screenplays or, you know, a movie that's actually been made. Do you know how rare serial killers are? How few of them are out there?"

"Jesus, Rose, we're not talking about Ted Bundy. We're talking about a man who saw the opportunity to kill two women and get away with it, and took it. Maybe he *has* killed other women. I don't know."

"But how could anyone kill anyone, anywhere, and have no one at all do anything about it? How could that even happen? Think about it."

"That's just it, Rose. It *does* happen. Maritime law screws the investigations up. The cruise ship companies don't want anyone to know what's really going on, so they pay people off and keep it quiet. And he knows what he's doing, Rose. This guy Ethan. We wouldn't even know about him if I hadn't found that phone bill in Sarah's desk drawer. She didn't tell you any details. We didn't even know his *name*, for God's sake."

"But *that's* just it. Sarah was with him. She liked him. Was attracted to him. Trusted him enough to go away on a trip with him. Are you saying she would've fallen for a murderer? I know love is blind, and all that, but I think she might have noticed."

"This isn't a fucking joke, Rose. Why are you being like this?"

"Like what? Realistic?"

"Like a *bitch*." I regretted it before I'd even uttered the "-tch" sound. "Sorry, Rose. Look—"

"I'm only trying to help you," she said quietly.

"I'm sorry. I know."

"Do you know what you sound like? I hate to say this to you, Adam, but a conspiracy theorist. One of those guys who think man never landed on the moon and 9/11 was an inside job. I think you've been taken in by this guy, and I don't blame you. You're dealing with a lot right now. There are people who prey on the vulnerable. That's why religious cults have a disproportionately high rate of members who have lost a spouse or a family member."

"Where are you getting all this from?"

"I believe they're called *books*."

"Rose, I'm just trying to find out what happened to Sarah."

"And I'm just trying to stop something from happening to *you*."

"Don't you want answers?"

"Of course I do, but am I going to get them from this random guy you met online? What about Sarah reading the WhatsApp message? What about the note? How does *that* fit into Peter's theory? You said the handwriting on it was definitely hers, and I agree."

"Ethan must have forced them to write them. Maybe at knifepoint. Then he addressed the envelope—that's why the writing is different— and posted it after he killed her."

Rose asked me then when I had last slept. I ignored the question.

"It couldn't be a coincidence?" she asked.

"Don't even mention that word, Rose."

"Okay, fine. Well, not to fan the flames of crazy, but let's pretend for a second that this Peter guy is right. What are you going to do now?"

"Find Ethan."

"And?"

"And then figure it out. I don't know. Get him to confess. Trick him into it. Or find evidence against him. Maybe he could have something of hers. Get more information to go back to the gardaí with, I suppose."

"But you said the gardaí have no jurisdiction."

"Whoever, then!" I snapped.

Rose sighed long and loud.

"You were there," I said. "In that room with Louise. You heard her outside afterwards. There's *something* going on. And everything Peter says, it fits."

"Well, if Psycho Peter says it ..."

"Rose, he lost his wife."

A pause. "Right. Sorry."

"This is all I *can* do," I said. "Isn't it? I mean, what else is there? I can get off the ship and go home and—what? Sit and wait? Wait for what? For how long? How long is enough? *How* am I going to wait?"

"We'll figure it ... Adam, I hear Moorsey at the door. Why don't you talk to him? Maybe he can—"

"No," I said. "It's okay. Tell him I'm okay. But I have to do this. We're about to set sail."

"Adam, no!"

"Listen, write this down somewhere. Peter's last name is Brazier. His wife was Estelle. She disappeared last August. You can look up the details online. Tell my parents and Jack and Maureen that I've just come to Barcelona to look around or something. To check the hotel. Don't mention anything about me going on the cruise ship, okay? Or the stuff I just told you. They've got enough to worry about right now. And no point giving them any news until we're 100 percent sure."

"Will you please just listen to me for a second? This isn't a good idea."

"I don't know if there'll be Wi-Fi at sea, but I've seen signs here for

Internet cafés. I'll check my email when I can, but my phone probably won't work. We'll be in Nice tomorrow and back in Barcelona Thursday morning. In the meantime, maybe you and Moorsey can try to find out as much as you can about Ethan. Last name Eckhart." I spelled it for her. "Cusack found him on a website for cruise ship workers, so I bet there's loads more out there. Facebook, Twitter, LinkedIn. Have a search. Email me anything you find."

"Adam, please just—"

"This is all my fault, Rose. I should've realized sooner that something was badly wrong. Not just after she left, but before. When she was … falling for him. There were signs; I can see that now. She was done. She was fed up. I'd had my finger on the pause button for long enough. She didn't want to wait anymore."

"Adam, it's not—"

"So I have to be there for her now. Be what she needs." More tears were coming; I needed to get off the line. "Please understand."

I ended the call.

While I recomposed myself, I scrolled through my list of recent calls. There were seven missed calls from Dan.

I glanced right and left to see if I was still alone on the path. Then I took a deep breath and hit RETURN.

"Oh, so you're *not* dead?" he said when he picked up. "'I'm so glad, because—"

I cut him off. "Dan, I'm going to talk now and you're going to listen, and this time *I* don't care what *you* have to say, okay? My girlfriend is missing. I haven't heard from her in over a week. She was supposed to be on a business trip in Barcelona, but I've traced her to a cruise ship off the coast of France, and I just met a man who thinks she might have been murdered. I'm on the ship now and I'm going to find him—the murderer. The cruise is for three nights, four days, and it leaves in less than half an hour. Obviously, finishing the rewrites is not on my list of priorities right now, and since *I* pay *you*, I'm not interested in hearing your thoughts on that. I don't care about the money. I don't care about my career. All I ever really cared about was this girl, about being with her, about sharing my life with her. Now I don't know where she is or how she is, or if she's even alive. I have to find out what happened to her, and I will. First. If the studio is unhappy about this, their options are to fuck off or wait longer. You can tell them that from me. When all this is over—if it ever is—I will call you and tell you that I'm ready. You don't call me. Are we clear?"

My palms were so slick with nervous sweat that the phone nearly slid out of my hand while I waited through the silence that followed. But Dan didn't have to know that.

"We're clear," he said eventually.

"Good."

"And I know you're not going to want to hear this, but can I just play the role of the blackened soul here for a second? It'd be a lot easier to get the studio to wait patiently if I told them about this, about what you're going through, because you know what? This has 'Oscar contender' written all over it. It's like *Taken* meets *Gone Girl* on a boat, only it's true, and you know how Academy voters love a good true—"

I ended the call.

Dan had secured a script deal for me, yeah, but it seemed his real talent lay in making me question my career choice.

I made my way back outside and looked to see whether Peter was still in the same spot. As I crossed the deck, I felt a faint, brief vibration beneath my feet, followed by a gentle lurch.

A cheer went up from the crowd. The *Celebrate* was sailing away.

We met Megan for the first time that night in Fizz, the cocktail bar where Estelle was last seen. From the view through its narrow floor-to-ceiling windows, Fizz must be in the stern—I'd lost all sense of direction on the twisty route here. Though it was still reasonably bright outside, it was dark in the bar, with partial drapes, soft lamps, and recessed spotlights all adding up to barely enough light to read a menu. Everything was purple, from the covers of the menus to the upholstery on the chairs.

Peter and I sat at the bar. We ordered hamburgers and Cokes from the bartender, Javier, whose favorite Blue Wave destination was Stockholm.

As he set our drinks down in front of us, Peter said to him, "A friend of ours works here. Somewhere. He doesn't know we're on board, and we'd love to surprise him. Maybe you know him? His name's Ethan Eckhart."

I kept my expression as neutral as I could, but I was shocked. I hadn't expected Peter to just start throwing the man's name around so soon, and so openly.

What if Ethan himself was nearby? What if he overheard us?

"It doesn't sound familiar, sorry," Javier said. "A lot of people work on this ship."

"How many is a lot?"

"Like, a thousand?"

"Our friend works in the Food and Beverage Department. Does that help?"

"Not really. F and B is every bar, restaurant, café, and ice cream stand on the entire ship. Room Service, too. We have more F and B crew than anything else. I'm sorry, but I think you'll just have to call your friend."

"But we *really* want to surprise him."

"I can ask my manager? Maybe he will know."

Peter smiled. "That'd be great."

Javier disappeared through a purple velvet curtain that must hide a passageway to the kitchens.

"A *thousand* crew?" I whispered to Peter. "We've only got four days. And are you sure it's a good idea to be throwing his name around so freely?"

"You didn't use your friend's Blue Crew, then?" a female voice said.

We both turned toward the source: a woman sitting three stools to my right.

I recognized her instantly. In real life, Megan of Megan's Muster Station seemed older than she did in her YouTube videos. Late twenties to early thirties, if I had to guess. She was slim and pretty, with short blond hair and a sun-kissed, outdoorsy look. There was a book open on the bar in front of her, but she was smiling at us.

"Pardon?" Peter said.

"His Blue Crew rate." The American accent was strong now that I knew to listen for it. "The Blue Wave employee discount for friends and family. If he doesn't know you're here, I'm guessing you paid the full ticket price."

"Oh, yes. Yes, we did," Peter said. "Unfortunately we don't know him *that* well." He gave a short, odd laugh.

"Shame," Megan said. "Mind if I join you?"

"Not at all."

She moved to the stool beside me and stuck out her hand. "My name's Megan."

"Actually, I know," I said. "I'm Adam, and this is Peter. I think I've seen one of your videos?"

"Oh, really? God." She blushed. "That's embarrassing." She reached across me to shake Peter's hand. "It's fine when you're at home uploading them, but then, when I meet a real live person who's seen them, it's mortifying. You're British, right?"

"He is," I said. "I'm Irish."

"Really? My mother's Irish. Like, has-an-Irish-passport Irish. She was born in Galway."

"Galway's nice."

"I must get there someday. What part of Ireland are you from?"

"Cork. Down in the very south."

"That's the *Titanic* place, right?"

"One of them, yeah. Built in Belfast, sailed from Cork."

"You're American?" Peter asked her.

Megan laughed. "How'd you guess?"

"I wasn't sure. I have occasionally made the mistake of saying that to Canadians."

"Which I bet they love."

"There have been some awkward silences, you could say."

"Well, I would take offense, too, but I guess it's just like the Irish-British thing, right? Sometimes you guys all sound the same to me."

"Are you doing one of your video things on here?" I asked her.

Megan smirked. "Yep. Busted. I'm on a junket. All expenses paid so long as I post a few videos. I'm actually not supposed to tell full-price-paying passengers that, but you two look trustworthy."

"Nice job to have," Peter said. "Do they let you bring someone along?"

"Unfortunately, no. I'm all on my lonesome. But it's okay, I've just met two really nice guys in Fizz."

She winked at me.

I looked at my Coke.

"Do they make you say nice things in return?" Peter said. "On your videos?"

"Let's just say I wouldn't get invited back if I said anything *too* nasty. But between you and me, I'll say whatever they want me to say. I make decent money from their affiliate program. I'm saving it up to go back to school."

"To do what?"

"Hospitality Management. So…" Megan turned to me. "How do you guys know each other?"

I opened my mouth to speak, then realized I was about to say, *Well, we don't really.*

"From university," Peter said.

"Oh, yeah?" She seemed dubious, probably because, going by appearances, Peter and I would have met at college only if he had been my professor.

"He was a mature student," I said.

Javier reappeared through the velvet curtain.

"You guys have friends in very high places, eh?" He wagged his finger at us in mock reprimand. "I hope you'll only be telling him very good things about me. Tell him I'm the best bartender, okay? Tell him I deserve a raise."

Peter and I looked at each other, perplexed.

"Your friend," Javier said. "He doesn't work in the F and B department. He *runs* it. Mr. Eckhart is our food-and-beverage director. You didn't know that?"

"No … no, we didn't," Peter said. "We, uh, haven't seen him in a while."

A director. That made sense, given Ethan's age. The average age of all the front-of-house staff we had encountered on the ship so far seemed to be somewhere between old enough to vote and old enough to rent a car. It was like *Logan's Run* around here.

Peter asked where we could find him.

"I don't know for sure," Javier said. "The director doesn't work just in one place. He moves around all the time, from restaurant to restaurant. If you want, you can give me a message and I'll—"

"I think we'll try finding him first," Peter said.

"Good luck, then. Lots of places to check on here. And you'll be moving around; he'll be moving around …" Javier shrugged. "The cruise is only four days, guys."

He moved away to serve other passengers.

"You know," Megan said, "you could just *ask* to speak with him. Go to one of the service desks and do it. You don't have to give your real name. You could even pretend you want to make a complaint. How funny would *that* be? Imagine his face then when he sees you!"

I imagined Ethan's face when I told him I was Sarah's boyfriend.

"Yes," Peter said. "That would be something."

"*Or* …" Megan rubbed her hands together like a stage villain. "We could sneak into the crew quarters."

I froze at the suggestion.

Peter asked how.

"I used to work for Royal Caribbean," she said. "I know *all* the tricks. And they have the *best* parties back there. Do you know the crew have their own pool? I don't think all three of us could manage it together, but maybe I could sneak one of you in."

She looked at me as she said the last bit.

Megan was flirting with me, I realized. I could feel it: the twinge, the pull of someone else's presence on mine. The subtext. *Come with me. Be with me. Stay with me.*

"I don't think that headache went away," I said.

"No?" Peter narrowed his eyes. "Didn't you take something for it?"

"I did. But I feel it creeping back now."

"I have something in my purse," Megan offered.

"It's okay. I have something in my cabin. I think I'll go get it." I started to slide off my stool.

"I'll see you in the morning?" I said to Peter. He just glared at me. I turned to Megan. "It was nice meeting you."

"Feel better," she said, patting my arm. "Nice meeting you, too."

I was already moving toward the door. Peter was pissed off at me, but I just wanted to get away. Because I couldn't do this. I wasn't cut out for this.

Breaking into crew quarters? Seriously? Me?

I was the sort that never stepped beyond the yellow line on the train station platform.

"Adam!" Peter had run out after me. "Wait. What are you doing?"

"Look, I'm sorry," I said when he caught up. "I just don't want to do this. I don't think I can."

"Do what? Find him? Because this is the finding-him bit."

"I'm not going to go sneak around crew quarters, Peter. We could get thrown off for that."

"That's the worst thing that could happen to you now, is it? Getting thrown off this ship?"

I said nothing.

"She's perfect, Adam. Megan is perfect. Come on. This is our lucky break! She knows the ship; she knows the industry. She used to be crew. And she obviously likes you. You should encourage that."

"Encourage ... *what?*"

"I'm not talking about doing anything. I mean, you know, let her think what she wants until we find Ethan."

"What are we going to do then? What's the actual plan when we find him?" I shook my head. "I'm not sure I'm cut out for this. When she said that about going into the crew quarters, Peter, I was ..." I didn't want to admit this. I wanted to be stronger. But the truth was, "I was scared."

"Of what?"

"Of *him.*"

Peter bit his lip, considering.

"Okay, Adam," he said. "Here's what we'll do. You go back to your cabin and rest. I imagine you haven't had much sleep in the past week. You could do with a solid eight hours. Then, in the morning, we'll start systematically searching the restaurants for him—from afar. We'll make sure we see him before he sees us. Once we locate him, I'll confront him. I'll do what needs doing. It's the least I can do. After all, you've paid for this. I couldn't have afforded to come aboard without you."

"It's fine," I said, waving a hand. "Don't worry about that."

Talking about who had paid for what was an excruciating torture for me in any circumstance, and this was my point. I was a guy who couldn't face a full and frank discussion about how best to pay for a shared taxi ride home. How in the hell was I supposed to confront a *killer*?

"Good," Peter said. "Now, go get some rest. I'll see you bright and early for breakfast."

I sighed with relief as he turned and went back into Fizz. I didn't know what I was going to do in the morning, but I did know that Peter was right: what I needed right now was sleep.

My cabin looked just as I had left it. There were no chocolates on the pillow; the Do Not Disturb sign had been heeded. I eyed the bottle of champagne on the desk. With a few glasses of that in me, it would be easy to get the full eight hours Peter had prescribed.

But my eyelids were already drooping. I didn't need it.

I went to close the curtains and stopped, looking out at the endless sea, shimmering in the moonlight. I couldn't help thinking it: she could be out there somewhere, floating, alone. Waiting for someone to believe that she was. Waiting for me to find her.

I pulled the curtains shut, kicked off my shoes, and climbed into bed, fully clothed.

And let myself sink into thinking about Sarah. About how it felt to fall asleep with her head on my chest. About waking up beside her in the morning. About how, when she came home in the evening, the first thing she always did was come to my desk, wrap her arms around me, and say, "Well? Did you get much procrastinating done today?"

Next thing I knew, it was morning, and the frayed ends of Sarah's navy-and-white scarf were on the bed beside me, tickling my face.

ROMAIN

Fleury-Mérogis, Paris, 2000

Romain sat on the bed his father had bought for him, and let his weight sink down into the deep, soft mattress. The new sheets still had creases in them from being folded into their packaging. They smelled clean and fresh. When he skimmed his palms over them, they felt soft and strong, not rough and thin like the ones he was used to. The pillows were thick, and there were three of them. If he piled them up on top of one each other, he would practically be sleeping upright.

A voice intruded. "Romain?"

He opened his eyes. His psychiatrist, Dr. Tanner, was sitting opposite, fingers steepled under his bearded chin, a six-inch-thick patient file on the tabletop in front of him. It had Romain's name on it.

"What were you thinking about?" Tanner asked.

"The bed my father is going to have ready for me in my new room."

"Oh? Have you seen it?"

"No, but I can imagine it."

"What do you imagine?"

"Something much better than you get in *this* place."

Tanner looked around and grinned. "For your sake, Romain, I hope so."

The chairs they were sitting on and the table between them were the only furniture in the room. Everything was steel-framed and bolted to the floor, its most recent layer of green paint chipped and peeling, the original smoothness of the material interrupted with the bumps and edges of older, deeper coats. The room was small and bare, the walls cinder block, their faded yellow paint pockmarked from old posters and blotched with stains, the only window narrow and secured with a metal grille. Behind Romain was a thick steel door, and behind that, an armed guard stood sentry.

"You're looking forward to leaving, then?" Dr. Tanner asked.

Romain made a face.

"Okay, okay." The doctor laughed. "Silly question. I suppose what I was really asking was, are you nervous, at all?"

"A little bit," Romain admitted.

"What are you nervous about?"

"Myself. What if it's all still there, inside me? What if it comes back up? What if all this hasn't worked?"

"Ah, come now. We've discussed this. It *has* worked. Which reminds me …" The doctor lifted up the patient file and took from beneath it a printout of several sheets paper-clipped together. He passed it to Romain. "This is the article. It was published in the journal yesterday. You're famous now."

Romain took the pages without mentioning that he was famous *already*, because Tanner knew that better than anyone.

The printout was a photocopy of a long, dense article. "Boy P and the Possible Curing of Psychopathy," the headline read. "Dr. Gary Tanner on the case study that looks set to rock the foundations of the psychiatry world." Above the text of the article was a large picture of the doctor standing in a garden in front of a big tree, smiling.

"*We're* famous," Romain said, tapping the picture.

"I think there will be far more interest in you than in me."

There was a sharp rap of knuckles on the door. A guard stuck his head into the room and said Romain's father was here.

"Off you go, then," Tanner said. "We'll meet again before you leave. Say hi to Charlie for me."

* * *

Three doors. That was all that stood between Romain and the outside world. The door behind the guard station that led to the corridor, the door at the end of the corridor, which led to the main entrance, and the door that separated the inside from the outside. He went through one of them now, into the visitors' room.

Only three doors.

It was something that Romain thought about often: about what a difference those three doors made, separating the world he experienced from the world everyone else his age did. He hadn't seen the third door, the farthest one, in five years, but in five days he would be allowed to walk through it.

Romain wondered what was going on out there—what he was missing. What he had already missed.

An electronic lock buzzed loudly, and his father came into the visitors' room.

Right away, Romain knew that something was wrong. His father didn't even look into his eyes until he was sitting down at the table and had no choice.

Today's visit was supposed to be about finalizing the plan for Romain's release, working out the last few details. What time Papa needed to come pick him up, what food he wanted to eat first, what he wanted to do to celebrate his eighteenth birthday.

Papa was in the process of moving from his apartment into a house. That way, there would be enough space for the two of them to live together yet still have some space of their own. The last time Papa visited, he had asked Romain to make a list of everything he thought he would need. Clothes, toiletries, posters—those kinds of things. Romain had the list in his pocket right now, but he didn't take it out. Something told him not to. Not yet.

"Hi, Romi," Papa said, giving him a big fake smile. Fake smiles were something Romain could identify now, thanks to Dr. Tanner. Had Papa forgotten that? "How are you? Looking forward to the big day?"

"What's wrong, Papa?"

His father frowned. "Who said anything was wrong?" He pushed his spectacles back up his nose, glanced back at the guards.

"What is it?" Romain asked. "Tell me."

"I don't know what you mean."

"I *know* something is wrong, Papa. You're a terrible liar. You can't do it at all."

His father looked as if he was about to argue, but then he changed his mind.

"Fine. There's, ah, been a change, Romi. To the plan. It's ... your mother."

"Is she dead? Did something happen to her?"

"What? No. No, she's fine. Why would you ... No, it's just ... We've been talking about you a lot. About our plans. The plans you and I had."

Had.

His father noticed that he had noticed, but he pushed on anyway, talking faster now.

"The thing is, Romi, she's told me that if I take you in, she won't let me see Jean and Mikki anymore. She still thinks ... Well, you know what she thinks. That it wasn't an accident, at the pond. I didn't tell you this before, I know, but I didn't want to upset you. Not when you were doing so well. She and I ... I've been seeing her a lot lately. We go out for dinner, and sometimes Jean comes with us, too. Jean is actually living with me for the summer. We're getting along well. Very well. Once all four of us went out for—"

"Four of you is not *all* of you," Romain said quietly.

"No." His father pushed his spectacles up again. They hadn't slipped down; it was just a habit. "No, that's right. I know. I just meant ..."

"I can't come live with you. That's what you're here to tell me, isn't it?"

"Well, it's a bit more complicated than that, Romi. Your mother and I have been apart for many years."

"You've been apart for as long as I've been in here."

"Yes. Yes, we have." Papa cleared his throat. He was sweating now. Beads of it glistened by his hairline. "Listen, I've always been here for you, and I'll be here for you now. I'm going to find a place for you to live, and one of the guys at work thinks he might have a job for you."

"Doing what?"

"I don't know yet. But he has a farm, so it'll be something to do with the animals, I expect. Would you like that?"

"How much does it pay?"

"You won't have to worry about money. I'll take care of you."

"Where will I live? Near you?"

"We might be able to get you something on the farm. That would be convenient, wouldn't it? And you'd be back out in the countryside, which you love."

"Where's the farm?"

His father waved a hand dismissively. "I don't want you to get fixated on the *farm,* Romi."

"You're the one who said it."

"It's only one possibility."

"Where *is* it?"

His father hesitated. "Ah, near Soissons, I believe."

Romain knew that Soissons was at least an hour's drive from where his father lived.

"Okay," Romain said. "I see."

"Also …" His father was shifting in his seat now. "Your mother thinks it might be better for everyone if we didn't come pick you up. Now, before you say anything, listen to *why* she thinks that. There'll be reporters there. And photographers. She doesn't want to remind everyone what she looks like. It's only recently that people have stopped recognizing her in the street and at the supermarket."

"*She* doesn't have to come."

"But it's better for you, too, you see. If we—or I—don't come for you, you can leave early in the morning before anyone is outside. Slip out before the press get here. You're a man now, Romi. You look nothing like the boy people remember. Isn't it better for you if people on the street don't know who you are, if they don't recognize you?"

"She told you, didn't she?"

Papa swiped at his forehead. "Told me what?"

"*That's* what this is about."

"Told me what, Romi?"

"Where I came from. Who I am. *What* I am. She only visited me once; did you know that? Just the one time. The first week I was here. She told *me* then. Can you believe that? Saying those things to a twelve year-old *boy*?"

"I ... I don't ..." Papa's voice trailed off, and Romain watched as his eyes moved up and to the left. Dr. Tanner called that *accessing a visually constructed image*. "I don't know what you mean."

Romain stared at him. He didn't want to push it. "Has she spoken to Dr. Tanner?" he asked.

"Many times."

"Recently?"

Papa said he wasn't sure.

"She doesn't believe him."

"Romi, it's not a case of believing him or not. This is science, and your mother ... She's been doing her own research, talking to some of the doctors who don't agree with Tanner. There are many of them, you know. Tanner's treatment is controversial. You're the only one he's treated. The other doctors, they say one person isn't enough to prove anything. Your mother tends to think so, too."

"So you're on her side now."

"There are no *sides*, Romi. There never have been. You know that. I'm just trying to keep the peace. I want the best solution for everyone. Don't you see? The best thing you can do is to show her that you're not what she thinks you are. Take the job. Stay out of trouble. Be responsible. Maybe in a year or two, we can talk about this again. She might agree to let you come live with us. Romi …" His father's voice cracked. "I just want my family back. Do you understand that? I just want my family back. Together. The way we were before … before all *this*."

Romain remembered the moment, six years earlier, when the verdict was handed down. *Guilty. Of murder.* Mama would have been allowed into the court—she'd already given her evidence; the trial was over—but she didn't bother to come. Only Papa was there.

Before they led Romain away, back to the cells to await transport, Papa had run from his seat, grabbed him by both shoulders and promised him that he would be there for him, on the other side.

"I'm going to make this right," Papa had said, his eyes glistening. "I know it was just an accident. I believe you, Romi. I do. Serve your time. You'll be eighteen before you know it. Then you and I, we'll make you a new life."

But now, just a few days before Romain was due for release, Papa had suddenly changed his mind. There could be only one explanation for it.

Mama had got to him.

"It's okay, Papa," Romain said now, pushing his chair back from the table. Hearing the scrape of steel on the concrete floor, one of the guards by the door stepped forward to escort Romain back to his cell. "It's fine."

"What do you mean?"

"You don't need to help me. I understand. I can put myself in your shoes and see what it's like from your perspective. Dr. Tanner taught me that. Do whatever Mama says, okay? I'll be fine. I can manage by myself."

"But I …"

"Really, Papa. It's okay. I mean it."

Romain stood up and walked around the table to Papa's side. Papa stood up, too, a little unsure at first, his brow furrowed in confusion. But when Romain moved to embrace him, there was no hesitation.

He held Romain tight and whispered into his ear, "No matter what happens, you'll always be my son. Remember that, Romi. No matter what happens, you will always be my son."

Romain said nothing.

He didn't need to see Papa's eyes to know that *that* was a lie.

* * *

Romain started his eighteenth birthday in a cell and ended it on a bunk in a city hostel owned by the prison service.

The social worker assigned to him— a woman named Marie who smelled of dirty clothes and talcum powder—said he could stay there for up to seven nights, and gave him a small envelope with a few hundred francs inside. It was his money. He had earned it by working in the prison library. She told him to keep it on his person and not to let anyone else know he had it, especially none of the other men in the hostel.

"*Other men*" sounded so strange. Was he a man now?

Romain lay awake all night that first night, staring at the ceiling. He kept one palm pressed against the envelope he had hidden underneath his sweatshirt. All around, strange and unfamiliar sounds threatened him from the dark.

There was another envelope hidden behind the first. It contained the handful of creased family photographs he'd had with him in prison, and a real estate agent's flyer for a three-bedroom semidetached house in the Parisian suburbs. Papa had given him the flyer months ago, when his offer was accepted. Since then, Romain had handled it so much that the ink began to fade and the paper to separate at the folds, but the street address was still legible.

Romain left the hostel at the break of dawn. Signs for the Metro sent him around two corners and then into a train station with a huge, curved roof that let the birds in. There were people everywhere.

A café on the main concourse displayed shelves and shelves of pastries that made Romain's mouth water and his stomach growl, but he didn't want to spend any money just yet. He didn't know how long it would have to last him. He could ignore his hunger for a while.

He *did* have to buy a Metro ticket. He went to one of the ticket desks because he didn't know how to use the machines, and asked for a day pass. The girl behind the desk let him have a student rate even though he had "forgotten" his student ID.

She smiled at him when she handed him the ticket. Remembering what Tanner had told him, Romain smiled back, mirroring her body language.

The Metro was easy enough to follow, although the noise of it made Romain's head hurt. There was so much going on out here in the world—traffic, television screens, people talking on phones they carried around with them—he was finding it difficult to concentrate. It was a relief to emerge from the RER station at the end of his journey to find himself on a quiet, leafy suburban street.

He found the house easily, not least because the FOR SALE sign was still in the garden. A SOLD! sticker was peeling off it.

Keeping his head down, Romain walked past it once or twice, trying to gauge whether anyone was currently inside. There was no car in the driveway, no noise coming from the house. A large window at the front gave him a view of a small, neat sitting room. The TV in the corner was switched off.

It appeared that no one was home.

Along the side of the house was a narrow alleyway, blocked by a wooden gate secured with a padlock. The gate was as tall as Romain. Using a nearby rubbish bin as a step up, Romain hoisted himself over and dropped down the other side.

Around back was a small, mossy patio and a set of patio doors. He tried the handle: locked.

Cupping his hands against the glass, he looked inside.

Romain could see a living room with a kitchen at one end. Packing boxes were everywhere, and leaning against the opposite wall was a large framed picture of Mama, Papa, Jean, and Mikki, huddled together in front of the castle at Disneyland.

There was a sudden burst of music from above Romain's head— something loud and angry. Rock, with indecipherable lyrics. More noise than music.

Romain looked up and saw that a small window on the first floor was cracked open. That's where the music was coming from. But who was playing it?

Could it be Jean?

The last time Romain had seen Jean, the boy was only eight years old. He had been sitting on a carpeted floor with shelves of green leather-bound books behind him, playing with his plastic wrestlers.

Talking about what had happened that day at the pond. Testifying against his own brother, via video link.

The brother who had only been trying to protect him.

Did Jean understand that? Did he remember? Or had Mama poisoned his thinking since? Papa was lost to him now, but Romain suddenly had an overwhelming need for Jean to know the truth, to know that he had done what he had done for his little brother.

Yes, things had gotten out of hand. Yes, the darkness had slipped out of him for a moment. But Dr. Tanner had taken care of that. He was good now.

Romain made his way back to the front of the house and rang the doorbell. He waited nervously for an answer. None came. He rang the bell again. A moment later, he heard movement on the other side of the door. Footsteps on the floor. Boots on wood, it sounded like. A beat of silence, perhaps while someone looked through the peephole. Then, finally, the turn of a lock.

The door opened to reveal a tall, thin teenage boy standing in the hall. Not as tall as Romain, but almost. His long, dark hair was disheveled, his face puffy from sleep, the laces on his black boots frayed and loose.

"Yeah?" he said, squinting in the daylight.

"Jean?"

A frown. "Who are you?"

Romain had no lie prepared. Perhaps he should have had. Perhaps he shouldn't have gone anywhere near the house until he had some elaborate story all worked out. He was a good liar when he was prepared. It would have worked. It could have.

But there was something about Jean, something about the familiar blue eyes of the boy he had known so well, now set into a young man's face. It broke open something inside Romain.

He thought of that same face at the edge of the pond, the fright the child had gotten when Bastian screamed at him. Earlier than that: Jean asleep on the bunk below, in superhero pajamas, his mouth hanging open. Back at the house in the countryside: Jean running after him on the path that led to the lake, to their fort, calling his name, begging him to wait.

It made him never want to go back to that awful hostel. He didn't want to have to fend for himself. He wanted to come home to his family. He wanted to stop paying for something he had done in one moment of madness, back when he was just a boy.

So he said, "It's me, Jean. It's Romi. Don't you recognize me?"

The look of sleep slid off Jean's face.

"I just want to talk to you," Romain said. "That's all. I don't know what Mama has told you, but we're brothers, Jean. Brothers. Nothing changes that. That day by the pond, I was just trying to protect you. I went too far, I know, but that was a mistake. Do you remember that day? Do you remember it, Jean?"

Jean took a step backward. Tripped on the edge of the doormat, recovered, and took another step.

"Jean, wait." Romain stepped inside. "You don't have to be afraid of me. I won't hurt you. I won't hurt anybody. They cured me. They found out what was wrong and they made it all go away."

"I'm calling the police."

Jean took another step back, retreating toward the kitchen.

There was a phone in there. Romain had seen it through the patio doors, on the wall by the fridge.

"There's no need, Jean. No need for police. It's just me. Romi. I only want to talk to you. We can talk about the day by the pond if you—"

"*Stop* calling it that!" Jean shouted suddenly. "'The day by the pond.' You *murdered a child*, you fucking psycho. You held him under the water until he stopped fighting and *drowned*."

"I thought you said you didn't—"

"I know what happened. The whole country knows what happened."

"It was an accident. I didn't mean to."

"Didn't mean to kill him when you pushed him underwater and held him there? What did you *think* was going to happen? Did you think he had *gills*?"

Romain felt the situation slipping away from him. Things weren't going according to plan. He should leave, but he couldn't let Jean call the police. He could say Romain had broken in or tried to attack him, and then, before you knew it, Romain would be back in jail.

Adult jail, now that he was eighteen. Romain took another step forward; Jean, another back.

"I was only a child," Romain said. "A *child*. If you'd just let me explain …"

"What's your excuse for Mikki, then? Was that an accident, too?"

"Yes, it was."

"That's not what Mama says."

"You can't believe everything she says, Jean."

"Oh, but I can believe everything you tell me? The convicted child murderer? The certified *psychopath*?"

Jean turned and ran, disappearing through the open door at the end of the hall and into the living room. But he went right instead of left, away from the phone. Then Romain remembered: *mobile phones.* Papa said lots of people had them now. Did that include teenagers?

A wailing siren startled him.

The house alarm. Jean had tripped it, which was actually quite clever of him, Romain had to admit.

He covered the rest of the hall in just a few strides, reaching the living room just as the patio door smacked loudly against its frame.

Jean had gone outside.

Romain followed him into the garden, picking up his pace now. The alarm company would be calling the house any second, and if nobody picked up and said the right words, the police would arrive soon.

He should leave. Right now. But …

Convicted child murderer. Certified psychopath.

He had to talk to Jean first, had to make him listen.

There was no sign of him at the back of the house, but there was only one place he could go.

Romain rounded the corner and saw the boy halfway over the side gate, legs swinging, struggling for purchase.

"Jean!" He ran to the gate and took hold of Jean's legs. "Come down from there. I just want to talk, for God's sake. You don't have to run from me. I'm not going to hurt you."

But Jean wasn't listening. He was wriggling and kicking and struggling to pull himself up and over the gate. Clearly, he had used all his energy getting up on it. His thin arms and bony shoulders suggested that he didn't have much to draw on in the way of strength.

"Jean, please. Stop."

"Get the *fuck* away from me," he yelled over his shoulder.

"Will you stop? Let me get something you can stand on." Romain looked around the garden. "Is there a ladder here?"

Jean, louder, scrabbling to get over the gate: "Help! Somebody help me!"

"I'll go around the front," Romain said. "I'll push the bin against the gate and help you over."

The legs went up and over.

Jean had pulled himself over the gate, but he must not have had enough energy left to control his descent on the other side.

He kept going, falling headfirst, and let out a yelp.

There was the sound of plastic rolling on concrete, and then nothing but the wail of the house alarm.

"Jean?" Romain called. "Jean? Are you okay?"

No answer.

"Jean?"

For a moment, Romain let himself believe that Jean had somehow managed to land on the other side, get up and dust himself off, and run away, all without making a sound.

But he knew that wasn't the case.

The darkness must be getting stronger. This time, it had only to propel him as far as the house. He had done the rest himself. Even when he was trying to be good, bad things still happened.

This wasn't his fault. But it was all his fault, too.

Romain pulled himself up to the gate and peered over the top. Jean was lying in a heap at the bottom of the other side, an apron of red, shiny blood oozing out from underneath him. He was completely still, and the eye that Romain could see was open, unmoving. The rubbish bin lay on its side a few feet away.

Another brother, gone.

Now Romain really had no one.

He heard them then, in the distance: sirens, getting louder. Coming this way.

ADAM

"Start from the beginning," Peter said. He was leaning against the desk, arms folded across his chest, looking toward my cabin door. I had it open five or six inches, just as it had been when I woke up a few minutes earlier. I had knocked on the wall to wake him up then, even though it wasn't even seven o'clock yet. "Did you lock it when you came in last night?"

"Of course I did."

I was sitting on the edge of my unmade bed, still in the clothes I had boarded the ship in. Holding Sarah's scarf in shaking hands. Navy with white butterflies. *A summer scarf,* Sarah would tell you. (I had made a joke about it—a bad one involving winter flip-flops. All I got was an eye roll.) The same scarf she had been wearing when she walked through the terminal doors in Cork. It was frayed and a little washed out, but I was nearly positive that was how it had looked when I last saw it.

There were no discernible stains.

"Someone came in here," I said. "Someone with a key. And they put this on the bed beside me. While I was *asleep.* And I think we both know who."

Peter looked dazed.

"Ethan *knows,* Peter. He knows we're here. Someone's told him. I knew it. When you asked that bartender last night, I *knew* it was a bad idea. And this …" I looked down at the scarf. "This is a message."

"Would he have a key, though?" Peter asked. "I mean, he's in the food department. Do they have keys?"

"If they don't, I'm sure he could've gotten one."

"Was anything taken? Did you check?"

"Everything's here."

It had been easy to determine: all I brought with me was my bag, and it contained only some crumpled clothes.

Peter crossed the room to sit on the sofa. He ran a hand through his hair. I had never seen him like this before. Nervous. On edge. Distressed.

"A message," he repeated. "Saying what, exactly?"

"Well, it's obvious, isn't it? He killed her." I surprised myself by how matter-of-factly I said it. "How else would he have the scarf? It's the one she was wearing when she left. How would he even know that if he wasn't the one to meet her on the plane, or at the other end?"

I pulled the material through my fingers. Would it still smell of her? She wore the same perfume all the time. Miracle or Miracles or something. Came in a pink bottle.

I started to lift the scarf to my nose, but stopped. That would be too much. That would break me.

"It's a threat," I said. "He's telling me he knows I'm here. He killed Sarah, he knows I'm here, and, if I stay, he'll kill me, too."

Peter's eyes widened. "You don't think he'd ...?"

"We're not safe here. We should go."

"*Go?*" He started shaking his head. "We can't *go.*"

Then I remembered something: this wasn't my cabin.

"Last night, at Fizz," I said. "Did you have to sign a receipt?"

"What?"

"For the food and drink. Was it charged to the room? Do you remember?"

"I ... I don't know. Oh, there may have been a slip I had to sign because I had a glass of white wine after you left." He looked embarrassed. "That's not in the all-inclusive, so it was added to the Swipeout account, and I had to sign for it."

"Which name did you put?"

"My own, of course."

I turned on the TV with the remote and pointed to the "Welcome Aboard, PETER!" message.

"You must have mixed up the Swipeout cards," I said as he frowned at the screen. "Doesn't your TV say, 'Welcome Aboard, Adam'?"

"I haven't checked."

"Something's wrong here."

"Adam, *everything's* wrong here."

"No," I said, holding up the scarf. "I mean something is wrong with *this*. This cabin is in your name. I doubt Ethan knows what I look like, and if he sneaked in here with this, he probably wouldn't hang around to check."

"What are you saying?"

"How come this isn't in *your* cabin? That's the one under my name."

"The reservation is in both our names. You're the lead passenger."

"But *your name* is on this cabin."

"You're presuming he's working off a list. The reservation system or the manifest or whatever. But he could have seen you. Watched you come in here. Followed you." A pause. "Followed *us*."

I didn't find it plausible. I had traveled back down to this deck in an otherwise empty elevator the night before and didn't remember seeing anyone else in the hall when I let myself into my cabin. And what were the chances that, barely an hour after the ship set sail, Ethan happened to be in the bar where Peter and I happened to go first? Far enough away for us not to see him, but close enough to overhear us mention his name?

But I didn't push the point, mostly because Peter seemed genuinely unnerved by this development. Scared, even. And who could blame him?

This should be the point where we call in reinforcements, I thought. Where, finally acknowledging that we need both help and protection, we contact an authority whose job it is to provide those very things.

But who could we call? There was no one.

I looked back down at the scarf. *Just do it.* I lifted my hands and buried my face in the material, breathing in deeply.

"This changes things," Peter was saying, almost to himself. "Perhaps we *should* go."

It did smell of Sarah, of her perfume. The scent was both a comfort and an exquisite pain. And strong! Strong enough to still have the underlying tinge of its alcohol base, the faint burn still detectable under the floral notes.

Too strong to have been sprayed on over a week ago.

The only explanation was that he had her things, too—that he had taken whatever luggage she had in her cabin, found the perfume, and sprayed the scarf just before he broke in and placed it on the bed beside me while I slept.

Who was this man?

What was he?

"Adam," Peter said from the sofa. "I have to tell you something. Something I should have told you long before now."

I lifted my head to look at him. "What? What is it?"

He didn't answer me right away. He looked as if he was deciding something.

"Peter, *what is it?*"

He stood up and went toward the door of the cabin.

"Come with me," he said. "I think it'll be easier for both of us if I just show you."

It took only a few minutes to cross the bay to Villefranche, a sliver of a village tucked into the side of one of the many rocky promontories along the Côte d'Azur. Its attraction was really the view it afforded: a small, secret bay of perfectly still sea, dotted with pleasure boats and yachts. In the distance, atop another rocky outcrop, the pink walls of the Villa Rothschild peeked out through a gap in the trees. Out of sight beyond it, Peter explained, farther east along the coast, were Bono's house in Èze, the glitzy principality of Monaco, and Ventimiglia, the first place across the Italian border where the trains stopped.

I didn't respond to anything he said. I wasn't interested in his local knowledge. I wanted to know what he hadn't told me and was still refusing to reveal.

The bus to Nice was packed with sweaty cruise passengers. I stood by the middle doors, clinging to a hand support, breathing deep and slow to ward off motion sickness—a futile endeavor when facing the wrong way in a bus as it snaked along the looping, twisting roads that climbed and descended the cliffs between Villefranche and Nice, sometimes at such a height and on such a narrow strip of tarmac that there was nothing but air between me and the shimmering water hundreds of feet below. We alighted in a large square paved in two colors of stone set in a checkerboard pattern, crisscrossed with tram tracks and overlooked on three sides by beautiful rust-colored buildings boasting row after row of yellow window shutters.

We hadn't been on the ship for a full day, and already the breadth of the view from this vast open space, the intense sun, and the fresh air felt like a revelation. I'd had enough of endless corridors, fluorescent lighting, and the faint smell of seawater lingering everywhere.

I had a sudden urge to run, to leave this place and not come back. I didn't want to go back on the ship. I could go home, find a way to survive.

I had my passport in my pocket because we'd had to get another set of Swipeout cards en route to the tender platform; we each were carrying a "wrong" key that matched the other's identity, and if we took different tenders back, we'd be in trouble without the "right" one. Sarah's scarf was in my backpack; everything else back in my cabin was either clothes or toiletries I'd be happy to leave behind.

I could go straight home from here, if I wanted to.

But first, I had to know what it was that Peter hadn't told me.

"It's a five-minute walk," he said, setting off across the square. "To, um, my place."

I stared at him. "You *live* here? In Nice?"

"Well, not exactly. I've been staying here. For the last four or five months. It was the place where Estelle was last seen, so ..."

I'd heard that Nice was famous for its promenade, but that was nowhere to be seen. We had entered the city via the port area, and with no line of sight to the sea, I soon lost all sense of direction. We walked fast in silence, along a wide, busy street lined with cafés, real estate agencies, and what must surely be an unnecessary number of pharmacies. I counted six in eight blocks.

Above the ground-floor shops and restaurants, the pale buildings with their bright window boxes were clean and attractive, with shiny brass plates affixed to their doors. At first, I studied them to see if I recognized any words—I didn't. Then I realized that it was dangerous not to look down. The footpaths were littered with piles and smears of dog shit.

We passed under an unsightly railway bridge that was all drooping power cables, torn posters, and graffiti, and then turned up a quieter residential street that sloped gently uphill.

"Here we are," Peter said cheerfully, stopping outside a set of glass doors fitted with a huge gold handle the size and shape of a dinner plate. Thin gold lettering was printed on the glass: BEAU SOLEIL PALAIS. Through the doors I could see marble steps, ornamental gold mirrors hung on cream walls, and rows of numbered mailboxes. Peter unlocked the doors by touching a small plastic key fob to them.

His apartment was on the third floor. We rode up on an elevator the size of a telephone booth.

As soon as I stepped inside Peter's place, I realized that "apartment" wasn't really the word for the space he was staying in. The outside of the Beau Soleil Palais had been impressive—regal, even—with gleaming common areas, but what lay behind Peter's door seemed to have been transplanted in from another building and left to rot.

It was one large, dark room, with what I presumed to be a small bathroom tucked away in one corner. The door was ajar, and I could see something black growing between the cracked off-white floor tiles. Back in the main room, a worn Formica table was pushed against the right wall, in front of a set of grimy French doors half-covered with a bedsheet. Atop a folding table sat a microwave, a hot plate, and a miscellany of crockery and pans. Tucked beneath it, a scratched compact fridge bore the remains of a collage of faded children's stickers. Above the table, a brown stain like rings in a tree stump was spreading out across the ceiling. To my left, an opaque curtain hid whatever space lay behind it.

The air smelled of stale things.

"It's a friend's," Peter said. "He's renovating it to sell, but the work won't start until September. He's letting me stay here until then."

"That's only a couple of weeks away," I said. "Are you going back to London then?"

"We'll see." Peter pointed to the curtain. "The, uh, living room, I suppose you'd call it, is through there. Why don't you go on in. I'll grab us something to drink and we can, uh, talk then. The thing I need to show you—it's all in there."

I looked at the curtain and felt a ripple of unease. What could Peter possibly need to show me that he was keeping in his *home*? Not even his home, but some rotting flat he was temporarily squatting in, in the last place his wife and my girlfriend had supposedly been.

"Go on," Peter said. "It's okay. It's all in there."

I felt for a gap and pushed the curtain aside.

At first, I saw only a battered brown armchair and a stack of old, warped Ikea shelves. Then more French doors, their white paint peeling back and the glass squares flecked with dirt and grime, leading to a little balcony. A house plant, dead for at least a week, sagged over the edges of its pot.

But then, once I was fully inside the room, I saw the boxes.

Piles and piles of them—the cardboard archive type, stacked on the floor and every other available horizontal surface in the room. All labeled with a marker pen, in the same handwriting:

WEST MED ASSAULTS & THEFTS 2009–2012.
CREW EVAL/SECURITY DEPT/ATLANTIC '06

JOHNSON SUIT: DISCOVERY (COPIES)

I counted quickly. There were at least thirty such boxes.

In a far corner, on a second armchair, lay pieces of Blue Wave–branded merchandise: a windbreaker, a baseball cap, a tote bag. Some of them sported the same logo I had seen on Sarah's note; others had the older blue outline of a boat. They were on a stack of newspapers tied together with string, and a collection of glossy brochures that looked about ready to fall over and onto the floor.

It was like an episode of that show *Hoarders* that Sarah so loved, only one where the hoarder had an unusually narrow field of interest and made an effort to catalog things.

In the middle of the room was an antique dining table with two laptops and a box of blank CDs on it.

On one of the closed laptops lay a yellow legal pad with a list scribbled on the first page. I went over to read what it said, but then saw the wall to my right and forgot about everything else.

Its original inhabitants, a series of generic, cheaply framed seaside prints, were on the floor, leaning against a table leg. They had been evicted to make way for a five-foot spread of maps, photographs, news clippings, and letters both typed and handwritten, all tacked to the wall. A schematic of something vaguely oval had been divided into hundreds of little boxes. There were smeared receipts, creased train tickets, and curling photographs. One sheet of paper had a grainy overhead image of a bar printed on it. I could just about make out two women sitting at the counter while a bartender stood behind it, in front of them. It looked like a single frame from closed-circuit television. A clear Ziploc bag was tacked to the wall, with a blue plastic key card inside it—an old Swipeout card by the look of it. My eyes moved across a bus timetable, a printout of a job description for a security guard on the *Fiesta*, and the cover page from an official-looking report: *Carter, P., v. Blue Wave Tours, PLC*. It was dated 2003. On a page torn from a reporter's notebook, a list of dates and times had been scrawled in pencil, and …

Sarah.

She was on the wall, too.

It was one of Moorsey's "Have you seen Sarah O'Connell?" posts—a printout of a screenshot from Facebook. There was a large picture of Sarah's cropped head and shoulders, turned slightly away from the camera, her mouth open in laughter, her eyes bright.

I stepped to the wall, reached out, touched it.

Sarah, what are you doing here?

Another photo was peeking out from underneath it. At first I thought it must be of Estelle, but it was of someone I'd never seen before. A blonde woman in her early twenties, slim and attractive. Scandinavian, maybe. She was wearing a tie-dyed sundress on a dark-sand beach, smiling at the photographer. Someone had written "SANNE VRIJS (*Celebrate* #1?)" on the photo in magic marker. Next to it was a yellowing newspaper article featuring the same photo, written in what looked like German or maybe Dutch. Several paragraphs were circled in red.

Behind me, Peter cleared his throat. I turned to see him standing in the doorway, holding two small bottles of beer.

"What is this?" I asked him.

"It's my research."

"Into what?"

"Into him. Ethan. Well, I didn't know he *was* Ethan until you told me. I hadn't identified him yet."

"What do you mean, you hadn't identified him? Who is this other woman? What *is* all this?"

"Why don't you sit down?"

"Why don't you just tell me what this is?"

"Sarah and Estelle," Peter said after a beat. "They're not the only ones."

Peter was right. I did need to sit down.

I pushed a bundle of Blue Wave merchandise off the armchair and collapsed into it, ignoring the stack of cruise brochures digging into my lower back.

"More than two hundred people," Peter was saying, "have disappeared without a trace from cruise ships in the last twenty years. We've only been keeping count that long, apparently. Some of these can be put down to tragic accidents—usually involving alcohol—and others, sadly, appear to be suicides. But many of them can't be explained at all. When Estelle disappeared and Blue Wave started stonewalling me, I started doing my own research into the statistics. In the last year, I've dug up every single thing I could find—every police report, internal memo, Internet forum thread—about cruise ship disappearances, trying to find similarities. Looking for a pattern, for any connections to Estelle's case. Searching for any disappearances that, in fact, might be something else. And so, when you contacted me about Sarah and told me about the passport and the note, just like Estelle ..." Peter cleared his throat. "Well, it wasn't the second time I'd heard of a woman disappearing from the *Celebrate*, and someone she loved back home getting sent her passport with a note stuck inside it. It was the third."

I looked at the young blonde woman's picture on the wall: "SANNE VRIJS (*Celebrate* #1?)."

Peter followed my eyes. "Sanne," he said. "Yes. She disappeared from the ship in June of last year, during its maiden voyage. She was crew. A bartender. A few days after she was last seen aboard the ship, her father received her passport in the post, at home in the Netherlands. This would have been just a few weeks before Estelle went missing."

The beer bottles were sweating on the table. I got up and grabbed one and took a long, cold swig.

"How do you know that?" I asked Peter. "About the passport?"

"I read about it in a news report. There was no mention of a note, so I tracked down an address for her father and got in touch. He said it was a private matter, and wouldn't tell me whether there was a note—which leads me to believe there *was*. Because wouldn't he have just said no, otherwise? And if it said the same thing as Estelle's and Sarah's, he might have interpreted it as a suicide note. Who would tell a perfect stranger about any of *that*?"

"What happened to her? To Sanne."

"She was on the opening team. They're the staff who come aboard the ship once it's been finished but before it opens its doors to the general public. They set up the rooms and the restaurants, clean and test things, complete their training. The first operational cruise is mostly friends and family members of Blue Wave employees, travel writers, et cetera, so anything that goes wrong won't go wrong on premium-paying customers. I think they offer last-minute discount tickets to fill up the rest. Blue Wave maintains that during this first cruise, Sanne got drunk at a crew party and fell overboard. Accidental death. No body, of course. And no CCTV. No witnesses, even though she supposedly fell during a party—which, by definition, requires the presence of a crowd. There's nothing to go on except for what Blue Wave says."

"But that doesn't sound anything like Sarah or Estelle."

"But it was on the *Celebrate*. And her passport was sent home. That's enough for me to assume that a note went with it. Yes, there are some differences, but I think they're down to the fact that Sanne was crew and that this was his first kill on this particular ship. He was probably still working things out. And he's crew, too, let's not forget. It makes sense that he'd target a colleague if he saw an opportunity. Perhaps he even knew her. He could have been involved with her."

"Then you think he's killed on other ships, too?"

"It seems likely, doesn't it? Ethan is what, late thirties? He didn't just wake up one morning last year feeling a compulsion to kill for the first time in his life. There are other unexplained disappearances of women from other companies' cruise ships, but no other incidents where family were sent passports and notes afterwards—not that I can find in the press, anyway."

"Doesn't that timeline strike you as a bit weird, though?"

"What do you mean?"

"Think about it. Sanne disappears in June, Estelle in August, and then Sarah in August again. What's he doing for the year in between?"

Peter looked at me pointedly, waiting for the penny to drop. It didn't.

"What?" I asked.

"We know that for some of it, at least, he was in Ireland. Courting Sarah."

I took another long swig of beer, swallowing it back until my eyes watered.

"He has it all worked out," Peter said. "On these ships, individual crimes go unsolved and sometimes even unreported. That's bad enough if these crimes are random. But what if the *same person* was committing crimes on a regular basis? What if they were all murders? Who would realize there was a pattern? Who would even have a *chance* to see that there was?"

Peter's eyes had taken on a wild, crazed look.

"*No one,*" he said, answering his own question. "No one has all the information, so no one can connect the dots. Brilliant for you if you're the kind of sick monster who enjoys ending lives, right? What better place to do it than on a cruise ship? Not only are you likely to get away with the individual murders, the cruise company will even *help you do it*. And you can practically be certain no one will ever say, 'Hey, doesn't this seem like the work of just one guy?' Not to mention the fact that you have a never-ending supply of fresh meat"—I winced at this—"and hundreds of dark corners and private balconies *designed* not to be overlooked, for Christ's sake, where you can commit your murders in peace, while everyone on board is busy drinking and having fun in holiday mode, under the gravely mistaken impression that they are safe. Oh, and there's an ocean all around you to dump bodies in, you work at night so the dark helps you, too, and you have *professional cleaning staff* to wipe away any evidence that might link you forensically to the crime. It's downright *perfect* for you, you sick bastard. You probably can't even believe your luck."

"I don't know," I said. "This all seems ..." *Too crazy? Too frightening? Too perfect a fit for the facts?* "Estelle and Sarah, yes. We can't deny the connection there. But this Sanne woman? Maybe the company sent her passport back with the rest of her belongings. I mean, did her father speak English? Are you sure he understood what you were asking him?"

"There is something else," Peter said. "Something the three of them have in common. None of them is American."

"What's *that* got to do with anything?"

"This maritime law, international waters thing—it doesn't work. How can it possibly? You get two police officers instead of a police force, they have to travel halfway around the world to get to you, and by the time they arrive, there's usually no physical evidence for them to examine, or witnesses to speak to. It's ridiculous. But it works for the cruise lines *because* it doesn't work. Nothing goes to court. No one gets charged. Justice is never served. And no one ever does anything about it—except for the United States. They changed the law—or, to be specific, they created their own law that supersedes the existing one. Now if an American citizen goes missing from a cruise ship, no matter where that ship is at the time or what country it's registered in or what the damn captain says, the FBI is awarded jurisdiction. It *automatically* becomes an FBI investigation. The FBI, who have the skill and resources to join the dots. Who have whole departments who would try to make connections. The foremost experts on serial murderers in the whole world."

Peter had started pacing up and down in a line parallel to his wall of research. "So doesn't it strike you as a bit unlucky for the law that here we are with a slew of missing women and yet not *one* of them is a citizen of the United States—the most enthusiastic cruising nation on earth? He's *purposely avoiding American victims.* Don't you see? He's found the perfect hunting ground, and he's doing everything he can to preserve it."

Peter's face was red.

"I think maybe *you* should sit down," I said to him.

He waved a hand dismissively. "No one cares about this. No one gives a shit about Estelle. About *my wife.* Do you think I can just let that go? If we were talking about a hotel or a holiday resort, it would have been burned to the ground by now. At the very least, some sort of investigative task force would've been assigned to it to find out what the bloody hell was going on. But because these things happen to float, no one even *knows.*" He stopped pacing and turned to me. "No one's interested in helping us, Adam. The law is a joke. Ethan has thought every bit of this out. Blue Wave's plan is to cover its corporate ass. It's up to us. Don't you see? You and me. We're the only ones who can prove that this is even happening, and you want to pack up and go home."

"Why didn't you tell me all this at the beginning?"

"Because you would've thought I was a nutter. One of those Internet freaks who prey on people like us—people who have lost loved ones. The psychics and the angel talkers and the alien abductees."

When he saw the look of recognition on my face, Peter smiled sadly. "Yeah, I got those, too. It was undeniable that Estelle and Sarah were connected, so I stuck with that. I said no more. And this *just* happened to you. I've had a year with it. If I had told you all this at the beginning, over the phone, well, we wouldn't be here."

"So why tell me now?"

"You were upset last night because you were scared. You *are* scared, I know. So am I. Sometimes, I think to myself that I'll just go home, back to London, and find a way to live alongside this pain. That even if I keep going, I may never know for sure what happened to Estelle. And I know that's what you've been thinking, too, right?"

I nodded.

"Ethan has killed at least two women already, Adam. We're the only two people who know. Who believe. So this isn't just about us anymore. It's about the woman he kills next. And the one after her. It's about his future victims. Their blood will be on our hands. Don't you want to stop this from happening to anyone else?"

"I want to," I said, "but how can I? Before all this, I sat at home in sweats all day. My main concern was when I would eat next and what I'd have when I did. I'm a terrible liar, I'm a coward, I'm—"

"Estelle was pregnant," Peter said.

"Oh, Jesus, Peter. I'm sorry."

"When I said I didn't want her to go on the cruise? That was the real reason why. The week before, I'd read about some norovirus outbreak on a cruise ship in the States. I didn't think it was a risk a pregnant woman should take."

"Estelle didn't agree with you?"

"She thought I was overreacting, but we'd been trying for so long …"

We fell into silence for a minute, thinking about what we had lost.

"My point," Peter said, "is that you don't have to do anything except help me find him. Once we do, I'll take care of the rest. This monster, he didn't just take my wife. He took my *family.* He took my future from me. He did it when I wasn't there, when I was sitting back at home, oblivious. I failed in my duty as her husband. I failed to protect her. But I'm not going to fail her now. I'm prepared to do whatever has to be done." He looked me in the eye with a steady gaze. "What I'm saying is, I don't have to go back. It's okay if I don't come out the other side of this the same way I went in."

"I'm not sure I understand."

"I want an investigation, Adam. An investigation and a trial. I want him put in prison, made to suffer for what he did. I want him to have to tell us *what* he did and why. If I can't make that happen, if it starts to look like that is an impossible task, then I'll settle for stopping this from happening to anyone else. I want you to know that. Not because I expect you to do the same, but so you'll know that if something happens, well, we both don't have to …"

I thought he was talking about risking his safety, about putting himself in danger, planting himself in the path of a killer to lure him out of the dark, if need be. I thought he was talking about ways to bring Sarah and Estelle's killer to justice, to find Ethan and get him to confess—trick him into doing it if we had to.

"What do you need me to do?" I asked.

"Get back on the ship with me now. Agree to use Megan, enlist her help. Under false pretenses, yes, but she's not in any danger. He avoids Americans, we know. We'll stick to our surprise-a-friend story with her. Three of us searching the ship will be better than two."

"Okay," I said. "I can do that. I will."

Peter looked relieved. "Good. Because I can't find him on my own, Adam. And time is running out."

Peter wanted to check the mailbox he had rented, and I wanted to check my emails, so we agreed to meet back on the ship. I got the distinct impression that Peter thought I was bailing on him, so I reassured him more than once that I would see him aboard. Then I wandered back down the wide street full of pharmacies, turned off onto a narrow, cobblestoned pedestrian street, and kept going until I spotted an Internet café. It was the kind that catered to gamers: high-spec equipment, comfortable leather chairs, and partitions between the consoles. I paid for half an hour and bought a coffee from the machine, then pulled my chair as close to the desk as my internal organs would allow.

Rose had sent me several emails since I spoke to her. The first couple had been written in all caps and sprinkled with typos—rants she had evidently fired off in a fit of rage after our last phone call. These had been followed by a couple of longer, more thoughtful ones, in which she had calmed down enough to give me all the logical reasons why I should return home straightaway. Finally, she had given in and done what I asked: searched for Ethan Eckhart online.

She found more profiles for him—Facebook, which he had locked down, and LinkedIn, which he had left mostly bare—and a much better, clearer picture, taken from a Facebook group for employees of something called Les Sablons, which appeared to be a campground on the southwest coast of France. It was dated nearly ten years back, but despite the much blonder hair then, the younger Ethan was easily recognizable. Rose had found no evidence of Sarah anywhere in his online presence, but interestingly, she *had* found a sample of his handwriting.

It was a screen shot of an Instagram post—Rose noted that he hadn't posted anything to the app for nearly a year, so pickings were slim there on the content front. But what she had found was a close-up of a coffee table on which a cup and a notebook had been artfully arranged, tinged with a sepia filter. The caption read, "To-Do List Time!" and "TO-DO LIST" was written in block capitals across the top of the notepad, above a line that read, "#1: Think of things to put on to-do list"—also handwritten but in cursive underneath. Rose had typed, "Recognize it? Passport envelope?" alongside the picture, but I didn't. But so what? He could have changed it on the envelope. Written it with his other hand. Got someone else to do it. We didn't even know for sure that the writing on the notepad was his. He could have snapped someone else's notepad, or that might be someone else's picture, which he had merely reposted. Both the handwriting and the setup looked feminine to me.

I went back to the picture of him at the campground. And had an idea.

I saved the photo to the computer's desktop. Then I navigated to the profile page Cusack had found—the one from which she had discovered that Ethan worked on the ship—and saved the picture from there, too.

Then I went to Google and searched for *"Estelle Brazier + Becky."* A list of news articles appeared, all dated from August or September of last year. I had seen them all before, when I first stumbled upon Peter's story on the Cruise Confessions website, and had gone to Google to search for more information.

I had to open three of them before I found mention of Becky's last name: Richardson.

Google found dozens of Becky Richardsons, and adding "London" to the mix didn't narrow it down much. I went back to the articles, opening them again until I found a picture of Becky and Estelle together. It looked as if it had been taken on Becky's wedding day. Estelle was in a pink bridesmaid's dress.

I saved that picture to the desktop, too. Then I went back to Google again and dragged it into the search box.

The only time I had ever seen Google's search-by-image function used before was on TV, to track down creeps with emotional problems who were pretending to be someone else—or multiple someone elses—online. But it worked. The top match was Becky's Facebook page, where the image had originally been posted. Her feed was filled with photos of her young children: a girl of about four or five and a boy who was just a toddler.

I decided against sending her a message through Facebook. Since we weren't friends, it would go to her "Other" inbox, which most users rarely checked. I needed to find out whether Becky recognized Ethan *now*, not in a few weeks' time. I scrolled down her profile page, looking for clues to where I might find an email address for her.

On the bottom left side of the page was a list of the public Facebook pages Becky had liked. A well-known clothing store, John Mayer, an artisan chocolate shop, a famous diet book, *Ideal Homes* magazine …

And Parkview High School, Kilburn.

Why would Becky "like" a high school's page if she didn't have children old enough to go there? Could it be because that was where she worked?

Back to Google. "Becky Richardson Parkview High School Kilburn London." Search.

The top result was the "Staff" page of Parkview High's website, on which Becky was listed as the school's librarian. Below a picture of it was an email address, which I copied.

Thank you, Internet.

I hit Compose and pasted Becky's email address into the "To" box. Then I typed a message explaining who I was, how Sarah had disappeared just as Estelle had, how I had gotten a passport and a note, too, and how Peter and I had boarded the *Celebrate* to try to find the man we believed was responsible for this: Ethan. Could she please take a look at his picture and let me know if she had ever seen him before, if she could remember seeing him on the ship last August? I explained that my phone probably wouldn't work at sea but that I would check my email as often as I could. Then I attached the picture and pressed Send.

I drummed my fingers on the desk. What else should I do while I was here? I ran through everything Peter and I had been talking about …

And stopped at Sanne.

Peter thought there was, in all likelihood, a note to go with her passport, but we didn't know for sure. Maybe I could find something about it online. I Googled her name and the word "*Celebrate.*"

Most of the results were in Dutch. I had put enough things through automatic translation programs to know that using them to make sense of anything was a fool's errand.

I thought there might be an easier way. A reverse way. I looked up the Dutch for "passport" and "cruise ship"—"*paspoort*" and "*cruise-schip*"—and put that into the search box along with Sanne's full name.

There were plenty of search results, but none of them contained all three things. There were several stories about Sanne and a cruise ship, but none that included both those things *and* mentioned a passport, too.

In fact, none of the Sanne stories that came back said anything at all about a passport. So how had Peter found out that her family had received it in the mail?

"Whatcha doin'?" Megan whispered into my right ear.

I bolted upright, knocking the coffee cup over with my arm. It spilled onto the desk—a thin caramel-colored lake expanding fast in the direction of the keyboard.

I heard Megan cry, "Oh, God!" while I scrambled for something to mop it up with. I looked over the partition to my left and saw a newspaper that had been abandoned on the next desk. I grabbed it and threw it on top of the coffee, stopping the flow, patting it so it would soak up all the liquid.

I turned to face Megan.

"I am *so* sorry," she said. She looked as though she was trying not to laugh. "I was sitting over there and I saw you come in. I thought it would be funny to creep up on you. I guess I didn't think about the coffee."

"Don't worry about it," I said. "It's fine. It just might take me a minute to get my heart rate back to normal."

Her eyes flicked to the screen.

"I was just finishing up," I said, hastily moving the mouse to close the browser window. "Are you heading back to the ship?"

"Not for a little while. I thought I'd get some lunch. Want to join me? I do owe you a coffee at the very least."

Just the idea of trying to make small talk while my brain whirred with thoughts of cruise ship crimes and passports and Ethan's face left me exhausted, but Peter had made it clear that we needed her help, and I had to agree with him.

"Sure," I said. "Let's do it."

"Great. There's a good place on Massena that does subs to go. We can take them to the beach." She leaned in close to me, lowering her voice to a conspiratorial whisper. "Then you can tell me who you and Peter *really* are, and what you're really doing on that ship."

We walked along the promenade until we came to a public stretch of Nice's pebble beach, pleasantly free of unsteady picnic tables, uniformed waiters, and bright-blue parasols. Unfortunately, it was covered in people and their beach-time accoutrements instead, and we struggled to find a gap in between the folding deck chairs and oily bodies. We ended up eating our lunch perched on a rise just feet from the crashing surf. The waves were retreating as the tide went out, turning and churning pebbles as it did.

"Okay," Megan said when we were both sitting cross-legged, having found a somewhat comfortable distribution of weight on the rocks. "Go."

I tried to sound as casual as possible. "Go with what?"

"Come on, Adam, I'm not stupid," she said with a wry grin. "Two grown men who aren't dating each other, going on their first cruise alone together? Who supposedly met in university even though you're from different countries and he's, what, ten to fifteen years older than you? My theory was that you were having an affair with each other, until I saw what you were looking up in that Internet café."

"You were *spying* on me?"

"I just happened to see your screen." Megan took a bite of her sandwich. With her hand in front of her mouth, she said, "Come on, then. What's the big secret?"

"There isn't one."

"Then why were you looking up cruise ship crimes?"

I took a big enough bite of my sandwich to make talking impossible, so I could think of a reply.

A lie based on the truth looked like the best bet.

"Peter and I came on this cruise to relax," I said, "and we *are* old friends who met at university. The reason I was looking up cruise ship crimes is because, when I woke up this morning, the door of my cabin was standing wide open, and I know I closed it before I went to bed last night."

"Huh." Megan made a face. "Careless cabin attendant?"

"Maybe. But I had a Do Not Disturb sign on my door."

"You think someone broke in?"

"I don't know. That's why I was Googling it, to see if there was anything on those cruise forums or wherever about something similar happening to someone else."

I watched her face. She seemed to buy it. "Was anything taken?" she asked.

"No, I don't think so."

The scarf was lying on the pebbles beside me, carefully stowed inside my bag.

But something was delivered.

"That's kind of weird," Megan said.

"Have you ever heard of anything like that? Break-ins on cruise ships? Or, you know …" I looked out at the sea. "Other stuff. Other crimes."

"Things happen, yeah. But nothing that doesn't happen on land."

"What kind of stuff?"

"Thefts. Assaults. People have accidents. They disappear. It doesn't happen very often, though."

"That's reassuring. How often is 'not very'?"

"I don't know. It's something like two hundred people since the midnineties. I read that somewhere, I think."

Peter had said almost exactly the same thing. "You don't sound very concerned," I told her.

"I'm not." Megan rubbed her hands together over the pebbles, cleaning crumbs from her fingers. "Did you ever hear the phrase 'guns don't kill people; people do'?"

"Yeah," I said. "And it's bullshit. A gun may need a person to point it at another person and pull the trigger, but it's infinitely easier to shoot someone in an instant than, say, spend a minute strangling them to death. Also, accidents. It's incredibly difficult to *accidentally* strangle someone, but people shoot other people by accident all the time. Therefore, guns *do* kill people, since more people die just because they happen to be around."

Megan was staring at me. "You done there, Mr. Gun Control?"

"Yeah," I said a little sheepishly. "Sorry."

"I was just going to make the point that theft, violence, murder, and all that jazz—they're all crimes committed by people. Wherever you have people, you'll have those crimes. And cruise ships are full of what, Adam? *People.* Thousands of them. What's the difference between them and hotels? Have you ever worked in a hotel?"

I shook my head.

"Well, I have. Lots of them. So trust me when I say that *all sorts* of crap goes down in hotels. They're a great place to commit suicide, for starters. You have a room you can lock yourself into, a nice, big bathtub to do the business in, and you know for sure that you'll eventually be found, and by a stranger. No loved one of yours has to live out their years with the image of your cold blue body tattooed on their brain. Opportunistic rapists love it, too. Do you know why most hotels train their housekeepers not to leave guest-room doors propped open while they work inside? Because any guy passing by could let himself in, rape them, and then leave again, and there'd be no proof he was ever in the room, because he didn't have to swipe his card or put his fingers on the door handle to get in there. Then you have stressed-out families who shouldn't even be together, let alone cramped in a hotel room ... The last place I worked? We had a woman call Security in the middle of the night, from a cell phone, to say she was thinking of hurting her children. Security had to call in everyone on its payroll to check every guest room, one by one."

"They find anything?"

"Thankfully, no. But just a couple of weeks later we had a murder-suicide. An engineer went into one of the suites because the one below had a water stain spreading across its ceiling, and found a guest who had slit his wrists in the bath. The rooms director was dealing with the coroner when he looked at the reservation and realized that *two* people had checked into the room. The guy's girlfriend was in a suitcase in the closet."

"That's awful," I said.

"That's *people.*"

"But don't you think it's worse on a cruise ship?"

"Why would it be?"

"Because it's easier to get away with things, isn't it? I mean, there's the whole maritime law thing."

"The what?"

I explained it briefly, leaving out the bit about how Megan could enjoy the protection—or at least attention after the fact—of the FBI.

She'd never heard any of it before.

"I suppose that makes sense, though," she said. "What I don't see is how that makes it easier to get away with things."

I repeated all the reasons that Peter had given me. From insufficient police resources to the sea being a perfect body-dumping ground.

By the time I had finished, Megan was eyeing me suspiciously. "You seem to have thought a lot about this," she said.

"Do I?"

"You know ..." She started folding up her empty sandwich

wrapper. "What you're saying—it's a little bit racist, don't you think? Like, why do you assume that a police officer from a country other than your own isn't as well trained or as good at his or her job as your own guys are?"

"It's not so much that, as that there would be only one or two of them. But maybe they *wouldn't* be as good. Maybe they wouldn't speak the language, for example."

"English, you mean."

"Well, yeah."

Megan rolled her eyes theatrically. "Do you know who Amanda Knox is?"

"The girl who went on trial in Italy for the murder of that British student?"

"The *American* girl, yes. If you were in the States during the trial, you just couldn't get away from it. It was everywhere. And running through all the coverage, every station, every interviewer, every talking head: the idea that Italy didn't know how to *do justice,* not like our fantastic country, the leading edge of democracy, the wonderful United States—which, the way people were talking, you'd think had invented the concept."

"You're saying I'm overreacting."

"To your cabin door being open when you woke up this morning? Possibly, yeah."

I had actually forgotten that that was the start of this conversation.

"I'd just like to know who it was," I said. "Or if it was anyone at all. I could've just forgotten to close the door myself, or failed to close it properly."

"I'll tell you what," Megan said. "I know someone who's in security on the *Celebrate.* I used to work with him on Royal Caribbean. If I can find him, I'll get him to check your lock activity. I think he's on shift right now."

"You'd do that?"

"What can I say? I'm a nice gal. Also, I think you're a little crazy, and I like to encourage that."

She winked at me.

"Well, thanks," I said. "Thanks a lot."

"It's going to cost you a drink, though. A proper one. Purchased for me, tonight, in the Horse and Jockey."

"What the hell is that?"

"A bar on the Oceanic Deck."

If she could get me a copy of my cabin door's lock activity, I reasoned, I'd do pretty much anything.

"Isn't the Horse and Jockey a strange name for a bar on a boat?" I asked.

Megan threw her head back and laughed. "Here's a tip, Adam: don't let anyone hear you call it a *boat*."

Shortly after that, we started walking back to the bus station. And between waiting while three buses to Villefranche came and went, already full, and then waiting again to get on a tender, Megan and I didn't reboard the ship until after six.

I knocked on Peter's cabin door to let him know I was back, but there was no answer. I slipped a note beneath it saying I'd meet him in the Horse and Jockey at seven thirty, half an hour before I had told Megan I would see her there. Then I went into my cabin to shower and change.

I knocked on Peter's door again before I left for the bar, but there was still no answer. I could see the tip of my folded note just under his cabin door.

He must not have come back yet. But where was he? The ship was due to sail in a matter of minutes.

And I needed him to get to the bar before Megan did, so I could fill him in on her offer to get the Swipeout activity and tell him about the Becky brainwave I'd had.

But when Peter finally did arrive, he was with Megan. He had only just gotten my note a few minutes before, and met her in the lift on the way there.

It was less than an hour later when Peter first complained of feeling unwell.

We were sitting at the bar, the three of us in a row, me in the middle. A line of pint glasses of beer filled to various levels sat in front of us. Peter was telling Megan a story about some unruly children who had been on his tender ride back from Villefranche.

I was only half listening because what I was really thinking about was the size of Megan's bladder. How long would it be before she needed the loo? That would be my only opportunity to talk to Peter alone, to fill him in. Women may get away with announcing that they were off to the bathroom together for some conspiratorial whispering and a shared urination experience, but I doubted Peter and I would. I didn't want to arouse any suspicions in Megan again.

Another passenger recognized her from YouTube and started waving manically at her from the other end of the bar. Megan smiled back sweetly—falsely, I realized now that I had spent a bit of time with her.

"This is the worst bit," she said to us, slipping off her stool. "I'll just go say hi and come back. If it goes past sixty seconds, come save me."

I watched her go, following the fall of blond hair down to the back of her neck, the outline of the dark bra visible beneath her white T-shirt, the swath of skin exposed in the space between her top and her jeans …

"Jesus Christ," I muttered.

Peter looked at me. "What?"

"Nothing. Listen—"

"It's okay," he said. "You can't control thoughts. It happens."

"Well, I'm …"

I had almost said, *I'm with someone.* But I wasn't. But then, I wasn't single, either. What was I, exactly?

In love with a girl who is gone.

The pain came in a wave. It felt like a physical force, trying to tip me over. Trying to pull me under. Trying to drown me.

I saw Megan turn to start heading back toward us. "I'll be back in a sec," I mumbled, standing up.

I crossed the bar and pushed through the swinging door marked "Gents." I leaned over one of the sinks, took a few deep breaths. Lifted my head to look at my face in the mirror.

I was fighting loneliness, I realized. That's what was going on. It was something that had never occurred to me before when I heard stories about people losing loved ones to tragedy or crime. I understood the horror of not knowing what had happened, yes, and the horror of knowing exactly what had happened, which in some cases could be just as awful, if not worse. I knew what people were talking about when they used terms like "grief-stricken" and "bereft" and "heartbroken." But it had never occurred to me until I was in it myself that there, on top of all those feelings, lay plain old generic loneliness because the one you love isn't there. It's a manageable feeling with an end date if that person is coming back, but a drowning depth of pain and hopelessness if they are not. It might be interminable. I couldn't even say whether it would ever end, or even fade. How could I even face the future like this? What if I always felt this way? How could anyone learn to live with *this*?

The door to the Gents swung open, and Peter walked in. *Stumbled* in, rather. His forehead was shiny with sweat. "Adam," he said breathlessly.

"What's wrong?"

"I don't know." He bent over one of the sinks and splashed water on his face. "I feel a bit … off, or something."

"Listen," I said. "I need to tell you what happened today. Megan says she has a friend on the crew who can maybe get a printout of the key-card activity on the cabin door lock last night. And I got a better picture of Ethan and I emailed it to Becky, asking her if she recognizes him, if she can remember him from when she was on the ship."

Peter straightened back up. "*Estelle's* Becky?"

"Yeah."

"You emailed Becky," he said flatly.

"Yeah. Is … Was that okay?"

There it was again: the hardening of his features, the shadow that crossed his face whenever her name came up.

Only this time, he didn't bother to hide it.

"She doesn't like me," he said, "and I don't like her. She's barely spoken to me since Estelle disappeared. Personally, I think it was because she couldn't stomach the guilt of knowing that *she* was why. Her and that stupid bloody party …" He stopped, bit his lip. "Adam, I think I might be about to throw up."

He pushed past me into a stall, kicking the door shut behind him.

A moment later, vomiting noises filled the air.

I waited a polite length of time before asking whether he was okay. Through the door I heard, "I'll be fine."

"There's something else," I said. "Megan, today—she might have caught me looking up a story about Sanne Vrijs. I went to an Internet café, and apparently she was in there already, and she snuck up on me and saw the screen. I made up a story about the door being open last night and me worrying about cruise ship crimes, and I think she bought it, but we should tread carefully there."

The stall door opened, and a grayer, sweatier Peter walked out. "Why were you looking up Sanne Vrijs?"

"I thought maybe I could find out for sure about the note."

Peter's eyes rolled back in his head.

I stepped toward him. "Peter?"

He fell, slumped back against the sinks. I caught him by the upper arms just before he sank to the floor.

"*Peter?*"

"I think I should go to bed," he mumbled.

"I'll take you. Here, throw your arm around my shoulders."

"I feel ... faint."

"That's okay. Come on."

"The ... drinks ... maybe ..."

"Can you try to stand?"

"You should ... talk ..." He stumbled, and again I helped right him. "Ask about ..." His words descended into incoherence.

Holding Peter up, I kicked the door of the Gents open with one foot ... and found myself face-to-face with Megan.

Her right hand was in a fist, raised in midair, as if she was just about to knock.

"I thought you guys had abandoned ..." She looked from me to Peter, then back to me. "Fuck. Is he okay?"

"Not really. He's been sick. I need to get him back to his cabin."

Megan quickly went to Peter's other side, lifted his arm, and ducked underneath it, helping hold him up.

"Okay," she said. "Come on. I'll help you."

We were in the elevator when I felt the headache coming on.

I opened Peter's cabin door with my "wrong" Swipeout card. The inside looked exactly like mine but with everything turned the other way around—a mirror image.

We got him on the bed and then, with gentle coaxing, persuaded him to lie down. Megan pulled his shoes off while I got the spare blanket from the wardrobe, to cover him.

When I pulled it down, a white envelope came with it—the kind greeting cards come in.

I had seen it before. It was the envelope that Peter kept Estelle's passport and note in. I laid it carefully on his desk. Bending over to do that turned up the dial on the pain at the base of my skull.

"Nice," Megan said. Now that Peter was safely on the bed, she was taking a minute to look around the cabin. "A deluxe exterior. Sea-facing balcony. Treating ourselves, are we? Is yours the same?"

"Yeah," I said. "I'm right next door. These were all that was left. We booked last minute."

"There were no interiors?" She raised an eyebrow. "When did you book?"

"Ah, a couple of weeks ago," I said, realizing that I shouldn't have said anything about that. The more detail I provided, the harder it would be to keep our stories straight.

I looked down at Peter, who had rolled onto his side, away from me. His breathing was deep and regular.

"Do you think he'll be okay?" I asked.

"Yeah, sure. It's probably just something he ate. You might want to leave him something to throw up in, though."

I pulled the plastic wastebasket from under the dressing table and set it down beside the bed.

"And water," Megan said. "Does he have any bottled stuff?"

"Can't you drink from the tap?"

She made a face. "Let's just say I wouldn't recommend it."

"I have a bottle in my room, I think."

I expected just to go and get the water and come back, but Megan followed me out into the corridor and then into 803.

I had bought a four-pack of small mineral water bottles earlier in the day. It was sitting by the bed, unopened. I started tearing at the plastic wrap, but it felt like a far more difficult task than usual, as if my fingers had suddenly grown thick and fat and the connection between them and my brain was only intermittent.

"Hey!" Megan said. "I thought you said this was your first cruise."

"It is."

I managed to free one bottle and started work on another.

"Well, there must've been a mix-up, then," she was saying. "Only returning guests get the bottle of champagne."

Her voice sounded odd to me. Distant, somehow, as if she were walking away. But when I looked, she was in the same spot, only a couple of feet from me.

"Did you talk to your friend?" I asked. "About the lock activity?"

"Oh, I forgot to tell you. It was *you*."

"What?"

Sitting down on the bed, I opened one of the bottles and chugged half.

"I couldn't get anything printed out, because apparently, there's a log for that kind of thing, but my friend had a quick look on the system. He said the door was opened at five thirty, or around then, and it was opened with your key card."

"But that's impossible," I spluttered. "I was asleep."

"Well, I don't know what to tell you."

When I closed my eyes, the beating pain inside my skull only grew more intense in the darkness.

"Adam, are you okay?" Megan crossed the floor and sat on the bed beside me. There was only a scant inch between us. I could feel her presence. "Now *you're* not looking so great. Do you feel like you're going to throw up? Did you both eat the same thing today? Adam?"

The room swayed around me. "Are we moving?" I asked.

"We're on a ship." Megan reached up to brush a strand of hair off my forehead, then pressed the back of her hand to my skin. Her touch felt electric. "I think you might have a temperature. You could be getting a flu or something. It happens a lot on board. Enclosed spaces and recirculated air ..." She moved her hand down to my shoulder, then up to my neck, then across to my cheek.

In spite of myself, I drifted into her touch, leaned into her hand.

"You poor thing," she said. "You'll have to tell Peter that his matchmaking efforts will have to wait for another night." She leaned over and kissed me, gently, on the lips.

"Peter?" was all I could manage to say.

Megan smiled. Her face was just inches from mine. "Are you going to pretend you had nothing to do with it?"

"With ... what?"

"He said that you liked me." Her voice was a playful whisper. Her hand was still on my skin, moving to the back of my neck, settling just below the epicenter of the pain that was threatening to crack open my skull with its shock waves. "But that you were too shy to show me." She sat back suddenly. "Unless he was just messing with me. I mean, no offense, I know he's your friend, and everything, but he's a little off, isn't he? There's something about him. He's a little intense. And tonight in the bar, I don't know how many times I caught him staring at me."

I slid my hand under one of the pillows and pulled out Sarah's scarf.

"Stylish," Megan said, "but is it really your color?"

"Sarah," I said, but it came out sounding like an indecipherable vowel sound.

"What was that? Adam, I think you need to lie down, too. I think you had some questionable buffet fare. It can be …"

I didn't hear the end of her sentence.

A darkness appeared on the edges of my vision and then swarmed in from all sides, reducing it to a pinhole.

Then there was only black.

PART FOUR

DARK WATERS

CORINNE

Everything looked so different at night. The corridors were low-lit and dim, while the public areas and open decks sparkled with twinkling lights and glowed with soft lamps.

The dim light might help her. She was breaking the rules by being off duty and out on the passenger decks. She had changed into the only halfway decent outfit she had brought with her—a delicate summer dress—and was wearing her hair down. Hopefully, if she *did* happen to meet one of her supervisors or another cabin attendant, they wouldn't recognize her out of uniform and without her hair pulled back.

She was on deck eight, methodically walking the corridors, looking for an open cabin door. Some of them had notoriously troublesome locking mechanisms—yet another bug on Blue Wave's brand-new ship—and she was hoping to happen upon one that hadn't locked properly when its occupants left.

But after searching for a full hour across five different decks, Corinne was getting anxious. Every minute she was out in passenger space increased her chances of getting caught there, and so far, every cabin door appeared to be securely locked.

Maybe she should give up and head back to crew quarters. Maybe even try to steal a master key, somehow.

A few doors up ahead, a young family emerged from their cabin. Two adults and four small kids: twin boys of about five or six, one older girl, and one younger. The parents were hissing at each other, muttering expletives under their breaths, while the children tussled playfully, oblivious to the tension. The older girl was the last one out, pulling the door shut behind her.

She didn't look to see whether it had locked.

It hadn't. It banged off the locking mechanism and didn't latch. Corinne knew the sound because she heard it at least a couple of times a shift.

She kept moving, walking past the cabin, noticing the sliver of light between the doorjamb and the door, following the family up the hallway.

Up ahead, the father suddenly stopped and turned around. "Did you lock the door, Jess?"

The older girl nodded slowly.

"Are you sure?"

"Yes, *Dad.*"

"I better check."

The father started back down the hall. He was steps away from Corinne now. She met his eyes, smiled at him.

"It is locked, sir," she said. "I heard the click."

He frowned at her just as she passed.

Damn it. She shouldn't have called him "sir." That was a mistake. But she was used to addressing passengers that way; it had just slipped out.

Corinne kept walking, past the rest of the family now, hoping the father wouldn't bother to go back. She didn't risk turning around to check.

Behind her, one of the children shrieked, "*Stop* it!" whereupon the mother admonished them all. A moment later, they were on the move again, following Corinne down the hall. At the end, she turned right, toward the stairs, while they turned left, toward the elevators. She stopped at a fire evacuation plan, pretending to study it, until the sounds of the family disappeared completely down the other end.

Quickly, she retraced her steps back to cabin 8091. The door was unlatched. The father hadn't gone back.

After checking the corridor, Corinne slipped inside and closed the door behind her, slamming it hard to make sure that this time, it locked.

She turned around, faced into the cabin.

Directly opposite Corinne was a frail, skeletal woman, just skin and bones shrunken inside a gaudy summer dress. Shocked, Corinne went to the mirror above the dressing table to take a closer look. She found red blotches on her neck and chest, blooming purple bruises on her arms. Her hair was thin and wispy, her eyes dull.

Dead already—that was how she looked. She had found him just in the nick of time.

The cabin was family style, with one double bed, two singles, and a child's cot. She found the phone mounted on the wall near the TV. Corinne pressed the button marked GUEST SERVICES and waited for the call to connect.

"Good evening, Mr. and Mrs. Blackwell," a female voice said. "How may I assist you?"

Corinne took a deep breath. This would have to be convincing.

"Thief," she said. "Thief. In cabin. Purse. Money. All gone."

Then she launched into rapid-fire French, trying to sound as anxious and panicked as she possibly could.

"Ma'am, I'm sorry. I don't speak French. Are you saying—"

"Thief. Took all money. Sending Security, please."

"Something is missing from your room? Is that it, ma'am?"

"Yes. Money gone. Security, please. Uh, *en Français, s'il vous plaît. C'est possible?*"

"Okay, ma'am. I'm sending someone now. Please wait there."

Corinne hung up the phone. So long as the *Celebrate* had only one French-speaking security guard on shift and the guest services operator didn't think too much about the passenger name registered to this cabin, "Luke" would be on his way here right now. She began to pace up and down the carpeted floor. What was she going to say to him? She sat down on the nearest bed to conserve her energy. Her breathing was labored, as if she had just climbed up several flights of stairs. There was a pack of bottled water on the floor under the desk. She took one and drank half of it in one go.

She had found him.

Or maybe, in the end, he had found her.

Either way, she wouldn't have to hang on much longer.

Her pulse was racing at the thought of seeing him again after all this time. She didn't know what she should do when he came in. Would he recognize her? Surely. He clearly knew she was on the ship. But would *she* recognize *him*? She had only the one photo to go by. He could have changed his appearance since it was taken. Should she embrace him? Would he let her? Should she call him by his real name when he must go by "Luke" now?

About five minutes after Corinne had hung up the phone, there came a single sharp knock.

"Security," a voice said through the door.

Unsure her legs would bear her weight at this moment, Corinne called out, "Come in!" in French.

There was a long pause before the door opened, and there he was, standing on the threshold. A perfect match with the picture.

It was him.

Corinne felt a surge of something in her chest. She had finally found him, with almost no time to spare.

He was staring at her, unmoving. He didn't look surprised. In fact, he didn't look *anything*. His expression was perfectly blank.

"Finally," she said in French. "I'm so glad to finally—"

"English." His voice was an alien's, deeper than she had ever heard. In her mind, he still had the voice of a boy. "I only speak English now. I know you can."

"Okay. That's fine. We can talk in English if you want. Of course."

He wore the uniform of a security guard: navy trousers and a white shirt. Thick, strong arms folded across his chest, raised veins rippling across pale flesh. Black hair, short on the sides, a bit longer at the crown. Thin lips. Eyes the color of glaciers. A perfectly normal-looking young man. Attractive, even.

That was the problem with these ordinary monsters: they wore no clues to their true nature.

He stepped into the cabin and closed the door behind him. Corinne was nervous, but not about that. Every request made to Guest Services was logged in a system that, in a few minutes, would ping a reminder to an operator to give the responder a call. "Luke" would have to report back on his visit to the room, and by beckoning him in, Corinne had forced him to use his key to unlock the door. There was now a record of his arrival. It would be stupid of him to do anything here, and whatever his qualities, stupidity wasn't one of them. The anonymous email she had received—it had been right. He had first been spotted aboard as a paying passenger but, in only a few weeks, had somehow managed to return as crew. The picture the emailer had included was his official crew head shot.

He walked into the cabin until he was just a foot from the end of the bed, towering over her, looking down.

She forced herself to lift her head and look him right in the eye. "Romain," she said. "Romi."

"It's Luke now. What are you doing here?"

He didn't sound angry or aggressive. His tone was entirely flat, matter-of-fact, emotionless.

He must have no love for her at all. And after what she had done, who could blame him?

"I came here to find you," Corinne said. "We need to talk."

"How did you know I was here?"

"I got an email."

"From who?"

"I don't know. The sender was anonymous. But I think maybe they worked here. Or they could have been a passenger. You know, there are documentaries on all the time these days. They have these channels now; they must fill twenty-four hours with crime shows …"

"Have you told the police?"

"Told them what?"

"That I'm here."

"Why would I do that? I told you, I just want to talk."

"About what?"

"I'm sick, Romi. Cancer. I don't have much time. And before I … before I go, there are things that need to be said. Things I need to say to you. That I should have said to you a long time ago. I just … I didn't know *how* to say them then."

Romain was peering at her as if at a puzzle he was trying to figure out.

"And after that, you'll leave?"

Corinne nodded. "Yes."

"Say them, then."

"Romi, this will probably be the last time I see you. I would like to have all the time I need. I shouldn't be here right now, and you are on duty … What time does your shift end? Could we meet then?"

He raised an eyebrow. "Is this about Lydia?"

"What? No. Why would—"

"Because I'm not going to hurt her, if that's what you think. I was just trying to find out why you were here."

"I … I know."

"Did you find the photo?"

"Yes. Why did you leave that for me, Romi?"

"To let you know I was here. That you were right."

"You could have just come and found me."

"I didn't know *why* you were here. I thought maybe you would just run."

"I want to talk. Properly."

"I finish at two," he said. "Where will we meet?"

"How about my cabin?"

"Okay," Romain said. "I'll see you there, Mama." He turned to go.

Mama.

It took everything Corinne had not to flinch at that.

ADAM

A booming voice. "… THIS MORNING …"

I was dreaming. Sarah was here. Alive. In love with me. She had never left.

The loud male voice was like an elbow to the ribs. I ignored it. I wanted to stay in the dream. I wanted to stay with Sarah.

But then it came again. Crackling. Louder.

"… IMPORTANT ANNOUNCEMENT …"

In the dream, I pulled Sarah closer. We both closed our eyes.

"… HAVE YOUR ATTENTION …"

It was no good. The two worlds had split. I knew I had been dreaming and that I was awake now, that Sarah was gone. I opened my eyes to see the speckled plastic ceiling tiles of my cabin.

"… MAKE YOURSELF KNOWN …"

Was there someone in the room with me? No, I realized. It was the ship's PA system.

The cabin was filled with daylight. It was morning. Past morning. The light in the room was soft; the sun must be overhead. Could it be so late in the day? Had I slept in for that long? Why hadn't Peter woken me?

Where *was* Peter?

"… YOU FOR YOUR ASSISTANCE."

More to the point, where was *Megan*?

I sat up, rubbed my eyes. I was still dressed. I had slept on top of the covers, an empty plastic water bottle by my side.

I felt as if I had a bad flu, a hangover, and my head encased in concrete. The headache was gone, but my brain felt sluggish, as if it were fighting to move through a fog. My muscles ached, and I had a crick in my neck. I must have slept funny.

I looked around the cabin. Everything seemed as it should be. I was alone. Nothing was out of place. The door was closed.

But hadn't Megan been in here? I put my hand to my cheek, touching the spot she had touched. Did she kiss me? What happened then?

Where did she go?

I poked my head into the bathroom. It was empty, too. I washed my face and brushed my teeth, hoping the taste of toothpaste would override the feeling of fur growing on my tongue while I had slept.

I pulled open the cabin door and stuck my head out into the hall. The Do Not Disturb sign was still on my door. A housekeeping cart was a few cabins down, a vacuum cleaner hanging askew at its end, a stripe of what looked like correction fluid dragged messily across its front. There was no sign of any cabin attendant or, in fact, any other passengers.

All was quiet. *Too* quiet. Even the low thrum of the engines, which I had grown used to, was missing. We had stopped. We weren't sailing. But wasn't today supposed to be spent at sea? Was I in the beginning of some post-zombie-apocalypse movie where a guy wakes from a coma to discover that everyone else has disappeared or turned into the walking dead?

I went to Peter's cabin and knocked so hard that his door shook. "Peter? Peter, are you in there?"

No response. There was a Do Not Disturb sign on his door handle, too.

I went to get my extra Swipeout card from my jeans pocket, but there was nothing in there except my own card—the one that opened my cabin. Had I taken them out last night? Had I managed to lose my "wrong" one?

Back in my cabin, I looked around, but there was only one Swipeout card that I could see: the one that opened my own door. As I laid it down on the desk, something about it snagged on an edge in my mind.

What was it that Megan had said?

The lock activity—that was it. She said *I* had opened the door, as in, my key had, very early yesterday morning.

And the champagne bottle. Hadn't she said something about that, too?

I thought you'd never been on a cruise before.

There was a sharp rap on the door. I rushed to open it, expecting to see Peter.

It was a security guard, dressed in navy-blue trousers and a bright white shirt, with a walkie-talkie beeping on his belt. He looked Italian, and when he spoke, his English had a thick accent. Behind him, another guard, in an identical uniform, was letting himself into the cabin across the corridor.

"Sir, I'm very sorry to disturb you," he said, "but we are conducting a cabin-to-cabin search of the ship for security reasons. Can I ask if you are alone at this moment?"

"Er, yes." I stepped back inside, motioned at the rest of the room with my hand. "I am."

The guard—Stefano, whose favorite Blue Wave destination was Naples—took a step into the room and looked around.

He pointed toward the bathroom. "Is okay?"

"Yeah," I said, nodding. "Sure."

I waited while he went to the bathroom door and ducked his head inside.

"Is something wrong?" I asked.

"There is a passenger we are unable to locate," he said brightly. "But surely it is not a problem. Maybe they are still in France, or sleeping in another cabin. Everything is okay, sir. Please, do not worry."

Something gnawed at my insides. "What's the passenger's name?"

Stefano smiled apologetically. "I'm afraid, sir—"

"You can't tell me."

"It is no problem. I am sure they will be found. Don't worry."

He moved back toward the main cabin door, and I stepped aside for him.

"Uh, actually," I said, "while you're here. I lost my key. Are you the guys who give me a replacement, by any chance?"

"You lost your key?"

"Yes."

"But you are in the room."

"In *this* room, yes, but I need to get into my friend's room. It's a bit of a long story. He's the one next door."

"I am sorry, sir, you must go to the purser. Only the guest whose name is on the cabin can have access to it, so if it's your friend's—"

"I know," I said. "But it's fine. You see, the names were actually mixed up. My name is on his cabin door, so that shouldn't be—"

I stopped.

My name was on his cabin door. Peter's was on mine. Meaning that if he went to the purser and said he had lost his key, the cabin he would have been given a new one for was mine. Enabling him to open my cabin door whenever he liked.

For instance, at five-thirty yesterday morning.

"Sir?" Stefano said.

"Were you just in there?" I pointed at the wall, the one I shared with Peter's cabin. "Have you been next door? Was anyone there?"

Stefano looked unsure whether he should tell me.

"It is empty," he said after a beat.

I thanked him, waved him off, and closed the cabin door, leaning back against it.

Had Peter come into my room yesterday morning while I slept?

Or had Ethan just made it look that way?

A burst of static from the speaker in the ceiling signaled the beginning of another PA announcement.

"Good afternoon from the bridge. May I please have your attention for a moment. Could our passenger Adam Dunne please make himself known to a crew member so they can escort you to the bridge."

I looked up at the speaker.

"This is a message for Adam Dunne. Please make yourself known to a crew member so they can escort you to the bridge. Thank you."

Why would *I* need to go to the bridge? Had they figured out who I was?

And where the hell was Peter?

I left the cabin, locking the door behind me, and started down the hall, toward the elevator bank.

What if this was *about* Peter? What if something happened to him? What if Ethan had drugged me so he could do something to him? I was supposed to be helping Peter. I was here to help keep us both safe. Had I failed him now as well as Sarah?

Had I failed them both?

A lump formed in my throat. Why did I ever come here? I couldn't handle this. I couldn't handle *life* unless it was easy and already going my way. That's probably why Sarah cheated on me: because she knew I was weak. I was such a worthless lump of shit. Sarah probably …

I stopped halfway down the hall.

Sarah's scarf.

I had pulled it out from beneath the pillow last night to show Megan. What had I said to her? For the life of me, I couldn't remember now. I also couldn't remember seeing the scarf in the cabin this morning.

I hurried back along the hallway to my door, fumbled with the key in the lock, tried to push open the door before it unlocked, tried again. Ran into the room. Checked the bed, tossed the pillows, pulled back the sheets. Turned a full 360 degrees to check everywhere else.

Dropped to the floor to look under the bed.

No scarf.

Where could it be? Did Megan take it?

I looked around the room again. The balcony.

There was something out there.

Forcing one foot in front of the other, I made it to the sliding doors. I moved as if underwater, even held my breath. I put my hand on the lock, flipped it open, and slid back the door. A cold breeze whipped at my face.

I stepped outside.

Beneath my feet, the thrumming of the engines far below. We were moving again.

The fabric flapped in the wind, blowing out, away from the ship.

One end of it had been tied in a double knot to the balcony.

Navy with white butterflies. Sarah's scarf.

Who would have put it out here—tied it to the railing like this?

I reached out a hand to touch the end of it, to be sure it was real, that it was really tied to the railing of my cabin balcony on the *Celebrate.*

It looked different from the last time I saw it. It was stained with something that had dried brown.

Blood.

What had gone on in my cabin while I slept? Had I really just been sleeping?

Megan, I thought. *It must be Megan who's missing.*

And then, *We've been set up.*

We'd been set up.

The thought crystalized en route to the Oceanic Deck. Peter was convinced the worst thing that could happen to us was that his theoretical serial killer might track us down and make sure to take us out next, but we had underestimated him. Drastically.

He could do much worse to us than that.

Now I was sure I knew what was happening. Ethan was indeed the killer we suspected him of being, and he had known from the start that Peter and I were here. It didn't make any sense that Peter would let himself into my cabin while I slept and then lie about it afterward, but it made *perfect* sense that Ethan had entered my room and then just made it look that way, made me think that it was Peter. Or maybe he didn't know we had accidentally switched over our cards, and just faked the Swipeout activity in my name to avoid detection. *He* had planted Sarah's scarf on my bed. Then, last night, he had followed Peter and me to the bar and, somehow, slipped something into both our drinks. Megan following me into my cabin may have been a lucky break for him, or perhaps he had engineered that, too. After all, it made sense that she would help me bring Peter back to his cabin.

Either way, I now had no recollection of most of last night. I had found Sarah's scarf, covered in dried blood and tied to my balcony railing, and I was being summoned to the *Celebrate*'s bridge, where I was about to be questioned about Megan's disappearance. I had no doubt now that she was the missing passenger security was searching the ship for.

Megan, a US citizen. Ethan was finally bringing the FBI here—only they weren't coming for him.

They were coming for Peter and me.

He had outwitted us. What fools we were for thinking we could just climb aboard and find him! What fools for thinking that it had been *our idea*! He had taken the women we loved, reeled us like fish onto this ship—*his* ship—and now he was going for checkmate: a move that would get rid of us all and enable him to keep on killing.

But he was doing something much worse than taking our lives. He was going to make it look as if I had taken someone else's.

A pair of security guards were standing, as always, opposite the elevator bank on the Oceanic Deck. I told them who I was, and they nodded.

"I'll take him," one said to the other.

He took me by the crook of my arm and steered me quietly toward the bow, toward the bridge, past sunburned passengers wrapped in beach towels and smelling of sunscreen, giddy children covered in face paint, and staff with pleasant expressions fixed on their faces walking purposefully in every direction.

I had never felt so alone.

I was on autopilot. *Walk forward.*

I felt no emotion. I was numb. My parents' faces, Moorsey's, Rose's, Maureen's, Jack's … When they tried to force their way up into my consciousness—*What will they think?*—I pushed them back down.

Keep walking. Just keep walking.

Eventually, we reached a door marked Authorized Persons Only Beyond This Point. It had a keypad. After the guard punched in a number, the door unlocked with a loud click, and he nodded for me to step through it.

They would say I was driven to it by grief. Or maybe anger. Sarah had cheated on me, after all. In fact, almost everyone else seemed to believe that she was out there somewhere, having escaped me, having chosen to leave. They would say I couldn't take it. That I had snapped.

We were on the bridge now. A wall of windows offered an expansive view of the jagged and mountainous Côte d'Azur. Its hills were rose colored again. It must be midafternoon at least.

How long had I been unconscious?

The coastline was getting closer, growing bigger in the windows. We were returning to Villefranche. They were bringing me back to land. Policemen would come aboard and arrest me. The FBI would be waiting on shore. My wrists would be in handcuffs. My face would be on the news.

Officers in navy trousers and white shirts stood in front of consoles, turning knobs and pressing buttons. Most of them turned to look at me now. Some nodded in greeting at my chaperone.

"Mr. Dunne?"

A man in a suit had stepped in front of me. Tall, broad-shouldered, middle-aged, with white-blond hair. A laminated lanyard hung from his neck. The name tag read "Director of Security." The name was obscured by his tie.

"Yes," I said weakly.

"This way, please."

He motioned toward a glassed-in office directly behind him. Inside were a table and two chairs. Something was on the table, though I couldn't make it out from here. Some kind of recording equipment? This was to be my interrogation room, then.

The director nodded to the guard beside me, who released his grip on my arm. I stepped forward, toward the office. Stepped inside its open door …

And saw that the device on the table wasn't a voice recorder at all. It was a telephone.

A phone that was off the hook.

What the ...?

"Take a seat," the director said. His tone was friendly. I did as I was told. He reached across me to pick up the receiver, put it to his ear, and said into it, "I have him here for you now ... Yes, you're most welcome ... Okay. Just a second." He held the receiver out to me.

I had no idea what was going on, but I took it.

"I'll just be outside," the director said. "Take your time."

I watched him leave. Then, slowly, I put the phone to my ear.

"Hello?" I said into the silence.

There was a rush of breath, of relief. Then a woman's voice, tremulous and uncertain. "Is this Adam?"

"Yes."

"Adam Dunne?"

"Yes. Who is this?"

"Are you alone?" A pause. "I mean, is Peter Brazier with you? In the room with you right now?"

"No, I haven't ... Actually, I don't know where he is. Who *is* this?"

"You sent me an email. My name is Becky. Becky Richardson?"

"Estelle's friend."

"Yes. I tried calling the number you gave me, but your phone seems to be turned off, and I wasn't sure when you'd get my email."

My phone. I thought back to the cabin. Had it been there? I didn't remember seeing it. I felt in my pockets with my free hand. I didn't have it with me. So that was gone, too.

"I knew you were on the *Celebrate*," Becky said, "so I thought a ship-to-shore call was best. To be honest, I wasn't even sure they did those anymore, but—"

"Becky," I said. "What's going on?"

"You can't tell him I called, okay? Peter. If you can't promise me you won't tell him I called, I'll hang up right now."

"I ..." My mind was a muddle. "Fine. Yeah, sure. I won't tell him."

"He's not going to find her," Becky said.

"How do you know? Do you know something he doesn't?"

"I know something *you* don't. I know Peter. My advice to you is to get off that ship as soon as possible, to leave all this be. Leave *Peter* be."

"My girlfriend, Sarah, she—"

"I know. And I'm sorry. But Peter isn't going to help you find her. How could he possibly?"

"Becky," I said, rubbing my temples. "I don't know what's going on here, but something is. Someone drugged us last night and broke into my cabin—"

"'Us'?" As in you and Peter?"

"Yeah."

"How is Peter now?"

"I don't know. I haven't seen him yet today. He's not in his cabin. But look, Becky, I don't know what you think you know, but I'm the one here with him, the one who's seeing all of this—"

"Adam, *I* had her passport."

"Her ... *What?*"

"I had her passport. Estelle's. I had it in my bag. She gave it to me for safekeeping after we boarded the ship. I'm the one who gave it to Peter."

"So she gave *you* the note?"

"Adam, no. Look ..." A pause. "Adam, I'm sorry, but there was no note. He must have just made that part up, along with the stuff about it being posted to him. To take advantage of you, is my guess. There's articles about you online, about the money you were paid for that film. Did you, by any chance, pay for the both of you to get on that ship?"

I thought of the boxes in his living room in the Beau Soleil Palais, the labels on them.

WEST MED ASSAULTS & THEFTS 2009–2012.
CREW EVAL/SECURITY DEPT/ATLANTIC '06.

JOHNSON SUIT: DISCOVERY (COPIES).

The writing on them was the same as on the note Peter had shown me that was supposedly from Estelle. I hadn't realized it at the time, because I'd been distracted by the boxes themselves, by what was in them. But I could see it now, clear as day.

And Sanne Vrijs …

My guess was, there was no passport there at all. That was why I hadn't been able to find any mention of it in the online news stories about Sanne's disappearance.

"Peter can't accept that Estelle isn't coming back," Becky said. "He won't stop this. He can't. He's lying to you. He's a desperate man taking desperate measures, and the only thing to do is to leave him to it. Like I said, you need to get off that ship as soon as possible. Get away from him now, before he pulls you down with him."

I thought about how, outside Fizz that first night, Peter had caught up with me.

She's perfect, Adam. Megan is perfect.

I had thought he meant she could help us find Ethan—and he did. But now I realized that we had very different ideas about *how* she could help.

"It's too late," I said to Becky. "He already has."

As soon as I hung up the phone, the door opened behind me and someone stepped into the room.

"Adam," a voice said. A voice I'd heard before. "Stay calm, okay?" Deep, with a distinctly American accent. "I just want to talk to you."

I turned to find Ethan Eckhart standing in front of me. I bolted up in an instant and made for the door.

"Wait," he said, grabbing my arm. "Calm down. I just want to talk to you, okay?"

"Get the fuck away from me."

I tried for the door again. This time, he stood in front of me, blocking my way. Over his shoulder, I could see some of the officers outside, looking in through the glass. One of them was frowning, his hand moving to the walkie-talkie on his belt as he took a step forward.

Ethan turned and waved at the man, smiled.

"People are looking," he said when he turned back to me. "Sit down." His body was still in front of me, his left hand still gripping my right. He looked just as he did in his head shot, though his hair was a bit lighter now and cut tighter. He wasn't in uniform; he was wearing jeans and a white T-shirt. "Adam, *sit down.*"

What could he do to me, here in this glass room with a bridge full of officers just feet away?

What *more* could he do to me?

Defeated, I sat back down.

"That's it." Ethan said. He leaned back against the wall, arms folded, his body still between me and the door. "I heard your name on the PA, so I came here to wait for you. I was going to knock on your cabin door, but I thought this might be better for you. More comfortable."

"Knock on my door *again,* you mean."

"What?"

"How did you know I was here, on board?"

"I searched the manifest for your name on embarkation day," Ethan said. "This one and the one before. I thought you might arrive on Monday, but apparently you didn't know yet that Sarah had been aboard. I knew that once you found out where she'd been, there was a danger you'd come here to look for me. And after you *called* me … Well, I figured it was only a matter of time. How did you find out?"

"How about fuck you?"

Ethan sighed. "I deserve that, I know. But, Adam, you have to believe me. I didn't mean for this to happen. I never thought I don't know what got into her, to be honest."

The rage boiling up inside me bubbled over and spilled right out of my mouth. "You fucking shit. You don't know what *got into her*? What could she *possibly* have done to deserve what you did?"

"What I … What *I* did?" Ethan blinked, gave me a blank look. "I don't know what she's told you, but *she* broke up with *me*. She said I'd just been a silly mistake. She picked you. Her words, exactly: 'I pick Adam.' Then she just left without even telling me she was going. Or telling you, it turned out. When you called me and said the gardaí were involved …" He shook his head. "Man, like I said, I don't know what got into her. Did she call you?"

I tried to clear a path through my thoughts. Half an hour ago, I was sure I was about to be frog-marched off the *Celebrate* and charged with Megan's murder. Five minutes ago, Becky Richardson told me that Peter never received Estelle's passport in the post at all, and that he told me that just so he could take advantage of me. That he wrote Estelle's note himself so he could extort from me the cash he needed to continue his quest to find out what had happened to his wife on this ship.

Now Sarah's killer and I were having a perfectly polite, human conversation, during which he told me that she had left him—alive?—and picked *me*.

"Go back to the beginning," I said. "Start at the start."

"Well, it's a long story."

"I have time."

"Do you want a coffee?" Ethan asked, inexplicably. I glared at him. "No?" He held up his hands. "Okay, man. Sorry. I was just trying to be polite."

Then he walked around to the other side of the table—the one farthest from the door—and took the seat opposite me. If I wanted, I could easily bolt out the door.

What the hell was going on?

When would I be able to stop asking myself that question?

"I want to say something to you first," Ethan said. "I know this is probably hard for you to hear, and I get that, but I'm in love with her. I don't know what happened that day in the office when we first met, but I just felt something. Some kind of connection. I'd never felt it before. My marriage had just ended, and she was feeling like you two weren't going any—"

"Wait," I said, holding up a hand. "You're in love with her?"

"Yeah. I thought she might have been in love with me, too, until we came here."

"You're *in* love with her."

"That's what I said."

"Present tense?"

"Huh?"

"She's alive, you're saying? Is that what you're telling me?"

"*Alive?* What the …?" Ethan sat back in his chair, shook his head at me. "Man, I think *you* should start at the beginning, because I don't have the first clue what the heck you're talking about." His eyes widened. "Wait. Do you ... Is she okay? Did something ... Did something happen to her?"

A minute ago, I would have said, *Yeah,* you, *you piece of shit.* But now I wasn't so sure.

I looked at Ethan as if I had never seen him before, as if I had no preconceived ideas about him, or any advance information on who he was. He looked ordinary, average, normal. Until we met in this room, I had been telling myself that this was deliberate, that he was an everyman so he could blend into the background, unnoticed.

But now I wondered whether he might be just ordinary after all. Maybe that was *all* he was.

Sarah? Sarah, is that you? Talk to me, please. Just talk to me.

"She came onto this ship with you," I said. "Boarded the *Celebrate,* the Monday before last."

"Yeah."

"You spent a night in Barcelona first, in a hotel."

"If we flew out from Cork on Monday morning, we wouldn't have made it to the port on time."

"You boarded the ship together. Did you share a cabin?"

"We were supposed to. I was on an educational—a comped staff trip. Every director gets one so they can experience the product like a customer—and Sarah was my guest."

That was why Blue Wave hadn't been able to find her reservation: because she didn't have one; she was on his. Ethan's had presumably been made in-house, at the corporate level, outside the normal reservation system.

And it would look doubly bad to have a crew member's cruise companion disappear off the ship, especially if he hadn't bothered to report her missing. Some tall tale about a computer glitch easily covered Blue Wave's ass on that.

"What happened?" I asked.

"I think Sarah …" A cough, a nervous throat-clearing. "Sarah was really unsure about the whole thing. Her and me, I mean. Well, I suppose you and her, too. She thought maybe we … When you're having an affair, there's the element of danger. The excitement of sneaking around, the novelty of the secret. Know what I mean?"

"Actually, no."

"Yeah, well … She was, uh, being weird all day. Wouldn't talk to me about it. I thought she might actually turn around and tell me she wasn't even getting on the ship, that she was going home instead. But she did get on, and then I had to go meet my new line manager, so she went to dinner alone, and then afterwards … Well, afterwards we had a fight. Out on deck. On Pacific by the Grotto Pool."

"I don't give a flying fuck where it happened, Ethan. Tell me *what* happened."

"She broke up with me, okay? She said it felt wrong and that it had all been a mistake, that she loved you and that … She said she couldn't believe she had hurt you so much already. She was going to get off the ship in the morning, fly straight home from Nice, and tell you everything. Ask you if you two could start all over again."

"How did you react?" I asked, trying not to react to what he had just said.

She was coming back to me. She was coming home.

"I didn't say anything," Ethan said. "I let her go. I said okay, fine. Whatever you want. That's what I told her. We agreed that I'd go find a chair in a corner of a lounge somewhere, or a bed in crew quarters, and let her have the cabin for the night. She said she'd go pack her stuff, and off she went. But then I started thinking about us, about how I didn't *want* to let her go. As I told you, I love her. And then I was like, is this a *test*? You know what women are like. They never actually *say* what—"

"So what then?" I said, cutting him off. "You went back to the cabin?"

"Yeah, but she wasn't there. Her stuff wasn't, either. Well, most of her stuff. She'd taken her suitcase, but she'd left some clothes behind in the wardrobe, and some makeup stuff by the bathroom sink. And there was the note."

"The … The *what?*"

"The note," Ethan repeated.

"For fuck's sake, *what* note?"

"She'd written me a note. It was stuck to the mirror over the desk."

"How do you mean, stuck?"

"It was one of those Post-it things."

"One of those …" I tried to gulp down some air, to inflate my lungs. They felt as if they were collapsing. "What did it say? What did the note *say?*"

"That she was sorry," Ethan said.

"Tell me the exact words."

"'I'm sorry,' signed the letter 'S.'"

"In block capitals?"

"Yeah. Wait, how'd you—"

"What happened to the note? Did you take it?"

"No, I left to go look for her. Went all over the ship, man. I swear. I searched everywhere. Came back to the cabin a couple of hours later and the note was gone. That was it. I didn't see Sarah again. I tried calling her and texting her, but I never got through. Her phone was switched off. So …" Ethan hesitated. "Well, I didn't think anything was *wrong*, you know? I thought she was just mad at me, and that turndown service had taken the note or it had fallen under the bed and I just couldn't see it, or something."

"You didn't report her missing."

"Missing? Why would I? She'd just decided not to spend that night in our cabin, and then she got off the ship the next day. I know she did. I checked her Swipeout activity."

"How?"

"I know a guy. He let me take a look."

"Why did you do that?"

"To make sure."

"What made you *un*sure?"

"*You,*" Ethan said. "When you called me."

"The first time I called you, you thought I was her."

"I just saw an Irish number. Figured she was calling to apologize or whatever but couldn't do it. So when she hung up—or when I thought it was her who had hung up—I called back and got you, and you were screaming about the police and her family and all *sorts* of shit. It got me worried, so I went to check if she'd gotten off the ship. The system said she had. So I figured, okay, I'm okay here, but obviously, after she got off she didn't go home like she said she was going to, and she's probably off somewhere trying to clear her head. But you're mad as hell, and if you have my phone number, what else do you have? You probably know all about me and, well, if I were you, I would've come straight here to find me, and probably beat the crap out of me. Which is exactly what you did. Well, the first part, anyway. And look, I appreciate—"

"I came here to find *Sarah,* you fucking dickhead."

Ethan shrugged. "Doesn't sound to me like she wants to be found, man. Sorry."

"What time was it when you went back to the cabin?"

"I don't know. Ten or eleven?"

"So it was dark?"

"Yeah, dark."

"You didn't notice anything unusual in there?"

"Other than the fact the note was gone, no."

"Did you find Sarah's phone?"

"No."

"There's a passenger missing from the ship right now, isn't there?"

Ethan was momentarily thrown by the change of subject, but then he said that yes, there was. "What's *that* got to do with anything?"

"Who is it?" I asked. "Do you know the name?"

"All I know is, it's some American girl. On a PR trip, so everyone's freaking the fuck out." So it *was* Megan. "Especially because of ..." Ethan trailed off. "Well, let's just say everyone's freaking out."

"Because of what? What were you going to say?"

"Just that, uh, there was a murder here, on one of the early cruises. Don't repeat this, okay? In the crew quarters. A real bloody one, apparently. Total horror show. One of the tabloids got wind of it, but they didn't have any pictures or names, so it didn't spread. Blue Wave is still holding its breath on it, though. If this girl is actually missing ... Well, they'll turn on the fans in the shit factory, if you know what I mean."

"What do you know about that murder?"

Ethan shrugged. "What I just said. That's all I got."

A murder in the crew quarters. I wondered whether that could be Sanne. But didn't Peter say that Blue Wave maintained she had fallen overboard? Had she really been murdered and they were just covering it up?

"What about the girl this morning?" I asked. "How did anyone know she was missing?"

"I heard someone reported it."

"Who?"

"I don't know. Maybe a crew member. Why are you so interested in her?"

I tried to focus. To think.

"Did your cabin have a balcony?" I asked. "The one you stayed in with Sarah—or were supposed to."

"Yeah."

"Did you go out there when you came back to look for her?"

"No, but I could see out through the doors. It was dark. If Sarah were out there, she would've turned on the outside light."

"But it was dark out there?"

"Right."

So someone could've been out on the balcony, hiding.

Like the man who had just finished killing Sarah by pushing her off it.

No.

It could have been Sarah, hiding from Ethan because she didn't want to talk to him. She waits for him to leave, thinks better of leaving the note, grabs it on her way out, decides she can't come home after what she's done, and sends the note to me instead.

Maybe she *was* alive. But then, where *was* she?

"Will you be here?" I said to Ethan.

"I'll be around," he said. "Listen, man, I *am* sorry. For all this."

"Yeah." I turned to leave. "So am I."

I had one foot out the door when I thought of it. I turned back around.

"Wait a second," I said. "You met Sarah in an office?" Ethan nodded. "Which office?"

"*Her* office. Anna Buckley."

"What were you doing there?"

"Er, same thing everyone else was doing: looking for a job."

"But why did you …" It dawned on me then. "Ethan, when did you start work on the *Celebrate*?"

"The day before yesterday, technically. This is my first cruise as crew."

"What were you doing before this?"

"*Right* before this? Managing a restaurant in a Dublin hotel. But I was looking to get moving again, and I heard Blue Wave was recruiting through Anna Buckley. That's why I went down there in the first place."

"So you weren't here last August? On the *Celebrate*?"

"No, man." Ethan shook his head. "Why is everyone suddenly asking me that?"

I felt my pulse quicken. "Who *else* asked you that?"

"Well, okay," he said. "Not *everyone*. But there was this guy in one of the restaurants the first night. A Brit. I thought he was maybe, you know, checking me out or something at first, because he kept staring at me, but it turns out he just thought he knew me from the last time he was aboard. Last August. But I told him the same thing I told—"

I was already out the door.

ROMAIN
Hersonissos, Crete, 2012

It was love at first sight.

She was walking in the door of Mikey's Place, searching for a face she knew, her pale skin standing out in the darkness, her long golden hair loose around her shoulders. She looked nothing like any other woman in the crowd that night—or any other night, for that matter.

Romain was mesmerized. He had never experienced anything like it before. An overwhelming warmth in his chest. A desire to touch her, yes, but more than that, too. He wanted to look after her. To be with her. To make her happy. He felt her presence in the room like a torch, and for the entire evening, without any real conscious effort, he kept track of where she was.

When she came to get a drink at the bar and smiled at him, he was relieved to be called away by another customer and let Freddy, the new bartender, serve her instead.

Romain didn't know what to do, and that made him nervous.

It wasn't as if he were a novice. There had been other girls. *Lots* of other girls. He was a strong, healthy, handsome twentysomething working as a bartender in one of the most popular bars on the island of Crete. That meant that every evening from April to September, he could take his pick. A different one each night, if he liked, although, after the initial novelty of it, Romain had quickly learned that there were advantages to being more discerning.

But a relationship? He had never managed to talk himself into one of those, and no one else had tried to talk him into it, either. It was such an odd idea—having someone who stayed with you all the time, someone who looked after you and who constantly told you how they cared for you— that it didn't seem as if it could ever be real.

Until this night. Until this girl.

Walking out with Freddy after closing, he saw her outside, smoking a cigarette and chatting with another girl.

Freddy nodded toward her. "There's the one who was hanging around at the bar all night. Here." He punched Romain lightly on the arm. "Watch *this.*"

Freddy walked up to the girl and her friend with a confidence that puzzled Romain, because Freddy was short, red-haired, and unattractive. He also had a whole arm covered in ugly tattoos, most of which he had done himself or started himself and that later had to be corrected. Lack of artistic merit aside, they all were embarrassing choices, too: religious shapes, his mother's face—Romain couldn't even *begin* to fathom that one—and a song lyric from one of last summer's big hits that made little sense when you were drunk enough to dance to it, and no sense at any other time.

And yet here was Freddy, striding up to two girls—one beautiful, one ordinarily attractive—with the confidence of a much more attractive man.

People puzzled Romain, even now.

"Do I know you?" Freddy said. It wasn't clear at first which girl he was addressing, but then he pointed to *her,* to Romain's girl. "You look really familiar."

The girl and her friend exchanged a glance.

"*Do* I?" she said to Freddy. "Imagine that."

Romain got the sense that she was just playing along, being polite. Hope rose in his chest.

"We don't know each other?" Freddy said.

The girl shook her head. "No, I don't think so."

"Then where do I know you from?" He made a big show of thinking about this. "Oh, wait, I know: from my *dreams!*"

"Really?" the girl said. "*That's* what you're going with?"

Freddy nodded. "Yep."

"Well, in that case, I'll meet you there later." The girls laughed, but it took Freddy a second.

"Oh, I get it," he said. He sounded cheerful. "Good one."

The girl's eyes flicked to Romain. "Does your friend have any better lines?"

"Ah, him?" Freddy gestured for Romain to join him. "*Lines?* Sweetheart, he wouldn't know what you're talking about. Luckily, the fucker doesn't need any lines. Have you seen his face? Ask him yourself, though, just to be sure." Freddy took a step to the right, making room for Romain to stand beside him, and addressed the second girl. "You know, *you* look kind of familiar to me, too …"

"Hi," the first girl said to Romain. "I'm Sanne."

"Hi, Sanne," Romain said. "I'm Luke."

* * *

Sanne had come to Crete with friends, on a short break from her job in Utrecht, where she was packing bags in a supermarket and saving money to go traveling around the world for a year. But only a week after returning to the Netherlands, she was back in Crete again, standing in the doorway of Mikey's Place, looking around—this time, for Romain.

This time, she was here to stay.

She moved into his room for the remainder of the summer season. In September, they found a place of their own: an old holiday apartment with a sea view if you leaned against the balcony railing and turned your head just right.

Romain had lost the concept of a home to his childhood; his only concern was a bed to lie in for the night. Now he watched as Sanne piled colorful cushions on their bed, hung framed pictures of them on the walls, and lit candles at night to make the place "cozy." She even decorated at Christmas, dragging a potted palm in from the balcony and twisting multicolored fairy lights around its trunk. She baked him a cake on his birthday, wrote in his card that she loved him.

She made a home for them, and whenever Romain woke up to her or came home to her or fell asleep beside her, she felt like a home to him.

Sanne got a job in a restaurant in town, and Romain was promoted to management at Mikey's. They stayed in bed well into the day, touching skin and stroking hair and kissing lips. They shared dinner at home, then went off to work for the night, before meeting up again in the early hours to party with their friends or to take a bottle of wine to the beach. They argued rarely and laughed often.

Sanne told Romain that he made her feel safe. Of course, she always called him Luke when she did that.

Romain, meanwhile, felt as though he had lived his life till now in a dark, constricting box. He had no idea that being alive could feel like this. Was this how other people felt all the time? Warm and safe and wanted and worthy? He wondered whether that was why he had been so different … before. Maybe everyone had darkness inside them, but this warm love kept theirs from ever coming out.

The darkness. Sometimes he wondered whether it was still there. It was all so long ago now. Mikki. The day at the pond. Sometimes, he thought about finding an address for Dr. Tanner, sending him a message to let him know that he had been right. The treatment *had* worked. Jean had just fallen off that backyard gate.

But Tanner probably didn't want to hear from Romain, not after what had happened. And anyway, Romain couldn't risk making contact.

He was thinking a lot more about Dr. Tanner these days. Being around Sanne, Romain's words and actions all felt as if they came from a deeper place. Before, when he laughed, it was because he had identified a moment when he was supposed to. Someone had paused at the end of the joke, or others were already laughing. His personality had always been a string of learned behaviors, each one discovered, studied, and acquired quite consciously, many of them during Tanner's treatment—a repertoire of reactions he could pull out and display as needed.

But with Sanne, it was different.

He didn't have to think about what to say or what to do, and whenever he *did* say or do something, it didn't come from just beneath the surface. It came from deep inside him.

He was becoming real. He was really being *good*.

Romantic love—both feeling it and receiving it—was an entirely new experience for Romain. So he didn't know there was a danger in throwing himself into it, in opening his heart wide, in thinking that his life with Sanne was his life forever now.

He couldn't have known, and it couldn't last—certainly not after she told him she was pregnant.

* * *

Romain said nothing at first. He was too stunned.

"I know we didn't plan this," Sanne said, "but it's happened. And it's not like we're teenagers, Luke. I'm twenty-three. I can have a baby if I want. Who's to say I can't? And wouldn't it be nice? A little person that we made together? We'd be a family."

Family.

The word stung Romain's heart.

"I know," Sanne went on. "Money. Yes, we probably can't afford to raise a child right now, but we have eight months to go, and I've been talking to Paul at the restaurant and he said there'll be a bookkeeping job coming up in—"

"Sanne," Romain said. "You can't do it."

"I can learn how to do accounts, Luke. It's not rocket science."

"No. I mean you can't have it."

Sanne's face fell. "What?"

"You have to get rid of it."

"What are you—"

"You just *can't have it,* okay?"

They were sitting side by side on their sofa. She put a hand on his cheek.

"Luke, I know this is scary, but just—"

"Listen to me, Sanne. You're getting an abortion."

She pulled away from him. Her eyes filled with tears.

"I love you, Sanne," Romain said. "You know I do. But you can't ... you can't have a baby with me."

"Why not?"

Because there'll be darkness inside it. Because eventually that darkness will get out. Because when it does, you'll make it feel the way Mama made me feel.

"I can't tell you why, Sanne. But there was something ... There was something wrong with my father, and the same thing was wrong with me. Before. If you have that baby—"

"But you're fine now, Luke. You're perfect. Are you saying you had a disability or something? A disease? Were you sick?"

"No."

"Then what is it?"

"I can't tell you."

"What? Why?"

"Because if I do, you won't love me anymore."

"Oh, Luke. Don't be ridiculous." She moved back to him, let him take her in his arms. She kissed his cheek, whispered in his ear. "I love you and there is nothing you could tell me that would change that."

This was a line Romain had heard spoken many times on TV and in movies. Or some version of it. It made him ball his fists, it was so stupid. Anyone who would say such a thing had to be willfully ignorant of the things that could happen in this world—of how things could go horribly, irreparably, frighteningly wrong.

Sanne needed to know how wrong she was.

"Romain Dupont," he said.

"What's that?"

"That's me. That's my real name."

"Your … your *real* name?" A nervous laugh. "Luke, what are you—"

"My name's not Luke. It's Romain."

"No." Sanne started shaking her head. "I don't understand."

"Romain Dupont." He spelled it out for her. "Look it up online. See if you still love me then."

But Sanne didn't move. She just sat there, staring at him.

Finally, he got up and got the laptop himself, powered it up, typed his name into Google, and pointed to a screen filled with results.

"Here," he said, handing the machine to her. "Tell me if you want any of the French ones explained."

He knew the stories Sanne was now looking at, because he had done this same thing himself many times.

Child Killer: "No Remorse" for Fourteen-Year-Old Victim … "Devil Spawn of Deavieux" Strikes Again … World's First "Cured" Violent Psychopath Murders Own Brother Twenty-Four Hours after Release … Interpol Launches Search for Romain Dupont … Disgraced Psychiatrist Loses License

Mixed in among them would be Romain's listing on a "Kids Who Kill" website, a link to a so-called true crime book someone had written about the case, and links to YouTube clips of the round of interviews Mama had done right after Jean's death.

Sanne's hands, resting on the laptop, started to shake.

"I didn't kill my brother Jean," Romain said. "He fell and hit his head while he was trying to get away from me. But the rest of it … the rest is true."

He reached over Sanne's arm and clicked on one of the YouTube links.

* * *

Mama was sitting in an armchair, looking thin and frail, shredding a piece of tissue between her fingers. She looked so old to Romain, and now she would be older still. She spoke so quietly, the interviewer had to ask her to speak up. She didn't cry at all.

The interview was for a popular documentary channel, so it was conducted in English.

"Tell us," the interviewer said, "about Romain's father." The woman asking the questions was as old as Mama, but she had lots of makeup on and her hair wasn't gray. "There's been some speculation in the press …"

"I was raped," Mama said flatly. "Walking home from work one night, just a few months after Charlie and I got married. I'd stayed in the city a bit later than I normally did, to have a drink with a friend—it was her birthday. And so, although I was taking the same walk home from the station that I had made I don't even know how many times already, that night I was walking the route a good deal later than I ever had. There were no people around, few cars on the roads, but it was such a short distance—five minutes at most. I thought it would be fine. Actually, I didn't think much about it at all. I had just turned onto this street where I noticed all the streetlamps were out, and I was thinking how odd that was, when I heard footsteps running towards me, and then …"

Mama paused here, took a breath in through her nose, steeled herself.

"Take your time," the interviewer said gently.

"A man grabbed me. He dragged me backwards, behind the garden wall of a derelict house. He hit me several times, in the stomach and on the sides of my head—to disable me, I suppose. I felt woozy after that, sleepy. Then he dragged me by my hair inside the house."

"How long were you in there?"

"It was light outside when he left."

"Were you … conscious?"

"Just."

The interviewer shook her head. "I can't even imagine."

"I wouldn't ask anyone to."

"Did they ever catch him?"

"I don't know. I didn't report it."

"Why not?"

Mama looked down at her lap, mumbled something. The interviewer asked her to repeat it.

"Because I didn't want my husband to know."

"Why not?"

"It wasn't the right decision, I know. But I was in shock. I was thinking, okay, this happened. I can't change that. But my body withstood it. My *mind* withstood it. He didn't win. I hadn't let him. Telling Charlie back then … To me it seemed like it would be an infection, that I would let this, this *thing* invade my life, let it spread beyond that one house on that one night. So I made up some story about how I'd fallen asleep at a friend's house and then tripped and fell running back home, and Charlie was in a rush to get out for work and he didn't question it, and by the time he got home that evening I had had a chance to put myself back together, to practice my story." Mama paused. "It was foolish of me, I realize now. I know. I should have gone to the police, let them collect evidence, get a description of him. But I was traumatized. That's what was happening to me on a clinical level: trauma. I wanted to push it down, to forget that it had ever happened. I didn't realize that doing so would mean repercussions for me in the long run. I thought I could just forget all about it."

"So you kept it a secret?"

"Yes."

"And then, when you found out you were pregnant …?"

"Then …" Another long breath in through the nose, out again. "Then it was too late for the truth. I couldn't—"

* * *

Mama's voice cut off in midsentence. Sanne had closed the lid of the laptop.

"Are you okay?" Romain asked.

He reached for her, but she shot up from the sofa and went to stand on the other side of the room.

"Sanne—"

"Don't speak, Luke. *Romain.* Just … just don't speak."

They stayed like that, in silence, for a long time.

"You killed a child," Sanne said eventually. It sounded as if it could be a question.

"When I was also a child, yes. I was even younger than he was."

"Why?"

"He'd been bullying me, and now he was saying things to my younger brother. Scaring him. Jean started to cry. And I got mad, Sanne. I got so mad. Don't you ever feel like that?"

"Not enough that I would kill someone, no."

"It was an accident. I didn't mean to."

"What about the other ones? Your brothers?"

"I told you about Jean. He fell. Mikki …" Romain sighed. "That was a very long time ago. He was crying, and my mother told me to make him stop. I'd seen her walk up and down the room with him, shaking him. I tried to do the same thing, but I was only seven years old and I didn't know that what I was supposed to do was *gently* shake him, and he … got a brain injury. From his brain moving inside his skull, hitting off the front and back. He died a few years ago, from an infection."

"Has there been anything else?"

"No."

"Are you lying to me right now?"

"No."

"How do I know what's the truth? All this time, you didn't even tell me your real *name*."

They fell silent again.

"Sanne," Romain said after a while, "the baby …"

"You think it'll be like you."

"Yes."

"And you think you did what you did because of your father."

"Yes," Romain said. "Possibly."

"What was your mother like?"

"She wasn't …" He sighed. "Not like a mother."

"But this is different," Sanne said. "This baby was made from love. Even if it wasn't real, that was the intention."

"It *was* real. It still is, Sanne."

"That's why you wouldn't come with me to Breda that time, isn't it? To visit my parents. You couldn't travel."

"I couldn't risk it."

"Do you even have a passport? ID? A birth certificate?"

Romain had gotten into Greece in 2005, on a passport he stole from a Danish guy in Seville. They looked vaguely alike, but it wasn't something he wanted to put to the test in an airport. He had been lucky enough to get through the sleepy guards at the ferry terminal on the way here.

"I have a passport, yes, but I don't want to use it unless I have to." He stood up, went to her. She turned her head away from him but didn't try to move. "Sanne, listen to me. I love you." He risked touching her. She let him. "All this, it was so long ago. I was just a child. Yes, I should have told you, but what would you have done if I told you before now? You would've run away. You would've left me. And why? Because of one minute of one day *nineteen years* ago. Because of something stupid I did when I was too young to know that it was. Because of a darkness that I haven't felt since, Sanne. A darkness that your love has *kept away*."

Tears were streaming down Sanne's face. Romain pressed his lips gently against her cheeks, trying to stop the flow.

"What about the baby?" she asked.

"My father—"

"It's not the same. *We're* not the same."

"What do you mean?"

"You didn't rape me." She turned to face him, met his eyes. "And I'm not like your mother. I will love this baby. *Our* baby."

Romain pulled Sanne to him, whispered into her hair, "But it scares me."

"It scares me, too." She put her arms around him, and he pulled her tighter again. "But we can do this. Together. I think we can. But only if there are no more lies. None. Not even little ones. Love isn't just touching and feeling, Romain. It's knowing. Knowing *everything*. And still having the feeling, even then."

"I will never lie to you again, Sanne." He meant it. "I love you."

"I love you, too."

He held her until he ached. He didn't know how long they stood there.

For the first time in his life, Romain felt like a real person. There was nothing inside that wasn't outside, no dark streak in his core. He had just been young, mixed up, and he had made mistakes. But now he had someone who believed in him, who loved him, who wanted to have a family with him.

A proper family, like the one he wished he'd had.

We can do this, Sanne had said. *I love you, too.*

But she didn't. It was all an act.

* * *

Sanne disappeared from Crete three days later, while Romain was on

[321]

a ten-hour shift at Mikey's. She had somehow found Romain's stolen Danish passport taped to the underside of one of the bed's wooden slats, and took it with her.

He thought she was at the restaurant, but no. She had been executing the escape plan she presumably began to hatch the moment she saw the search results for Romain Dupont. Everything that had happened since had been a lie, a way for Sanne to extricate herself from the situation without getting hurt.

Romain understood this now.

Had she gone to the police, too? If she hadn't already, she would once she was away.

What about their baby? They'd had seventy-two hours to talk about the future, to discuss names and make plans and get excited. Romain couldn't even contemplate the idea of a baby without feeling a strange lump in his throat. Imagine: a child, maybe even a son, to whom he could give everything that Mama had denied him, everything she had kept from him because she started regretting her decision to have him the very moment he was born, maybe even before that.

A child who would feel about Romain the way Romain had once felt about Papa.

But now Sanne was gone, and that didn't bode well for the life in her belly.

That night, Romain packed a bag, wiped the apartment of any trace of him, and walked into the night, stopping only when he reached the beach. He slept on the sand and, the next morning, talked his way onto a fishing boat headed for Essaouira, convincing the captain to stow him away for five hundred euro—nearly all the money he had in the world.

Romain hated Morocco. Essaouira was dirty and noisy, with bird shit as common there as drunk, sunburned tourists had been back in Greece. The place was infested with seagulls and stank of rotting fish. But he kept his head down and his end goal in mind. Within a few weeks, he had enough money to afford new, better papers and to buy a plane ticket back to Europe.

A ticket back to Sanne.

He knew exactly where she was. He had spent nearly all his days off in Essaouira's Internet cafés, searching for her.

She hadn't called the police. He had checked day in, day out, for weeks but had come across no new alerts, news stories, or other mentions of himself online, and absolutely nothing tying him to Greece. This gave him a very valuable piece of information: if Sanne hadn't told the police about him, it was unlikely she had told anyone else about him, either.

Romain created a fake Facebook profile using the name of one of the waitresses from Mikey's Place, Claire, who apparently didn't already have one. He happened to have a photograph of Claire and Sanne, arms around each other's shoulders during a night out a few months ago. He uploaded it as "Claire's" profile picture, thus establishing a connection to Sanne without Sanne's knowing a thing about it or having to click anything to authenticate.

Then Romain started systematically sending friend requests from "Claire" to every one of Sanne's friends. Some of them accepted them; some didn't.

He bided his time.

Four weeks after his arrival in Morocco, a girl named Kelly, who was friends with Sanne and "Claire," posted a status update about how excited she was to finally be getting on the *Celebrate* after a month of training.

Underneath the status it read, "With Sanne Vrijs."

Kelly had tagged Sanne in her status—an action that millions of people performed on the site every day. She had probably thought nothing of it. Maybe even Sanne thought nothing of it, not realizing that Kelly was connected, through "Claire," to Romain.

It was all Romain needed.

He deleted "Claire" and determined that the *Celebrate* was a Blue Wave cruise ship readying for its maiden voyage, due to begin the following week. More Internet searching returned photos of Sanne, in a Blue Wave T-shirt, on something called Tumblr, and he even found a video she appeared in momentarily on someone else's blog. In one of the pictures of her published online, Sanne was helpfully wearing a name tag that, when Romain enlarged the image, clearly read "*Fizz Cocktail Lounge.*"

You could try to protect your own privacy, yes, but you couldn't really count on those around you to do the same.

Once he knew where she was, the next part was easy. He booked himself onto the *Celebrate* and boarded the ship at Barcelona. He had gotten a discounted ticket because this was its very first cruise. His new passport was worth every penny, passing every checkpoint with flying colors. On embarkation day, he went to his cabin, slept for a few hours, and then, as soon as Fizz opened that evening, made his way to Sanne.

She wasn't pleased to see him.

"I'm not here to make a scene," Romain said to her. "I just want to talk to you. You don't have to be afraid. I won't hurt you. I don't do that anymore, Sanne. I wasn't lying about that."

"You need to leave," she had said through clenched teeth, trying to keep her face neutral. A number of passengers were sitting at the bar alongside them. A male colleague of hers stood at the other end of the counter, polishing glasses and watching them out of the corner of his eye.

"Sanne, I just want to talk. That's all. Five minutes."

"Go away or I'll call Security."

"What about the baby?"

"*Baby?* There is no baby, *Romain.* I did what you said."

"What did you do?"

"What I had to."

"You mean you …"

Sanne looked him right in the eye. "What choice did I have?"

The bartender started walking toward them.

"Everything okay here?" he asked.

"Fine," Sanne said. "It's fine."

"Are you sure?" The bartender looked to Romain. "This guy isn't bothering you, is he?"

"No, he was just leaving."

With both of them staring at him—and other passengers turning now to look—Romain turned and walked out of Fizz. He had no choice.

After that, he walked the ship for hours, circling every deck several times, thinking about what to do next. He had no loving feelings for Sanne anymore. It was as if someone had flipped a switch.

But the baby …

Was she telling the truth about that? It had been only a few weeks. Maybe she hadn't done it yet. Maybe she was just lying to him, to get him to leave. Still, a job on a cruise ship seemed an odd choice for a young woman who was pregnant.

Before he let her get away again, he had to be sure.

The lights went off in Fizz just after three in the morning. A few minutes later, Sanne emerged alone to pull down and lock the metal shutter that covered its entrance overnight.

Romain watched her from a dark corner a few feet away—a nook that housed a little ATM.

When she was done, she pocketed the keys and started toward the stairs. Romain followed her up to one of the open decks.

It was practically deserted up here, what with the hour and the weather. It was the middle of the night and cold outside, with flurries of rain and a bracing wind. Sanne kept away from the brightly lit area by the rail, instead walking in the shadows cast by the lifeboats hanging overhead.

Romain followed her from a safe distance, looking for security cameras as he went. After a minute or so, he realized that all the cameras were on the other side of the promenade, on lampposts close to the rail.

Sanne was intentionally avoiding them and the lights. But why?

Then it came to him: *because she was crew.* Crew in uniform. She wasn't supposed to be up here at all.

And it was the middle of the night. And they were at sea.

And no one knew that a convicted murderer named Romain Dupont was even on this ship in the first place.

That was how it happened. There was no great plan, no real premeditation. He had intended just to talk to her—or at least, to try that first.

But then different ideas moved into the foreground of his mind like pieces sliding across a chessboard. Coming together. Forming a new, better idea.

One the darkness *really* liked.

Near the end of the deck, Sanne crossed to the rail and leaned against it, looking out. She pulled a pack of cigarettes from a pocket.

Romain didn't think Sanne was the type to smoke while she was pregnant, but that alone wasn't proof of anything. After checking for cameras pointed her way, and for other passengers—and finding neither—he made his move.

As quickly as he could, he stepped up behind Sanne, threw one strong arm around her waist while wrapping the other across her chest, clamped his hand roughly over her mouth, and pulled her head back.

The cigarettes fell into the darkness beyond the rail. Sanne didn't get a chance to make a sound.

She did, however, begin to jerk and struggle.

Keeping his right hand over her mouth, and her body locked against his, he ran his left hand down to her abdomen, up under her T-shirt, down inside her waistband, pressed it against her bare skin.

She felt the same.

If she was pregnant, she would be at least a couple of months along by now, maybe three. Wouldn't she be bigger there? She felt the same as she always did, but then, it was difficult to tell when she wouldn't keep still.

Romain pushed his hand lower, inside the front of her trousers, down over the front of her underwear.

And felt the bulge of a sanitary pad. Sanne had her period.

She had gotten rid of his baby.

What's the point?

That was what the darkness wanted to know. It demanded to. It pressed Romain for an answer as he stood there, holding Sanne against the railing on the *Celebrate*'s deck, keeping her in an armlock, the wind whipping at his face, nothing but the abyss of black ocean all around.

What's the fucking point?

He had spent his childhood trying to please a mother who hated him before he was even born, who should never have had him in the first place. Then spent his adolescence doing time for a crime that was really only a moment of madness. Bastian had provoked him. He had been asking for it. Romain was only trying to protect Jean. But Mama didn't see it that way, of course. She even testified against him at the trial, weeping about how she regretted not doing something with him before, back when he hurt Mikki. Then he had agreed to Tanner's experimental treatment and done everything he was told, only to be abandoned by his father and falsely accused of Jean's murder just a day after his release, destroying both his own freedom and Tanner's reputation. Then Sanne had changed everything, but now she had changed everything back again.

What *was* the point?

There was none, as far as Romain could tell. There never had been. He closed his eyes and let the darkness in, let it crash down on him in waves and splash up against him and cover him, soak him, drench him.

It felt warm and comforting, like a hot bath.

He relaxed into it. He wouldn't resist it anymore. The darkness was all he had left.

Then he opened his eyes, bent at the knees, picked Sanne up, and threw her over the rail.

All his life, Romain had tried to be good. He was done with that now.

ADAM

The signs were there, if you knew to look for them. Crew members hurried about, eyes solemn above their smiles. Those stationed behind bars, poised beside restaurant tables, and manning cash desks whispered to each other, their expressions serious. Their trademark aggressive friendliness and toothy smiles were dialed back a notch. The number of visible security guards moving through passenger areas seemed to have doubled, and they all strode past with one hand on their radios, anticipating a sudden burst of communication. Passengers who queried why France was getting big in the windows again were taken to one side and spoken to in calm, reassuring tones. There was no anger or outrage, only wide eyes and understanding nods. Whispers about helicopters and the French coast guard, a young woman thought to be tragically lost at sea.

I saw this happening in every corner while I walked the ship, searching for Peter, moving systematically from lounge to restaurant to store. Then I walked the corridors, took the elevator up a deck, and started again. When I reached the top, I started working my way back down, repeating the process in reverse.

But I didn't find him.

Meanwhile, the sun sank in the sky.

By the time darkness fell, the *Celebrate* had settled back in the bay of Villefranche, dropping anchor in much the same spot where it had the day before.

A PA announcement informed passengers that the ship was dealing with a security issue, which would mean a minor delay in the itinerary. Complimentary drinks were being served on the open decks, and if anyone had any questions, they should feel free to approach the nearest crew member. Sincere apologies, circumstances beyond our control, we'll endeavor to keep guests informed of this ongoing situation, and so on.

Sarah had had none of this. But then, she wasn't American.

Just before nine o'clock, exhausted by my search for Peter and all out of ideas where I might look for him next, I returned to my cabin.

Everything looked exactly as I had left it, except for the deepening dark outside. I turned on a few lamps and checked to make sure. Earlier, I had untied the scarf from the railing, put it inside the plastic wastebasket liner, and stuffed the lot down to the bottom of my bag. I had washed my hands in the bathroom sink afterward and then left the cabin. Now I retraced my steps with a small bottle of hand sanitizer I had picked up in the Crescent Store, hoping it would be enough to remove fingerprints or DNA or whatever else the FBI might find.

I wasn't going to let Peter lead them to me. Instead, I was going to lead them to Peter.

I swung my bag over one shoulder and went out onto the balcony. I had to get inside Peter's cabin, and if I couldn't go through the main door, well then …

Frosted-glass privacy screens were all that separated my balcony from those on either side. The screen ran from the floor right up to the underside of the balcony above. The only way to get to Peter's cabin was to go around.

I stood for a second, facing my half-open sliding door, looking at my reflection in the glass. Was I really going to do this? I was planning to climb from one balcony to another, eight decks up on a gigantic cruise ship, with nothing below me but open sea.

Do you think you can do this?

It didn't matter. I had to. For Sarah. And now for Megan, too.

Making sure I had a good grip on the railing's top rung, I stepped up onto its bottom rung and leaned as far left as I could. It offered me a view of part of Peter's balcony, but not of his sliding door.

Damn it.

I would just have to take the chance that he hadn't locked it from inside. If he had, well, I'd cross that bridge—or railing—when I came to it.

I stepped up onto the bottom rung with both feet.

I tried not to look down or think about not looking down. I tried to put all thoughts of "down" out of my mind altogether.

I swung one leg over the top of the railing and onto the other side. The *outside*.

If I fell, I would not only fall to almost certain death by drowning, but I might well ricochet off a few things on the way down: canopies of lower balconies, lifeboat fixtures, the hull of the ship.

Don't think. Just fucking do it.

I swung the other leg over.

I was now clinging to the outside of my balcony's railing, with nothing but air and my death below me. Outside the balcony's shelter, the wind had picked up.

I couldn't help it. I looked down.

The water was several stories below my feet. If I hit my head and so hit the water unconscious, I would have no chance whatsoever of surviving the fall. In the dark, no one would see me drop. They would never find my body.

I shuffled to my right, ducked my head around the privacy screen. Peter's cabin looked empty, but then, he might just be in the bathroom.

I took a breath, held it, and moved my right hand from the railing on my side of the screen to the one on Peter's as quickly as I could.

Then I moved my right foot over, too.

Okay, okay. I exhaled slowly. *So far, so good. You're practically halfway there. Halfway done. Just keep calm.*

The gear bag began slipping from my shoulder. The wind was picking up.

Before I could think too much about it, I pulled my left hand and leg off the railing, shifted my weight, and tried to replace them on Peter's stretch of railing before I plunged to the sea. My hand caught the top rail okay, but my foot slid off, leaving me with one leg dangling off the side of the *Celebrate* for a second.

A second too long.

Somehow, I kept calm, kept my grip, and kept breathing, all at the same time. Then, with some effort, I managed to hoist myself back up to a standing position with both feet firmly on the bottom rung of the railing, still on the outside, staring into Peter's cabin. I could see no movement inside.

I had done it. I'd made it across. Now I just had to make it *in*.

I climbed over the top of the railing, slowly but steadily, sweating and panting, and then let go, falling back onto the floor of Peter's balcony, spent and exhausted as much from the stress as from the physical exertion. The adrenaline that had fueled me this far dissipated in an instant, and I started to shiver violently.

Hold it together. Don't lose it now.

I stood up and ventured a peek over Peter's balcony railing. Christ, it was a long way down. I felt sick just looking. I shook my head and turned to try the handle on the sliding door.

It gave.

Thank fuck for that.

I let myself into the cabin. It was empty. I dropped the bag on the floor and took out the bloodstained scarf, careful not to touch it without keeping the plastic bag I'd wrapped it in between the scarf and my skin at all times.

I dropped it on the carpet and pushed it under Peter's bed with my foot.

Then I stood there for a long moment, thinking.

Was I really going to do this? Was this really me? Planting evidence in someone's room? But then, it wasn't planting, was it? It was *returning*, and the evidence would only be doing its job: tying the right man to Megan's murder.

I pictured Sarah's face, smiling at me in the car outside the airport the Sunday morning before last.

She had chosen me, Ethan said. She had picked *me*.

I slung the empty bag back over my shoulder and started to leave the cabin the easy way: through the door.

But then I saw the white envelope lying on the desk.

It was the same envelope I had accidentally pulled out of the wardrobe with the blanket last night, the one that contained Estelle's passport and the fake note.

I picked it up now and carefully withdrew the items inside, wanting to see for myself that my memory was correct, that the writing Peter had pretended was Estelle's was the same that I had seen on the archive boxes back at the Beau Soleil Palais.

I flicked to the last page of the passport. The note was still stuck in there:

I'M SORRY—E.

It was so obvious, now that I studied it. The writing was identical. How could I possibly have missed that? Why hadn't Peter made more of an effort to disguise it? Maybe he didn't normally write in block capitals and had forgotten about the labels on the boxes. Or maybe he thought showing it to me right after sharing his theory that the same man had murdered both his wife and my girlfriend would be effort enough.

And he had been right, hadn't he?

I didn't hear the door open behind me.

I hadn't realized that Peter was back, until I heard his voice.

"Adam, what are you doing in my room?"

I looked up and saw his reflection in the balcony doors. Peter was standing behind me, his Swipeout card in his hand. He had already closed the door behind him.

I turned around.

"I'm making sure the FBI gets the right man," I said.

No response. He just looked at me.

I studied his face and saw no emotion in particular. He didn't seem scared or nervous, nor was he angry or threatening. He didn't even seem surprised. He just looked ... *resigned.*

"You killed her, didn't you?" I said.

His eyes dropped to the floor.

"Last night," I said. "You weren't sick. You were just faking it. But *I* wasn't faking it. You slipped something into my drink. That's what you did after I left you at your apartment, right? Went and got something to knock me out? What did you give me?"

Peter didn't respond.

"Then, when I went to the bathroom, you whispered something in Megan's ear, telling her I liked her but was too shy to say so. We had to bring you back to your cabin, and then, when I started to feel unwell, too, she helped me into mine. Once I was unconscious, you let yourself in. You had a key because of the mix-up with the Swipeout cards. You did that on purpose when we boarded, so you would have access to my cabin, too. That's it, isn't it? That's how you got in to leave the scarf, to leave the door open. We didn't pick up the extra set of keys until the next day, but that was fine, because the first night, you were able to go and hand over your ID, and *presto,* here's a key for the cabin that Peter Brazier is supposed to be staying in, which is actually mine. Then last night, after I was knocked out, you came in and"—my voice cracked—"you *killed Megan.*"

It was the first time I had said it out loud. Bile followed the words up into my mouth.

"What did you *do?*" I demanded. "Push her overboard? What did you do before that? Where did you get all the blood that was on the scarf? How could you even ..." My voice cracked again. "That's what you meant, wasn't it, back outside the bar? When you said she was perfect. I thought you meant it was great that she could help us, but you meant it was perfect that *she was American.* Her disappearance would bring the FBI. You told me that yourself. And the FBI are the only people for the job when it comes to catching a serial killer, right? That's what you were talking about with all that shit about doing 'whatever it takes.' Was it just a coincidence that we happened to sit at the same bar as she did that night? That we randomly crossed paths on a ship this size?"

Still Peter said nothing.

"You killed Megan," I said, "to find out what happened to Estelle, and you lied to me so you could get on this ship in order to kill Megan. I know about the passport, Peter. I spoke to Becky. I know you found Ethan the very first night. And I know what he told you. He couldn't have had anything to do with Estelle's disappearance—he wasn't even here. And Sarah left him the first night of the cruise, and she left *him* that note in their cabin."

Peter flinched.

I pushed on. "What's the endgame here? What happens now? An American is dead, the FBI is coming, and what? All the evidence points to me so I can take the fall? How does that work in your grand scheme? Is it because I'll protest my innocence by telling them every-thing? That I'll have to convince them there's a serial killer murdering women aboard the *Celebrate*, because if I don't, it'll be my freedom that's at stake? Have you done this to me so I'll have no choice *but* to make them listen? Where will you be? Waiting in the shadows to find out the truth? Is that your plan? Is it, Peter? *Is it?*"

Peter's legs crumpled beneath him, and he sank to the floor. He put his face in his hands.

"I'm so sorry, Adam," he said through his fingers. "I'm so sorry."

"Oh, don't apologize to *me*. It's Megan's family you should be apologizing to. Shit ... Oh, God. Oh, shit." I started pacing. "Peter, you've killed an innocent woman. Do you realize that? Do you even realize what you've *done*? You're just as bad as he is—this man, this *monster* we've been searching for. Do you get that? Do you get that you've made Megan suffer *just as much* as Estelle did? That you've taken an *innocent* life, just so you could find your wife? Jesus Christ, Peter. I can't even ... I don't know ... What the *fuck* were you even *thinking*?"

"I'm so sorry," Peter said. He took his hands from his face. His cheeks were wet with tears. "I'm sorry, Adam. I ... I thought she was American."

"What? But she *was* Ameri ..." I stopped.

No.

The champagne bottle in my cabin—a cabin registered in Peter's name.

A perk that was only for returning passengers, Megan said.

"She didn't suffer," Peter said. "I made sure of it. I promise. She didn't suffer. I did it quick. I don't think she even knew what was happening. I'm so sorry, Adam. I am, really. But I thought she was American! I thought it because *he* was."

The passport started trembling in my hand.

No.

I looked down at it, at the note:

I'M SORRY—E.

Just like mine, except for the initial:

I'M SORRY—S.

If Peter had written it, if he'd just made it up to get my attention, to forge some link between his missing wife and my missing girlfriend …

Then how did he know what to write?

"I thought she was American," Peter repeated, "because *he* was."

How could he possibly have known what it was that *my* note—Sarah's note—said?

No.

The cabin interior blurred in front of me as my eyes filled with tears.

"I'm so sorry, Adam. I'm so sorry. *He* was, so …"

"Who was, Peter?" I knew the answer, but I wanted to hear him say it. I wanted there to be no mistake. "Because who was?"

Peter looked up at me, his face streaked with tears. "Ethan," he whispered. "Ethan."

I don't remember walking out onto the balcony, but I ended up there, looking out over the dark sea.

This was the starboard side. The hills of Nice were hidden from my view off beyond the *Celebrate*'s stern. The tiny village of Villefranche was a mile behind me. All I could see was a seemingly endless expanse of dark sea and, above it, darkening sky.

I gripped the rail with both hands, gulping down deep breaths, trying to slow my pulse, trying to think, trying to think, trying to think.

Peter killed Sarah. And he killed Megan, too.

All in the search for Estelle.

I felt his presence behind me, his hand on my shoulder. "Please, Adam. Let me explain."

I swung around in a fury.

"Explain? *Explain* why you *murdered* my girlfriend and then pretended to want to help me find her killer? Used me for the money to get on this ship so you could *kill someone else*—an innocent woman whose only crime was having an *American accent?*"

"I couldn't ..." Tears ran down Peter's face. "I couldn't *go on*, Adam. I just couldn't! Not with that monster out there who had taken Estelle. I nearly ... I nearly ended it all. That was true, what I told you. But then I read this newspaper article that talked about the US Congress passing a law so American citizens would get the FBI. And

I thought, FBI? They're the *experts* when it comes to serial killers! If anyone can find him, they can. I just … I needed them to come to the ship. I needed them to come to the *Celebrate*. Once they started investigating, once they started looking back, they'd find Estelle. I knew they would. Even though she was British, they'd have to investigate that, too, because they'd connect all the disappearances from the ship. They're the only ones who would."

"Tell me," I said. "Tell me what you did."

Peter hesitated.

"*Tell me,*" I said again.

"I was on the *Celebrate* with Sarah. Behind her and Ethan in the boarding queue. I heard him talking about how she'd be on her own that night because he had to meet someone. His accent—he was obviously American. You'd be surprised how few of them you find on European cruises, especially the very short ones like this. When they go to the trouble of coming all the way over here, they want to sail for a week or two. I thought she was American, too. Really, Adam. Otherwise I never would have—"

"I don't give a *fuck,*" I said, biting my lip with the vehemence of the *f.* "Tell me what you *did to her*!"

"I followed them." Peter talked faster now. "Well, I followed *her*. I stayed at a distance so she wouldn't notice. That's why I didn't hear her speak. She met up with him afterwards, out on deck. They looked like they were arguing. She went back to the cabin alone. I … I waited outside. When she opened the door to come out again, I pushed her back in." Peter was crying hard now. "And I had a … I'm sorry, I am. I had put some chloroform on a napkin, like you see in the movies …"

I thought of Sarah, eyes wide with fear, a hand clamping a piece of white cloth over her mouth and nose.

"She was unconscious in seconds," Peter said. "She didn't feel anything; I know that. I did it as quick as I could, and I told her …" An anguished sob. "I told her I was sorry. I told her I was doing it only because someone else had done it to the woman I loved; some monster had taken the woman who was carrying my baby, my child. I pulled her out onto the balcony, and then ..." He looked away from me. "Then I heard a noise."

"No," I said. "No."

"It was Ethan, coming to look for her. Their balcony was the same as this one." Peter pointed to the exterior wall between the frame of the sliding door and the next partition. There was a space, two or three feet, where a person could stand and not be seen from inside the cabin. "I hid there, holding Sarah's ... holding Sarah, waiting for him to leave again. He did. Then I pushed her." Another sob. "I pushed her, Adam. I'm so sorry."

I put one hand back on the railing and gripped it until my knuckles were white.

"What then?" I asked through clenched teeth.

"I took some of her stuff, but not all. Just like Estelle. Everything had to look the same. I saw the note on the mirror on the way back in. I took it because ... well, Estelle didn't leave a note. It was only afterwards I realized that Sarah's phone was in her handbag—I'd taken the handbag. I was going to throw it away, throw it in the sea when I disembarked, but then all these calls and texts started coming through, and your message, and all the numbers had Irish country codes. I checked online, and I found something on Facebook. An appeal for information. That's when I realized she wasn't American at all; she was Irish." He straightened up, looked me in the eyes. "Adam, I know I should never have—"

"So then," I said, "you went to plan B."

"No one believed me about Estelle," Peter said. "No one. Blue Wave didn't care—about Estelle *or* Sarah. You told me they said Sarah got off the ship, right? Well, she *didn't*, did she? We know that for sure. They just told you that to mollify you. This is what they do. So then I knew that despite what they said, Estelle hadn't walked off the ship, either. I was convinced more than ever: someone *had* murdered Estelle. Maybe the same person who had killed Sanne Vrijs—who Blue Wave didn't give a shit about, either. I knew I still had to try to get the FBI onto the ship. They were the only ones who could solve this, who could find him and stop him. Who could tell me what happened to Estelle. I'd made a mess of things, yes, but there was still time to set things right, to do this right. But I had no money left. I couldn't get on the *Celebrate* to … I looked you up online, and it said you'd just signed this big movie deal or something. Six figures, it said. You were *rich,* and your girlfriend was missing from the *Celebrate.* I figured if I could convince you beyond all doubt that Sarah and Estelle were connected … So I found Sarah's passport in her bag, and I put the note I'd taken from the mirror inside, and posted it to you."

The wind had picked up. I turned away from it and leaned back against the railing.

Peter was standing in front of me, leaning on one outstretched arm against the sliding door. He removed it now, straightened up. His hand left a smudge of moisture on the glass.

"How did you know where I lived?" I asked him.

Peter looked surprised that I didn't know the answer. "You're in the phone book. I looked it up online."

"Then you, what, waited for me to contact you? I might never have."

"I thought of that," Peter said. "I actually sent you some messages through the Facebook page—not under my own name, of course—bringing up how similar the two cases were. You mustn't have seen them. I waited a while, thought maybe you'd stumble upon it yourself. If not, I was going to get in contact with you, pretend *I'd* stumbled on *your* case. Anyway, I needn't have worried. That woman Sarah met at dinner led you to Blue Wave, and then you did your own research and you found Estelle's case. You got in contact with me and—"

"You pretended that Estelle had sent you a note, too," I finished.

There was a pause, filled with the whistling of the wind.

"Yes." Peter said eventually.

"But you'd written it."

"Becky had Estelle's passport. It was never missing; she gave it to me. I had some stationery from the *Celebrate* from the time ... from the time with Sarah. I thought you were going to figure it out, Adam. I did. There was the logo change. I thought you might ask why Estelle's paper was the same as Sarah's. They should've been different, right? If Estelle was on the ship a year ago and Sarah was here last week? But you said nothing about it. Then when I swapped over the keys, that was the other thing: I didn't realize that return guests got a bottle of champagne in their room. At check-in, even, back in the terminal, I thought something might come up and the girl would say, 'Welcome back, Mr. Brazier,' and I'd have to think of some way to explain that. And then Ethan. I found Ethan that first night—I kept looking until I did—and he told me it was his first week working on the ship. And I knew then that if you found him, he'd tell you the same thing and it would all be over. It was nearly over anyway. You wanted to leave. So I delayed you, made you stay. And then last night ... I had to see this thing through to the end. I had to take Megan."

To take Megan.

He made it sound so small, so unimportant. A simple task. An errand.

"The scarf," I said flatly. "Was it even Sarah's?"

Peter bit his lip, shook his head.

"No," he said. "I threw her clothes overboard. Got rid of them before I disembarked from the ship last week. But I remembered the scarf. It was easy enough to find another one like it—it was from a high-street chain. And I remembered the perfume. That was ... my backup plan in case, once we got aboard, you changed your mind about all this."

I glared at him. "Seems like you thought of everything."

"I'm not proud of it, Adam, but yes, I tried to. I've had a year to think of nothing else."

"Except Megan died in your cabin. You swapped the keys over. Your name is on my cabin. If you killed her there—"

"It doesn't matter," Peter said. "You're the one who's been seen with her. Were undoubtedly caught on CCTV. Seen chatting with her in the bar—maybe even seen going into your cabin with her."

"I'll tell them," I said, "I'll tell them what you did."

"Honestly, I don't care if you do. I just needed to get Megan to a place where I could do what I had to. Say what you like. So long as it's the FBI asking the questions, and they're on their way here as we speak. When they arrive, they'll arrest you. You can tell them all about Megan and Sarah—in fact, please do. Then they might make the connections. Do what no one else has ever done: actually see what's happening on this ship." Peter looked past me, out over the sea. "I don't care what happens to me. I just want justice for Estelle. And for that to happen, Megan must be connected to Sarah, and Sarah must be connected to Estelle. She's the only one I care about. You're a nice guy, but I don't care about you. I can't. And I couldn't care about Sarah—"

It all happened so fast.

I saw hands on Peter's chest and realized they were mine. I was gripping him, pulling him by the shirt, turning him around, pushing him up against the balcony, bending him back over it.

"You're not going to do this, Adam," he said. "This isn't you."

I looked at him and thought about what he had done. I saw Sarah, eyes filled with terror, wondering what this man who was whispering apologies to her could possibly have to do with her life. And something just boiled over inside me.

I couldn't keep it in, couldn't let it go.

I couldn't forgive him.

Then Peter was gone, over the balcony. And in that instant,

I realized what I had done. I shot out my arms to catch him and screamed his name, but there was only air.

And then I was on the railing, standing on the first rung, then the second, looking over, and then—

CORINNE

Just after two o'clock the next morning, Corinne's son stood in the doorway of her crew cabin.

"Hello, Mama."

She invited him in, motioned for him to sit down beside her on her bed, the bottom bunk. There was nowhere else in the tiny space for him to sit.

"You know," she said, "you're the only one left who can call me that. 'Mama,' I mean."

"Mikki got pneumonia?"

"Over Christmas 2003."

"I read about it online."

"How did you hear about Papa?"

"On the news," Romain said. "I was still in France then."

"Where have you been since?"

"I went to Crete."

"Why did you leave there?"

Romain turned to look at her, and then she at him.

He said, "How do I know that you're not recording this?"

Corinne laughed softly. "Why would I bother with the police now, Romi? There's no one left to protect. Mikki, Jean, Charlie—you took them all out, one way or another. There's only me left, and God has already handed down my sentence."

"What is it?"

"Cancer. In my liver and my lungs. 'Six months,' they told me eight months ago. I can't have much time left."

"How long have you known I was here?"

"A few weeks. I got the email back in July. I was going to come aboard as a passenger, but then I realized that if you were crew, you may not necessarily be in passenger areas. Even if you were, it might take years of me walking loops around these decks, waiting for the one time that I, one of two thousand passengers, might happen to run into you, one of a thousand crew. I don't have that kind of time. So I applied for a job instead."

"But how can you do it if you're sick?"

"I just had to do it for long enough. And I've managed that, haven't I? How did you know I was here?"

"We make the new crew ID cards. I saw your picture come up last week. Then your name. You use your real name still?"

"What other one do I have? I'm not like you, Romi. I'm no master criminal. I wouldn't even know where to get a fake passport, let alone have the nerve to use one."

"Mama ..." He stopped.

"What?" Corinne said. "Is this the part where you deny everything?"

Romain's hands were in his lap. He looked down at them.

"I didn't kill Jean. Really, Mama, I didn't. I mean, yes, it was probably my fault. He was climbing over the gate trying to get away from me, but I wasn't trying to hurt him or anything. I wouldn't have. I just wanted to talk. If Papa ... If he did what he did because he felt guilty, then I can't be responsible for that."

"Why would he feel guilty?"

"Because he lied to me. In the prison. He said he was going to bring me to live with him when I got out, but then he ... changed his mind."

"What about Mikki?" she asked gently. "Was that an accident, too?"

"I didn't want to hurt him. I was only trying to get him to stop crying."

"Are you sorry for it?"

"Yes," Romain said, after a beat.

"And Bastian. Are you going to claim that was an accident, too?"

"I wasn't much older then, but no. That wasn't an accident."

"I didn't think so."

"There's a darkness, Mama. It comes in. I can't stop it."

"Was it always there?"

A pause.

"Yes," Romain said.

"What about Sanne Vrijs?"

His jaw clenched. "How do you know that name?"

"Did you kill her, too?"

"I said how do you *know that name*?"

"The person who emailed me," Corinne said. "He was a friend of hers. Worked with her here, on the ship. Was working with her the night she disappeared. Saw you harassing her at the bar, he said. After you were asked to leave, she told him who you were. Said you were the infamous Devil of Deavieux, the child murderer known as Boy P. He'd never heard of you. She didn't tell him your new name, but he took what he had to the authorities. They didn't follow up. I believe the company said she was drunk at a party and fell overboard? He didn't believe that, but he couldn't do anything about it. Then, a few weeks later, he's sitting eating his lunch in the crew mess when he looks up and sees you there. In uniform. He knows there's no point in going to Blue Wave. He doubts the French police will believe him, and anyway, I don't think anyone is too concerned with hunting you down there anymore. He looks up your new name in the crew directory. Sends it and an updated picture to me. He watched my videos, you see. After Sanne disappeared. He learned everything about you. The *old* you, I mean." She paused for breath. "So?"

"So what?"

"Sanne?"

"I did kill her," Romain said.

"Why?"

"Because she killed our baby."

"She was pregnant?" Tears sprang to Corinne's eyes. "Oh, Romi. Was she your girlfriend?"

"Back in Crete, yes."

"Did she know …?"

"That's why she did it. She was afraid it would be like me and that she would be like you."

Corinne couldn't speak.

"It's not the same, I know," Romain went on. "Your situation— that was different. But even though I knew that the child could be like me, I still wanted it. I wanted to take the risk. Because it could have also been like Sanne. *More* like Sanne, if we tried hard enough."

"*I* tried, Romi."

"How hard?"

"You don't know how difficult it was to look at you."

"But I was just a baby, Mama. How could you blame me for what *he* did?"

"Because I thought …" Corinne bit her lip. "Because I thought you were like him. I was afraid you were. Your father was a monster, Romi. He raped me. Repeatedly, for hours. He … He cut me. Inside."

Romain flinched, looked away. She could see his jaw working.

"I remember looking into his eyes at one point, and there was nothing there. Nothing. No life. His eyes were just like little dark marbles. I didn't tell anyone, because I wanted to forget that it had ever happened. That was the only way I could go on. And your papa … How could I tell your papa? How could I put those images in his brain?" Corinne shook her head. "No. I couldn't. So I said nothing. And then I found out I was pregnant with you. Pregnant with the seed he had forced inside me, pregnant with what was going to be a living, breathing reminder, for the rest of my life, of what happened to me that night. I could never forget it, because it would always be there. Running around my house, sitting at my dinner table. But what choice did I have? It was too late to … to take care of it. The only other option was to ruin Charlie's life, to break his heart. I loved him too much to do that to him, so I said nothing at all. The man who … your father. His coloring was a lot like Charlie's. I thought I might get away with it. And I did. At least, until … until you started taking after him in other ways."

"But which came first, Mama?"

"Oh, Romi, the things you did when you were just a boy. Do you remember? Hurting animals? Walking around like a robot, copying Jean? And then Mikki …"

"You told him, didn't you?"

"Who?"

"Papa. That day he came to see me, just before I was released. When he told me that he and I weren't going to live together anymore. You had just told him, hadn't you?"

"Yes." There was no point in lying now. "He was talking about getting the family back together. *All* of the family. He went on and on and on. Finally, I just cracked. I screamed at him. I told him that his family was already together. He could gather us all in one room, right then and there."

"What did he say?"

"Not much. He was upset. He left. I didn't see him for a couple of days. But when he came back, when he was a bit calmer, he told me that on some level, he had always known." Corinne sighed. "He said we were all going to live together again. All of us, his …" She glanced nervously at Romain. "His real family. We'd move somewhere new, without you. Move on with our lives. Have the life our family was supposed to have before I walked down that street that night. But then Jean died. Charlie went six months later. Mikki is gone now, too … Did *you* know? That he wasn't your father?"

"Not until the day you came to the prison."

"Yes, well, after you were found guilty, I thought there was little point in keeping any more secrets. You didn't suspect before?"

"No."

"Never?"

"I didn't really think about it."

"But the darkness —did you not wonder where it came from?"

"I thought it was inside of everyone."

"Have you hurt anyone else?"

"There's been some fights. I worked in a bar for a long time. People get drunk, say stupid things. But aside from that, no. I haven't killed anyone else."

"But you came back to work here. Why?"

"Because no one came for me after Sanne. Nothing happened at all. It was almost like it had never happened. So if the darkness comes ..." Romain looked away. "This is a safe place for me to be."

"Don't you want to resist it, though? Don't you want to be good?"

Romain shrugged. "It's not about what *I* want."

"Tanner," she said. "Did any of it work?"

"I thought it did, at first. But over time, I realized that I could do what he told me, act like he showed me, and yet, underneath I was still the same. He couldn't test that, couldn't see what was inside me. He couldn't see into my head. He just *thought* he could."

"You were faking."

"Basically, yes."

"Tell me one more thing." Corinne took as deep a breath as she could manage. "When you murdered Bastian, do you remember how it felt?"

"Why do you want to know that?"

"I just do."

"It felt ... good, Mama. Like I'd been sitting in the same position for a really long time and I'd just got up and stretched. Like all this stuff had been building up inside of me and then someone opened a vent."

"It was a relief, you mean?"

"Yes."

"Is there something building up inside you now?"

"No," Romain said.

Corinne didn't believe him.

"Well, Romi." She put a hand on his arm. They hadn't touched since he was a boy of eleven. She would take the opportunity now, while she could. "The past is over. There's little future left. I just wanted to tell you that I'm sorry. My decisions weren't your responsibility. You were just a child. I shouldn't have blamed you. I should have tried harder with you, tried to love you. For a long time, I told myself that I couldn't love you, because of what you were. But maybe, if I had loved you, I could have changed who you became. But by God, Romi, didn't you make it *so damn difficult.*"

Next to her, Romain nodded silently.

"I know, Mama, and I'm sorry. So, what hap—"

He stopped abruptly, looked down at the knife sticking out of his side, blinked in the light reflecting off the blade.

He looked back up at Corinne, eyes wide in bewilderment. "Mama?"

"I'm sorry for this, too," she said. "But I have to do it." She pushed the knife in farther. Blood pushed its way out of Romain's lips and trickled down his chin. "I shouldn't have brought you into this world, Romi, so before I leave it, I'm going to take you back out."

Corinne pushed the knife in the rest of the way, to the hilt, tried to twist it. Felt it meet resistance—a bone.

"I don't care what happens to me," she said, "but I doubt anything will. There's a reason I didn't wait for you to go ashore on a day off, or finish your contract and travel somewhere else. I came aboard for the same reason you did. Because out here, you can end someone else's life and get away with it." Romain was still looking at her, but she didn't think he was seeing her anymore. His eyes were unfocused, glazed. "This, I've realized, is the only way. It always was. I just wish I'd done it sooner, before you took my family from me. Mikki. Jean. And that poor boy, Bastian. That girl, Sanne. The life that was inside her."

She stood up and went to sit on Romain's other side, the one that didn't have a ten-inch butcher knife sticking out of it, or a pool of wet, glossy blood sinking into the sheets.

Then Corinne did something she had never done before and would never have the chance to do again.

She put an arm around her firstborn and pulled him close. And she waited for him to die.

ADAM

I jumped before I had decided to.

Air whistled past my ears as I plummeted toward the sea, dark but for the panes of moonlight breaking into tiny shards on its surface. At first, I seemed to be moving in slow motion and the surface seemed miles below; then it was rushing up to meet me faster than my mind could follow.

I had to find Peter. I had to save him. If I didn't, he and I would be the same.

A fragment of a memory: *hitting water from this height is just like hitting concrete.* I tried to straighten up, to grip the back of my thighs with my hands, but I was too late. I hit the water at an angle, and every nerve ending on the left side of my body was set ablaze with white-hot pain.

I closed my eyes.

When I opened them again, I was underwater.

It was nowhere near as dark as I expected. My shoes had come off, and now, beyond my bare feet, was blackness. But above my head, just beneath the surface, it was brighter than it had appeared looking down. It was clear, too. I could see no dirt or fish.

But I couldn't see Peter, either.

Was Sarah down here, too? I thought about it: if he had pushed her into the water late on the first night, where was the ship then? Miles and miles and miles away from here, surely. It would have only just left Barcelona. She might be in the same sea, but she was nowhere near me.

All I wanted was to go back to her. Let her come back to me, as she was planning to do.

Now I knew for sure I would never be able to.

As I looked up through the water, the hull of the *Celebrate* loomed to my right, the lights of the Oceanic and Atlantic decks twinkling, tinny music drifting down.

I started to sink. Pressure began to build in my chest. I moved my arms to swim toward the surface and—

Fuck.

A red-hot poker of pain, deep inside my shoulder joint. I must have dislocated it with the force of the impact.

My lungs felt as if they were about to burst. I had to take a breath. I moved my legs; they felt all right. I started kicking, propelling myself slowly to the surface. But I had never been a strong swimmer, and I went nowhere fast.

I saw a familiar shape bobbing on the water: a life ring. Someone must have thrown it in. Who? Had someone seen us? *What* had they seen? What if Peter was still alive? What would he tell the FBI when they came to question us? Would he still try to blame me? Would he tell them I had pushed him off?

The bloody scarf was in his room, but Megan was all over mine. He had killed her on my balcony. I had spent half the day with Megan, unwittingly building the case against me, collecting witnesses for the prosecution.

I needed to get out. I needed to survive.

I needed to be sure I would be around to tell them my side of the story. I kicked faster toward the life ring, my lungs feeling as if they were ripping apart, the pain in my shoulder making me want to scream out, my muscles burning with exhaustion.

I punched through the surface.

Coughing and spluttering, I opened my mouth to suck down as much air as I could.

I was alive. I was okay.

Where was Peter?

I was close enough to the life ring to reach out and touch it, but when I gripped it with my right arm and threw my left—hanging limp, the elbow at a disconcerting angle—over it, it started to flip. I realized it was providing only assistance, not rescue, and that even though I was already exhausted I had to keep my legs moving to keep my head above water.

Looking at the life buoy now, up close, I saw that its color was faded, its surface scratched and ripped. A chunk of seaweed was wrapped around its rope, and the rope itself was frayed and unfurling. No one had thrown it in. It had been here already, floating in the sea.

No one had seen us.

I looked around, turning. Scanning the surface in all directions. I saw nothing but the white foam of breaking waves.

Then, faint in the distance, I heard it for the first time: *whump, whump …*

I knew the sound; I just couldn't remember what made it.

I saw something maybe fifteen or twenty feet beyond my left arm: a dark shape bobbing on the surface.

Whump, whump, whump …

The noise was getting louder.

Watching the shape, I caught a glimpse of short brown hair. Hair, I knew, was a lighter color when it wasn't soaking wet. It was on a body floating facedown in the water.

It was Peter. Dead. I let out a sob.

Peter was dead because I had pushed him over, because he had killed Sarah because he had loved his wife.

Should I go and get him? Try to save him? Was it already too late? Would it do any good?

Whump-whump-whump-whump …

A glare so blinding that for a second it seemed as if the sun had shot up into the sky. But the glare moved, and I could see the dark shadow above it.

A helicopter.

That was the sound. The FBI had come for me.

No, wait. They couldn't possibly have gotten here by now. I had just gone in the water a minute or two ago. It must be the French coast guard, come from Nice to help look for Megan. Instead, they had found me.

Whump-whump-whump-whump-whump …

It was directly above me now, the helicopter, blowing waves out from the center of its downward blast, splashing water up in my face. The sound was thunderous, tunneling through my brain, pounding in my chest.

I couldn't see Peter's body anymore. It was drifting away, the spray making it impossible to track its movement.

I had to decide what to do. Should I let Peter go?

Should I pretend I knew nothing?

I could say that I fell. Or jumped. Grief had driven me to it.

Grief? the FBI would ask. *Grief over who?*

My girlfriend, I would tell them. *Sarah, my girlfriend. She disappeared from this ship nearly two weeks ago. After she did, a man contacted me. I came to meet him in Barcelona. We boarded the ship. Yesterday, we met Megan, the woman who was reported missing this morning.*

They would know what to do.

The helicopter's beam had stopped on me. They could see me; they knew exactly where I was. A rope ladder was dropping down. But what about Peter? His body bobbed in the dark waters somewhere just beyond the light. They hadn't seen him yet.

I felt the grip of a hand on my arm and turned to find myself face-to-face with a man in a wet suit, wearing a thick mask over his face.

He was saying something to me. He looped an arm around my rib cage, and I stopped having to kick, stopped having to keep my head above the water. Just as well, because I didn't have the strength anymore.

If I was going to try to save Peter, I had to tell them now. Or maybe not telling them *was* saving him—saving him from the things people would say, the things they would think. If I said nothing now, no one would ever know what he had done. I could say he disappeared while we were on the ship, that I climbed into his cabin to look for him, but he was gone. There would be no trial, no justice for Sarah or Megan. But what would it change if there were? They were gone, and they weren't coming back. The man responsible was floating, most likely dead, in the sea not fifty feet from me.

A red basket was being lowered on a cable.

The man in the wet suit shouted something at me, but I didn't understand it, so he moved closer, shouted it again right into my ear.

"Is there anybody else in the water?"

I wouldn't be like Peter. I could never be. I had pushed him in a fit of rage, but then I jumped in, too. I had intended to save him. I hadn't meant to do what I had done.

But he had.

He had *planned* to kill Sarah. And Megan.

"Did you see anybody else in the water? Did you go in alone?"

We had reached the basket and another man in a wet suit. Together, they lifted me up into it, securing me with webbing and carabiners.

I was facing the night sky now, the stars swinging before me like a cosmic pendulum.

Sarah was gone forever. I knew that now. Somehow, I would have to learn to live with that. To live without her. To move on. To pick up the dreams that had cost me so much—that had cost me *her*.

I would have to learn to live with that. Did I believe there could be a way?

"Can you hear me? Can you hear me?"

I turned my head toward the man in the wet suit and nodded.

"Were you alone in the water? Did you see anyone else?"

Above me, the helicopter's rotor spun. *Whump-whump-whump-whump-whump-whump.* The pain in my shoulder was unbearable. I started to shake.

Where is she?

Now I knew, and knowing was enough. It would have to be.

"No," I said finally. "It was only me in the water. There's no one else."

The man in the wet suit nodded. The basket began to rise.

ADAM
Six Months Later

We arranged to meet in a bar in Gatwick's South Terminal. I had a couple of hours to kill before my afternoon flight to Los Angeles, and Becky had said it wouldn't take her long to drive out from the city. I got there first and took a seat facing the doors. When she arrived, I recognized her straightaway. She looked just as she had in her Facebook pictures—short and soft, with dark eyes and caramel skin—only, here in the flesh, solemn and nervous instead of happy and smiling.

She was bundled up in a heavy wool coat, scarf, and gloves. As she peeled off the various layers, we talked about the bitter January cold and how lucky I was, not to have tried flying out a couple of days before, when the runway got snowed in. We ordered coffee and joked awkwardly about how awful it tasted. I asked Becky about her job and explained why I was traveling to Los Angeles.

"To go to meetings," I said, "which I was really excited about until I found out that that's basically all anyone does there, all the time, and rarely does anything come out of it. Still, they're flying me out and putting me up in a hotel, and the sun will be shining, so …"

"And how are you?"

So many things were different now, in this After life. That question was one of them. Before, it was just good manners. A polite inquiry.

A flippant "Fine, thanks, and you?" was all anyone expected in return. But now people actually wanted to know *how I was.*

"Well, I'm seeing someone," I said. When I saw the flicker of surprise cross Becky's face, I added, "A therapist, I mean. Once a week."

Becky waited for a PA announcement about unattended bags to finish before she asked, "Is it helping?"

"I don't know." I looked down at my cup and noticed a little smudge of … jam? On the inside of the handle. We hadn't ordered any food, and there were no condiments on the table. I pushed it away. "I thought it would be more … prescriptive, I suppose. Like, he'd tell you what to do, how to cope. But he just sits there and listens."

"Back when I was in college," Becky said, "my older brother died. Suicide."

"I'm so sorry."

"People didn't know what to say, so they'd just go with variations of 'time heals all wounds.' Everyone kept telling me that the longer I waited, the less it would hurt."

I nodded in recognition. I'd been hearing that a lot lately, with the occasional "At least you're still young" thrown in. I wondered sometimes whether these supposed well-wishers could hear themselves speak.

"They were wrong," Becky said. "It's been almost fifteen years now, and it feels just like it did the day we found him. But the thing is, it does get … not *better*, exactly, but easier. Even though it hurts just as much. A grief counselor at my university said it's like, when it first happens, you fall into a hole of grief. You can't do anything. You don't *want* to do anything. All you can do is focus on the next five minutes, or the next hour, or just today. Then, over time, you suddenly find that while you were pulling yourself through time in these little increments, you also managed to climb out. The hole is still there—it always will be—but you learn to live around it. You can. You *will*."

"Yes. Well." I looked at my watch. "It's just after eleven. She should be here by now, right?"

Becky didn't call me on my blatant change of subject.

"I'll call her," she said instead, picking up her phone. There was a pause while the call connected. "We're here," she said into the receiver. "Where are you? … Okay. Well, we're upstairs in the Wetherspoon's. The stairs by Marks and Spencer. You know where? … Okay. See you in a sec." She ended the call and looked at me. "She just got off the train. She'll be here in a minute or two."

I took a deep breath in, let it out slowly.

"It'll be okay." Becky put a hand on my hand. "*You'll* be okay."

"What am I going to say to her?"

"Trust me when I tell you that she's more afraid about what she's going to say to you."

"Why?"

"Because she thinks this is all her fault."

"Don't be ridiculous," I said. "She had to do what she did. The way Peter acted afterwards, everything that happened—it only *proves* that."

"That's what I've been saying to her."

"Peter did this. No one else."

"I know." A pause. "And I hope you know that, too, Adam."

I raised an eyebrow. "Meaning …?"

"That email you sent me, right after you got back to Cork. It sounded like you were blaming yourself for Sarah being on that ship."

"It *was* my fault she was on that ship. If I'd been better to her, better for her, if I'd kept my promises, she wouldn't have gone looking anywhere else. She wouldn't have started something up with Ethan. And so she wouldn't have been on that ship."

"But, Adam, you can't—"

"But what I've realized is that the ship wasn't the problem. Sarah should've been able to get on it and get back off it again in one piece. She should've been able to come home. It shouldn't have been a dangerous thing to do. It was *Peter* who made it that way. It was *Peter* who did this. It doesn't matter what the chain of events was that led up to him doing it. He could've stopped at any time. So I can't blame myself. I won't. And she shouldn't, either."

"Well," Becky said, "that was a good speech."

"It was, wasn't it?" I smiled. "Sometimes I even believe it myself."

"Regardless, I think it would mean a lot if you said that to her. That you don't blame her. She's been struggling ever since it happened. She didn't ever imagine for a second that he'd be ... like he was. That he'd go to those lengths just to ..."

I didn't hear the rest of Becky's sentence, because I was looking over her shoulder at the woman who had just arrived in the bar.

She was standing in the doorway, her head turning to search the crowd. The long, glossy blond hair was gone, replaced with a mousy brown color and cut clear of her shoulders. Gone, too, were the stylish, expensive clothes I'd seen her wearing in pictures. She was wearing jeans, sneakers, and a brightly colored winter jacket of the kind skiers wear. A squishy-looking bundle was perched on her hip: a toddler so well insulated against the winter weather that his arms and legs stuck out like the rays of a starfish. Only his flushed face was visible. One mittened hand was reaching for his mother's hair while the other gripped a toy truck.

She saw Becky first; then her eyes came to rest on me.

I will admit it. I did feel, just for a second, a beat of resentment. What if she hadn't stayed for as long as she did? What if she had never married him? What if she and Becky had come up with a different escape plan? What if, after it became clear that he wasn't going to stop until he found her, she had contacted him somehow and told him the truth? Sarah would still be alive.

But then I caught myself. Corrected myself. She would never have had to do any of this if it weren't for Peter. This was nobody's fault but his.

She started walking toward us.

I pushed back my chair and stood up, just as Becky turned and saw her. She stood up, too, hugging her friend and whispering something in her ear. I thought it might be the same thing she had said to me.

It'll be okay. You'll be okay.

The toddler squealed.

"Hello, Christopher!" Becky said brightly. "Do you want to go for a little walk?" She took him in her arms. "Come here and we'll go for a little walk. Let Mummy talk to this nice man for a minute."

Then we were alone.

"I don't know what to say," I admitted.

She shook her head. "Neither do I."

"How about we start with the basics?" I stuck out my hand. "I'm Adam. It's good to finally meet you."

"I was surprised that you wanted to, after … Oh!" She suddenly remembered my outstretched hand and grasped it. "It's good to meet you, too, Adam. It really is. I'm Estelle."

AUTHOR'S NOTE

At the time of this writing, maritime law is applied in the real world just as it is in this novel: cruise ship passengers sailing in international waters are subject to the authority of the country where the ship is registered, with the exception of citizens of the United States, who fall under the jurisdiction of the FBI. Although, thanks to a 1976 environmental agreement called the Barcelona Convention, no part of the Mediterranean Sea is *technically* classed as international waters; in practice the nations bordering it still lose their jurisdictional claims and responsibilities twenty-four miles off their own coasts. The less-than-riveting nature of this author's note thus far is why, in *Distress Signals*, I took some artistic liberties and simplified the situation somewhat.

For more information on maritime law, real-world cruise ship crime, and the fight for better passenger protection and improved safety for all at sea, visit www.InternationalCruiseVictims.org.

ACKNOWLEDGMENTS

To my superagent, Jane Gregory, and everyone at Gregory & Company in London; my editors extraordinaire Stephanie Glencross, Sara O'Keeffe, and Michael Carr; and the entire team at Blackstone, especially Josh Stanton for bringing *Distress Signals* to the US and Kathryn English for designing an amazing cover for it to wear here: you all are lovely, talented, hardworking life-changers, and I thank you for all you have done for me and for this book. Go team *Distress Signals*!

Special gin-laced thanks to Sheena Lambert and Hazel Gaynor for pushing me to get this show on the road and then keeping me sane during the journey, even while I was asking things like "How winey is that wine?" at the BGEIBAs. (I *told* you I'd get that in.) Thanks to Niamh O'Connor, Patricia McVeigh, and Cliona Lewis for their help with some of the crime-and-cruising details, and to Vanessa O'Loughlin of Writing.ie for her years of generous support, not just of me, but also of countless other Irish writers at all career stages. (I hope Sam Blake gets to collect on all the good karma now!) Thanks also to Ellen Brickley, Eva Heppel, Elizabeth R. Murray, and Andrea Summers for all the encouragement that came in the form of coffee, cocktails, and cheesecake. To all the writers, publishing professionals, booksellers, bloggers, tweeters, and baristas I've gotten to know in the past few years: thank you. You are a very lovely bunch.

The seed that grew into the idea for *Distress Signals* was planted by "Lost at Sea," an article by Jon Ronson, which first appeared in the *Guardian Weekend* magazine in November 2011 and was later